Ladies' Night

Ladies' Night

Edited by

JESSICA ADAMS,
MAGGIE ALDERSON,
IMOGEN EDWARDS-JONES
AND CHRIS MANBY

HarperCollins*Publishers*

HarperCollins*Publishers*
77–85 Fulham Palace Road,
Hammersmith, London W6 8JB

www.harpercollins.co.uk

A paperback original 2005
1 3 5 7 9 8 6 4 2

Compilation © HarperCollins Publishers 2005
Copyright © in individual contributions remains with the contributor

The moral right of all of the contributors has been asserted

A catalogue record for this book
is available from the British Library

ISBN 0 00 721136 8

Set in Sabon by Palimpsest Book Production Limited,
Polmont, Stirlingshire

Printed and bound in Great Britain by
Clays Ltd, St Ives plc

CONTENTS

One evening, back in 1999, authors Chris Manby, Jessica Adams and Fiona Walker met up for a few drinks and had – as you do after a few drinks – one of those thoughts that seemed like a good idea at the time: why not publish a volume of short stories, featuring the great and the good in women's fiction and donate the royalties to Warchild? Then they sobered up – and it *still* seemed like a good idea.

That book was *Girls' Night In* and was so successful that it spawned a follow-up, then another – and this is the fourth in the series. Featuring stories from Adele Parks, Fiona Walker, Mike Gayle, Belinda Jones, Chris Manby and many more, this is a brilliant read. But it's much more than just that.

All the authors' royalties will be donated to two charities, Warchild and No Strings, both of which work to alleviate the suffering of children in the most disadvantaged and wartorn areas of the world.

Conflict is created by adults but children are the ones who suffer. To date, the *Girls' Night In* series has raised almost a million pounds which has been used to make a tangible difference to the lives of thousands upon thousands of children.

You are continuing to make that difference. By buying this book, there is a child somewhere in the world whose life you've just helped to improve.

Marian Keyes

ACKNOWLEDGEMENTS

Thank you to all the people who have made the Girls' Night In series work so well:

The fantastic authors who've generously contributed the great stories that make up this book.

Our wonderful UK editor, Katie Espiner, plus Lynne Drew and all at HarperCollins UK. Susan McLeish and Julie Gibbs, at Penguin Australia. Red Dress Ink USA.

Our esteemed English agent, Jonathan Lloyd, plus Camilla Goslett, Alice Lutyens, and all at Curtis Brown. Eugenie Furniss at William Morris. Our American agent, Laura Dail. Our founding American agent Deborah Schneider. Our founding agent in Australia, Fiona Inglis. And our queen of contracts in Australia, Tara Wynne.

Julian Carerra and all at War Child UK. Johnie McGlade and all at No Strings. Our Australian editor, and Chair of War Child Australia – Nick Earls.

Our energetic American and Canadian editors, Carole Matthews and Sarah Mlynowski. Our founding American editor Lauren Henderson. Our founding editor in England

and Australia – Fiona Walker. Our generous webmaster, James Williams.

And, above all, you, whoever you are, for buying this book and helping to make a difference.

Jessica Adams
Maggie Alderson
Imogen Edwards-Jones
Chris Manby

WAR CHILD

War Child is an agency dedicated to helping children in war zones around the world. War Child believes that children should never be the victims of armed conflict.

Since War Child began in 1993, we have worked in areas such as Afghanistan, Democratic Republic of Congo, Sudan, Bosnia, Kosovo and the Solomon Islands. As the organisation has grown, it has undertaken large and small scale projects, one of the first being a mobile bakery which fed 30,000 people a day throughout the conflict in Bosnia.

War Child also established a mobile bakery in Herat, Afghanistan that made more than five million breads for displaced people. Since establishing the bakery, War Child's work in Afghanistan has included the building of a kindergarten in Herat for 500 children aged between 6 months and 6 years. These children now have an opportunity to meet and make friends with other children and to start their education.

War Child joined with other agencies to rehabilitate the children's hospital in Nasiriyah, Iraq after it was damaged by battle and looting in 2003. We are currently focused on rehabilitating two drop-in centres in Iraq (in Nasiriyah and Basrah) to provide a safe space for vulnerable children and assist them to access education, skills and training. As well as providing emergency relief and working with communities to develop sustainable projects in areas such as education and agriculture, War Child is very concerned about the rights of children in conflict-affected areas. Recently, War Child was involved in negotiating the release of children from detention centres in Herat.

War Child is currently working in the Democratic Republic of Congo supporting centres that care for children who have been abandoned, separated from their families or made homeless by war. War Child provides training to staff of the centres to help with family reunification and reintegrating children into the community and also assists the organisation running the centre to generate income to contribute to the children's school fees and medical costs.

If you would like to find out more information about War Child please visit our website:

www.warchild.org

NO STRINGS

Miss Piggy, Fozzie Bear and the Muppets are household names, but in 2003, long time Muppet Designer and Producer, Michael K Frith, and his wife, puppeteer, Kathryn Mullen decided to use their years of Muppet expertise and experience to do something more serious.

Their idea was to teach children affected by war about the dangers of unexploded landmines using live puppetry and video. And with help from staff and volunteers drawn from some of the world's best known aid agencies – including War Child, GOAL and HAAD – No Strings was born.

Their first project is a landmine awareness video for children in Afghanistan, created in partnership with OMAR (Organisation of Mine Clearance and Afghan Rehabilitation) – and money raised from the sale of *Ladies' Night* will fund completion and distribution of the first 40-minute video, which is being translated into the two main languages of Afghanistan. UNICEF have already agreed to field test the video, and No Strings hopes to distribute it throughout local schools, television stations and cinemas.

As more money comes in from *Ladies' Night*, further projects will follow – including HIV awareness videos for Africa.

To see photographs of the No Strings puppets, and recent press coverage in *The New York Times* and the *Independent* please visit www.nostrings.org.uk

Thank you from everyone at No Strings for buying *Ladies' Night*. Although No Strings has had massive support so far, it is still very new – and exists on a tiny budget. Contributions from *Ladies' Night* will help to get the charity off the ground.

HEAVEN KNOWS
I'M MISERABLE NOW

Jessica Adams

Half way through Justin Rushcroft's funeral (1970–2005), his ex-girlfriend Jo McGee (1975–present) realised that she had left her mobile phone on. Worse, the offending phone (and it really was offending, as it vibrated and flashed pink at incoming calls) was now playing a jaunty version of the *Austin Powers* theme.

'Shit, bugger, shit!' Jo hissed, as she scrambled for it in her handbag.

On the other side of the church, Justin Rushcroft's other ex-girlfriend, Philippa Earl, (1969-present) crossed her legs and smiled. She was glad she had gone all the way to London to buy a new black suit, she thought. It made Jo's leather jacket look even cheaper than it actually was.

While the congregation kneeled to pray for Justin's soul, Philippa kept one eye open and shot a careful look at Jo's feet. As she expected – she was wearing her habitual fake tan and trainers. In the middle of autumn.

'As one of Brighton's most familiar broadcasting voices, and one of its best-loved DJs, it is no surprise to see so many

1

of Justin's fans, as well as his family and friends, here today,' boomed the priest.

What fans? Philippa thought, as she failed to see anyone who wasn't a relative of Justin's or one of his former shags. In fact, she realised, for the entire time she had managed the station where Justin worked, she had never seen a single fan.

Occasionally, a mad woman from Wivelsfield posted used cat-food cans to Justin, requesting that he sign them and send them back, but apart from her – nothing.

In her peripheral vision, Philippa could see another of Justin's ex-girlfriends. She was blonde, too (they were all blonde. When it came to women, Justin was like some low-rent version of Rod Stewart) but shorter, and – frankly – much fatter than any of them.

Her name was Kate Tickell, and she had been their summer temp at the radio station. *Why was the bloody woman crying so much?* Philippa thought. She knew for a fact that Justin had viewed her strictly as the most casual of all his casual sexual conquests. *Nothing more*, Philippa thought, contemptuously – *nothing less*.

Kate Tickell, meanwhile, was sobbing so hard that she was now down to her last scrunched-up tissue, and reduced to wiping her nose on her hand. All she could think about, as she stared at Justin's coffin, was the fact that she had given up her job at the radio station for him – the best job she'd ever had in her life. God was a bastard, Kate decided. She had sacrificed her whole summer for Justin, waiting, every single day, for phone messages and e-mails that never came.

And now look, Kate thought, as she blew her nose. *After all that effort, the insensitive wanker had gone and died anyway*.

Was it just her, Kate wondered, or did funerals make

2

everyone think about the most inappropriate things? Wiping her eyes, she stared fixedly at the coffin and tried, unsuccessfully, to stop herself remembering the way Justin had always yodelled, *Sound of Music* style, at the point of orgasm. And then there was his bottom, she remembered. It had looked exactly like her grandmother's balding hearth rug.

Across the church, Jo triple-checked that her phone was switched off, shoved a cinnamon Tic Tac into her mouth, and tried to concentrate on the priest, and Justin's coffin, in that order. The whole *Austin Powers* theme song/flashing phone experience just now had been completely humiliating. She had never received so many filthy looks in her entire life.

She looked down at her feet, noticed that her fake tan stopped in a line above her ankles, then looked up again – and saw that her trainers were filthy as well. While everyone else was praying for Justin again, Jo shot a surreptitious look at Philippa. As she expected, she was wearing a black designer suit to match her black designer handbag. And a string of pearls. *If only Philippa had worn a bat as well*, Jo thought savagely, *the magic transformation from station scrubber to Jackie Onassis would have been complete.*

Jo decided that she hated her, as she had seldom hated any other woman, and she wanted to ring up one of her friends right now and bitch about her – for the duration of the funeral, if necessary.

Even if Philippa hadn't been her boss, Jo thought, she still would have loathed her. Even if she hadn't stood between her and Justin, she still would have despised her.

While the congregation tackled another hymn, Jo wondered idly if she could ever work her way up from announcer, to station manager, and take Philippa's job. It suddenly seemed like the best idea she had ever had. It wouldn't be too hard to supersede Philippa, Jo decided. The woman knew nothing about working in radio – and even less about music.

Jo remembered a Christmas playlist Philippa had suggested at a staff meeting last December. It had consisted of *Agadoo* by Black Lace, The Gypsy Kings, Kylie, Britney, various other people whose names ended in *ie* or *ey*, a fat bloke who had won *Pop Idol*, Phil Collins, Cher and Classics on '45.

Bloody Philippa had never even heard of The Clash, Jo thought, in disgust, but she had still worn some ripped designer T-shirt bearing their name to last year's Christmas party.

Then Jo looked at Kate Tickell, and realised that not only was she openly sobbing, she was also out of tissues. And for what? Jo thought. Justin Rushcroft had been nothing more than a womanising wally-brain, with buttocks like the less accessible parts of the Amazon jungle. And the noise he used to make when he came! It was like listening to Julie Andrews stuck on some remote Swiss mountain peak.

Jo wondered if everyone else thought inappropriate things about the dead at funerals – then decided they didn't, and it was probably just her. She had to thank Justin for one thing, though, Jo realised – and that was the drivetime slot he had just left vacant. She couldn't wait to get her hands on it.

'Justin was also a popular member of his local cricket team,' the priest droned, while his family wondered why – if Justin had been so popular with his fellow cricketers – none of them had bothered turning up.

Above the sound of the church organ, Philippa heard Kate Tickell sobbing, and flinched. It was the most extraordinary noise, she thought. Like someone having their sinuses cleared with a dredger. Was it just her, she pondered, or did everyone

else think sinful thou
pumping away on top
with his bottom rota
in a car-wash, drifte

Stop it! Philippa
hymn rolled on, all
high-pitched, unden
Hee Ho!' of her fo

I'll never, ever s
as she rubbed her
last chance to see l
too. Even if we did only do it three times. And I ...
– much, much more than anyone else here did. At that
moment, Kate wished she'd had his baby after all.

She remembered her long and lonely day at the abortion
clinic in London, and put her face in her hands. This was
hell, she decided. It was bad enough to have lost Justin's
baby. But to lose him as well? For the second time that
morning, Kate decided she hated God. She didn't care if
Justin had mucked her around. She didn't care if he'd had
a photograph of one ex-girlfriend above his bed, and
another in his glovebox. She didn't care that he never called
her, or that he behaved exactly like one of the depressing
example men in *Men Are From Mars, Women Are From
Venus*.

She didn't even care, she decided, that Justin had said mean
things about her weight when they were in the shower
together. At that moment, as Justin lay dead in his coffin,
Kate Tickell decided that she could forgive him almost everything, if only he would come back. Then another mobile
phone rang, from the other side of the church – this time
playing the theme song from *The Simpsons*.

eone tutted. And then – at last – the

n the coffin had been taken to the cremator-
kell made a decision.

she said, walking up to Philippa, who was
g the wreaths.

n. Hello, Kate.'

'I'm sorry I made such a fool of myself in church. And
after all – Justin was your boyfriend. Not mine. I don't know
why I got so upset. I'm sorry. Let me buy you a drink,' Kate
whispered.

Philippa sighed. Had she sacked her, or had Kate resigned,
in the end, after all those sick days? She couldn't remember.

'Just go home Kate,' she told her.

'I can't.'

'Justin's gone now. Move on.'

'I can't. And I don't like it when people say move on. Why
don't you come and have a drink at Heaven with me? I'm
the night manager there, now. I can have anything I want,
from behind the bar.'

'But it's three o'clock in the afternoon!' Philippa was
shocked.

'Bollinger. Moët. Whatever you want. And get Jo to come,
too.'

'What?'

'Ask Jo. She likes Heaven. I see her in there sometimes.
I'm sure she'd like a drink with us.'

'What's bloody Jo McGee got to do with it?'

Then they both realised Justin's mother had moved closer,
and was unashamedly eavesdropping.

'That's a nice idea,' she said, squeezing Kate's arm.

6

'Well, it's just an idea,' Kate shrugged.

'Well, I think it's lovely,' Justin's mother agreed. 'All you girls, together, having a wake. I'm sure Justin would have liked it. Oh – Jo!' she spotted her by the chapel, and waved enthusiastically. 'Jo!' Come over here! The girls are going for a drink!'

'What?' Jo mouthed, feigning ignorance.

'*Drink*!' Justin's mother mimed.

'*Aah*,' she said, when Jo came over at last, in her muddy trainers. '*Aaah*. Look at all you girls! I think I'm going to cry again. Justin never had a chance to get married, you see. He died too young. Never had a chance to have a baby.'

Except Justin's mother was wrong about that, Jo thought, as the three women said their farewells to her, and headed for Philippa's car. Kate Tickell had been through an abortion, and everyone at the station – except Justin, of course – had guessed it.

Under grey Brighton skies, in jet black jackets (Prada, Top Shop and Monsoon) the three women drove to Heaven, in Philippa's company car.

'I've got to be back at the station by five,' Jo said, as she and Kate walked into the club, ahead of Philippa.

'Well I'll get the champagne out now, then,' Kate said.

'Oh,' Jo cheered up, as she noticed the jukebox in the corner. 'And I might put a song on.'

Music, she thought. Music and alcohol. As opposed to hymns and Holy Communion. That's what she needed right now. She had been brought up as a Catholic, but all church services gave her the creeps. She put money in the jukebox, and sniffed the air – the place stank of stale beer, vomit, ashtrays and piss – like all nightclubs, during the day.

'I'd forgotten how awful Heaven is,' she told Philippa,

once she had arrived, and Kate had gone to the loo. 'Look at those clouds they've painted on the ceiling. And the *jukebox*. It's themed. Every song's got heaven in the title.'

'Oh yes,' nodded Philippa, as *Heaven Knows I'm Miserable Now* began booming through the speakers. 'There's that song by The Cure.'

'It's The Smiths, actually.'

'No, it's The Cure.'

'It's the bloody Smiths.'

'No, I'm sure it's that man with the big eyebrows and the mad brother. The one who married Gwyneth Paltrow.'

'God, Philippa. You don't have a bloody clue, do you?'

Then Kate came back from the loo, carrying two bottles of champagne and three glasses, and they saw him.

'Justin! Oh my God. Justin.'

At the end of the table, still in his old jeans and white T-shirt, Justin Rushcroft – looking translucent, but otherwise well – smiled, and waggled his fingers in greeting.

'Shit!' said Jo.

'No!' said Philippa. 'No, no!'

'I've decided to stay here,' Justin explained, looking up at the ceiling, with its painted angels and plaster harps. 'In Heaven.'

'But you shouldn't even be here,' Jo said, once she could breathe.

'Why not?'

'Because this is a club,' she said. 'And because, if you stay here, you'll be – haunting it.'

'Oh, Justin,' Kate sighed. 'You've come back. I prayed you would.'

Then Philippa spoke. 'Are we dreaming?' she asked her ex-boyfriend.

'Nope.'

'Has someone put something in my drink?' She confronted Jo.

'Wrong again,' Justin smiled.

Then, at last, Jo spoke.

'Justin,' she said quietly, 'since you had the accident. Since you – how shall I put it – *died*. Well. Have you actually tried to get into the real heaven?'

'Oh, come on!' Justin made a face at her.

'Well – have you? I mean, what are you actually doing here?'

'Boring,' Justin said. 'Next question.'

'I bet he has tried to get into heaven,' Philippa glanced at Jo and Kate. 'I bet he has tried to get in – and his name's not even on the door.'

'Crap!' Justin cut her off.

Then suddenly, every light in the club blew, and The Smiths ground to a halt on the jukebox.

'*Aaargh*!' yelled Jo, as Justin laughed at her, and the mirrored ball above her head started spinning wildly on the ceiling.

'How do you like the dark, Jo?' he baited her. 'You were always afraid of the dark, weren't you?'

'You remind me of something,' Jo said to him, defiantly taking a swig of champagne, while Kate found some candles.

'What's that?' Justin grinned.

'My niece's Little Mermaid night-light. You should see yourself, Justin. You've gone pale green.'

Despite herself – she tried very hard not to find anything Jo said funny – Philippa laughed. Then, after that, she steeled herself to look at Justin properly.

He had died in a car crash, coked out of his brain, and

gone straight through the steering wheel. Now, however, there wasn't mark on him. She wondered, vaguely, if his buttocks were still like a front doormat as well, and then stopped herself, in case Justin could also read minds as well as affect electricity.

'I heard that!' Justin smirked.

Then Jo got up from the table, and sank to her knees on the floorboards, clasping her hands in prayer.

'What on earth are you doing?' Philippa confronted her.

'Our father, who art in heaven,' Jo recited, then she went blank. 'Oh God. Does anyone know the rest? Something about bread. Trespassers, bread, kingdom come. Bollocks.'

Then her champagne glass flew off the table and smashed onto the floor.

'Jo!' Philippa screamed, 'make him stop it!'

'No, let me try,' Kate insisted. 'I can stop you,' she turned to Justin. 'Because I can help you go to heaven. And I know I can do that – because I love you.'

'What?' Justin looked horrified.

Slowly and carefully, Jo got up from the floor. 'I've remembered why I stopped going to Mass now,' she said. 'It's the pain.'

'Don't pray for me,' Justin swore at Kate, as she got down on her knees.

'It's the best thing,' she said.

'Oh well. While you're down there –'

'I love you,' Kate smiled. 'Even when you say things like that.'

'Crap,' Justin said. 'You hate me as much as she does –' he pointed at Jo. 'And her!' he added, pointing at Philippa.

'We don't hate you,' Philippa interrupted him. 'Or at least,

I don't hate you. Not properly. I just forced myself to think of you as a bastard, so I could get over you.'

Then she put her champagne down, and knelt on the floor next to Kate.

'Come on, Jo,' she beckoned her over.

'Our father, who art in heaven,' Philippa began.

'Hallowed be thy name,' Jo added.

'Thy kingdom come,' Kate remembered, suddenly. 'Thy will be done.'

'Whatever,' Justin shrugged. 'You have to believe in it, if it's going to work. And none of you,' he said triumphantly, 'believe in it!'

'Go to the light,' Philippa heard herself saying. Was she repeating something she had seen in *Poltergeist*? Or was it *The Sixth Sense*?

'Yes!' Jo seized on her words. 'Go to the light, Justin.'

She wished she had never stopped going to Mass, she thought. She wished she had never stopped believing. If only she'd kept it up, she realised, it might not be quite so dark in here now. Without lights, or candles, Heaven felt more like hell.

Then –

They all saw him at once, suddenly appearing in a flood of light – a tall, grey-haired man, in a knitted cardigan and tie, with his hand on Justin's shoulder.

'Oh no,' Justin said. 'Dad.'

'I've not been able to get through to you before,' the tall man said, in a Northern accent.

'I'm dead, Dad.'

'I know,' his father shrugged. 'Though we don't call it dead over here. We call it your second innings.'

'Really?' Justin said.

11

The blinding white light in Heaven grew steadily, as the electricity suddenly came back on again all over the club, and Talking Heads replaced The Smiths on the jukebox.

'Christ!' Justin complained, shielding his eyes. 'It's so bright!'

'You're just halfway to heaven,' his father said. 'Keep going.'

Then Justin's own light began to fade, and started merging with something so powerful that neither Kate, nor Philippa, nor Jo could look any more.

'Goodbye, Justin,' Philippa said, as she watched his father take him.

'I love you!' Kate shouted.

'Have fun!' Jo said, then realised how stupid this sounded, as if she had just been farewelling him to Ibiza.

Then the three women got up off the floor, as David Byrne sang a song about heaven being a place where nothing ever happens; followed by Hot Chocolate singing a song about heaven being in the back seat of their Cadillac; and Tavares singing a song about heaven missing an angel.

'Wait for it,' said Jo, as the jukebox jumped from song to song. 'Any minute now, we'll get Led Zeppelin.'

'It's stuck,' said Philippa. 'It needs a repair man.'

'There!' Jo punched the air, as *Stairway to Heaven* replaced Tavares.

'Maybe Justin's stuck in there,' Philippa said hopefully.

'It's divine punishment if he is,' Jo smiled. 'Imagine being trapped between *Stairway to Heaven* and bloody Tavares for the rest of eternity.'

'Ha!' Philippa laughed, feeling strangely pleased with herself as she finally understood one of Jo's music jokes.

'Any chance of getting my job back?' Kate asked her, half

an hour later, as they opened their third bottle of Bollinger. 'Of course!' Philippa promised, swaying slightly under the mirrored ball. 'Besides, Kate, neither Jo nor I can let you work in Heaven any more. It's pure hell.'

Before embarking on her writing career, Cecelia Ahern completed a degree in journalism and media studies. Her first novel, *PS, I Love You*, was one of the biggest-selling debut novels of 2004 and a number 1 bestseller, as was her second novel, *Where Rainbows End*. Her third novel, *If You Could See Me Now*, will be published in December 2005.

Cecelia lives in County Dublin. For more information on Cecelia Ahern and her books, please visit www.ceceliaahern.ie

THE END

Cecelia Ahern

Let me tell you what this story is about before I get into the finer details. That way you can decide whether you want to read it or not. Let this first page be my synopsis. First of all, let me tell you what this story is *not*. This is not an 'and they all lived happily ever after' story. It's not about life-long friendships and the importance of female relationships. There are no scenes of ladies whispering and sharing stories over cups of coffee and plates of cream cakes they swore to themselves and their weekly weightwatchers class they wouldn't eat. Drunken giggles over cocktails do nothing to dry the tears or save the day in this story.

What if I told you that this story won't warm the cockles of your heart; that it won't give you hope, or cause you to blame escaping tears on the sun cream as you lie by the pool reading it? What if I told you that the girl doesn't get the guy in the end?

Knowing exactly how it ends, do you still want to read on? Well, it's not like we don't venture into things without knowing the end, is it? We watch *Columbo* knowing his misguided representation of himself as a foolish old man will help him solve the case. We know Rene Zellweger decides that she will be the one to go with Tom Cruise and the fish in *Jerry Maguire* every single time we watch it,. Tom Hanks always sees Meg Ryan at the end of *Sleepless in Seattle*. James Bond always gets the girl. In *Eastenders*, every once happy marriage will end in death, destruction or despair. We read books knowing that the character will blatantly and predictably fall in love with the guy as soon as his name is first mentioned . . . but we still watch them and read them. There's no twist in my story. I genuinely mean it when I say it: I do not live happily ever after with the love of my life, or anyone else for that matter.

It was my counsellor's idea for me to write this story. 'Try to keep an air of positiveness,' she kept telling me. 'The idea for this is to enable you to see the hopefulness of your situation.' Well, this is my fifth draft and I've yet to be enlightened. 'End it on a happy note,' she kept saying as her forehead wrinkled in concern while she read and reread my attempts. This is my last attempt. If she doesn't like it she knows what she can do with it. I hate writing; it bores me, but these days it passes the time. I'm taking her advice though; I'm ending this story on a happy note. I'm ending it at the beginning.

I'll tell you, just as I told her, that my reason for doing so is because it's always beginnings that are best.

Like when you're starving and it feels like you've been cooking dinner for hours: the smell is tickling your taste buds, making your mouth water, and it teases you until you take that first bite, that first beautiful bite that makes you feel like giggling ridiculously over the joy of having food in your mouth. You can't beat the first relaxing slide into a warm bath filled with bubbles, before the bubbles fade and the water gets cold; or your first steps outside in a new pair of shoes before they decide to cut the feet off you. The first night out in a new outfit that makes you feel half the size, shiny and new before you wash it, the newness fades, and it becomes just another item in your wardrobe that you've worn fifty times. The first half hour of a movie when you're trying to figure out what's going on and you haven't been let down by the end yet. The half an hour of work after your lunch break, when you feel maybe you have just enough energy to make it through the day. The first few minutes of conversation after bumping into someone you haven't seen for years, before you run out of things to say and mutual acquaintances to talk about. The first time you see the man of your dreams, the first time your stomach flips, the first time your eyes meet, the first time he acknowledges your existence in the world.

The first kiss on a first date with a first love.

At the beginning, things are special, new, exciting, innocent, untouched and unspoiled by experience or boredom. And so it's there that my story will end, for that is when my heart sat high in my chest like a helium-filled balloon. That is when my eyes were big, bright, innocently wide and as green as a traffic light all ready to go, go, go. Life was fresh and full of hope.

And so I begin this story with the end.

The End

Feeling desolate I looked around the empty wardrobes, doors wide open, displaying stray hangers and deserted shelves as though taunting me. It wasn't supposed to end this way.

What had only moments ago been a room overflowing with sound and tension, with pleas and desperate begs for him not to leave, with sobs and squeals, wails and shouts coming from both sides, was now a chamber of silence. Bags had been thrown around, violently unzipped. Drawers were pulled open, clothes dumped into sacks, drawers were banged shut, and zips made ripping sounds as they closed. More desperate begs.

Hands holding out and pleading to be held, hearts refusing, tears falling. An hour of mass confusion, never-ending shouts, boots heavily banging down the stairs, keys clanging on the hall table as they were left behind, front door banging. Then silence. Stunned silence.

The room held its breath, waited for the front door to open, for the softer surrendered sound of boots on the stairs to gradually become louder, for the bag to be flung on the ground, unzipped, drawers opened, to be filled and closed again.

But there was no sound. The door couldn't open; the keys had been left behind. I slowly sat on the edge of the unmade bed, breath still held, hands in my lap, looking around at a room that had lost all familiarity, with a heart that felt like the dark mahogany wardrobe. Open wide, exposed and empty.

And then the sobs began. Quiet whimpering sounds that reminded me of when I was five years old, when I had fallen off my bicycle all alone and away from the safe boundaries of my home. The sobs I heard in the bedroom were the frightened sobs that escaped me as a child running home sore and scared and desperate for the familiar arms of my mother to catch me, save me and soften my tears. The only arms now were my own wrapped protectively around my body. My heart was alone, my pain and problems my own. And then panic set in.

Feelings of regret, gasps for breath in a heaving chest. Hours of panic were spent dialling furiously, redialling, leaving tearful messages on an answering machine that felt as little as its owner. There were moments of hope, moments of despair, lights at the end of tunnels shone, flickered and extinguished themselves as I fell back on the bed, the fight running out of me. I'd lost track of time, the bright room had turned to darkness. The sun had been replaced by the moon that had turned its back on me and guided people in the other direction. The sheets were wet from crying and the phone sat waiting to be called to duty in my hand, and the pillow still clung to his smell just as my heart clung to his love. He was gone. I untensed the muscles in my body and I breathed.

It was not supposed to end like this.

And so I won't let it.

The Middle

Oh sweet joy, the joy of falling in love, of being in love. Those first few years of being in love, they were only the beginning. Twenty phone calls a day just to hear his voice, sex every night until the early hours of the morning, ignoring friends, favouring nights in curled up on the couch instead of going out, eating so much you both put weight on, supporting one another at family do's, catching roving eyes as they studied one another in secret, existing only in the world to be with them, seeing your future, your babies in their eyes, becoming a part of someone else spiritually, mentally, sexually, emotionally.

Nothing lasts forever they say. I didn't fall in love with anyone else, nor did he. I've no dramatic story of walking in on him, in our bedroom with the skinny girl next door. I've no story to tell you of how I was romanced by someone else, chased and showered with gifts until I gave in and began an affair. You see, I couldn't *see* anyone but him, and I know he couldn't see anyone else but me. Maybe the dramatic stories would have been better, better than the very fact that nobody and nothing, living in a state of lovelessness and heartbreak, seemed more appealing to him than me?

We had one too many Indian takeaways on the couch together, had one too many arguments about emptying the dishwasher, I piled on one too many pounds, he refused one too many nights out with his friends, we went one too many nights falling asleep without making love and went one too many mornings waking up late, grabbing a quick coffee and running out of the door without saying I love you.

You see, it's all that stuff at the beginning that's important. The stuff that you do naturally. The surprise presents, the random kisses, the words of caring advice. Then you get lazy, take your eye off the ball and before you know it you've moved to the middle stage of your relationship and are one step closer to the end. But you don't think about all that at the time. When it's happening you're happy enough living in the rut you've carelessly walked yourself straight into.

You have fights. You say things you definitely mean but afterwards pretend you don't. You forgive each other and move on, but you never *really* forget the words that are spoken. The last fight we had was the one about who burned the new expensive frying pan, that's the one that ended it. It stopped being about the frying pan after the first two minutes. It was about how I never listened, how his family intruded, about the fact he always left his dirty laundry on the floor and not in the basket, about how our sex life was non-existent, how we never did anything of substance together, how crap his sense of humour was, how horrible a person I was, how he didn't love me anymore. Little things like that . . .

This fight lasted for days, I knew I hadn't burned the frying pan, he 'could bet his life,' on the fact he hadn't even used it over that week and, 'of course he didn't seeing as I was the one who did the cooking around here,' which according to him was, 'an admission to burning the pan.' Years of a wonderful relationship had turned to that? He went out both nights that weekend and so did I. It was like a competition to see who could come home the latest, who could ring the least, who could be gone for the longest amount of time without contact, who could go the longest without calling all their friends, family and police, sick with worry. When you train yourself not to care, the heart listens.

One night I stayed out all night without telling him where I'd gone. I even turned my phone off. I was being childish; I was only staying in a friend's house, awake all night turning my phone on and off, checking for messages. Waiting for the really frantic one that would send me flying home and into his arms. I was waiting for the desperate calls, to hear I love you, to hear the sound of a man in love wanting to hang on to the best thing that had ever happened to him. As proof, as a sign that there was something worth holding on to. No such phone call came. That night taught us something. That I had stooped that low and that he hadn't cared or worried like he should have.

We had an argument and he left. He left and I chased.

You know those moments at the end of movies when

people announce their undying love in front of a gasping crowd? When there's music, a perfect speech, and then he smiles at you with tears in his eyes, throws his arms around your neck and everyone applauds, feeling as happy about the end result as you are? Well imagine if that didn't happen. Imagine he says no, there's an awkward silence, a few nervous laughs and people slowly break away. He turns away from you and you're left there with a red face, cringing and wishing you'd never made that speech, taken part in the car chase, spent the money on flowers and declared your love in the middle of a busy shopping street at lunch hour.

Well, where do you go from there? That's something the movies never tell you. And not only is the moment embarrassing, it's heart breaking. It's the moment when your best friend, the person who said they would love you forever, stops seeing you as the person they want and need to protect. So much so that they can say no to you in front of the gathering crowd. It's the moment that you realise absolutely everything you shared is lost because those eyes didn't look at you like they should have and once did. They were the eyes of an embarrassed stranger shrugging off the begging words of an old lover.

Faces looks different when the love is gone. They begin to look just how everyone else sees them, without the light, sparkle – just another face. And the moment they walk away, it's as though the fact you know they sneeze seven times exactly at a quarter past ten every morning means nothing. Like your knowledge of their allergy to ginger and their penchant for dancing around in their underwear to Bruce Springsteen isn't enough to hold you together. The little things you loved so much about a person become the little things they are suddenly embarrassed you know. All that while you're walking away in that awkward, uncomfortable silence.

When you return home feeling foolish and angry to a house that's being emptied you begin to wish all those dark thoughts away. I began to wish that we were still together and feeling miserable rather than having to go through goodbyes. He still felt part of me, I was still his, I was his best friend and he was mine. Yet there was just the minor detail of not actually being *in* love with one another and the fact that any other kind of relationship just wasn't possible. I begged and pleaded, he cried and shouted, until our voices were hoarse and our faces were tearstained.

Feeling desolate, I looked around the empty wardrobe with its doors wide open, displaying stray hangers and deserted shelves as though taunting me. It wasn't supposed to end this way.

The Beginning

He used to get the same bus as me. He got on one stop after me and got off one stop before. I thought he was gorgeous from the very first day I spotted him outside after wiping the condensation from the upstairs window of the bus. It was dark, cold, raining, seven o'clock in the morning in November. In front of me a man slept with his head against the cold vibrating glass, the woman beside me read a steamy page of a romance novel, probably the cause of the fogged up windows. There was the smell of morning breath and morning bodies on the stuffy bus. It was quiet, no one spoke, all that was audible were the faint sounds of music and voices from the earphones of Walkmans.

He rose from that staircase like an angel entering the gates of heaven. His hair was soaking, his nose red, droplets of rain ran down his cheeks and his clothes were drenched. He wobbled down the aisle of the moving bus sleepily, trying to make his way to the only free seat. He didn't see me that day. He didn't see me for the first two weeks but I got clever, moving to the seat by the staircase where I knew he would see me. Then I took to keeping my bag on the chair beside me so no one could sit down, and only moving it when he arrived at the top of the stairs.

Eventually he saw me. A few weeks later he smiled; a few weeks on he said something; a few weeks later I responded. Then he took to sitting beside me every morning, sharing knowing looks, secret jokes, secret smiles. He saved me from the drunken man who tried to maul me every Thursday morning. I saved him from the girl who sang along loudly with her Walkman on Wednesday evenings.

Eventually, on the way home on a sunny Friday evening in May, he stayed on an extra stop, got off the bus with me and asked me to go for a drink with him. Two months later I was in love, falling out of bed at the last minute and running with him to the same bus stop most mornings. Sleeping on his shoulder all the way to work, hearing him say he had never loved anyone else in his life as he loved me, believing him when he said he would never fall out of love with me, that I was the most beautiful and wonderful woman he had ever met. When you're in love you believe everything. We shared kisses that meant something, hearts that fluttered, fingers that clasped, and footsteps that bounced.

Oh sweet joy, the joy of falling in love, of being in love. Those first few years of being in love, they were only the beginning.

Maggie Alderson was born in London a long time ago, and is the author of three bestselling novels, *Pants on Fire*, *Mad About the Boy* and *Handbags and Gladrags*, which have been translated into many languages. Moving to Sydney was the inspiration for the first two, while *Handbags and Gladrags* is set at the designer fashion shows of New York, London, Milan and Paris, which she has been covering as a glossy magazine editor and newspaper fashion writer, for over 15 years. She moves a lot and is currently shacked up back in the UK, by the sea in Hastings, with her husband and young daughter. This is the second anthology she has co-edited in aid of Warchild.

ARE YOU READY, BOOTS?

Maggie Alderson

'*Dang diddy dang diddy dang diddy dang . . .*' I sang to myself as I zipped the boot up to my knee, the soft black leather stretching to hug my calf. I got up and looked at myself in the full-length mirror.

'Nancy Sinatra eat your heart out,' I said to my reflection. 'These boots were made for me.'

I couldn't believe my luck. Not only were these killer boots 50% off in the Barneys shoe department sale, they were even my size. And they weren't just boots – they were actual Manolos. Here I was in New York City, shopping just like Carrie. Sex was the word for it – and for these very high-heeled, very black, very pointy boots.

Boots so high and black and pointy indeed, that all I could do after admiring myself in the mirror was to turn round to my pal Spencer and growl.

'Grrrrrrrr,' I said, copping a vamp pose with my booted leg forward, my teeth bared.

'Good Lord in the foothills, Miss Lulu,' said Spencer, in his hilarious southern accent – real: he had come to New

York from Charleston when he was seventeen. 'You are such a true minx in those boots, I swear I am quite afraid of you.'

Now totally overexcited – Spencer always had that effect on me, not unassisted by the second bottle of Cristal he had insisted on ordering for us at lunch – I asked the nearest sales assistant for the other boot.

I zipped it on and set off stalking up and down the shoe department, working those heels like RuPaul.

'These boots were made for strutting,' I sang to Spencer.

'Yes, ma'am,' he agreed. 'So why don't you just strut right off and pay for them? It is nearly the cocktail hour and Spencer is one thirsty boy.'

I was still admiring the boots – while the sensible side of my brain tried to reason with the champagne-fuddled one, which was insisting they were a bargain – when my other great New York pal, Betty, came shuffling over in a pair of red patent mules which were clearly three sizes too big for her. She looked like a little girl dressing up in mummy's clothes.

'What do you think of these?' she asked us. 'They're only $95, down from $400.'

'They'd be real nice on The Hulk,' said Spencer.

'If only the size had gone down along with the price they'd be great on you,' I added. 'But look – check out these boots. Aren't they totally perfect?'

'Wow,' said Betty, momentarily distracted from the tantalising bargains on her own feet. She was famous in our crowd for never paying the full price for anything; it was like a religion with her. 'Those are so hot. They look great on you. How much are they?'

'Who cares?' I answered, strutting around a bit more. 'They make me feel like a Bond girl, I totally have to have them.'

I finally came to a halt in front of a full-length mirror, where I was quite mesmerised by how good I thought the boots made me look. They seemed to lengthen and slenderise my legs. They made me look browner. They made me look richer. Kinder. More intelligent. I felt like I had won the shoe lottery.

'These are the boots I'm going to be wearing when I meet my husband,' I proclaimed.

And they were. Kind of. I didn't wear my kinky boots – as Spencer had dubbed them – for six months after I bought them. Even though they were real Manolos and truly beautiful and half price in the sale, I felt so sick and ashamed about how much I had spent on them – money I could ill afford after blowing two months' rent money on that four day trip to New York – I couldn't bear to look at them, let alone wear them.

They were still in the Barneys carrier bag, which I had brought home in my suitcase as a style souvenir, stuffed under my bed.

And that's where they stayed until one dreary winter Sunday evening. Spencer was over in London for one of his hectic visits and he called up to tell me I was coming out with him and six of his favourite boy pals that night to the launch of a new restaurant.

'But it's Sunday, Spencer,' I whined at him. 'We went out last night, we went to brunch today and then to an exhibition, and we're having drinks again tomorrow. It's not like I haven't seen you and it's not like you have no one else to go with. You've got your usual posse of poofters lined up, haven't you? Why do you need me?'

There was silence on the other end of the phone. A loud silence I knew all too well from the three years I had shared a flat with Spencer, before he had moved back to the States. He could say more just breathing than most people could put over with RADA coaching and a Hollywood script.

'Spencerrrrrr,' I whined, stretching out on my sofa. 'It's already past seven, it's a school night, it's drizzling, I'm knackered, my hair's dirty and I have nothing to wear. Nothing.'

'I'll pick you up at eight, Missie Lulu,' said Spencer, firmly. He paused, then continued. 'Why don't you wear those kinky boots you bought in Barneys that time? They made you look like a trailer park Honor Blackman. I like that look on you.'

As always with Spencer, who had a personality so charismatic he could have set up his own evangelical TV ministry, I did what I was told. I put the pointy boots on. Standing in front of my mirror wearing nothing but them and my undies, I had to say, they looked pretty damned good.

Inspired by their sex kitten appeal I backcombed my filthy hair and tied it up into a Bardot-esque high ponytail, with my fringe falling over one eye. Then I threw open my wardrobe and raked through the hangers for something good enough to wear with my special boots.

Almost immediately I found the perfect thing: a vintage Pucci-esque (i.e. psychedelic bri-nylon from a charity shop) mini kaftan. I slipped it over my head and felt immediately compelled to dance the pony with myself. It was a great look, but I couldn't hack it.

Apart from anything else, the restaurant was in Mayfair and the nylon mini was definitely not a West End look. So instead I played it safe with a classic black shift dress and some Jackie O-style ropes of pearls, with my kinky boots as a wicked statement at foot level. I pouted at my reflection one more time and ran downstairs.

* * *

It was the usual night out with Spencer and his merrie men. Hilarious laughter, totally unnecessary nastiness about everyone else there, and far too much to drink.

I was on my way to the loo after about five glasses of champagne in half an hour when I first spotted Charlie. You couldn't miss him. He was seriously handsome with a great tan and floppy blonde hair, and wearing a beautiful suit. He was standing alone in a corner of the restaurant and as I passed I could feel him checking me out.

When I came out of the ladies, he was still there, still incredibly handsome, still – incredibly – alone, and still looking at me. And I could tell by that look that he definitely wasn't gay. He wasn't admiring my dress or my French manicure – he was admiring me. I felt a bit giddy.

I went back to the boys, but found it less easy to concentrate on their antics, even though Spencer had cranked himself up into his most evil mood and was doing impersonations of people simultaneously as they walked by. It was hysterical, but my gaze kept returning to the mystery man in the corner. Still there. Still gorgeous. Still alone.

I'm sure it was the boots that made me do it, because I can't remember my brain actually forming the thought, but suddenly my feet were on their way over to where Mr Cutie Dream Man was standing,

'Hi,' I said when I got there. 'You've been standing alone for ages. I've come to keep you company.'

His broad smile revealed perfect white teeth as he held out his hand to me. His eyes were very pale blue.

'Great,' he said. 'I was hoping you would. I'm Charlie March-Edwards. How do you do?'

*   *   *

Well, I did very well, and from that moment on we did very well together. That first fated encounter led to a drink after the party – Spencer and the boys hardly even acknowledged my departure, as they had spotted a group of Argentinean polo players in the corner – and a chaste kiss as he dropped me home.

From that we moved on to a couple of dinner dates, a walk in the park, an exhibition, a movie and finally into a relationship. A boyfriend. I really had a boyfriend. A good-looking boyfriend with a really good job in the City. He even had a Porsche. He was the full 99 with a Flake, sprinkles and raspberry sauce. Amazing.

Even more amazingly, Charlie seemed to understand how it all worked. He was very cuddly, always rang me when he said he would, and after a few weeks of seeing a lot of each other he said the words every single woman most dreams of hearing.

'I want to be your boyfriend, Lulu, your proper boyfriend. Are you cool with that? Will you be my girlfriend? Will you come and meet my parents? I've told them all about you.'

I smiled like a watermelon.

Needless to say, Spencer didn't approve.

'I don't know, Miss Lulu,' he said, when I rang to tell him about the weekend with Charlie's parents at their beautiful house in Berkshire.

I was furious and gave him a taste of his own silence routine, until he continued.

'See, honey, I know all you girls think you want to marry stockbrokers and live in Chelsea and drive around in cars like trucks with two little tow-headed kids in back, and I do grant that Charles is way over on the handsome side of pretty, but are you sure he isn't just an eensy weensy bit straight for you? That's straight as in dull, darlin'. You know, boring?'

'You're just jealous,' I said.

I couldn't believe Spencer wasn't happy I'd found the perfect man. He had always been trying to set me up with people before, but I figured he just didn't like the fact that I had found Charlie all on my own.

But while I was furious with Spencer at the top level of my brain, I soon began to wonder if hadn't planted a tiny seed of doubt at a lower level. I started to notice little things about Charlie which hadn't bothered me before.

For one thing, he told jokes. He didn't *crack* jokes like Spencer and I did – off the cuff, spur of the moment one-liners. He repeated formulated jokes people had told him. And some of them were a little bit sexist and a little bit racist. I tried to dismiss it as one little fault in an otherwise perfect package, but then other things started to annoy me, too.

Like the skiing stories, and the anecdotes about his so wild (so not) days at school. We'd both left school over ten years earlier, but Charlie was still talking about it. And then there were his friends, most of whom he had known since he was at that stupid snobby school, with their own repertoires of offensive jokes and un-hilarious skiing and drinking stories.

So the doubts were there, but they were only small annoy-ances in an otherwise glorious scenario, and Charlie didn't seem to have any such problems with me. He was truly a loving and affectionate man and his parents seemed to like me too. So I wasn't really surprised when he asked me to marry him.

OK, so it wasn't the most original proposal – he took me away for the weekend to our favourite country house hotel and went down on one knee beneath the rose arbour, but it was still thrilling. And it was a huge diamond. I accepted.

We went back to our room, called his parents and mine with the good news, made love with the ardour appropriate to the occasion and then started to get dressed for dinner.

I'd had such a strong inkling that the big question was going to be popped that weekend that I had packed the kinky boots and the shift dress and pearls I'd been wearing the night we met, as a bit of fun. I thought it would be rather witty to put them on and see if Charlie noticed.

He did.

'Oh no,' he said, coming out of the bathroom with a towel around his firm brown waist. 'You're wearing those awful boots. I hate those boots.'

I was too stunned to speak. Charlie continued.

'Please don't spoil this special night by wearing them, Lulu darling,' he said. 'They're so tarty. They nearly put me off you the night we met. They're chav boots. I was so relieved when you never wore them again.'

I looked at him and for the first time saw right through the dashing, handsome exterior, to the bigoted bore inside. Spencer had been right. Charlie was a handsome ass.

As he opened the wardrobe to get out his Savile Row suit, lined with cyclamen pink, his Paul Smith shirt and his Hermès tie, I folded my arms and looked down at my kinky boots. They were so great.

'Are you ready boots?' I said to them. 'Start walking.'

Lisa Armstrong is fashion editor of *The Times* and divides her time between New York, Paris, Milan and her garden shed. Her best-selling novel *Front Row* uncovered the frocks and feuds of the fashion world. Her fourth novel, *Deja View*, recently published by Hodder and Stoughton, does pretty much the same thing with a ménage à trois.

THE COMMON TOUCH

Lisa Armstrong

I owe everything to Clare.

I've always made that absolutely clear whenever journalists ask. I think it pays to be scrupulously honest in these situations, don't you? As scrupulously honest as these situations allow.

And it's true. I don't have any illusions about it. Without Clare I could have been stacking shelves in Morrisons, or trapped in some piss-soaked lift with four snot-faced brats and a crack habit. It's my common touch apparently. It was always going to be all or nothing with me.

The funny thing about the common touch is that it's bloody rare. Or it is in my line of work. Tony Blair had it when he first came on the show, flirting with Clare, flirting with the viewers, flirting with his mug of tea. I'd made that tea, but I take no credit. He'd have flirted with Simon if hadn't been for the Christian vote.

Kate Moss has it. She could sell halitosis to a dentist. It's not actually about being common. It's about accessible classiness, apparently – and I'm going by the focus groups here.

It's about reaching out from the screen to grab the nation by the goolies just as it's sitting down to a lunch of cut price baked beans and sliced white bread that tastes like the foam inside one of those bargain kids duvets from Woollies – and giving them a bit of easily digested glamour to drizzle on top.

Or that's what Gil, our producer, always said. 'Know why the opposition's sinking without a trace?' he would crow every time the new viewing figures for Lunch with Simon and Clare came in. 'Cos that Miss Frigidaire on the other side looks like she's got a poker shoved up her Elle MacPhersons. Alright so she's going out with a soap star and she's always at the right parties. But viewers can't take that much glamour at one o'clock in the afternoon. They want to see a bit of humanity.'

Then he would rake his fingers through his transplant in mock sympathy for the losers running the other side and chuckle. 'They thought they'd pulled off such a coup getting that skinny cow to present, but all it's done is rub the public's noses in precisely how scummy their lives are'.

Clare had the common touch. The battle with the weight. The bad hair months. The procession of pictures in all those celebrity magazines showing her so-called misguided wardrobe choices. I don't know how the witches on those magazines sleep at night. How would they feel if their every tiny ripple of cellulite and wrinkle got blown up like soufflé on the cover of their rags?

But Clare was brilliant. She'd worked out exactly how to turn the taunts to her advantage. I've sometimes wondered whether the flicky hair-cuts and the harsh shade of news-reader chrome blonde that made her pale, crumpled, face look like a pummeled grapefruit were deliberate. It wasn't as if she couldn't afford to go to the best salons – or get a tan and some Botox come to that. I bet it was part of the game plan, like the mascara that smudged whenever one of the callers got halfway emotional. Jesus, it's been thirty years since the first breakthroughs at Maybelline.

She's much cleverer and more sophisticated than anyone's ever given her credit for. You try sitting at the other end of those endless bleeding-heart calls while three cameras slice away your flesh to get at the sincerity and see what it does to your Magdelene College education. Not that anyone knew about the degree, apart from Gil, and possibly Simon. I didn't even know about it for a while. Clare had a problem with elitism.

She had no problem with sincerity, however. Politicians would kill for that brand of sincerity. And I include Tony Blair – I saw the way he stared at her that time. Clare thought he was flirting and the menopausal flush that spread from her chins (she was going through one of her heavy phases) right up to her freshly bleached roots made it onto the front pages of all the tabloids the next day. For the first time I understood why she never bothered with fake tan.

The *Sun* called her a Clare Babe and said it wasn't surprising that she and Tony had such chemistry. The Fashion Editor of the *Mirror* concluded that despite, or maybe because of, the occasional dodgy outfit and puffy ankles, Clare was every man's ideal woman.

No one can deny she was good. Every viewer who ever called in to talk about their botched hysterectomy, their obese teenagers and their balding, farting, shiftless pets would get the same sympathetic, owly smile and watery, hazel-eyed nod of sympathy. At the end, the caller would give a satisfied little snivel and then, nine times out of ten they'd say something like, 'By the way, Clare, I saw you at those awards the other night and those so-called fashion critics don't know what they're talking about. You looked gorgeous'.

And Simon? Simon would look at Clare adoringly, fidget with his Paul Smith shirt collar and nod. Though once, halfway through a particularly harrowing call from a woman who'd had the wrong kidney removed, the camera caught him picking his cuticles.

Alright, so I'm exaggerating about the crack and the crappy supermarket job. It wasn't as if I'd grown up on a sink estate, as my step-dad points out with monotonous regularity on the increasingly rare – thank God – occasions the family gets together. Maybe not. But the pinched, miserable, plywood '70s cul de sac we grew up in – rusting Austin Allegro in the garage, nylon fitted sheets on the bed – wasn't exactly a gas either. And it doesn't even make good copy. You realize these things after a while. It's part of the job. You name a publication and I can tailor good copy to suit it. If a tabloid asks how much I value Clare's friendship, I say something like 'I'd give my right ovary to save her'. Usually gets a laugh from the hack at the other end of the phone, and it always makes it into the paper. If it's *In Style* I say something like, 'I love her so much, I'd let her have the last Prada dress in the shop'. Prada? That's a laugh. It doesn't have the common touch you see. And it goes without saying that it wouldn't fit her.

Personally I don't know why they're still so obsessed with Clare and me. I'd like them to just drop the whole thing and start afresh.

*   *   *

Starting afresh was exactly what I did the first day I walked into Clare's dressing room. She didn't share with Simon because she said his pathological untidiness made her nervous, but really, as I discovered later, it was because she wanted to listen to classical music – and I'm not just talking Mozart and the *Schindler's List* music, but serious, headache inducing stuff – and he wanted to listen to Dido.

Just getting to that room was a triumph. I almost didn't get the application in on time. The pathetic printer in the library had been out of order and the closing sign had already been flipped round in the post office. But I'd pleaded with the hatchet-faced drone locking the door, spun him a story about this being a once in a lifetime chance, batted my admittedly sparse lashes, and said he wouldn't want me to end up on the scrap heap of society for the sake of two minutes, would he?

I couldn't have been the most qualified for the job. Working in a kennels doesn't give you an obvious edge when it comes to being a PA for one of the country's most successful TV presenters. But I'd been really good at typing and secretarial skills at school. And I was excellent at shovelling shit.

Simon wasn't the only one mystified by his wife's choice. But he was the only one I overheard vocalizing his dismay.

'Christ Clare, you could have got someone a bit more . . . presentable.'

There was a pause. Clare had one of those smiles you could hear though a closed door. I could hear it now. 'Whom are we going to be presenting her to?' she asked eventually, in her neutral, TV Personality of the Year accent. 'She's our invisible back-up. No one who matters is ever going to see her. She's . . . stolid. She'll organize us. And she'll sort out your dressing room. I wouldn't be surprised if she doesn't stumble across a few dead bodies in there. We don't need Julia Roberts for that.' She laughed. 'Honestly, how a man can emerge from such squalor looking so immaculate I'll never know.'

'You're the one with skeletons,' sulked Simon. 'I don't think I can stand having her galumphing round my dressing room.'

'Don't be petulant,' Clare soothed, in her missing-kidney tone. She lowered her voice. 'I told you, Simon, no more mini-skirts.'

'Christ, not if she's the one wearing one. On that my precious, we can both agree.'

I was a bit lardy in those days. Simon's comments were like oil off a whale's back. They don't ever mean much when men say them because half of them secretly fantasize about chubby chasing. But I didn't lose weight for them. I did it because Clare's comments about me being stolid – God, what a Cambridge sort of word – had made me break down and weep.

After a year or so the weight had dropped off. The gruelling hours. And God knows there were enough diet experts on the show to make Clare's excess poundage look like a wilful act of stubbornness.

I worked like a demon. I wasn't going back to those kennels ever again. I sorted out Clare's schedule, helped with her scripts, found her a hairdresser who could do stylish and accessible, and when she went into hospital for her hysterectomy – cue a six page exclusive in the *Sun*, a huge boost in viewing figures and a mega publishing deal for the rights to her *Life Without a Womb* book – I moved on to Simon's bombsite.

I looked a lot better by then. It wasn't just the weight. You only had to study Clare to see what didn't work. Simon's kindled interest – inviting me round to cook supper while Clare was in hospital – was simply confirmation of what I already knew. I wasn't interested in him though. He was as transparent as the sheer bronzer he sometimes wore on air. As for his skeletons, everyone already knew about his weakness for leggy blondes in mini-skirts. I was far more interested in digging up Clare's. It would take me another two years.

I couldn't believe it when I finally found out about Clare and Gil. They'd been at it for years apparently. And no one knew. Not even Simon. What a joke. All that synthetic sympathy in the press for Clare every time Simon was caught out with another blonde and all the time she was having it off with a toupee. I suppose they got turned on by each other's Oxbridge qualifications. But I'll hand it to them, they were careful. I only found out myself after I'd followed her out of the office one night – I'd become a bit obsessed with her at that point. I felt betrayed frankly. It was like being in a really bad car crash. By then I'd become everything to her. I bought her CDs, filled in her medical records, chose her company car, advised her about her underwear, booked her theatre tickets and holidays and told her which magazines to read and which to avoid that week. We were friends. She owed me trust at least.

I won't pretend I didn't feel betrayed. Still, it's no excuse for sleeping with Simon. But he certainly wasn't worth working up a guilt complex about – too worried about rumpling his Paul Smith suits. In a way I was doing Clare a favour – better a meaningless screw with me than a fling that might turn into something with one of his mini-skirted blondes. Not that it ever would. I know the press could never understand what he was doing with a mumsy-looking sack like Clare, but the point about Simon was that all he wanted was a mummy. When he went mini-skirt chasing, he was just temporarily looking for a younger mummy.

I'd been on *Lunch With Clare and Simon* about four and a half years when the unthinkable happened. The ratings began to slip, gradually at first. But within a year, like an old whore desperate for new tricks, it was down on its knees. They all rushed around – Gil, Clare, Simon and the executives, manic smiles plastered across their disintegrating faces, trying an increasingly desperate roster of gimmicks and competitions. I had to put them out of their misery. It was so obvious – to anyone under thirty. I went to see Gil one day and told him straight that the public had grown up. They didn't want blowsy looking sympathy. And that clichéd old formula of having some frumpy woman in need of a facelift, flanked by a too-smooth-by-far bloke who could be her son didn't begin to intrigue. Nor was it any good having some geriatric male presenter slumped on a sofa next to some twenty year old bimbo. The public wanted a self-possessed presenter with long legs, a glamorous lifestyle and a date of birth this side of the Crimean War. That's why those losers on the other side were trouncing us. The funny thing is, I think he was taking it on board when Clare walked in.

Shortly after that I was moved to the TV production company's new shopping channel. I didn't get a say in this, you understand. I didn't even see Clare for three weeks after I got the letter. She was back in hospital. With a cancer scare, would you believe? When I finally confronted her she pulled that bleary-eyed mascara thing on me, told me how much she'd miss me but that she couldn't hold me back any longer. She was becoming too dependent on me for our own good and that this was a once in a lifetime opportunity for me.

Call me ungrateful, but flogging crap to the bed-ridden, the brain-addled and the insomniacs struck me as being barely one step up from serving up poor man's Winalot in the kennels. It was hardly as if I was one of those desperate-to-be-on-tv-at-any-price girls who hung around outside the offices with their CVs all day. I didn't even want to be a presenter. I just wanted to help Clare. But I did it. I sold anti-wrinkle potions that didn't make a blind bit of difference; creams that purported to banish 'dirty eye-lid syndrome', gels that got rid of 'puffy finger problems' and exercise machines that were bigger than the average ground floor and were never likely to be unpacked from their excessive, planet destroying packaging. I encouraged women to thrash their credit cards, smash their fat, and convinced them they had problems they'd never previously dreamed of. I was brilliant. And Clare never once bothered to watch me. She didn't send me so much as a postcard when I got Cable Presenter of the Year. She didn't even return my call.

It was an act of kindness really when I tipped off one of the tabloids about her and Gil. By then I'd stepped down as a presenter and got what I really wanted, which was the producer's job. As for *Lunch with Simon and Clare*, it had been languishing in the ratings gutter for so long that the press had stopped bothering even to mock it. It wasn't worth the column inches. I got them more press that week than they'd had in the past two years.

I got rid of Gil and Simon when they brought me back to the station. They were just pathetic camp old caricatures. I kept Clare on though, in a five minute weekly agony aunt slot. I put that skinny cow in as presenter, gave her a clothing allowance that was bigger than Clare's new salary and put it about that she might be a dyke.

Clare and Simon divorced – I think Simon's breakdown on a reality celebrity show was the last straw for Clare. I understand he's got some kind of one man act on cruise ships now, which should suit him perfectly. They didn't have kids so you can't feel too sorry for them. And that was another myth – that they were desperate to have babies, when the reality was Clare didn't feel like sharing her job with children.

'Times have changed,' I told the shareholders and crew at the first annual meeting after I'd taken over the running of the new lunchtime format. Not that they could complain after the ratings I'd just delivered. 'I'm very grateful to the previous generation,' I flashed my newly whitened teeth at the room. 'I know they felt they were doing the right thing, hiding their bushel under a populist light. Feeling the nation's pain, and sharing their flab. But it's not like that any more. A presenter, even a daytime presenter, doesn't have to pretend to be less intelligent than they really are. Or more . . .' I looked across at Clare and forced her to meet my eyes, '. . . stolid.' I shook my head. 'What a waste.' And for a moment I meant it. I owe everything to Clare. Perhaps that's why I despise her.

Tilly Bagshawe is a novelist and journalist. Her first novel, *Adored*, was published in 2005 by Orion in the UK and Warner Books in the US where it went straight into the *New York Times* Top Ten. A Cambridge graduate, and single mother at eighteen, Tilly has contributed numerous articles to *The Sunday Times*, *Daily Mail* and *London Evening Standard*. Now thirty-one, she divides her time between London and Los Angeles.

For more information about Tilly Bagshawe and her books, please visit her website at www.tillybagshawe.com

DOG LOVER

Tilly Bagshawe

The irony is that I've always thought of myself as a dog lover.

No, really. Even as a kid, I was crazy about them. Dogs, I mean. Particularly Chihuahuas, funnily enough. That's partly why I took the job in the first place. Well, that and the enormous salary, the guest house in Beverly Hills and the free use of the boss's Bentley Continental on weekends. But it was mostly the dog.

I can remember the advertisement now, word for word. I can even remember the taste of the big, delicious, gooey slab of carrot cake I was eating at The Coffee Bean as I read it (a cake that, by the way, I gave a good twenty percent of to the cute little Bichon Frise tethered to the table leg next to me. I hate to see dogs tethered, don't you? No? Well, I do. Because whatever anybody says, I have always, ALWAYS loved dogs. If you don't believe me ask . . . well, ask whoever you like. Because what happened was *totally* out of character for me, I assure you. Totally).

Where was I? Oh, yes, the advertisement. 'Housekeeper required,' it said. 'To provide domestic assistance for single lady in early sixties. $50,000 p/a, including guest house accommodation and use of car. No kids. One dog. Only animal-lovers need apply.'

Well, I mean, it was written for me, wasn't it?

Written. For. Me.

I called up then and there, right from the coffee shop. It was a bit awkward if you must know, because the Bichon Frise had thrown up, poor little mite. Apparently she was allergic to sugar, but I mean, really, how was I supposed to know that? The guy who owned her was *extremely* rude to me as a matter of fact. I can give you a description of him if you like? No? Well, I *will* tell you that he was cursing and yelling so much I had trouble concentrating on the call. I ask you! Some people!

Anyhoo, long story short, I called and I got an interview for the very next morning.

What was that? Was that the first time I met Mrs Andrews? Well of course it was, silly! Never seen the woman in my life until that moment. Of course, now I wish I'd never seen her at all. Amazing how *wrong* you can be about someone on a first impression, isn't it? I mean some people think that, just because I'm a little heavy, I have no self-control! How ridiculous is that? Let me tell you, just because someone battles with their weight, that's no reason to make assumptions about . . . hmm? Oh, yes, sorry. Mrs Andrews.

Well, I met her at the house and she seemed like a nice enough lady. A little quiet, perhaps. Softly spoken. Very well dressed. You know, genteel. Not all Beverly Hills-y with one of those stretched-out surgery faces and too much make-up and jewellery. She asked me a bunch of questions. Just regular stuff, you know, my background, references, experience I'd had with dogs, that sort of thing. And then she had the maid bring him in.

Nebuchadnezzar.

On a red velvet pillow.

Wearing a crown.

You probably think I'm exaggerating, but I swear to you on my departed mother's grave, God rest her soul, that was exactly what happened. A *tiny* little Chihuahua, not much bigger than a jumbo avocado. On a pillow! With a crown!!

Of course I know what you're going to say: Why didn't I get out then and there? Go on. Say it. 'Why didn't you get out then and there, Mrs McIntyre?' I mean, if the writing was on the wall . . . But you know what I say to that, Detective? *Hindsight is 20/20!* That's what I say. *Hindsight is . . .* Oh, well, alright. There's no need to lose your temper. If you'd just let me finish without interrupting all the time . . . OH YES YOU ARE YOUNG MAN! . . . I'd get to the point a mighty sight quicker.

So anyway, in comes Neb. (You'll understand I couldn't keep calling him Nebuchadnezzar, although Mrs A insisted upon it whenever she was around. Poor woman. She loved him, but she was obsessed. *Obsessed!* I mean, I ask you. What kind of a name is that to saddle a dog with? Thank the Lord the woman never had children, that's what I say. Oh she did? A daughter? That's funny. She never mentioned her. Oh well, my mistake Detective, I stand corrected!)

So at first I felt sorry for him. For the *dog*. Do try to keep up Detective. Truly, I did, I actually pitied him. With that ridiculous crown squashing his little ears. Oh, and he had leg-warmers on. Did I mention that already? Little pink legwarmers shot through with silver thread. He looked like a Kid from *Fame*. Did you ever see that show? With Leroy, the dancer? He's dead now, you know, poor man. Aids. Turned out to be one of those, you know, doo-dahs. Fairies. Anyway Neb reminded me of Leroy. Except, obviously, he was a dog. And as far as I know he'd never taken a modern dance class, although knowing what I know now, nothing would surprise me!

I think she picked the legwarmers up at Chateau Marmutt. Do you know that place? On third? No? Well, I do. When I think of the hours, not to mention the *thousands* of dollars she had me spend in that store. Two words for you Detective: *Emotional Torture*. Write that down, would you? I want it on record: what I suffered in that job was *abuse*. I swear to God, if I saw that place now, I think I'd have a panic attack. Little doggy sweaters and diamond collars and silver nail clippers and Lord knows what else they have in there. It's a crazy world we live in Detective. A crazy, crazy world. Not everyone's as nice and normal as you and me.

So, needless to say, I took the job. If I hadn't I wouldn't be sitting here now, talking to you, now would I? I took the job and the next morning I arrived and I'd barely finished unpacking in the guest house . . . have you seen Mrs A's guest house by the way?

Guest House? Doll's house more like!

I should have sued her then and there for false advertising, but you know what I always say. That's right! *Hindsight is 20/20*. Now, I grant you, I may be a smidgen over my ideal weight – oh! Detective, here, have some more water! Did something go down the wrong way? – but honestly, Calista Flockhart McBeal would have had a tough time squeezing into that so-called Queen Size bed. Queen of the dwarves maybe! Queen Ant! Queen . . . oh, right. My statement.

So anyway, I'd barely finished unpacking when Mrs A came over and handed me my 'List of Duties'.

Oh, look, you have it right there in your hand. How funny! Is that Exhibit A? Ha ha ha! Exhibit A, like on Court TV, geddit? What was that? It *is* exhibit A? Oh. Dear. Well, take a look at it would you, and you'll see my point.

3am: Check on Nebuchadnezzar. If his doggie blanket has slipped, re-cover him gently. Make sure room temperature is set to a constant sixty-eight degrees.

6am: Check Nebuchadnezzar again. If he stirs, see if he wants to go pee-pee. I prefer him to use his tray, but if he wants to go outside, make sure he's wearing his cashmere wrap. The blue one.

8am: Breakfast. Please follow the menu cards provided. If Nebuchadnezzar is reluctant to eat, taste a few mouthfuls yourself first to reassure him. Make sure you do this on all fours or he may take fright.

It goes on for eight pages. Eight pages! Look. The last entry isn't until midnight.

12 midnight: Insert Chihuahua womb-sounds CD into player. This helps Nebuchadnezzar sleep soundly through the night.

Womb sounds? Can you imagine Detective?

At first I thought it was a joke. I mean all these doggie duties were on top of my regular work as a housekeeper, you understand. But Mrs A looked deadly serious.

Hmmm? No, no I didn't say anything about it at the time. Well she was my new employer wasn't she? I wanted to make a good impression. And, like I say, at first I felt sorry for Neb. I thought perhaps if I stayed, I could help him, have him lead a more normal, carefree dog's life. Because, you know, I have always, ALWAYS loved dogs, whatever anybody might tell you. But of course, all that was before I got to know him. Before I found out first-hand what an evil, Machiavellian little *snake* he was.

And still is.

Oh, yes! You may look surprised Detective. But he planned all this you know.

Who? What do you mean *who*? Neb, of course.

Indeed I am serious! Don't you watch Court TV? *Hmmm*. Well perhaps you should. If you *did*, you'd know that the first question every good detective asks himself is: *Who stood to gain the most from the crime?*

Go on. Ask it. Ask that question!

See? Am I right or am I right? There you have it! You have your prime suspect right there.

Yes, I am aware that he's a dog. There's really no need to take that patronizing tone with me. I don't mean to be rude Detective, but *wake up and smell the coffee*, would you? Don't you see? That's exactly what he *wants* you to think. Poor, cute little Chihuahua, wouldn't hurt a fly! Butter wouldn't melt, that's what you're thinking, isn't it?

Isn't it?

I suppose I can't blame you for being sceptical. He had me fooled at first too. So much so that I actually figured I could *help* him – *ha!* That's why I took Mrs A's list with a pinch of salt. I suppose I thought that I'd be on my own with Neb for much of the day, and she wouldn't know the difference if I took him to Toy-Breeds-Yoga or out for a walk in the park. Plus, she wasn't hauling her bony ass out of bed at 3am every night to check on the dog, was she? So how would she know if I did? And yes, if truth be told, maybe I was also thinking about the money. Fifty thousand is a good salary after all. OK, yes, and a little bit about the Bentley too. Maybe. I wanted to drive it by the Coffee Bean at the weekend, you see, and put one over on that dreadful, abusive little man with the Bichon Frise.

Who's allergic to sugar now, asshole!!

But I digress. I'm not a vengeful person, Detective, as you know. Nobody can accuse me of that. No, no. Neb's welfare, at that time, was my main concern.

Anyhoo, long story short, for the first couple of months everything worked out just fine. I stuck to the parts of the list that seemed most important. I gave the dog the specially imported Fois Gras and the truffle oil, just as Mrs A asked. I made endless, and I mean *endless*, trips to Chateau Marmutt for all his little accessories. I even brushed his teeth for him, morning and night, with the tiny silver brush she'd had specially made at Fred Leighton. And believe you me Detective, that is *humiliating*, even for a dog lover like me: sticking your hand into its mouth and pulling out all the left over pieces of pate and whatnot? *Eeeugh*!

But what can I say? Neb was the woman's life, her reason for living, her *world*. And I tried to respect that, Detective, truly I did. Within reason.

No, any complaints the old lady had about me at that time were nothing to do with the dog. I'm sorry? Oh, well, it was nothing really. A silly misunderstanding. Those little things, foibles, what have you, that always come to the surface when one starts a new working relationship. What *exactly*? Well, if you must know, she complained – and I mean this is quite ridiculous, there was no basis for it whatsoever – but she complained that I talked too much. *Me!* Can you *imagine* Detective?

Well, yes, I suppose if you're going to be literal, she did say that once. That I was driving her to suicide. With my constant prattle, yes. But you know, it was said in a very *light-hearted* way. It's really not at all what you're implying . . .

Gosh, now you're *really* blowing this up out of all proportion. No, I'm not denying it as such. She *may*, in the heat of the moment, have threatened to sack me. And make me homeless, yes. But she wouldn't have *done* it Detective. Don't you see? Mrs A and I got on like a house on fire! Two peas in a pod we were! And we would have carried on that way, for years and years, I'm convinced, if it hadn't been for Neb stirring the pot with his evil, pink legwarmered paws.

It all started going wrong when she brought in the pet-psychologist. You see, I'd started to introduce a little discipline into Neb's life, and he didn't like it one bit. Not that I was cruel, you understand. Far from it. But when I saw him, just minutes after we'd got home from walkies, deliberately lower his little ass over my brand new Victoria's Secret pink mohair slippers . . . Oh yes, he shat in them Detective. Cool as a cucumber, looking right at me. It was quite deliberate I can assure you. Well when he did that, I told him 'no!' in a firm voice and I smacked him on the bottom. In fact, I wouldn't even say it was a smack. You can cross that out. CROSS IT OUT! It was a tap. It was nothing, really. But *boy* did he not like that! I saw a different side to him from then on Detective, yes indeed. And things went from bad to worse.

Whenever Mrs A was around he would ham it up, moping and rolling his eyes, cowering whenever I came near him as if I were about to hit him. I mean *me*, Detective. Me, who has ALWAYS loved dogs. Especially Chihuahuas! Neb as good as told the old lady that I was abusing him! Well, no, obviously he couldn't speak. That would be ridiculous. He's *dog*. But he didn't have to, did he? His eyes, his evil, scheming little eyes – they said it all.

Anyway, in the end Mrs A hired Dr Maxton, an animal shrink, to take a look at him. Dr Doolittle I called him. You know why? Because he *did little*! Geddit? In fact, scratch that. He did *nothing*. Dr Doonothing! Neb had him twisted around his little manicured paws from day one. He'd be right as rain, playing with his so-called friends down at Tumblepups (I say 'so-called' because there was no loyalty there Detective. None whatsoever. Neb didn't understand the meaning of the word friendship. *Uh uh*. He was rotten, rotten to the core!) But then he'd come home, take one look at Dr Doonothing, and start sulking and whining like someone forgot to give him his Prozac.

And the shrink fell for it! Not that I blame him entirely. Neb gave an Oscar winning performance. Forget Leroy from Fame. He was Lawrence Olivier! He was Marlon Brando! (Before he got fat, obviously. Poor man. People are so quick to judge heavier citizens, Detective. In the old days it was blacks and Jews and doo-dahs, but now it's the plus-sized that have become America's pariahs. Let's face it, that has a lot to do with me being here right now, doesn't it? If someone has to be blamed, it may as well be the fat woman, right? RIGHT?)

Sorry. It's just sometimes, the *injustice* of it all . . . What? Yes. Yes, after that Mrs A did let me go. *Uh huh*, yes, on the doctor's recommendation, although of course legally she couldn't give that as the *only* reason.

The other reasons? Oh, I can't remember Detective. Some trumped-up nonsense about me talking too much – I mean, *please* – and skimping on my agreed duties. Well, yes, if you're going to get literal about it I did cut back on The List a little, but who wouldn't? And as for what she said about pilfering petty cash and taking the Bentley during the week without permission, well that was outrageous. Totally groundless.

Sorry? The mid-week episode at the Coffee Bean? Oh, you mean the assault charge? Yes, yes, yes, but that got dropped. It was all a silly misunderstanding, I can assure you. No, it was Neb who got me fired, Neb who turned her against me.

That was why I had to act.

Don't you see? I had no choice.

I got the arsenic off the internet believe it or not. Amazing thing, the internet. Have you ever been on, Detective? Ever *surfed the web*? See, I've got all the lingo! I can show you if you like. It's a wonder! You can buy just about anything you want there nowadays: fancy Christmas gifts, furniture, intimate feminine apparel, lethal poisons. But I was very careful. I only bought a small dose – enough to kill a household pet, they said – and a little bit extra, to make doubly sure I got the job done cleanly. I wouldn't have wanted to leave him suffering you see, Detective. I'm not a cruel person. But I couldn't just let him think he'd gotten away with it, could I? When we start letting animals Lord it over us, it's a slippery slope, isn't it? I had to take a stand.

But then . . . then . . . oh Detective it's all so *horrible*! And it's all Neb's fault. He could smell the poison somehow, I'm sure of it. And he stepped back and took his chance. He seized the moment.

How was I supposed to know she'd get down on her hands and knees and taste his food?

Or that she already had a weak heart?

And why, why in the name of Jesus, did she go and eat all of it?

Anyway Detective, I think I've said enough. Like I said, I don't really want to say anything about this until my lawyer gets here. But you are *terribly* easy to talk to. I feel we really connected on some level. Don't you?

All I *will* say is that this whole idea that I was taking my revenge on poor, dear Mrs Andrews is absolute codswallop. It was Neb! It was all Neb! He's the one who should be in here calling his lawyer, not me.

You do realize that she left him everything, don't you? The house, the car, the art collection? Oh yes. Nebuchadnezzar cleaned up.

It all worked out exactly the way he planned it.

Faith Bleasdale grew up in Devon, studied history at Bristol University, and then moved to London where she decided to put her passion for writing to good use. She now writes full time, and is currently based in Singapore although frequently returns to the UK to get her London fix. Her novels include *Deranged Marriage*, *Peep Show* and *Agent Provocateur*, the last of which was published this year.

THE TAMING OF THE PLAYBOY

Faith Bleasdale

It was more than unbelievable. When my mother called me to tell me that my brother, Tim, was getting married, I thought it was some sort of joke. Because Tim had always said marriage was for mugs. He said that all women wanted to tie men down, but he was cleverer than most men, and wouldn't be trapped. He said he was dedicated to being a playboy.

He was a man who ran away from commitment the way the rabbit runs away from the dogs on a greyhound track. He even moved to Singapore to get away from one poor girl (well he was offered a good job there, but the timing was a bit suspect). I told my mum that she must be wrong, and I hung up on her to get the news straight from his mouth.

'Yes,' Tim said. 'It's true, and I can't wait.' While I was shocked into silence, he then went on to extol the virtues of his bride to be, Angela. She was beautiful, intelligent, very caring, sweet, and he spoke about her with such pride in his voice that I wanted to know where my real brother was.

The engagement was not going to be a long one, which

again surprised me. My 'real' brother would have waited at least a year to see if he got bored, or if someone better came along. But no, they were getting married in a couple of months. In Singapore.

As we prepared to fly out there (my parents and I were staying for a month leading up to the wedding), an official engagement photograph arrived. Grinning inanely, Angela and Tim were wearing matching outfits, and had their arms around each other. This wasn't like my brother; he ruthlessly mocked people who did things like that. My mother thought it was lovely and showed everyone she knew; my father commented on how gorgeous Angela was. And she was. But still, nothing was as it should have been. I felt that I was in my own twilight zone.

I actually felt bitter about the whole situation. The way Tim had always been so cynical about relationships and love had ruined every relationship I'd ever had. Or so I believed. For some reason I attracted men like my brother. Every man I dated followed the same path. Didn't call on time, let me chase them (I was verging on becoming the world's best stalker), didn't believe in romance, stood me up on various occasions and then completed my humiliation by callously dumping me. Honestly, every one. And their behaviour mirrored my brother's. I suppose I could have taken comfort in the fact that now my brother was settling down, there was hope for me. But I wasn't feeling like taking comfort, I was feeling betrayed.

Tim had been in Singapore for just under a year and because of work I hadn't visited him yet. So, despite the fact I wasn't keen on the reason for going, I was looking forward to it.

When we arrived, Tim met us, alone. He looked like my

brother, and as he kissed my cheek and told me that I looked haggard, he even sounded like my brother. Tim explained that Angela felt that it was important that he had some time alone with us before we met her. My parents thought that this was the most considerate thing they'd ever heard.

After the twelve hour almost sleepless flight, wedged in between my mother and father like a child, I was too tired to ask him all I wanted to know. My interrogation would have to wait.

Tim lived in a condo. It was a brand new, tall, skyscraper type thing. It reminded me of those TV shows set in the future. In London my brother had lived in a bachelor pad. It was sparse, messy and looked about as inviting as his dirty laundry. I knew he'd probably have cleaned up for our coming but as he opened the door and ushered us in, I wasn't prepared for what we faced. Apart from the fact that the apartment was huge, stunning, all marble floors and dark teak furniture, there were fresh flowers everywhere, a number of plants were thriving and warm-coloured pictures decorated the walls. There were even cushions for goodness' sake.

A tour of the place proved that this wasn't the only room that had been made delightful. I knew who the culprit was, and it wasn't Tim. I know by now you probably think me slightly evil, but I was just confused and displaced. My brother lived in a flat that I would live in. Actually he lived in a flat I could only aspire to live in.

'I suppose that this is what happens when you live with a woman,' I said. My mother gave me a dirty look; I must have sounded surly.

'I don't live with a woman,' Tim replied.

'But . . . Angela?' I asked, confused.

'No, she lives with her parents. It's not appropriate for

her to move in until we're married.' My mother actually cried and hugged him. I almost cried, but for a completely different reason.

We freshened up, had some coffee, and waited for Angela to appear. My mother was keener than ever, my father was pretty excited and Tim was more enthusiastic than I'd ever seen him. I was the only normal member of my family, although I was probably the only person in the world who saw it like that.

Angela arrived. My mother immediately pounced on her. More tears and kisses and hugs. My father was slightly more formal and shook her hand. I gave her a half-hearted hug; Tim gave me a dirty look which I very much ignored.

'I'm so glad to meet you all,' she said. In a flash she was part of our family. My mother immediately started talking to her about wedding plans. Flowers, dresses, bridesmaids, cars. Then Angela formally asked me, as her future sister, if I'd be one of her bridesmaids. Luckily everyone else was too busy gushing to notice my ingratitude. As the time wore on, it became clear that this was no joke. My brother treated Angela like a princess. He couldn't stop staring at her, touching her, and he was constantly making sure she was alright. If I wasn't so evil, I would have said that there was no doubt that they were in love. But I still didn't understand. Angela was nice enough, and she was gorgeous, but I still couldn't quite get why my brother had changed his entire personality for this woman. And you might think that I'm exaggerating, but as soon as he had his first girlfriend, my brother had been all about breaking hearts. It took up so much of his time that he didn't really have an awful lot else going on.

So in between jetlag, having fittings for my bridesmaid

dress (dusky pink, and although it wasn't ugly, it definitely wasn't me), watching my parents literally fawn over Angela, like a detective I tried to work out for myself what was going on. Luckily as Angela didn't live with Tim, I had plenty of opportunities to confront him about it. Unluckily I chose a time when I'd had a little too much to drink.

'What do you see in her?' I demanded. I was slurring as I waved my glass of wine around precariously in his pristine apartment.

'What do you mean?' My mother replied, diving and snatching the glass from my hand.

'She's not that special,' I said, which wasn't nice, I know. My mother called me wicked, then she wondered where she'd gone wrong with me, and finally demanded that I become more like Angela. My brother refused to speak to me. My father's eyes were full of disappointment.

Of course it was Angela who healed the threatened rift. Apparently she ever so reasonably told my brother that it was hard for me, as I'd never met her before, learning they were getting married. In fact she used the word over-whelming. It was also Angela who said that she would take my parents to see her parents while Tim and I spent some time alone. My hatred for this perfect being grew. Especially as she'd replaced me as number one daughter in the eyes of my parents.

Tim took me to a bar. He ordered cocktails and he asked me what my problem was.

'It's not that I don't like her. I mean what's not to like,' I started. 'But Tim, it's just not you. You went down on bended knee, and you told me that you'd never do that. You've known her five minutes, Tim, try to understand why I'm so confused.' I was almost in tears. I felt as if everything I knew as certain had suddenly been taken away from me, leaving me with foundations that were very shaky.

'Becks, I fell in love. It's that simple.' He didn't even choke when he said the 'L' word.

'But you don't even believe in love,' I argued.

'I do now. Listen, sis, I met her and I just knew. Well I didn't, but after dating her for a month I did. She's everything I want in a woman and I didn't want to let her get away.' My brother had never really opened up to me before, something else that had changed. He poured his heart out and I began, reluctantly, to understand.

He met Angela through a work event, (they both work in banking). She bumped into him; he fancied her and started chatting her up. Before he knew it they were dating. So far, so my brother. But they quickly discovered that they had everything in common. She liked to look good; he liked her to look good. She loved to cook; he loved to eat. She loved football, and kept him supplied with beer whenever they watched it. She was great fun and enjoyed going out with his friends, who were all incredibly jealous of him, and she never minded if he wanted to go out with the boys on his own. She was compliant in most things he wanted, but not all. She made it clear early on that co-habitation wasn't on the cards. She told him that her respect for her parents prevented her from doing that. He liked that she was old-fashioned and had values. In fact, he confided after a few more cocktails, she was a virgin until they got engaged. And who wouldn't want to marry a virgin he asked? I had no idea.

It all began to make sense. My brother had fallen in love with a sweet, innocent girl who wanted to take care of him in the old-fashioned way. To such an extent that they'd decided that she was going to give up work when they were married, so she could concentrate on being a good wife. Well, with all that on offer I probably would have married her too.

As my brother got drunk, he made it clear that he was one lucky bastard, to have got everything he could possibly want in a woman, and very importantly know that no one else had had it before him. So, my brother hadn't actually changed as much as I thought. His life with Angela would be better and I didn't doubt that he loved her, but had she not been this subservient little thing, then there was no way he'd be getting married. He was pretty much marrying a very attractive doormat.

I almost felt sorry for her after that. I was much nicer. We bonded over shopping, (she wouldn't buy anything unless she was sure that Tim would approve), and lunch and finally I showed an interest in the wedding plans. Still being a little evil, I even tried to teach her about feminism, but she thought that it was a joke. I'm sure I saw her look at her huge diamond rock and then at me with pity as I told her about equality. I still wasn't in love with the idea of Tim getting married. I certainly panicked at the idea that in order for me to get married I'd have to be like Angela, but I decided to accept things for what they were. Even my single status. Although, that didn't detract my mother from trying to ascertain which of Tim's friends were single and which wouldn't mind a strong-minded woman like me. Apparently none of them, was the answer. So then she decided that if I didn't talk when introduced to them, I might be in with a chance. Her behaviour was like something out of an Austen novel.

Despite this, I began to enjoy my holiday and Singapore. It was incredibly hot, and I was immune to the humidity.

My brother's condo complex boasted a swimming pool which I sat next to quite happily for hours on end. Angela had given up work by now, but refused to tan, apparently it's not a popular look in Singapore. I carried on regardless, although my mother fretted that a tan might make me even more unlikely to find a mate.

While Tim was at work I reverted to being a child and went sightseeing with my parents. We went to the zoo, the bird-park, out to the man-made beaches of the East coast, museums, and when we weren't sightseeing we helped out with wedding plans. Well my mother did; I sat by the pool. Sometimes Angela joined us, and the bond between her and my parents grew.

Jealousy is a bad thing, we all know that, but it's also quite natural. So where I'd spent a week or so making an effort and being almost happy about the wedding, now I wasn't. Angela was like this dream girl. She made me look bad even when I wasn't being. My mother criticised the way I dressed (ten year old sarong and plastic yellow flip-flops mainly), my hair, the fact that I didn't wear enough make-up, everything about the way I looked. My personality didn't escape either. My sarcasm made me highly unattractive, I didn't smile enough; my humour was too base, no man would ever want me unless I learnt to be less opinionated. Throughout these attacks, no one stood up for me. Except for me, of course. I was getting to the stage where I just wanted the wedding to be over and for my life to resume some normality. I began to think that Singapore was putting spells on people and I wanted to escape before it got me too.

The wedding day arrived. I donned my dusky pink amidst extreme excitement at Angela's parent's apartment. The other three bridesmaids, two friends and a cousin, were all giggling as our hair and make-up was expertly applied. The other bridesmaids were all beautiful and slim, and although I was only a size ten I felt frumpy next to them. My mother obviously felt the same. She looked incredibly worried for my prospects.

I have to admit to feeling a lump in my throat when Angela was ready. Her satin white dress (which in all fairness she almost had a right to wear), was so incredible. She looked breathtaking. Even my evil side couldn't find fault. And as everyone was so nervous and excited, I got caught up in the middle of it.

In Singapore you have to go to the Registry of Marriage. They'd done that bit already so they were in fact legally married, but it was official and unromantic, according to Angela, so this was their blessing, which was treated as their proper wedding. It was held in the grounds of a lovely hotel, and was beautiful. It went without a hitch. My brother stood there, tall, handsome and proud and I actually shed a tear – whether out of happiness or sadness I'm unsure. Afterwards we had champagne outside while the photographs, which were the horribly cheesy kind, as all wedding photos seem to be, were taken. But Tim didn't seem to mind as he picked Angela up and fed her champagne and they stood looking lovingly into each other's eyes by the flowers.

Finally, the heat got to us so we were allowed to head inside for the air-conditioned reception. The food was wonderful, the speeches mercifully short, and the drink flowing. Although my mother told me that I really ought not to eat and definitely not drink if I had any chance of finding a man.

I didn't. I met Tim's new friends who were politely disinterested in me. I re-met his friends from the UK who didn't bother with politeness as they'd known me most of my life.

My mother looked so upset that at one point I'm sure she was trying to persuade a waiter to ask me to dance.

I sat in the corner getting drunk as I watched my brother dancing with his bride. The other bridesmaids dancing with his friends. Angela's friends dancing with the rest of his friends. Even my mother had decided to ignore me. I'm sure I heard her tell one of Angela's family members she had no idea who I was. So I sat in the corner with a bottle of champagne and a very bruised ego.

A woman around my age came and sat next to me. She smiled shyly and introduced herself as one of Angela's cousins, Sasha. I gave her some of my champagne and wondered why she wasn't dancing.

'I'm tired. It's been fun, but I needed to rest. You're Tim's sister aren't you?'

'Yes, Becky. How come we haven't met before?'

'Angela and me, well we aren't very close anymore. It's a bit tricky.' She turned red and I became very interested. I plied my victim with more champagne and did the same to myself. Finally I was ready to interrogate.

'Why aren't you close? It seems that everyone loves Angela.' I hoped I didn't sound bitter.

'Oh they do. Too much. She stole a boyfriend from me when I was twenty-five and she was just eighteen. It broke my heart. I wouldn't have come today but my parents made me.' She turned redder. Emboldened I refilled her glass and looked sympathetic.

'That's awful. But she was young.'

'No, it's not that. I shouldn't tell you.'

'Please do.' I was almost begging. There was a long pause.

'She is a bitch.' Wait. I stared at my new friend incredulously. I indicated that she should carry on, and she hesitated for just a second before she did so. 'She always has been. She manipulates men and chews them up. I know you wouldn't believe it to look at her but . . .'

'You must be talking about someone else. Angela's compliant, that's what my brother says. And she cooks for him, and takes care of him.'

'Of course she does. She met him and decided that she was going to marry him. That's what she did. She knows that a way to a man's heart is through his stomach – and his ego.'

'Are you saying that it's an act?'

'Well, yes. She hates football but is always boasting about how you can hook many men by saying you like it. And she hated her job, so she told Tim that it would be better for him if she quit.'

'Are you telling me that my new sister-in-law knew what she was doing with my brother?'

'Oh yes, she knew about his reputation with women, my other cousin told me, you know, the bridesmaid. Well, she did her research and she presented herself to him, with the goal of today in mind.'

'You mean my brother, who thought that he was the clever one by marrying her, has been played.'

'Don't get me wrong, I think they'll be happy enough. Apparently she's very good in bed.' Sasha turned bright red; I stared open-mouthed.

'But she didn't sleep with my brother until they were engaged. She was a . . .' the penny fell from a great height.

'She told him she was a virgin. I know, but it's not true. She's clever.'

'My brother thinks she was a virgin, thinks she isn't going to cause him any trouble, thinks he's got a doormat, but all the time she was in control? She tamed the playboy?'

'Yes.' I was stunned; astonished. I stood up. My legs were slightly wobbly, either through the drink or the shock. 'Are you going to tell him?' she asked. I thought of my brother, how happy he was, of my upset, of my loveless life, of my future.

'No bloody way. I'm going to get some lessons.'

Elizabeth Buchan lives in London with her two children and her husband. She read for a double degree in English and History at the University of Kent at Canterbury and began her career writing blurbs for Penguin Books. She later became a fiction editor at Random House but decided after a couple of years that she should do what she wished to do: write. For her first two novels, she took as her subject very typical watersheds – the French Revolution (*Daughters of the Storm*) and the Second World War (*Light of the Moon*). The latter followed the fortunes of a woman SOE agent in occupied France. Her third novel, *Consider the Lily*, is the story of a woman in the Thirties who comes to terms with her unhappiness through gardening. *Perfect Love* explored the bargains and accommodations that have to be made in any relationship. *Against Her Nature* reworked Thackeray's *Vanity Fair* set against a backdrop of the Lloyds disasters during the Eighties. They were followed by *Secrets of the Heart* and *Revenge of the Middle Aged Woman*. The latter has sold all over the world and has been made into a television film for CBS. Her latest novels are *The Good Wife* and *That Certain Age*. She is currently writing the sequel to *Revenge of the Middle Aged Woman*.

KINDNESS

Elizabeth Buchan

At Rome airport, Sable Farrer climbed into a coach labelled 'Euro Culture 'n' Fun Ltd'. She was dressed in her customary muted way – a matching knitted caramel coloured sweater and skirt which could have been elegant, but on Sable looked dull and lumpy. Already, it felt far too hot.

As usual, she kept her head down. This was, in part, due to her terror of being noticed but, as she had grown older, in part a deepening desire not to look at things too closely. The world did not, in her view, bear too much close examination. Nevertheless, she knew perfectly well that several pairs of inquisitive, speculative eyes would be sizing her up.

She carried her hand luggage awkwardly to the back of the coach and slipped into an empty double seat. 'I wish more than anything I was not on this bus,' she thought. 'I wish I was not in Rome.' Above all, Sable wished she was not scheduled to endure a week in the company of strangers. Yet, in a moment of uncharacteristic impulse, and on a depressing winter's day in the office where she worked as a billing clerk for a utility firm, this was precisely what she had chosen to do and, furthermore, *paid* for. Why? Outside had been rain-lashed, her stomach had been a little bilious and she had discovered the pamphlet advertising the trip in her in-tray. She remembered its thin, glossy texture as she held it between her fingers. *We promise you marvellous things*, it seemed to say.

The coach jerked forward and Sable clutched at her tote bag which had toppled over. A woman in the opposite seat reached over to help and said: 'I had no idea it would be so much warmer than home. It's only April, after all.'

Sable waited for the woman's gaze to fixate on the lower part of her face which she knew from thirty-five years of experience would take approximately ten seconds. (She could see: *what happened to her?* slide like news-tape across the mind of any observers.) Sable almost never satisfied their curiosity. It was nobody's business but her own as to what had turned her mouth from the pretty childish pink bow which it had once been, into the twisted thing that marred her adult face. Equally, since she had no family, not even a cousin, there was no one who could supply chatty asides such as: '*Of course, Mary was heartbroken by what happened*' or '*it was just one of those things*' or any other nuggets of information to anyone who was interested. As far as most people were concerned, Sable was a blank sheet. Puzzling, but definitely blank. That was the way she preferred it and, occasionally, when someone proved too curious, too invasive with their questions, she could be quite ferocious in her rejection. A psychologist might have concluded that Sable was allowing a trick of fate to cut her off from full participation in reciprocal relationships. Sable would have replied. 'It's none of your business. No one has the right to know what goes on inside me.'

The woman opposite looked puzzled at the lack of response and Sable made an effort. 'Yes it is surprising,' (which was not the case, for they were in Italy). She pitched her tone to suggest she was willing to be polite but had no desire to continue the conversation. It was a neutral tone, as neutral as Sable had schooled herself to appear. Rebuffed, the woman settled back into her seat and concentrated on the view.

It was early evening. The traffic clogged the roads and progress was inch by inch. 'To your right, is an example of *cypressa sempervirens*, the Italian cypress . . .' droned the tour guide who had introduced himself as Paddy, 'the man on whom you must rely'. In the becalmed coach, Sable stared hard at a slender, green exclamation mark of a tree which had been planted on a roundabout. Didn't '*sempervirens*' mean 'to live forever'? This did not strike her as a welcome proposition.

In the foyer of the Merry Bacchus Hotel, a bald modern building so ugly Sable felt like crying out in protest, Paddy issued them with instructions, including the exhortation to appear at seven-thirty sharp for dinner. As she hoped, no one spoke to Sable as she hauled her luggage up to the tenth floor and into a room from which all individuality had been carefully – and successfully – planned out. She swept back the curtains from the plate glass window, sat down on her bed and watched the traffic roar up the Via Aurelia which snaked past on the way into Rome's centre. With a bit of luck, she could contrive not to speak to anyone much for the entire trip. After that, she would return home to the flat on the housing estate and the office in the utilities firm, and drop back into her routine and out of sight.

The following morning, Sable ate breakfast with her eyes

fixed on the sugar bowl in the centre of the table. She must have counted the packets in it at least ten times. Her silence and hunched shoulders did not go unnoticed and when the group assembled (many of them breathing out the fumes of strange coffee overlarded with toothpaste) for the morning's outing, Paddy drew her aside and asked. 'Is everything in order?' Sable now riveted her gaze on Paddy's feet which were shod in suede lace-ups, the kind she considered that only cads wore. 'Everything's fine,' she replied. 'Quite fine.' Paddy was too harassed to take it further. He had done his duty and moved swiftly on to question a fit-looking couple dressed in matching green shorts and polo t-shirts.

Very quickly, it became apparent that Euro Culture 'n' Fun was a tour company that believed in quantity as opposed to quality. To this end, it floated the sights of Rome as fast as possible past its clients, so neatly captive in the coach. The itinerary was rapid and furious. 'To your right,' Paddy crooned through the microphone, 'is the Palatine Hill, home of the Roman emperors.' He threw in the additional sop. 'Up ahead is the Coliseum.'

'Can you tell us about the gladiators?' A man three rows ahead sounded bewildered. 'Do you know any details?'

'Yup, that's where the gladiators fought,' said Paddy.

This, clearly, was to be the sum total of information which he was going to grant the group and, with a blare of its horn, the coach accelerated. As to what the Coliseum was, or had been, was left to private conjecture.

In this manner, Rome slid past in a blur . . . the Pantheon, Piazza Navona, St Peter's, the Tiber – colours, shapes, and smells melting into one another, nothing distinct, nothing sharp – much as Sable, on her bad days, hoped that her own life would pass. In fact, was passing. *Soon I'll be thirty-six, then forty, then forty-five . . . and it will all be over*. In this respect, the holiday suited her very well.

'Day Three,' declared Paddy, on day three, 'is our villa day, ladies and gentlemen. We take a break from the city in order to enjoy the delights of the country around the capital.' He herded them onto the coach and they were driven up into the hills at Tivoli. Formerly an ancient playground for wealthy Romans, the town scrambled up the slope, offering a cool summer retreat from the baking plain and relief from the stew and swelter of the streets. Later, in the sixteenth century, it provided a playground for the rich (and no doubt) spoilt cardinal who had built the Villa D'Este and laid out its fabled garden.

Still, concluded Sable, intrigued despite herself by the beautiful sight-lines of the garden which was constructed on several levels and by the ingeniousness of the fountains, the cardinal had possessed great taste. And she wondered more than a little about a man of God who had been so enamoured of the good things of the world that he had devoted such energy to them. Surely the cardinal should have been concentrating on the next world?

Perhaps it was fatigue, perhaps it was the rebellion of the over shepherded, but the group displayed a tendency to fragment and wander in different directions. 'Over here,' cried Paddy more than once. 'Over *here*.' Under her unsuitable jersey jumper and skirt, Sable felt the sweat force its way from her armpits down her body. It was so warm, hot even, and the smell of jasmine mingling with dust and new growth was so very invasive. Its sweetness, its suggestion of heat and languor, were unsettling. Sable's nerve endings were quivering with feelings and yearnings with which she was unfamiliar, and for which she had no explanation.

She made her way to one of larger fountains, sat down on the marble lip which surrounded the pool and willed herself to think of nothing very much. It was cool here and, if she remained quite still, she could imagine herself merging into the background of green box and oleander. Merging so completely until she, too, turned into a shade from the past, like those men and women who used to walk up and down these paths in their rich, colourful garments, talking and laughing, plotting and planning. If that happened, if Sable faded into nothing, became merely a memory, then everything would be over: all the grief and boredom and disappointment of being what she was. *Why am I thinking like this?* But she knew why. If Sable was truthful, if she dug right down into the dark of her sub-conscious and looked properly at the mysteries which lurked there, she would find anger. *I am angry that I have not been bolder and braver about myself.*

Sometimes, in her better moments, she planned to make changes. Of course she did. 'One day,' she promised herself, 'I will take myself by the scruff of the neck, give myself a good shake. Instead of looking at a glass and perceiving it as half empty, I will declare it half full.'

That would be a sensible, positive attitude to life.

Then (ran her fantasies), a new Sable would emerge: a bright, confident woman who would say things such as: *my mouth? I never think about it.*

'I'd say, Dora, that she's had plastic surgery . . .' said a voice, and continued with a triumphant inflection, *'which went wrong.'* It was a rich voice, full of humour and dark velvety tones. If one had to describe it as a metaphor, this voice was a fruitcake stuffed with cherries and raisins.

Sable stiffened.

'Rubbish, Margaret. She doesn't look the type. Still, you can never tell.' This second voice lilted: it ran like a stream, light-hearted and almost girlish.

Haven't you seen the ads in the magazines? You can have your bottom rebuilt Dora, if you wish. If you are prepared to pay enough.'

'My bottom?' said Margaret. 'They'd have a job.'

'Girls nowadays don't know if they're supposed to be mothers or that Jo-Lo person. I pity them. Very confusing. Paddy says you can't get a word out of her.'

'Plastic surgery,' said Margaret. 'I wonder what she asked for? Lips like my settee?'

'It doesn't matter what she asked for, it's what she got that's the problem.'

Sable turned her head in order to identify the speakers. But she already had a suspicion. And, yes, it was the two women who always bagged the front seats on the coach. They wore brightly coloured cotton shirts and trousers in which they seemed completely comfortable, and big straw hats. They had capacious handbags and guidebooks which they read out to each other. On the return to the Merry Bacchus the previous evening, they had led the coach party in a group sing-song. '*We're all going on a summer holiday.*' They had sung the words with gusto, and swayed from side to side, and Dora had seized the microphone in order to whip up a response from the rest. 'Come on,' she admonished, looking straight at Sable on her back seat. 'Everyone join in.'

It went without saying that this Dora and her friend Margaret were talking about her. Or rather, the mouth – Sable had reached the stage when she could no longer think of it as 'her' mouth, for it had a life of its own. This discreet, separate existence to which Sable played host was an insoluble conundrum for, wherever and whenever she strove to make herself as inconspicuous as possible, she found herself continually thrust into the spotlight of speculation.

This is what Sable imagined.

No, not imagined. At work, on a station platform, queuing for tickets at the cinema, she knew the disaster of her face always triggered speculation. But why was the urge so strong for explanations in people? For her part, she had no interest as to why Mrs Whatson next door was seen frequently stuffing empty whisky bottles into the refuse bin. Or in the rumour that her boss, Damien, was probably having an affair with his assistant. It was no one's business but theirs, and Sable respected the boundaries. Grief and love were private. Feelings were private, and not to be shared. Everyone was alone. Everyone was an island. And that was that.

But she knew, she well knew, that she *was* an object of pity, conjecture, malice even. On those better-moment days, she wondered if she might be – just – developing a sense of humour about the subject. But on the cold, despairing days, she shook with rage and humiliation at the way these chatterers and speculators helped themselves to her story without her permission *and got it wrong*.

The two women moved in the direction of where Sable was perched. Their shirts were loose and bright, so *appropriate* for the temperature. Their cheeks and arms were sheened with sweat, their feet sensibly shod. They were making no concessions towards beauty or fashion and they wore smiles of complete enjoyment.

Margaret transferred her capacious bag from one shoulder to the other, and plumped down on the rim of the fountain. Dora followed suit, and they sat closely together, with the closeness of friends who knew each other through and through and she heard: 'You'd better ask her Dora, then we can sort it out. *Was it plastic surgery?*'

Sable looked down at her reflection in the water. Somehow (a trick of the refraction?) the scar was not so obvious and a watery portrait of a woman with large and rather beautiful eyes stared back at her. *A bold, bright confident person?*

All around, the warmth was insistent and the scents of spring and growth beguiled.

She opened her mouth and from it issued words which had rarely been uttered. 'If you must know,' she said, 'it was my mother.'

The two women whipped round and Sable had the satisfaction of witnessing the colour storm into their cheeks.

'Yes,' she continued. 'My mother was a failed actress but she liked to keep her hand in. She was demonstrating to my father just what Lady Macbeth should have done with the knife and, unfortunately, I was in the way. It must have been a vicious swipe, but I was too young to judge.'

'Oh,' said Dora.

Margaret was quite silent. Red, but silent.

'She died not long after,' added Sable.

Dora's hand flew to her own mouth. 'What a terrible story.'

'It's funny,' said Sable, 'how wrong you can get things.'

More silence.

'I didn't ask for it,' said Sable, who was experiencing an extraordinary sensation. Inside her, a tap was gushing forth, rather like the fountain behind her, and she wondered how on earth she was going to stop it. 'And for your information, I have had two operations to put it right, but it won't *go* right, and I am stuck with it.' She looked down at the water. 'People think they can talk about it, as if they owned my problem. But they don't.'

It was Margaret who collected herself first. 'No, they don't,' she said. 'And, even if they did, they have other things to think about.'

'*You* were talking about me.'

'We were,' Margaret moved closer to Sable, plump and determined, but, on closer inspection, a kind looking woman. 'But only because you've let your mouth spoil your looks.'

And Sable heard herself exclaim. '*What* looks?'

She felt the weight of the other woman's good intentions and flinched. She hated that more than anything: kindliness bestowed as a duty, as a form of moral obligation.

But Margaret appeared bent on an instant crusade: to put Sable right. 'You've got it wrong, love,' she said. 'Now that I look properly, I can hardly see anything noticeable. Anyway, you should look up. Then we can see your eyes.'

She took Sable by the arm and made her turn round to face the fountain which was composed of several marble figures – a god, a couple of nymphs, a flying dolphin – over which the water arced and flowed.

Attended by a few loyal stragglers, Paddy came into view. 'Over here . . . now this fountain has been extensively restored . . .' He paused, gesticulated irritably in the direction of the three women, and then moved on. 'Over here . . .'

'*Do* look up, love,' insisted Margaret, in the voice which dripped plums and satiny warmth. Sable considered flight. She considered flinging herself into the fountain. But actually what Sable did was to raise her eyes. 'Go on, give yourself a treat,' said Margaret. 'See that little nymph.'

As Paddy had pointed out, the cracks and repairs to the figures were obvious. They were particularly marked on the face of the smaller nymph, who crouched at the feet of the god bearing a triton. Whereas her larger sister was untouched and glowed with a frozen, somewhat cruel, beauty, this one's nose had crumbled, and a chunk had fallen out of her chin. Her face was half-shielded from the onlookers and yet, thought Sable, and yet the expression on the marble features was of a quiet, and secret, humour. *Too bad*, that expression said. *I don't mind. I have what I have. I know what I know.*

Sable stood between Dora and Margaret, feeling their solid bodies press against hers. A living, breathing solidarity.

'Isn't she pretty,' said Margaret. 'Much prettier than the other one.'

Dora captured Sable's hand and patted it. 'Why don't you join us?' she invited. 'We're going to have an ice cream at the cafe.'

Sable felt the sun beat down on her neck, smelt the sharp spicy smell of the hedge, heard the splash of the water. She shaded her eyes and looked down the avenue at the solid outlines of the box hedge, the softer tracings of the olive trees and, behind them, the villa, and they registered so vividly and clearly that it was as if they had sprung into focus for the first time.

'We're not the only ones who were wrong,' added Dora. 'Don't you think?'

And, then, something happened. Sable felt her mouth stretch in a novel fashion. The muscles in her lips were tight and unwilling and unpractised but, eventually, they yielded. 'Perhaps you're right,' she agreed, and the smile she directed at Dora and Margaret held the beginnings of an unfamiliar and novel joy.

Meg Cabot is the number one *New York Times* best-selling author of the *Princess Dairies* series, as well as teen favourites such as *All American Girl*, *Teen Idol* and the *Mediator* and *1-1800-Where-R-You* series. She also writes books for older readers, such as *The Boy Next Door*, *Boy Meets Girl*, and *Every Boy's Got One*. Like the character in her story for this collection, Meg hates parties. She currently divides her time between New York City and Key West, Florida, with her husband and one-eyed cat, Henrietta.

For more information about Meg Cabot, visit www.megcabot.com

PARTY PLANNER

Meg Cabot

To: All Employees of *The New York Journal*
Fr: Charity Webber <charity.webber@thenyjournal.com>
Re: Company Holiday Party

Just a reminder that all departments will close at 4:30PM today
so that employees can get an early start on their holiday merry-
making. We hope to see all of you at Les Hautes Manger (57th
and Madison) for cocktails and hors d'oeuvres (not to mention
entertainment by the nationally acclaimed Magical Madrigals)
from 4:30 to 8PM. All you need to bring is your holiday cheer!

Charity Webber
New York Journal Events Coordinator

To: Charity Webber <charity.webber@thenyjournal.com>
Fr: Natasha Roberts <natasha.roberts@thenyjournal.com>
Re: Holiday Party

Char–

How in the hell did you get old Pinchpenny Peter Hargrave to shell out the bucks for a swank shindig at a top restaurant like Les Hautes Manger? Last year's Christmas party was in the senior staff dining room, where the refreshments consisted of non-alcoholic eggnog and pigs-in-a-blanket. Now suddenly we're having cosmos and salmon tartare someplace where ties and jackets are required? What gives?

You didn't talk the guys in Tech Support into diverting funds from office supplies into the events budget again? Char, don't you remember what happened last time you did that? You ended up spending five Saturday nights in a row watching *Robot Wars* with the likes of Danny 'When's the last time you updated your software' Carmichael. Do I need to remind you that Danny volunteered to *marry* you when you had too many rum and Diet Cokes and were bewailing the fact that there are no good men left out there? I believe he said that the two of you could live in his mother's basement in Long Island until he'd saved up enough to get his own place . . .

Didn't you swear to me then that you would never again exceed your departmental budget? *Didn't you?*

Just wondering,
Nat

To: Natasha Roberts <natasha.roberts@thenyjournal.com>
Fr: Charity Webber <charity.webber@thenyjournal.com>
Re: Holiday Party

Shut up! I told you never to mention the *Robot Wars* incident to me again. That was *years* ago.

Well, okay, two years ago. Still, don't you think I've learned my lesson?

Besides, sometimes I think I did the wrong thing, turning Danny down. He would have made an excellent husband. I mean, at least if I ever needed my hard drive defragmented, I'd know who to ask.

And I hear his mother is a great cook.

In any case, it wasn't 'Pinchpenny' Peter Hargrave's idea to have the party at Les Hautes Manger. It was his nephew Andrew's idea. You know Andrew's taken over day-to-day operations since his uncle's by-pass surgery. Everybody's saying Mr H is going to announce his retirement after New Year's, and that Andrew will be taking over as the new chief exec.

I just hope nothing goes wrong tonight. It'd be just my luck to screw up my first party under the new chief exec. I really want to make a good first impression on the new boss . . .

Although I don't see what was so bad with last year's party. I happen to like pigs-in-a-blanket.

Oh my gosh! An email from the soon-to-be new CEO himself! Gotta go –

Char

Meg Cabot

To: Charity Webber <charity.webber@thenyjournal.com>
Fr: Andrew Hargrave <andrew.hargrave@thenyjournal.com>
Re: Tonight

Just a quick note to let you know how much I appreciate the great job you've done planning this year's holiday party. I know it must have been a lot more difficult for you to set up than in previous years when the event was held in the Senior Staff Dining Room.

But I think having the party off-site will be a real morale booster for the staff, who certainly deserve it after all the hard work they've put in this year, outselling the *Chronicle* for the first time in the *Journal's* history. Les Hautes Manger is one of the best restaurants in New York and I'm hoping the staff will appreciate it, as well.

I look forward to meeting you tonight. I've heard nothing but great things about you from my uncle, and am glad I can count on you to provide a memorable and smooth-running event for our hard-working staff.

Andrew Hargrave

To: Natasha Roberts <natasha.roberts@thenyjournal.com>
Fr: Charity Webber <charity.webber@thenyjournal.com>
Holiday Party

AAAAAAAAAAAAAGHHHHHHHHHHH! He's counting on me to provide a memorable and smooth-running event for our hard-working staff! He's looking forward to meeting me! What if I screw it up??? What if I make a bad first impression?
Oh, God, why me????
C

To: Charity Webber <charity.webber@thenyjournal.com>
Fr: Natasha Roberts <natasha.roberts@thenyjournal.com>
Re: Holiday Party

What could go wrong, you schmo? You've only done a million of these things since you started working in this god-forsaken hellhole. So what's the problem?

And how could you make a bad first impression? You know perfectly well everybody loves you. They can't help it, you're one of those types. You know, all bubbly. What are you worried about?

Oh, wait, a minute . . . this doesn't have anything to do with the fact that you and Andrew Hargrave have already MET, does it? Didn't you run into him once last month, down at the newsstand? Oh my God, I remember now: you were buying Skittles, and so was he, and the two of you laughed about it, but you were too nervous to introduce yourself because he was so tall and cute and single and had a really nice butt, or something, so you ran away?

Is THAT where all this worry about making a good impression is coming from? Because you're warm for his form?

Nat

To: Natasha Roberts <natasha.roberts@thenyjournal.com>
Fr: Charity Webber <charity.webber@thenyjournal.com>
Re: SHUT UP

SHUT UP SHUT UP SHUT UP

This has nothing to do with that. Well, not the butt part. He's just REALLY cute. And nice. And he likes Skittles! Who else do you know who likes Skittles? I mean, besides me? No one!

Oh, God, this party just HAS to go well . . .

I have to write him back and I want my response to sound witty and professional yet breezy and casual. But now all I can think about is his butt. Thanks a lot.

C

To: Charity Webber <charity.webber@thenyjournal.com>
Fr: Natasha Roberts <natasha.roberts@thenyjournal.com>
Re: No, YOU shut up

Hee hee.

Nat

To: Andrew Hargrave <andrew.hargrave@thenyjournal.com>
Fr: Charity Webber <charity.webber@thenyjournal.com>
Re: Tonight

Dear Mr Hargrave,

Thank you so much for your note. Please don't worry at all about the party tonight. I'm sure it's going to go well. The staff at Les Hautes Manger seem imminently professional, and almost everyone here at the paper is delighted that we won't be having pigs-in-a-blanket again this year.

Looking forward to meeting you as well,

Charity Webber
Events Coordinator

To: Charity Webber <charity.webber@thenyjournal.com>
Fr: Andrew Hargrave <andrew.hargrave@thenyjournal.com>
Re: Tonight

Glad to hear it! And please, call me Andrew. See you tonight!
  A

To: Natasha Roberts <natasha.roberts@thenyjournal.com>
Fr: Charity Webber <charity.webber@thenyjournal.com>
Re: No, YOU shut up

ANDREW !!!!!!HE SAID FOR ME TO CALL HIM ANDREW!!!!!!
Oh my God, maybe this evening is going to turn out fine after all
. . . Maybe Andrew and I will meet at the party and our hands
will touch as we both reach for the same cosmo, and he'll gaze
into my eyes and realize I'm the Skittles girl from the newsstand
downstairs, and it will be like we can see into each other's soul!!!
And he'll ask me to go on a carriage ride with him in Central Park
and afterwards we'll go back to his penthouse and make sweet
tender love and then he'll ask me to marry him and we'll move
to Westchester and have three kids and have big bowls of Skittles
in EVERY ROOM . . .

To: Charity Webber <charity.webber@thenyjournal.com>
Fr: Natasha Roberts <natasha.roberts@thenyjournal.com>
Re: No, YOU shut up

You do realize that the scenario you just described is this
bizarre mixture of *Maid in Manhattan* and *Charlie and the*

Chocolate Factory, don't you? But far be it from me to rain on your parade.
  Nat

To: Natasha Roberts <natasha.roberts@thenyjournal.com>
Fr: Charity Webber <charity.webber@thenyjournal.com>
Re: No, YOU shut up

A girl can dream, can't she???
  Oh, God, things just HAVE to go well tonight!!!!!!!!

To: Charity Webber <charity.webber@thenyjournal.com>
Fr: Frank Leonard <frank.leonard@thenyjournal.com>
Re: Holiday Party

Ms. Webber,
  The guys down here in shipping and receiving want to know if they have to dress up for this thing tonight or not. Are they gonna get thrown out of this place if they don't have ties on? Cause I looked it up in Zagats and it's one of those capital letter places. And I know they usually like you to wear ties at those capital letter places. So maybe I should run out and buy a bunch of ties? Can I expense that, do you think? Let me know.

Frank Leonard
Scheduling Manager

To: Frank Leonard <frank.leonard@thenyjournal.com>
Fr: Charity Webber <charity.webber@thenyjournal.com>
Re: Holiday Party

Don't worry about buying ties for your guys, Frank. We are renting the entire restaurant for the evening so there shouldn't be any complaints about the dress code. Tell your guys to come as they are. All they need to bring is their jingle balls!

Charity Webber
Events Coordinator

To: Frank Leonard <frank.leonard@thenyjournal.com>
Fr: Charity Webber <charity.webber@thenyjournal.com>
Re: Holiday Party

Obviously, I meant jingle bells, not balls. Please ask your staff to stop faxing me their interpretations of what jingle balls might look like. Although they are amusing, they have offended some members of my staff.

Charity

To: Charity Webber <charity.webber@thenyjournal.com>
Fr: Antoine Dessange <adessange@leshautes.com>
Re: Event tonight

Chere Mademoiselle,
    I don't know what you may have been told by our events hostess Chantelle but there is no possible way I can provide

salmon tartare for three hundred. There is a nationwide salmon shortage due to a recent act of sabotage by the People for the Ethical Treatment of Aquatic Life. They broke into the salmon farm from which our restaurant receives its supply, and released all of the fish there back into the wild! Attempts to recapture the escaped salmon have been in vain, and it will be weeks before the farm can hope to replenish its stock.

In the meantime, there will be no salmon on our menu. We could, if you wish, substitute crab-stuffed mushroom caps for the tartare. However, this will significantly increase the cost of tonight's event.

Please let me know as soon as possible what you would like us to do. I remain, as always, yours faithfully,

Antoine Dessange
Manager, Les Hautes Manager

To: Charity Webber <charity.webber@thenyjournal.com>
Fr: Cara Polawski <cara.polawski@thenyjournal.com>
Re: Party tonight

Dear Ms Webber,

Hello, it's me Cara from the lobby reception desk. I know you are probably busy planning the big party and all, but I was wondering if you could tell me whether or not Bobby Hancock down in Shipping and Receiving had RSVP'd. Because if he RSVP'd yes, I just want you to know that I have a restraining order against him and he's not allowed to come within five hundred feet of me. So unless this restaurant is big enough that he can stay five hundred feet from me I want you to know that

I will be obliged to call the police if he shows up. Please call me if this is a problem.

Sincerely,
Cara

To: Charity Webber <charity.webber@thenyjournal.com>
Fr: Bobby Hancock <robert.hancock@thenyjournal.com>
Re: Cara Powalski

Dear Ms Webber,
   Cara told me she emailed you about us and I just want to make sure you know that whatever she told you is lies. She doesn't have a restraining order against me – her ex-husband does. I'm not allowed to go within five hundred feet of the guy because of an unfortunate incident involving his eye, which got in the way of my fist last month.
   But the judge didn't say anything about me hanging around Cara.
   So I'll be at the party tonight, wearing my jingle balls, just like you said to.
Bobby

To: Natasha Roberts <natasha.roberts@thenyjournal.com>
Fr: Charity Webber <charity.webber@thenyjournal.com>
Re: Where ARE you????

I hate everyone. Why aren't you picking up?

Meg Cabot

To: Charity Webber <charity.webber@thenyjournal.com>
Fr: Bernice Walters <bernice.walters@thenyjournal.com>
Re: Tonight's Party

Dear Ms Webber,

Hello, I don't think we've actually met, but my name is Bernice and I work in Ad Circulation. I just wanted to let you know that I have a severe shellfish allergy. If I so much as smell crab, lobster, or shrimp meat, I go into anaphylactic shock. I do hope you aren't planning on serving anything at tonight's event that contains shellfish. I've noticed that it tends to spoil the holiday mood when I go into convulsions!

Although I do carry an epi stick with me just in case. If you should happen to see me grab my throat and collapse, would you kindly remove it from my purse and stab me in the thigh with it?

Many thanks,

Bernice Walters
Ad Circ

To: Charity Webber <charity.webber@thenyjournal.com>
Fr: Sol Harper <s.harper@madrigalmagic.com>
Re: Tonight

Just a quick note to let you know that the singers you requested for this evening's event are running a little late due to the traffic in and around the Holland Tunnel. Apparently everybody and his brother decided to drive into the city today to see the tree at Rockefeller Center.

But never fear, they'll be there on time, gridlock alert or not.

98

Nothing can keep OUR knights and fair ladies from 'wassail'ing the house!

Sol
Manager, Madrigal Magic
****Don't hire a DJ for your next party. Let our medieval madrigals 'wassail' you with traditional song in traditional medieval costume! 'Simply the best madrigals this side of the Rocky Mountains!' – *New York Chronicle*****

To: Natasha Roberts <natasha.roberts@thenyjournal.com>
Fr: Charity Webber <charity.webber@thenyjournal.com>
Re: Killing self now

Not that you care, obviously, or you'd have e'd me back by now.

To: Charity Webber <charity.webber@thenyjournal.com>
Fr: Daniel Carmichael <daniel.carmichael@thenyjournal.com>
Re: Party Tonight

Hey, Char! Just wanted to let you know me and the guys up here in Tech Support are really excited about the party tonight. We hear it's at a real happening place. I think it's a real good choice for a company holiday party. According to Zagat's, it's the kind of place where a lot of marriage proposals take place, because it's so romantic. I just hope I don't get too carried away by the romance in the air and propose to anyone! Especially since my grandma left me her two-carat diamond cocktail ring and I just happen to have it in my pocket *right now*.

  See you at the party.
  Danny

To: Charity Webber <charity.webber@thenyjournal.com>
Fr: Antoine Dessange <adessange@leshautes.com>
Re: Event tonight

Chere Mademoiselle,

It pains me to have to inform you that despite the unusually warm weather, the back garden will not be open for use by your guests, due to the fact that at lunch today the fountain there was vandalized by members of the Yardley Middle School French Club, who poured a box of Mr Bubble into it when their teacher wasn't looking.

As the garden area is the only place in the restaurant where diners may legally smoke under New York City law, any members of your party who wish to indulge will now have to do so in front of the restaurant. I hope this will not be an inconvenience.

I remain, as always, yours faithfully,

Antoine Dessange
Manager, Les Hautes Manager

To: Natasha Roberts <natasha.roberts@thenyjournal.com>
Fr: Charity Webber <charity.webber@thenyjournal.com>
Re: Still killing self

I don't know where you are, but I just thought I'd let you know that I'm leaving for the restaurant now. If you want to hook up later-you know, like after the party – you'll be able to find me floating in the Hudson . . . if the cement block I plan on tying to my ankle fails to do its job, I mean.

This party is going to be a complete disaster. Andrew Hargrave's first official act as CEO is undoubtedly going to be to fire me for organizing such a completely screwed up event. There's zero chance now that we'll ever get married and move to Westchester to raise little bitty Skittles-lovers. I should have known it was all just a pipe dream.

Goodbye, cruel world.

Char

To: Charity Webber <charity.webber@thenyjournal.com>
Fr: Natasha Roberts <natasha.roberts@thenyjournal.com>
Re: I'm so sorry!!>

I was in an art meeting. They just let me out. Have you left yet? I tried to call and just got your voicemail. I hope you check your Blackberry.

I'll be there in ten minutes. Don't start drinking! Remember how you nearly became Mrs Danny Carmichael after all those rum and Diet Cokes? We don't want a repeat performance of that now do we? Especially if you're saving yourself for Andrew Hargrave, aka Mr Skittles.

See you there.

Nat

To: Andrew Hargrave <andrew.hargrave@thenyjournal.com>
Fr: Peter Hargrave <peter.hargrave@thenyjournal.com>
Re: Holiday Party

What's this I hear about your having the annual holiday party at some restaurant? What's wrong with the Senior Staff Dining Room? We always had a good time there. The staff really seemed to like the pigs-in-a-blanket.

I hope you know what you're doing. Those boys down in Shipping and Receiving have a tendency to go a little nuts when there's an open bar.

Peter

To: Peter Hargrave <peter.hargrave@thenyjournal.com>
Fr: Andrew Hargrave <andrew.hargrave@thenyjournal.com>
Re: Holiday Party

Don't worry, Uncle Pete. Charity Webber has it all under control. That girl's a real firecracker, just like you said. Well, not that I've gotten a chance to meet her, yet. But I'm leaving for the party now. And don't worry about the boys in Shipping and Receiving. With Charity in charge, I can't imagine anything could possibly go wrong.

Andrew

New York Journal Employee Incident Report

<u>Name/Title of Reporter</u>:
Carl Hopkins, Security Officer

<u>Date/Time of Incident</u>:
Thursday, 5:30PM

<u>Place of Incident</u>:
Company Holiday Party
Les Hautes Manger Restaurant
57th and Madison

Persons involved in Incident:
Robert Hancock, Shipping and Receiving, aged 29
Cara Powalski, Reception, aged 26
Fred Powalski, Security Officer, aged 29

Nature of Incident:
Security Officer F. Powalski, on door duty at company holiday party per the request of C. Webber, Event Organizer, asked R. Hancock what he was doing at company holiday party.

R. Hancock said he was enjoying the company holiday party, as was his right as an employee.

S.O. Powalski stated that R. Hancock had no right to be at company holiday party, as S.O. Powalski has retraining order against him.

R. Hancock said if S.O. Powalski doesn't like it, why doesn't he leave?

S.O. Powalski replied because he was on duty and could not leave, but R. Hancock under no such obligation.

R. Hancock refused to leave.

S.O. Powalski attempted to physically remove R. Hancock from the party.

R. Hancock punched S.O. Powalski in the face.

C. Powalski begged them to stop fighting and not to embarrass her in front of her coworkers.

S.O. Powalski threw R. Hancock through plate glass window.

Follow-up:
New York Police Department alerted, arrived, arrested R. Hancock, S.O. Powalski.

To: Charity Webber <charity.webber@thenyjournal.com>
Fr: Sol Harper <s.harper@madrigalmagic.com>
Re: Last Night

Dear Ms Webber,

The Magical Madrigals are a group of musical professionals who are not in the habit of being groped like Hooters girls, but that's what they tell me happened at your party last evening. Suggestive comments were made to both the flutist and harpist, and one of my singers says she was frequently implored to 'take it all off', apparently in reference to her kirtle, which some guests appeared to mistake for a chastity belt.

I'm afraid I will be unable to offer the services of the Magical Madrigals at any future events at your company. You should be aware that my lute player is considering filing a sexual harassment suit against your firm.

Sol
Manager, Madrigal Magic
****Don't hire a DJ for your next party. Let our medieval madrigals 'wassail' you with traditional song in traditional medieval costume! 'Simply the best madrigals this side of the Rocky Mountains!' – *New York Chronicle*****

To: Charity Webber <charity.webber@thenyjournal.com>
Fr: Antoine Dessange <adessange@leshautes.com>
Re: Event Last Night

Chere Mademoiselle,

Please note that, in addition to the cost of food and beverage, I must add a damage fee of $1,560.47 for repair and replacement of the plate glass window, $532.67 for replacement of one of our art deco wall sconces, and $267.53 for regrouting the tiles in the back garden fountain, which were loosened when a number of your guests felt compelled to leap into the water.

Additionally, I would like to mention that Les Hautes Manger will no longer be available for private parties of any size. Please remove our card from your Rolodex.

I remain, as always, faithfully yours,

Antoine Dessange
Manager, Les Hautes Manger

To: Charity Webber <charity.webber@thenyjournal.com>
Fr: Bernice Walters <bernice.walters@thenyjournal.com>
Re: Many Thanks

I just wanted to say thanks one last time for giving me that shot last night. I had no idea that was crab meat inside those mushroom caps! They were delicious. It was almost worth going into shock for. That is one good restaurant. Thanks again.

Much love,
Bernice

To: Charity Webber <charity.webber@thenyjournal.com>
Fr: Daniel Carmichael <daniel.carmichael@thenyjournal.com>
Re: Last Night

Listen, I know after the fight and the arrest and that fat lady going into shock and all, you had a few drinks, and maybe weren't quite feeling like your normal self last night. So I just thought I'd ask one more time:

Are you SURE you don't want to marry me? Because the offer still stands. My mom even promised to move her circular saw collection out of the basement if we do decide to tie the old knot.

What was that you kept saying about Skittles, anyway?

Danny

To: Charity Webber <charity.webber@thenyjournal.com>
Fr: Frank Leonard <frank.leonard@thenyjournal.com>
Re: Holiday Party

Just wanted to say thanks from me and all the boys for inviting us to such a swell soiree last night. We took a vote, and we all agree – it was the best office holiday party any of us has ever been to!

And I'm sure you'll be interested to know – in the drinking contest between us and Budget, well, we won! Bet they can't wait for a re-match next year!

By the way, we all think you look real good wet.

Well, thanks again!

Frank

and all the guys in Shipping and Receiving

Ringing their Jingle Balls

To: Charity Webber <charity.webber@thenyjournal.com>
Fr: Cara Polawski <cara.polawski@thenyjournal.com>
Re: Last Night

Dear Ms Webber,

I hope you know that you've ruined my life. My Bobby's in jail, and it's all YOUR fault! Why didn't you look at the last names of the officers security sent down to guard the doors at the party? Couldn't you have guessed that Fred Powalski is my ex?

Thanks for nothing,

Cara

To: Andrew Hargrave <andrew.hargrave@thenyjournal.com>
Fr: Peter Hargrave <peter.hargrave@thenyjournal.com>
Re: Holiday Party

What's this I hear about a brawl at the party last night? And an arrest? And people making lewd suggestions to Christmas carolers? And someone stripping naked and jumping into a fountain? Is this really the kind of behavior we want to encourage at our company holiday parties?

I sincerely hope you plan on doing something about all of this, Andrew.

Peter

To: Peter Hargrave <peter.hargrave@thenyjournal.com>
Fr: Andrew Hargrave <andrew.hargrave@thenyjournal.com>
Re: Holiday Party

Don't worry, Uncle Pete. I'm on it.

Andrew

To: Charity Webber <charity.webber@thenyjournal.com>
Fr: Natasha Roberts <natasha.roberts@thenyjournal.com>
Re: Last Night

Oh my God, are you all right? You look TERRIBLE. How many drinks did you have, anyway? I TOLD you to stay away from that bar.

Although I can't really say I blame you. If that had been MY party, I'd have had a few, too. Could you BELIEVE all that?

Though the topper, if you ask me, was you jumping into that fountain.

Nat

To: Natasha Roberts <natasha.roberts@thenyjournal.com>
Fr: Charity Webber <charity.webber@thenyjournal.com>
Re: Last Night

WHY ARE TRYING TO TORTURE ME???? My head is POUNDING. I could hardly WALK this morning. And you're teasing me about jumping into some fountain?

Nat, my CAREER is probably over. I'm probably going to be FIRED today. Someone at my party got THROWN THROUGH A PLATE GLASS WINDOW, and then arrested. Somebody else went into anaphylactic shock. One of the Magic Madrigals smacked a wall sconce with her pointy cone hat trying to get away from some pervert in Accounting, and now the company has to pay to replace it – not to mention the sexual harassment suit, if she sues us.

And who knew so many of our fellow employees were alcoholics! The Budget department alone drank, if my estimates are correct, a thousand dollars worth of liquor.

And to top it all off, apparently I only just avoided becoming Mrs Danny Carmichael again.

PLEASE, do not torture me about some non-existent dip in Les Hautes Manger's back garden fountain. You don't have to. My reality is quite bad enough.

Char

To: Charity Webber <charity.webber@thenyjournal.com>
Fr: Natasha Roberts <natasha.roberts@thenyjournal.com>
Re: Last Night

Char, I'm not trying to torture you, I swear. Last night, you DID jump into the fountain. And a number of our colleagues immediately followed suit, particularly the guys from Shipping and Receiving.

I can't believe you don't remember. I TRIED to get you out, I swear. But Char, that's not even the worst part:

When I tried to reason with you, telling you it was too cold to go swimming, and that you were getting your clothes all wet, you said, 'Well, I'll just take them off, then' and started unbuttoning your blouse . . .

. . . right as Andrew Hargrave came outside to introduce himself.

Please, please don't shoot the messenger.

Nat

To: Natasha Roberts <natasha.roberts@thenyjournal.com>
Fr: Charity Webber <charity.webber@thenyjournal.com>
Re: Last Night

I DID NOT!!!! YOU ARE LYING!!!! I DID NOT DO ANY OF THOSE
THINGS!!! I DID NOT JUMP INTO THE FOUNTAIN! I DID NOT
TAKE OFF MY TOP!!!

AND ANDREW HARGRAVE DID NOT WALK OUT JUST AS I
WAS DOING SO!!!!!

Please tell me you're making this up. Please. I'm begging you.

To: Charity Webber <charity.webber@thenyjournal.com>
Fr: Natasha Roberts <natasha.roberts@thenyjournal.com>
Re: Last Night

Sorry, Char. But it's the truth. Thank God you were wearing a
bra.

If it's any comfort to you, it looks as if those spin classes
you've been taking at the Y have really been paying off.

Nat

To: Natasha Roberts <natasha.roberts@thenyjournal.com>
Fr: Charity Webber <charity.webber@thenyjournal.com>
Re: Last Night

NOOOOOOOOOOOOOOOOOOOO!!!!!!!!!!!!
Oh my God. It's all coming back to me now. After Bobby Hancock
went through that window, I grabbed a drink off the first tray that
passed by me – a cosmo, I think. I must have had six or seven

more as the evening went on . . . Those bubbles. They just looked so inviting . . .

WHAT DO I DO NOW???? He's going to fire me!!! What choice does he have? Oh, God, Nat!!! WHAT SHOULD I DO????

To: Charity Webber <charity.webber@thenyjournal.com>
Fr: Natasha Roberts <natasha.roberts@thenyjournal.com>
Re: Last Night

Might I suggest groveling?

To: Andrew Hargrave <andrew.hargrave@thenyjournal.com>
Fr: Charity Webber <charity.webber@thenyjournal.com>
Re: Last Night

Dear Mr Hargrave,

I just want to apologize for the appalling way that I behaved last night. I want to assure you that I am normally much more levelheaded than my actions last night might have led you to believe. I will admit to having been slightly unnerved by a few things that occurred during the course of the party last evening, and for that reason may have imbibed more than I'm used to. I just want to make it clear that what happened last night in the fountain behind the restaurant was a complete anomaly, and will never happen again.

And I would also like to say, on behalf of my fellow staff members, whose behavior last night you might also have found somewhat circumspect, that we've all been under a lot of stress this year, and I think they really, really appreciated the effort and expense you exerted on their behalf, and were only letting off a little steam.

I will perfectly understand, however, if under the circumstances, you feel you cannot keep me in your employ, and will tender my resignation at once.

Very sincerely yours,

Charity Webber
Events Organizer

To: Charity Webber <charity.webber@thenyjournal.com>
Fr: Andrew Hargrave <andrew.hargrave@thenyjournal.com>
Re: Last Night

Dear Charity,

You're kidding me, right? That was one of the best parties I've ever been to! And exactly the kind of shot in the arm this company needed. And I'm not the only one who thinks so. People around here can't seem to stop talking about what a great time they had. That fight breaking out not to mention you saving that lady, the one who went into convulsions – were definite highlights.

But your jumping into that fountain was a stroke of genius. Who knew cavorting in foam could be such a bonding experience? Departments that were barely civil to each other all year were actually having fun together – exactly what I've been trying to achieve since I started working here! After all the money my uncle spent on expensive corporate retreats and management seminars, you proved that all we needed to come together as a company was a fountain and a box of Mr Bubble.

By the way, I realized last night that – though you probably don't remember it – we've actually met once before. I ran into you some time ago down at the newsstand. We were both buying, of all things, bags of Skittles. I tried to get your name then, but you disappeared, and I thought I'd never see you again. Although admittedly you were wearing considerably more clothing then than you were last night, I recognized you right away: I never forget the face of a fellow Skittles fan. We're a dying breed.

If you have time next week, maybe we could have lunch? I believe there's a party or two in my future that I'm going need your help planning.

Andrew

Jill Davis is the author of the bestselling novel, *Girls' Poker Night*. She is a former writer for *Late Show with David Letterman*, for which she received five Emmy nominations. She lives in New York with her husband and daughter.

Visit her website at www.jilldavis.com

NEW YORK

Jill Davis

MONDAY

My boss is a nightmare. She resembles every gym teacher I've ever had.

Anyway, this is my first day on the job – my very first day on the job. She calls me into her office. It's time for the traditional welcome aboard speech. The if-you-need-anything-just-ask speech. I know that my assigned response is to reiterate how excited I am to be here at IT magazine. IT's such an honor to make so little, yet work so hard.

Instead, the boss had a warning for me: 'Anne, you need to spiff it up,' she says.

'Excuse me?' I say.

'Your blazer. It's not pressed,' she says.

OK, admittedly, not the welcome I was expecting.

She takes a deep breath, annoyed that I haven't coughed up an excuse or apology.

'You represent us. Me. This magazine,' she says.

'In my cubicle . . .' I say.

'And in your cubicle you'll stay – dressed like that,' says Carly.

It's a fine cubicle. I've got no complaints about the cubicle. But I think the implied demotion is what's troubling me. All based on a slightly creased jacket?

'What if we need to send you to interview someone? We simply couldn't. Not dressed like that,' she says.

I didn't sleep in it for fuck's sake.

'Point taken,' I say. 'Thank you for bringing it to my attention.'

I dart for door in complete humiliation. Her voice grabs me before I reach the door.

'There's more,' she says. This is followed by a very long pause, which gives me time to slowly turn around and face my tormentor.

'The hair . . .' she says.

'The hair,' I repeat. I use a knowing tone, indicating I know exactly what she is talking about. We are conspirators in this recognition of disgrace. Except – I do not know what 'the hair' means.

Is there hair on my blazer? Are we discussing leg hair? Is 'the hair' possibly a nickname for one of our co-workers who I've yet to meet? The hair on my head? Could we be talking about the hair on my head? I've never discussed hair of any kind with any boss – so I know not of what hair she speaks. Besides, and this is the chilling part: today is a very good hair day for me – not that I've ever been the type to borrow pop moronic phrases like 'good hair day' but in this situation I think it applies.

'Who does your hair?' she says, in a voice that suggests she might be considering filing a restraining order against him so he can do no more harm.

'Who does *your* hair?' I ask.

Carly scribbles the name Fabian on a piece of paper along with a phone number. At lunchtime, I trot off and spend $150 on a haircut I can't afford. And now . . . I look like a gym teacher, too.

New York is harder than I thought it would be. And New York is easier than I thought it would be. After lunch I go to the ladies room to check out the new haircut for the, well, let's be conservative and call it the fifth time. The other women from the lifestyle department pack into the bathroom waiting patiently to puke up their lunch. This is the female version of the shoeshine line. They just shoot the breeze, read newspapers, and file their nails until it's their turn to heave.

They all dress the same. Wear the same perfume. And they're all named something deriving from the name Elizabeth: Liz, Lisbeth, Beth, Betsy, Lizzie, Liza, Lisbet', Bizzy.

They drop to their knees at the altar of thinness and heave up their lattes and salads. If you're going to heave it up, why not go to town and have spaghetti with meatballs?

You can never overestimate the importance of being thin in New York City. And the Elizabeths are no slackers. When it comes to blowing lunch, these women rule.

When I'm at my desk, I can hear the sounds. The disgusting puking sounds. But by mid-afternoon, it's white noise. The noise of my new landscape. There is a rhythm to it.

If the Elizabeths harnessed all of the energy they spend in pursuit of inexpensive frozen margaritas and 'cute boys', they would own the magazine. And in a way, they already own the world. This shiny corner of it. I guess I should be grateful that they haven't confused pretty with capable, though I think they could get away with it.

TUESDAY

I've spent the better part of today doing exactly what I did on day one ... writing lame blurbs under photographs of glamorous parties.

I use words like pensive, sultry, myopic. The Elizabeths describe dresses as fun, and sassy, and 'this season's must have' clogs ... clutch ... jumpsuit.

I've decided I may begin smoking out of sheer boredom. If you're a smoker, you get a break every few hours and you get to go stand out on Fifth Avenue and inhale carcinogens with other disgusting people who smoke. *Any* club is better than no club?

Someone said they saw Andy Rooney almost get hit by a car today. I'll never see stuff like that sitting all the way up here.

The good news is that earlier I looked through the Yellow Pages and I found three hypnotists. Would they be willing to hypnotize me and use the power of suggestion to get me to start smoking? Two said no. One said, 'Yes, for $40.'

Did I mention that since getting my new haircut, I'm the darling of IT Magazine? I find popularity unsettling and hope it will soon pass. And then I will get to long for it and crave it.

The gym teacher could not be nicer to me. But maybe that's all part of her diabolical plan.

It's after lunch – congratulate me. Thanks to the wonderful world of hypnosis, I'm now a smoker. After all of the hocus-pocus I immediately walked over to Nat Sherman's and bought some mint cigarettes and the most adorablicious (actual word invented by one of the Elizabeths to describe a dress that just wasn't just adorable, and not just delicious but a happy marriage of the two) sterling silver pocket ashtray. If I'd known about the cute little ashtrays I'd have started smoking years ago. I feel like a coma victim, waking up to discover she'd squandered the most precious years of her life.

Anyway, I started smoking my mint cigarettes on the way back to the office and the cutest boy in the cutest suit said: 'You know, each one of those cancer sticks will take seven minutes off of your life'. So cute, but sooo stupid!

The seven minutes is a reference to the amount of time if takes to smoke a cigarette, bonehead.

'Let's talk about it over dinner,' he says.

'As long as there's a smoking section,' I say.

I know what you're thinking. What? She's meeting men on the street, now? Forgive me: a smoker who looks like a gym teacher hasn't the luxury of playing hard to get.

After smoking all of those cigarettes I threw up. Apparently smoking is like exercising. You need to approach it sensibly. I never should have smoked an entire pack. But they really are like yummy chocolates. Have just one? How can you! My heaving put me in good favor with the Elizabeths. They believe I am a convert to their eating disorder.

WEDNESDAY

I've got some great news! Or, in Elizabeth-speak, funtabulous news! Carly, a.k.a. the cow, liked the piece I wrote about being hypnotized to smoke. Thought it was clever. She said to make some small changes and then it's a go.

I called home and my father said it was terrific news. And that the ashtray and the hypnotist are both tax deductible. If that's how it works, perhaps my next project will be a gals' guide to top shelf liquors.

When it hits the stands my father says he plans to buy up every copy. They don't sell IT magazine back home. But it was nice of him to say. I am picturing my byline. Anne S. Wheeland (the woman who has no one to share her joy with but her parents).

You know how everyone says New Yorkers are nuts? Well, at dinner Henry didn't seem so nuts. Then he let it slip that he was born in Hoboken.

He took me to his 'club' because it's the only place left in New York to smoke, he says. I told him we didn't really have to go somewhere that allowed smoking. He insisted. He said it was the polite thing to do.

Back home the men are polite, too. But they're different. They could be falling in love with another woman and still tell you that they love you. They're dangerous men. And I always did fall for the dangerous ones.

I keep remembering when I left last Saturday. Her voice. I hear it perfectly.

'No stunts,' she said. 'Problems are patient, they'll be waiting for you when you come home.' The screen door slammed behind me. I threw my suitcase into the back of the taxi. I looked up at the house for a moment. I memorized my mother's silhouette in the doorway. My father glanced up from his drink, and the TV, and waved.

'I love you,' I said. And then I promised myself I'd never go back. Not to them, and not to him.

No stunts, mother said. No stunts. I cannot travel far enough away from that voice. I want to cry when I think of her saying that to me. One bad decision and I am a person who pulls 'stunts'.

THURSDAY

Today the piece was typeset. Fourteen column inches! Now I am absolutely certain I will die before the next issue hits the news-stands.

I've been alive a little more than two decades and I have done nothing. I would like to have my obituary set in 78-point type, to take up a lot of room and make it look like I actually *did* something while I was here. Except there's no one in my life who likes me enough to get that creative on my behalf. How sad.

Everyone pads obituaries. It's a well-known fact. It's done everyday. So and so was a lifelong member of the Kiwanis Club . . . yeah, yeah. Sure. Sure. Who's going to check?

I have lunch with Carly and the publisher Samuel Manley. Hell of a name for any man to have to live up to each and every day. But I can't focus on that because I'm obsessed with what seems like must have been a mix-up, in that I was invited to this lunch at all. But I didn't mention it, and neither did they. We were all in cahoots and too embarrassed to bring the mistake to center stage.

'Most new employees are too intimidated to touch the computer the entire first week they start working here,' Mr Manley says. And you Anne, on your second day write a column that we will feature in our next issue. That my dear – sorry, that Anne, is why we are having this celebratory lunch,' he says.

Good cover up, I'm thinking.

'Wait,' I say. 'You mean I could have done *nothing* – for a few *weeks*?'

He laughs. I used to be able to make Nick laugh, too.

'Carly says great things about you,' he says.

'Thank you, Mr Manley. I could not be more grateful to you, Carly and IT magazine,' I say. 'Truly, I mean this. As you are aware, it has long been a dream of mine to work for your magazine. When I say 'long' I mean since September of 1997 when your fine example of gloss was launched.'

They laugh. I'm not exactly sure why. And it's all sort of true. When the magazine was first published I had a subscription. And I read it not for its content, but for its massive number of typos which was really something of a marvel.

Anyway, the Elizabeths – they all hate me now. I didn't even have a chance to hate them. They seemed OK to me. I mean, OK enough to have coffee with now and then. OK enough to see a movie with.

When I got to work this morning there was a package waiting for me. Inside was a gold pen from my father. 'Dear Anne, The keeper of words wise and sweet, be true in verse and heart. Love, Dad.' It was so warm and melodic and it reminded me that he is one of those dangerous men. Sometimes I'm just sure you never really know anyone.

FRIDAY

The entire city smells of trash. Carly assures me it's only this smelly in the summer. I feel like my lungs are being coated with toxic dust. Like my organs need to be vacuumed. I imagine my blood is thick and sticky with bugs and germs just stagnating in it. And when I blow my nose black soot comes out.

I got my first paycheck today. Depressing! I'll never be able to afford rent and cigarettes. I still have some money left from my work at the newspaper. But I didn't want to spend that money just yet. That's my run-away-from-the-world, don't-ever-call-home money.

On my lunch break I sat on the steps of the Public Library with the cement lions. Every other man who walked by looked like Nick. And it made me want to go home. Not home actually, but to be some place familiar. To be in a car and know where I am going. To drive by and see Mrs Hathaway's white house, and see her balancing on her tip-toes, hoisting a watering can over her head and drenching the hanging geraniums on her porch.

Good news. Carly just called me into her office. She promoted me to general assignment writer. Gave me a raise. I'm happy to report that my allegiance to smoking has been renewed.

'Don't let them bother you,' she says. 'They're just parking here until they get married. They're too worried about breaking away from the pack.'

I wanted tell her I am just like them. I'm terrified of not being liked – but if I tell her, maybe she won't like me.

The next thing I know Carly and Manley and I are sitting, eating $30 hamburgers at the 21 Club. And then, a fourth person joined us. Carly's husband James. Apparently she doesn't wear a ring for fear the street goons will cut her fingers off or something.

'Isn't it more about not letting people know you aren't really married to your job?' I say.

That silences the table. What's wrong with me?

'So Anne, I hear you're on some kind of meteoric rise at the magazine,' James says. 'How is it that you came to New York?'

'James,' I say. 'It's no big secret. There are these tin things nowadays called buses.'

There is no polite was to tell this kind man, or anyone else, the truth. My unfaithful husband. The mental hospital. The hairdryer incident. The good thing about the bin, I could have explained, was not having to decide what to wear every day. But it never got that far. I should have stayed long enough to acquire a charming story or two.

Mr Manley . . . it's so depressing that I think of him as Mr Manley and that I come from a backward place where women call men Mister . . . even if he's only ten years (a guess) older.

He stared at me. Those big brown eyes. They were just focused right on me throughout the whole meal. Perhaps he instinctively knew he was dining with an out-patient and was being careful not to let the knives out of his sight. To use a ninth-grade description, it felt at though he was eavesdropping on my soul.

'Knock it off,' I say.

He smiles.

Carly blushes. James blushes. And of course, I just about die.

SATURDAY

I didn't get up until noon. Went shopping for a nice big heavy ashtray for my new office . . . newest office.

I bought blinds for the windows in my apartment. The

poor guy across the street will have to buy a TV or something, now. The phone rang six different times. I was happy not to answer it. It allowed me to imagine who it could have been.

SUNDAY

I can't help but think about Nick. Uninvited, he has a way of creeping across my thoughts. Then I looked at the date on the newspaper. Today is our first wedding anniversary. And there is something sad about Sundays anyway.

There's someone out there for everyone. But what if there is only *one* someone for everyone? What if I was meant to live in my hometown with a dishonest man?

There are things to run away from. And there are things to confront. Nick was someone to run from, and for a day or two maybe I thought I was going crazy. And I did attempt to check myself into the State Hospital, but when they tried to take my hairdryer away, I snapped out of it. It turns out, that in many cases, mental hospitals are for people who can't afford a few days at Canyon Ranch.

I was staring at the hairdryer. Contemplating.

'Why would you take this away?' I asked the intake nurse.

'You might try to injure yourself with it,' she said.

'It's a hair dryer . . .' I said.

'You could hang yourself. Scald yourself. Electrocute yourself,' the nurse said, bored, and then she continued on in greater detail.

'I could have done those things at home with any number of objects,' I said. 'Besides, I'm no engineer. I couldn't figure out half of the things you just described.'

'Maybe you need a drink, not a hospital,' she said.

We went and had a beer during her break. That's when I decided to move to New York. I was always afraid to move to New York. Now I had nothing to fear. I'd already made the biggest mistake of my life.

The day before I left for Manhattan, Nick called. My mother handed me the phone. She wore a hopeful look. Her happiness makes me want to do things that don't insure my happiness. Perhaps reconciliation was not out of the question, her eyes said. Maybe New York City *was* out of the question.

'Hello, Nick,' I said.

'I don't know what to say,' he said.

Sure, sure. Turn my life ass-over-tea-kettle and then call me and try to get me to do all of the talking and make you feel OK.

'You deserved better,' he said. It sounded like a question. You deserved better . . . I'm not even sure I did. After all, I married a man who had a tattoo of Sylvester the cat on his thigh. A permanent child. I run toward red flags.

Of course, it's not Nick who I can't forgive. And it's not Nick I need to prove something to.

Henry calls. Just in time. Yes, I'm free, I tell him. Dinner at Da Silvano? Yes, sounds great.

Replacing one drug with another is no way to live one's life. I know that. But he's cute, and today is my first wedding anniversary. The wedding will count as paper.

Stella Duffy has written ten novels, including *Parallel Lies* (Virago) and *Mouths of Babes* (Serpent's Tail) both published in 2005. She has written over twenty-five short stories, including *Martha Grace* (Tart Noir, co-edited with Lauren Henderson), which won the 2002 CWA Short Story Dagger Award. She lives in London.

SIREN SONGS

Stella Duffy

Ryan moved into the basement apartment with a heavy suit-case and a heavier heart. And the clasp on his suitcase was broken. And the clasp on his heart was broken, shattered, wide open, looted, empty. When Ryan moved into the base-ment apartment he was running away from a broken heart. Slow, loping run, limping run, with no home, job or car. Never a great idea for your beloved girlfriend to have an affair with your boss. The new apartment was cold, dark, dingy and not a little damp. It suited his mood, suited his budget, suited him. The bedroom had a small bed. Double certainly, but small double, semi-double. As if the bed itself knew what a mess Ryan and Theresa had made of things and kept its edges tight to remind him of where he had once been, the expansive stretch of past love. And where he was now.

Where Ryan was now was as bad as it had ever been. There had been other break-ups of course. Ryan was a grown man, he'd broken hearts, mended his own, broken again. But this one was different. He had loved Theresa,

129

really-properly-always. Love with plans, love with photo albums full of future possibilities, love made concrete by announced desire. Loved her still. And she had loved him too. But not enough. Just not enough. Not enough to wait while he worked too late, not enough to stay quiet when he shouted, open when he closed, stay faithful when he played first. Ryan had played first, but Theresa played better. Ryan lost. His fling was a one night forget-me-quick, hers was his boss and a fast twist of lust into relationship-maybe into thank you goodbye. Goodbye Ryan, hello new life.

Ryan did not blame Theresa, he blamed himself and his past experiences and his present ex-boss and the too-grand future he had planned for her in the lovely big apartment with the lovely big rent. The plans and hoping and maybes and mistakes first tempted and then overtook them both. Ryan believed in the future and Theresa was swamped by it. Either one could have been left out in the cold. In this case it was Ryan. Cold in damp sheets and small apartment and no natural sunlight and tearstained – yes, they were, he checked again, surprising himself – tearstained pillows. Saltwater outlines on a faded lemon yellow that desperately needed the wash-and-fold his new street corner announced so proudly. And they'd get it too, these depression-comfort- able sheets – once Ryan could make it back up the basement steps into the world. From where he lay now, a decade didn't seem too long to hide. He lost some weight, bought some takeaway food, felt sorry for himself and listened to late- night talk shows. He followed the pattern. Waited it out. Morning becomes misery, becomes night and then another day, almost a week, and eventually, even the saddest man needs a bath.

Ryan stumbled his bleary, too much sleep, too little rest,

too little Theresa way through the narrow apartment. Touched grimy walls, glared at barred windows, crossed small rooms with inefficient lighting. But then he came to the bathroom. The Bathroom. A reason to take the place at his lowest, when the bathroom looked like a nice spot for razorblades and self-pity. Ryan checked out just two apartments before he moved in to this one. The other was lighter and brighter but only had a shower, a power shower in a body-sized cubicle. Good size, it would take even his boy hulk bulk, but Ryan needed more. Needed to stretch into his pain, luxuriate in his sadness. And while heartbreak was pounding in his chest, Ryan's prime solace was the picture of himself in a bath of red, Theresa's constant tears washing his drained body. It was a tacky image to be sure, a nasty one, bitter and resentful and 'you'll be sorry when I'm gone'. Entirely childish, utterly juvenile, ludicrously self-pitying.

It worked for Ryan. He paid the deposit.

The glorious used-to-be-a-bedroom bathroom, highest window in the apartment, brightest room in the gloom. Bath with fat claw feet, hot and cold taps of shiniest chrome, towered over by an incongruously inappropriate gold shower attachment, smooth new enamel to hold his cold back and broad feet. A long, wide coffin of a bath, big enough for his big man's frame, deep enough to drown the grief. Maybe. Picture rail and intricate cornices and swirling whirl of centre ceiling rose, peeling and pockmarked but still lovely, fading grand. Set high into the flaking plaster of the wall was a grille. An old-fashioned cast iron grille; painted gold, picked out, perfect. The ex-owner had started to renovate the whole place, got as far as the bathroom plaster, the golden grille, and stopped. Dead. Heart attack while painting the ceiling.

One corner remained saved from his endeavours, nicotine-stained from the bath-smoking incumbents of years gone by. Ryan liked it, the possibility of staining. Considered taking up smoking. And then decided death-by-cancer would take too long. And he couldn't count on Theresa to rush back to him in a flurry of Florence Nightingale pity. (Though pity would do. Love had been great, but right now, ordinary old pity would do just fine.)

The first time he managed to get out of bed, away from the takeaway cartons, the television, the radio, the box-set DVDs and a wailing Lou Reed on a self-solace soundtrack (Ryan was in mourning, he hadn't stopped being a boy) he ran himself a bath, poured a beer and poured his protesting body into the welcoming water. Ryan was still picturing stones in his pockets and blades on his wrists, heavy stones, long vertical cuts, slow expiration. He had loved her. So very much. But he'd known nothing and the truth had all been proved to him in the end. Love's not enough, he wasn't enough, siren songs only last as long as the mermaid keeps her hair. Theresa had her hair cut a week before she dumped him. He thought it was for her new job. Seven days later he knew it was for her new man. James was a good boss, but he did have this thing about small women in sharp suits with short haircuts. Theresa had been wearing suits for a couple of months, lost a little weight, tightened up her act, her arse. Ryan noticed the clothes, the body, he read the signs, he just didn't know they weren't for him. The hieroglyphs of Theresa, roadmaps to a new desire.

There he was, in the bath with blades on his mind, but the water was hot and his skin was beginning to crinkle and in the comfort of the beautiful room, the only beautiful room, he thought – for the first time that week, for the first time since – that he just might make it through. Through this night anyway. And of course, truthfully, he wasn't going to cut his wrists. Not really, not even slightly scratch in actress-poetess-girlie style. He was just picturing escape from heartbreak and the possibility of Theresa running her hands through his hair in the hospital, in the coffin. Just the possibility of her hands in his hair. Ryan likes his hair. Theresa loved it. Maybe he should cut it off and send it to her. She could make a rope of his hair and climb back to him. If she wanted to. She didn't want to. Theresa on his mind, in his hair. Theresa on his hands, time on his hands, nothing to do but think of her.

And then the singing started. Soft singing, girl-voice singing, slight held-under, under the breath, under the weather, under the water, coming from somewhere that was not this room but close. Coming through the steamy air, the curled damp hair, and into his water-logged ears. Coming into him. At first Ryan thought it was from next door. Another dank basement on either side of his, one more out back across the thin courtyard too. But it was three in the morning. And the left hand basement was a copyshop and the right hand one a chiropodist. No reason for middle night singing in either of them. Across the courtyard then. Past the rubbish bins, over the stacked empty boxes, around the safety-conscious bars and through the dirty glass. But although the window was high and bright, it was also closed. Shut tight against the nameless terrors that inhabited his broken break-in sleep without Theresa. And this voice was floating in, not muffled through walls or glass, but echoing almost, amplified. And gorgeous. So very gorgeous. Just notes initially and then the mutation into song, recognisable song. Peggy Lee's *Black Coffee*. Slow drip accompaniment from the now-cold hot tap. Gravelly Nico *Chelsea Girls*, Ryan soft-soaping his straining arms. Water turning cold and dead skin scummy to Minnie Ripperton *Loving You*. And finally, letting the plug out and the water drain away from his folds and crevices while a voice-cracking last line Judy Garland saluted *Somewhere Over the Rainbow*. Torchsong temptress singing out the lyrics of Ryan's broken heart.

Ryan dried his wrinkled skin and touched the steam-dripping walls of the bathroom. Reached up to the golden grille. The grille which ran the height of all four apartments this old house had become. The grille that was letting in the voice. The voice that woke him up.

Ryan went to bed. Slept soundly. Arose with his alarm clock. (Midday, no point in pushing too far too soon.) Ate breakfast. (Dry cereal. Sour milk.) Tidied the apartment. (Shifted boxes and bags, some of them actually into the rubbish bin.) And, with a cup of coffee in hand, made a place for himself on the low wall opposite his building. He waited three hours. Buses passed him and trucks passed him, policemen talking into radios at their shoulders passed him. Schoolchildren passed him shouting and screaming at each other, entirely oblivious to Ryan's presence, his twenty years on their thirteen making him both invisible and blind. Deaf too. An old man passed him. Stopped, turned, wanted to chat. The weather – warm for this time of year, the streets – dirty, noisy, not like they used to be, young women – always the same. Ryan did not want to converse, did not want to be distracted from his purpose. So he nodded and smiled. Agreed to the warmth, shrugged off the noise, and couldn't help but engage with the women. The conversation took fifteen minutes, at most. In that time Ryan looked at the man maybe twice. But the man didn't think him rude. He thought him normal. The man was old after all. Didn't get many full-face chats any more. Nannies passed with squawling babies in buggies. Dog-walkers passed, pulled on by the lure of another thin city tree, the perfect lamppost. And one cat, strolling in the sunshine, glanced up at the sitting man and walked off smirking. Tail high in the air, intimate knowledge of Ryan's futile quest plain and simple. And laughable. Ryan knew it was laughable. But still, at least he was laughing.

At six in the evening, as the sun was starting to go down behind the building opposite, with a red-orange glint battering his eyes, a woman rounded the corner. She was young. Very young he thought. Too young to be living alone, surely? Scrabbling for keys in the bottom of her bag she walked right past him, turned abruptly, looked left and then right, crossed the road and walked up the steps to the door that let into the thin shared hallway and then the dark staircase to all three of the apartments above his. On her back she carried a backpack. In her backpack she carried a sleeping baby. The girl didn't look like she sang lullabies. Not often. And he'd heard no crying baby through the grille. He watched the lights go on in the front room of the top floor apartment, her blinds fall down the window, crossed her off his list. Shame. Too young, too mothering. Nice legs though.

He waited until midnight. It was time for dinner, supper, hot chocolate, bed. No one else came. The young mother turned off her lights. The other apartments stayed empty and dark. He was cold, late spring day turned into crisp still-winter night. The woman in the top apartment needed to be careful of her window boxes. This hint of frost wouldn't do her geraniums any good. He could tell her that, when he found her, if he found her, if she sang the songs. He crossed the road and let himself into the hallway. Looked at the nondescript names on their post-boxes. Wondered which and who and went downstairs to the darker dark.

Ryan turned on every light in the apartment and ran a long bath, made a fat sandwich of almost-stale bread and definitely stale cheese (cleaning was one thing, proper shopping was definitely a distant second on the getting-better list) and lowered his chilled body into deep water, sandwich hand careful to stay dry. And just when he'd finished the first mouthful a door upstairs opened and closed. Then footsteps, more muffled. Another door. A third. He waited. Swallowed silently, chewed without noise, saliva working slowly on the wheat-dairy paste, teeth soft on his tongue. And then, again the water was cold, the food done, his arms just lifting water-heavy body from the bath, he heard it again. Singing through the grille, slow voice through the steam. Billie Holiday tonight. A roaring Aretha Franklin. And surprise finale: theme tune to the Brady Bunch. Sweet voice nudged harsh voice twisted slow and smooth into comedy turn. He leapt even further then. Wet hand reaching to the grille, stronger determination to find her. Bed and alarm set for six am. Maybe she worked late, left early. He would too. Theresa was there, in his bed, in his head. But she wasn't hurting just now. Or not so much anyway. He must remember to buy some bread.

For a full week Ryan follows the same pattern. Gets up early, runs to the closest shop, buys three sandwiches, takes up his post opposite the house. The young mother comes and goes. Smiles at him at first and then gives up when he doesn't smile back, when his gaze is too concentrated past her, on the steps, on the windows, up and down the street. The old man passes every morning and every afternoon. Each time a new weather platitude, a new women truism. Ryan thinks he should be writing these down. The old man is clearly an expert in the ways of women, in the pain of women, the agony of women-and-men. Ryan changes his daily shifts by two hours each time. In twelve days he will have covered all the hours, twice. There are two other occupants of the house. One of them is the singer. He will find her. Theresa is fading. Still there, still scarring, but fading anyway. There is something else to think about, something else to listen to. It does help. Just as they always say so. Just as the old man says so. She left him a message yesterday morning, Theresa. And he only played it back five times. It was just a message, some boxes he'd left behind, when he planned to pick them up. She had nothing more to say to him. Even Ryan, even now, knew it didn't need playing more than five times.

And in the night, when he hasn't yet found the other two, caught the other two, followed their path from the door to hallway to specificity of individual window, while all he still knows for sure is the young, young mother, at night Ryan listens to the songs. Every night a new repertoire. Deborah Harry, Liza Minnelli, Patti Smith, Sophie Tucker, Nina Simone. A parade of lovelies echoing down the grille and into his steamy bathroom, through the mist to his eyes and ears, nose and mouth, breathing them in with the taste of his own wet skin, soap suds body, music soothing the savage beast in his broken breast. Ryan is really very clean. His mother would be proud. (She never much liked Theresa.)

The following Sunday, his eyes switching from one end of his street to the other, the old man just passed ('Never trust a pretty woman in high heels, either she'll trip up or you will'), about to start on his cinnamon bagel, he sees the door open on the other side of the street. The door to his maybe. A woman comes out. Middle aged, middle dressed, middle face between smile and scowl until she checks out the sky – it is sunny, she turns to smile. She is dressed to run. Locks the door behind her. (She has a key! She is one of them!) Makes a few cursory stretches, jogs down the steps, up again, down, stretch and away to the west end of the street. Ryan notes the time. Twenty minutes later she is back. Red-faced, puffing hard, she is not running fast now, did not start off fast either, a slight lean to the left, lazy – or unaware – technique, bad shoes maybe, she stops at the steps. Sits, catches her breath. She takes off her shoes, removes a stone from one, replaces the sticky insole in the other. Runs fingers through her hair, red fingers, red face, faded red hair. She is his mother's age maybe. Ryan has a young mother, but she is his mother's age all the same. He is both disappointed and comforted. If she is the singer, then they are lullabies. Not the young mother lullabies to the wailing baby, but this older woman's lullabies to him. And they work. He is soothed. Would sleep in the bath but for the cooling water. She wipes sweat from her forehead. She is not beautiful, or particularly strong. She does not look like the singer of the songs. He watches her go inside and some minutes later follows. In the hallway, before descending the dark stairs to the basement (a lightbulb to replace, time to do it now, time and inclination) he catches the scent of her in the air. Woman older than him and more parental than him and sweatier than him and under all that a touch of the perfume she must have worn yesterday, last night. A stroke of the perfume she will wear again, proud to have been out and sweating, pleased with her slow progress towards firmness from age, flushed through with the pumping blood. Ryan scents all this in the hallway.

And is happy to think of something not himself. Not Theresa.
Brand new.

Then the songs change again. Britney and Whitney and
Christine and Lavigne and other songlines he doesn't know
the name of but knows what they look like, what they all
look like, MTV ladies of the night, little bodies and lithe
bodies with low pants or high skirts and bare midriffs,
flashing splashing breasts beneath wide mouths with good
smiles. They are uptempo these songs and they don't soothe
him any more, but they do excite him, awake him a little,
remind him of what else and possibility and – when they rail
and rant and proclaim and damn (mostly men, mostly boys,
mostly life) – Ryan is reminded he is not the only one. The
identification with sixteen year old girls may be a little
unusual, but he is not the only one. He is glad to be joined
in his suffering-into-ordinary. Glad to have companionship in
his ordinary-back-to-life. And, given the choice, he feels
happier shouting along with the Lolitas than looking on with
the old men. Ryan has never done letch very well. Naked
and wet, he is all too aware of his own vulnerability.

Ryan decides the third woman must be her. The She. The
Singer. The One. Of course, either of the other two might be
the singer, but he just can't see it. Not the young mother, tired
as she seems to be from the baby and the college books she
carries in and out every day. He knows they are college books.
He has stopped and asked her. Helped her with them once,
when the baby was screaming and she couldn't find her keys,
and then another time too, when it was raining, summer rain,
hot rain, and she needed to get the baby and her shopping
and her books all inside at once. She asked him then if he

was always going to sit on the low wall opposite the house. If he didn't get bored. And Ryan wondered before he answered, what it must look like, him there, every day. How to answer her question without sounding insane. Or frightening. He told her that it was dark in the basement flat. He wanted to be outdoors. And she nodded, agreed. She used the fire escape herself quite often. Not that it was very safe. Not that she'd ever let the baby out there. But she needed to see the light sometimes, have it fall direct on her skin. And then she went upstairs. Grateful for his help with the books and the baby. And he smiled, realising he'd told her the truth.

It couldn't be the older woman either, his singer. Not that she didn't have a good voice. He'd heard her as she ran. She was getting better at running, faster, a cleaner stride. After the first few times listening to her own panting, she decided music would be easier and played tapes to keep herself going. Show tunes mostly. He heard her coming round the corner. Of course she had the slightly out-of-tune twist that comes from only hearing the sound in your ears and not your own voice as well, even then though, he knew she could sing. But she was a high, very soft, sweet soprano. Quite breathy. Perfectly nice but not strong. And the siren who sang down into his bathtime sang with a low growl, a full-throated roar, a fierce, passionate woman's voice. This older lady was sweet, but she wasn't the one. She nodded at him now, as she had started to do when she got back to the house, wiped her brow, loosed the pull of her shoelaces. He heard the click of her tape recorder and the *42nd Street* tap-skip-hum as she made her way up the steps.

Ryan nearly missed Carmella the first time. He'd almost given up waiting. Was worried about what it looked like to be sitting there day after day. Was worried that the old man thought he was a fixture, that Ryan himself was a fixture like the old man. Was worried he needed to get a job. The redundancy package that left him without Theresa and without an apartment only left him with three months of feeling sorry for himself as well. And he'd wallowed through the first and now sat through another. He needed her to be the one. And, just as he was thinking now might be the right time to get up from the wall and walk to the shop and buy a newspaper, look for a job, there she was. Tall and slim and gorgeous. She'd been singing it last night, *Girl from Ipanema* in her swinging gait. Walking slowly down the stairs from her apartment, out of the gloom of the hallway to the glass of the front door. She stopped to check her mailbox. Long perfect nails, each one pretty pink. And Ryan knew this was her, she, the one, his singing angel. He started to get up from the wall. He didn't know what he would say but he knew he had to say it, must make a move, he'd lost Theresa, this wouldn't, couldn't happen again. She opened the door, he had his foot on the bottom step, she pulled the door back, he was looking up, she down, brown eyes met blue eyes, she smiled, he smiled, he started up, she started down. And kept coming, she fell on the second of five steps. Ryan decided it was meant. She fell into his arms, they tumbled to the pavement, arms and legs, hands and feet. When he sat up she was leaning against him, his right hand holding her left shoe. She smiled again.

'How kind. If you wouldn't mind?'

And he knelt to replace the shoe and knew with a startling clarity that this time, this one, this vision . . . was a man. A beautiful, tall, delicious, perfect, angelic . . . man. Ryan replaced the size ten shoe and looked up.

'You may stand. If you wish.'

He did. Both.

'I'm Carmella. I live on the second floor. I'm a singer.'

'Yes.'

'I have to go. I'm sorry. I have a show.'

'Yes.'

'Thank you so much.'

She walks away. Ryan calls after her 'No. Thank you.' Except that he doesn't. When he opens his mouth there is no sound. She has stolen his sounds. And then Ryan laughs and gives in. Maybe the dream woman is not waiting for him on the other side of the grille. Maybe she isn't really there. But she has woken him anyway.

That night Ryan lies in the bath and waits for his siren. She comes through the mist, singing of dreams and awakening. Of perfect men and wonderful women. The next day, waiting by the doorstep at the appropriate time for the appropriate woman, Ryan asks each one of them out. He asks the young woman to breakfast – on the way to the nursery, via the park, then quick to college.

'Thanks, I'm really busy, but . . . yeah. OK. Thanks. Anyway.'

The older woman agrees to lunch. An hour – and then another half – grabbed from the office, damn them, why not, why shouldn't she, after all?

'I'm never late back. Who'd have thought? Late back? Me!'

And then with Carmella to dinner. In her high heels and short skirt and no need to catch when they fall.

The young mother is delighted and charmed and astonished to be treated as anything other than Jessie's mum. The older woman is delighted and charmed and astonished to be treated to anything by a younger man of Ryan's age. And Carmella who is Colin is delighted and charmed and astonished to be treated generously by such an obviously good-looking, obviously straight man. (And it's such a long time since Ryan thought of himself as good-looking that he too is astonished, charmed, delighted.)

There is eating and drinking. They are nice, good to do. There is music and singing. Of course there is singing. Time passes. Because it does. Ryan feels better. Because he can. Life goes on. It cannot go back. The baby grows, the young woman takes on another year at college. The older woman enters a six-kilometre fun run. It takes her ninety-eight minutes to complete the course and Ryan waits for her at the finishing line. Carmella gets another gig, a better show, learns a whole new repertoire. And buys a new wig, lovely shoes. Ryan gets a job, one he thinks he might like, where the office is high above the street and floor to ceiling windows let in the light missing from his home. He begins to date again: good dates and inappropriate dates and wildly misjudged dates. And then the right one comes along when he isn't even looking, when he has a paper to be worked on this minute, before lunch, right now. Passes his desk. Stops for a chat. Stays for coffee. Ryan has met another woman. Carmella sings into the night. A right woman, a good woman. Carmella sings clean through the morning. And Ryan tries harder and the new woman tries harder and it works. Carmella tries out her opera routine, segues into slow ballad, then fast rock, hint of lullaby calm. Ryan and the new woman are giving it a chance. For now, for as long as it can, for as long as they will. As is the way of these things.

* * *

And, in the basement apartment with the deep claw-foot bath and the sound of possibility echoing down the golden grille, Ryan and his new love Chantal bathe happily ever after. More or less.

Imogen Edwards-Jones is a journalist, broadcaster and honorary Cossack. She is the author of four novels: *My Canapé Hell*, *Shagpile*, *The Wendy House* and *Tuscany for Beginners*. She is a fluent Russian speaker and has also written a travel book: *The Taming of Eagles – Exploring the New Russia*, as well as the best-selling exposés *Hotel Babylon* and *Air Babylon*. She was co-editor of the previous War Child anthology, *Big Night Out*, and is currently working on the BBC TV Drama series of *Hotel Babylon*. Her new book, *Fashion Babylon*, will be out in 2006.

A BLAST FROM THE PAST

Imogen Edwards-Jones

Claire takes the train to London to get away from her husband. It's eight months since they got married and quite frankly, things have become a little dull. After all the excitement of the wedding, with the dress, the presents and all that lovely attention, married life is turning into something of a letdown. Living in the countryside, away from all her friends, the great big happy ending isn't quite as great or as big or as happy as she'd expected.

No one had warned her that the first year of marriage was not a bed of elegantly sprinkled rose petals. In fact, none of her friends had ever really discussed marriage beyond the altar at all. Viewed as an end in itself, something to aspire to, along with a flat stomach, size ten jeans and a Balenciaga handbag; marriage was just another one of those things to tick off on your lifetime achievement board.

In fact, the only marriage that Claire had witnessed up close and personally was that of her parents. Three decades of quiet compromise and disappointment, it ended in the most banal and passionless of solutions – an amicable divorce – when Claire was twenty-five. And Claire, sitting in her country cottage in the middle of nowhere, can't help but think that this is exactly where is she is headed. All she really has to look forward to is thirty years of domestic drudgery, peppered with occasional bouts of polite sex with her less than dynamic husband, Howard.

So last Thursday, when she saw Jefferson's name hidden in a group email sent by an old friend, it was like a life-saving bolt from the blue. And Claire grabbed it with both hands. You see, Jefferson represents everything that Howard is not. Jefferson is her ex-boyfriend from years back. He was glamorous, he was intelligent, he was drop-dead handsome. He was American, good in bed, hedonistic, tanned, toned – and totally reminded her of her youth. Not that Claire is at all old, mind you. She is thirty-two. But let's just say that in the recent past, catalogues have become much more interesting, and cropped-tops from Top Shop are increasingly out of bounds.

It took her all of ten seconds to reply. Her tone was flirtations, racy – and let's be honest here – for a recently married woman, it was rather forward:

Jeff, darling! It's been a long, long time. Still as sexy as ever? Still playing the guitar? Still travelling the world? Still got that little tattoo? Still single? Wld love to hear from you. Love Claire.

She held her breath for a second before she sent it. What if Jefferson didn't reply? What if he didn't remember who she was? What was she thinking? She smiled. Of course he would. Jeff was one of the great loves of her life. If it hadn't been for circumstances beyond both of their control, they'd be together right now. He was one of those significant lovers that Claire tended to talk about when she was sharing with girlfriends, drunk, at two in the morning. And the mere idea of him put a spring in her stride. She pressed send and sat back in her chair.

That night, when Howard came home from the coalface of estate agenting, he found his wife was unusually chatty. She'd had a bath, washed her hair, and put some make-up on. She was altogether different from the tracksuit-wearing, monosyllabic woman he normally returned to. She'd even done some cooking. Not the sort of Nigella cooking that she'd produced in the early days of their relationship, but she had cut open a few sauce bags and jazzed up a chicken breast in his honour, and he was pleased.

To be honest, Claire had become a little difficult of late. She had changed from the carefree soignée girl-about-town that he'd married into this rather tetchy, grumpy, withdrawn woman who could barely be bothered to speak to him when he came home. Howard had been so worried about the change in her, he'd spoken to his mother about it from work. He always spoke to his mother when he was concerned about things. She always gave such great advice. His mother had originally suggested that Claire might be pregnant, and when he said that there was no chance of that, his mother suggested that he give her a wide berth. 'The first year of marriage is difficult,' she warned. 'There are lots of teething problems. Particularly for a girl who had a career and a life in London, before moving to the country. Give her some space and she'll find her feet.'

So Howard had been giving Claire space. Plenty of space. So much space, in fact, that they hadn't had sex in six weeks. As a result, Claire was under the impression that her husband no longer fancied her, and Howard thought that he was being a caring, sharing New Man.

However, that night, after their chicken supper, Howard thought that perhaps Claire might have had enough space and suggested that they get an early night. But Claire politely refused, saying she had a few emails to send.

Sitting in the darkness, her husband asleep in the room next door, Claire hoped against hope that her ex-lover had replied. She stared at the screen as the computer dialled up: a message from her sister. A spam offering her Viagra. An invitation from her old boss. And then, there it was – Jefferson Allen's reply:

Hey there sexy!!!!!!! – long time no hear – definitely still single, still playing the guitar, still got the tats, am coming over 2 ur neck of the woods nxt wk, poss record contract, u still there? U still got great tits? JA.

Claire could hardly contain herself. Jefferson's response was so quick, so funny, and so flirtatious. He'd always been such a laugh. He'd always been so entertaining. And he was coming over next week. Claire leant forward on the desk and smiled. She ran her hands through her blonde hair and looked down at her cleavage. She did still have rather nice breasts. Round and pert and rather under-wired, she'd always been quite proud of them. She was pleased that he remembered them too. But then he would, wouldn't he? They were meant to be together. So he would remember every inch of her, as she remembered every inch of him. His dark hair. His blue eyes. The way his lips curled when he smiled. His smooth back and his long, strong legs. She'd lost count of the number of times she'd lain in bed at night and imagined him, poised above her, at the point of penetration. She curled a strand

of blonde hair around her finger and bit the end of her nail.
And he was still single.

J – can't believe u r coming over here nxt wk. Of course I'm still
in town. Where else wld I be? Let's meet up? C.
PS tits still great.

It took another flurry of flirty emails for Claire and Jefferson
to finalise the rendezvous. It was hard for Claire to keep the
arrangements from Howard. She had to get up early to make
sure he didn't check their shared email before she'd had the
chance to delete the messages. And she had to go to bed late
to ensure the same. Howard thought that her behaviour, and
sudden interest in computers, was a little erratic, but nothing
dramatically out of the ordinary. However, the tension in the
house was something else. Claire's temper was even shorter
than usual. She seemed to be sighing out loud a lot, and she
was overly critical of everything he did. The way he brushed
his teeth seemed to annoy her. The way he blew his nose.
The way he ate. The way he laughed. The way his socks
never quite made it into the laundry basket. In short, all the
little habits that she used to find endearing now apparently
got right up her nose. So when Claire said she wanted to see
a girlfriend in London, and that she planned to spend the
night, Howard was only too pleased for her to go.

Sitting on the train, looking out of the window, Claire's heart
is racing. Her hands are clammy, her top lip is moist and her
desire is mounting with each mile travelled. She hasn't felt
this excited since her wedding day. There is only an hour to
go before she sees Jefferson again. Will he be the same? Will
he still fancy her? It's taken ten years for their great love to

be reunited. All she has to do is keep herself together for a little while longer.

She exhales through her mouth, trying to relieve some of the tension, and looks at her reflection in the glass. Perhaps she should lengthen her bra straps? She's pulled them so short and pushed her breasts up so high, she can practically lick her own cleavage. She tweaks the collar of her white silk shirt and undoes another button. Now is not the time to be subtle, she thinks. Jeff has got to realise immediately what he has missed out on. She takes out her handbag and starts to rattle around inside for her compact. Her mobile rings.

'Hello?' she answers.

'Hi. It's . . . me.'

'Who?' she asks.

'Me. Howard. Your husband?' he says.

'Oh, Howard,' she stutters. 'Sorry. I was miles away.'

'You sound it,' he replies. 'Um, I was just calling to wish you a great evening. I hope you have a wonderful time and I can't wait to hear all about it. Oh, and send my love to Sue.'

'Right,' says Claire, fighting the hot wave of guilt that suddenly engulfs her. 'Will do.'

'Love you,' says Howard.

'Um, thanks,' is all Claire can manage in reply.

She hangs up just as the train pulls into Marylebone Station. The fuss, the confusion and the rush for a taxi fortunately prevent her from dwelling on her lies and duplicity all that much. And by the time she's in the back of the cab on her way to Duke's Hotel, the anticipation and the adrenalin have more than taken over. Pulling up outside the hotel, Claire checks her appearance once more. The tight black pencil skirt, sheer black stockings and high black shoes teamed with the white silk shirt all make up the slim, sexy secretary look that she is after. She smoothes down her hair, adds some extra lip-gloss and, finally, removes her wedding ring, popping the gold band and diamond solitaire engagement ring into her purse.

She is the requisite ten minutes late as she walks into the quiet, panelled bar. It smells of tradition and old cigars. She searches the leather-padded armchairs. There's a fat bald bloke in the corner. Is that him? She looks confused. There's a couple talking. A man in a suit. A woman on her own, staring expectantly at the door. Where is he?

'Claire!' comes a familiar voice with a Boston brogue. She turns around to find Jefferson sitting in the corner. Her heart stops, her mouth goes dry, her heart is racing. He is . . . oh? A little shorter than she remembers. Dressed in jeans, with a blue jacket and a white t-shirt, he's thicker-set, older, with more lines, less hair and round, horn-rimmed specs.

'Jeff!' she exclaims, making a step backwards as she takes it all in. 'You look . . . exactly the same,' she lies.

'So do you,' he lies right back.

'How great to see you,' she leans in and kisses him. Even his skin smells different.

'God, it's great to see you too,' he grins. His bright white, heavily orthodontised teeth haven't changed at all. 'So how have you been? Still working hard?'

'Absolutely,' she lies again, perching down next to him. 'I've had such a busy day in the office.'

'Well, you need a drink,' he says. 'Waiter!' He clicks his fingers. Claire blushes slightly. A charming, white-jacketed waiter approaches. 'A martini for the lady,' says Jeff. 'And another one for me.'

Jeff and Claire sit there, eating peanuts, drinking their

incredibly strong cocktails, searching for topics of conversation. Claire shifts uncomfortably, Jeff laughs too loudly, and a ten-year gap yawns before them. He tells her about his music career, omitting the fact that it is still going nowhere. She fills him in on her stunning rise through her legal firm, not mentioning that she gave it all up to get married and move to the country.

They order another drink. Claire cracks open her first packet of cigarettes in six years. She keeps staring down at her left hand; her wedding ring finger looks rudely naked and vulnerable. She drinks some more vodka. They resort to talking about old times. Claire leans forward, pushing her breasts together. Her lips are wet with booze.

'God,' she drawls. 'Do you remember when we made love in that little hotel in Paris and you covered me with bits of chocolate?'

'No,' laughs Jeff, leaning in. 'Did I really?'

'Yeah,' says Claire. 'You licked them off, crumb by crumb.'

'Really?' says Jeff, smiling away. 'I don't remember that at all!'

'How about when we were on holiday in Spain?' suggests Claire.

'Oh,' he replies. 'That was great.'

'And we drank all that sangria . . .'

'Oh yeah,' he nods.

'And we made love on the beach . . .'

'Yeah,' he nods again.

'And we swam naked until dawn . . .'

'Did we?' he grins. 'God . . . you've got a great memory.' He laughs.

'I have,' smiles Claire. 'So many great memories.'

'We've got plenty of those,' says Jeff. He leans over and

starts to run his hand up and down Claire's leg. The feeling is electrifying. She can hardly move, breathe or concentrate. 'You do look really great, you know, Claire,' he mumbles, looking directly in to her eyes. 'Just like I expected . . .'

Claire's stomach lurches. All the old familiar feelings come flooding back. She and Jefferson were always made for each other.

'Why did you never ask me to marry you?' she says suddenly. 'Why did you never ask me to run away with you? Back to the States?'

'What?' he says. His face falls with confusion. He snaps back into his chair, withdrawing his hand. 'Ask you to marry me? Why would I do that?'

'Because we're soulmates.'

'We had a fling.'

'Because you love me.'

'It was just sex.'

'Sorry?' says Claire. The colour drains from her cheeks as she begins to feel sick.

'Yeah,' he says. 'Sex,' he repeats. 'That's what I always loved about you. We had great sex but with no commitment. Don't tell me you didn't get that?'

'Well . . .' Claire struggles. She looks around in her handbag for another cigarette.

'That's one of the things that I loved most about you,' continues Jeff. He rubs his hands together, warming to his theme. 'You were so strong, so independent, so clever and sexy and we did it like rabbits all over Europe. Happy days,' he smiles. 'You were one of the best flings I ever had.'

'Flings,' repeats Claire.

'Yeah,' he nods. 'I have no idea where you got this marriage thing from. It was the last thing on my mind.' He starts to laugh. 'You're not marriage material, Claire. You're far too filthy.' He grins and gives her thigh a squeeze. 'What are you thinking?'

'You're right,' says Claire, getting out of her chair and draining her glass. 'What am I thinking? Listen,' she says. 'It was nice to see you. Rekindle an old fling, that sort of thing, but I'm afraid I've got to go.'

'What?' says Jeff, sounding a bit surprised. 'I thought we might . . . you know . . . for old time's sake.'

'Well, you thought wrong,' says Claire. 'I'm afraid I have a train to catch. And a husband to see.'

'You do?'

'I do.'

'Someone married you?'

'They did.'

'Well, he's a brave fellow.'

'I know,' smiles Claire. 'It's just a shame it's taken me this long to realise it.'

Claire calls Howard a few times from the train but there is no reply at the house. She wishes she'd listened more this morning when he was saying goodbye, because then at least she might have an idea where he is. She calls again from the cab but there is still no response. His mobile is switched off. Maybe he's working late? If only she could remember.

Letting herself back into the cottage Claire suddenly shivers. The air is remarkably cold. Turning on the lights, she looks around the sitting room and it all looks a bit bare. Have they been robbed? There are bits and pieces missing. Empty shelves, missing objects. She runs upstairs to check on the computer. It's still there, purring away in the darkness. She turns on the light. The window is open and there are reams and reams of curling paper blowing in the wind. As she walks across the room to close the window she looks down at the paper on the floor. '*Of course I'm single!*' she reads. '*My tits are still great!*' '*I can't wait to see you.*' '*It'll be just like old times.*' '*Remember the night of the chocolate chips?*' The sentences swirl around her feet. Claire cups her cheeks at the horror and slowly sinks to the floor. She didn't totally delete the emails. The full extent of her undoing slowly dawns on her. As tears of self-pity crawl down her face, she looks up at the desk and there stuck to the screen is a note, written in Howard's neat, controlled script:

You're a liar and a cheat. I want a divorce.

Harriet Evans' first novel, *Going Home*, is published by HarperCollins in November 2005. She lives in London.

THE PANTS OF SHAME

Harriet Evans

They were down to the last box of the day. Feeling like she had done this journey a thousand times, Clare heaved it wearily out of the van, up the path, into their new sitting room, and sat it gingerly down on the wooden floor.

'*Phfff*,' she said, flopping onto their new sofa. 'That's it. Where's the kettle? I'm dying for a cup of tea.'

Marcus appeared in the doorway. 'That may take some time. Not sure.' He smiled at her. 'All done, then? Shall I take the van back?'

Clare pulled his belt loops so he fell onto the sofa next to her. 'In a minute.' She kissed him. 'I can't believe it. Here we are.'

'At last,' Marcus said. Clare rested her head on his shoulder. She felt strangely serene and comfortable, despite the fact she was aching all over and covered in dust. They were silent for a moment as the spring evening sun shone gently through the French windows from the garden.

Suddenly Marcus said, 'Hey, what's that?'

Clare followed his gaze to the battered old cardboard box

on the floor. The side of the box was torn and the corner of a frame was sticking out.

'Oh my god,' she said quietly. 'That's where it is.'

'Where what is?' Marcus said.

Clare slid off the sofa onto the wooden floorboards. 'The . . .' she stopped, and bit her lip. 'God.' She reached into the box and started pulling things out. 'Just . . . girl stuff. You know.'

'Not really,' said Marcus.

'From when I was still at the agency,' Clare explained. 'It must be nearly ten years ago now. Look.' She pulled out an old photo album, some theatre programmes and then the frame.

'What the hell is that?' Marcus said.

'The Pants of Shame,' Clare said, laughing. 'The frigging Pants of Shame.' She propped the frame up against the box and looked at it.

'What are The Pants of Shame?' Marcus said, looking on in total bemusement. There, in the centre, was a pair of black shiny M&S pants with a tiny gold teddy bear in the centre. The pants were saggy, the elastic frayed. The gold was peeling off. The waistband was far too high. And underneath the pants, which were pinned delicately onto the mount, were the words:

Clare Garfield
. Fran Elwood
Helen Muswell
Jane Hitchin
The Pants of Shame
1996–2001

And at that moment, in her beautiful new home with her gorgeous new husband, with the boxes of their new life waiting to be unpacked, Clare felt strangely alone. She was remembering the girl she used to be and The Pants of Shame. It felt like a long time ago and she missed it. She hadn't realised, but she missed it.

'Just us,' she said. 'Just me and the girls at the old company. When we were young, and stuff. Weird. I haven't thought about it for ages. I miss them.'

'But you're seeing them for supper next week, aren't you?' Marcus said, totally confused now.

'Just Fran,' Clare said, vaguely. She stood up and brushed the dirt off her jeans. 'It's – it's different now. I haven't seen Helen and Jane for a while.'

'You should get them over too then.'

'Oh . . . I don't know. Sometimes I do miss them. We were all so close once. But it's nothing special. Just – when you're young. First job in London, and all that. Silly stuff.'

'I see,' said Marcus tolerantly, though he didn't, but he was used to Clare's daydreaming by now. He left to find the kettle, but Clare stayed in the sitting room, staring at the frame, thinking. Various scenes and stories flew through her mind, things she hadn't thought about for too long. She stayed there as the sun slipped behind the gabled roofs of the houses beyond the garden.

1996, Clare: just dumped by Andy, the account manager at Faraday PR.

'I hate him!' Clare sobbed, resting her head on the table. She sat up and hiccuped. 'I think I'm going to be sick.'

'Oh god,' said Helen glumly. 'That's all we need. She's *fine*,' she said firmly to the landlord of the Carthorse, who was glaring at them suspiciously from behind the bar.

It was a Tuesday night in November, and the girls were drowning their sorrows at the local boozer, a tiny old pub in a courtyard behind the financial PR firm where they'd been working together for over two years. Without realising it, they'd become a foursome. The girls from work. Who were being called upon now to cheer poor Clare up, since she'd just found out Andy, her boyfriend of six months (and incidentally, kind of her boss), had got back together with his old girlfriend.

The four of them spent a lot of time in this pub, one way or another. Jane and Helen – the unlikeliest of friends, Jane being spiky and rather chippy, Helen being a traditional gal at heart who just wanted to marry her Tony and move to the suburbs – had been banned for a month earlier in the autumn after they danced on a table to En Vogue's *My Lovin'*. Fran (who loved a dust-up) had nearly got into a fight with the barman after he tried to charge her for a sachet of brown sauce to go with her chips. And Clare had once hidden in the Carthorse loos for an hour after Jez, aka Fat Spotty Post Room Boy, whom she'd snogged by accident at the work Christmas party, had showed up looking for her. It wasn't a great pub by any means. It was just the place where they'd become friends.

'She don't look fine,' the landlord said suddenly. 'If she chucks up, I'm having you lot, I tell you.'

'Did he just say I was fat?' Clare said, raising her tearstained face and looking at them with a wobbly expression.

'No, of *course* he didn't, you idiot,' Jane said briskly, pouring out the rest of the wine. 'Don't be stupid. You're the thinnest person I know in real life.'

'No, I'm not,' said Clare tragically. She downed the rest of her glass and gasped. 'You . . . *you're* the thinnest.'

'No, *you* are,' said Jane.

'Crap!' Clare bellowed.

Fran came back from the bar carrying some crisps and another bottle of wine. 'Crap what?' she asked.

'I was just saying Clare's the thinnest person I know,' Jane said.

'I think Jane is,' Fran said. 'You're the thinnest.'

'No way!' said Helen. '*You're* the thinnest.'

'No, *you* are.'

'No, *you're* the thinnest.'

'No *you*.'

The landlord leant on the bar and looked over at the corner table in bemusement. Women. He would never understand them, not if he lived to be a hundred.

Jane topped up the glasses again. 'Cheers, ladies,' she said. 'To Clare. Glad you've got rid of that creep, who cares about him, eh? *And* you're the thinnest.'

'He dumped me, I didn't get rid of him,' Clare said, her lip trembling.

'Who cares!' said Fran, slurring slightly. 'He wore shiny suits! He was a wanker! Hurrah!'

'Hurrah!' Jane and Helen bellowed, clapping fervently. 'Clare?' Jane said, looking round. But Clare had passed out on the banquette.

They did the 3–2–1 hand movement at the table to determine who was most sober and who could be trusted to take Clare home with them, as they couldn't send her home alone like this. So, as the 98 night bus trundled back to Fran's flat, Clare slept on her knee and Fran gazed out of the window and tried to pretend she was sober too. Fran was nice enough, when they got back home, to pull off Clare's shoes, throw a duvet over her and put a glass of water by the sofa for the raging thirsts.

'I'm so sorry,' said Clare the next morning, rubbing her panda-eyes. '*Ow*.'

'I know,' said Fran. 'I want to die. I'm never –'

'– drinking again,' Clare finished. She pushed the duvet feebly over her head again. 'What time is it?'

'Eight thirty,' Fran said, wincing. 'Loz and Alex have already gone to work.'

'God,' said Clare. 'I'm so sorry about being so crap last night. Did I really blow my nose on your scarf?'

'Yes, but don't worry,' said Fran, remembering the previous month when she'd poured beer over Clare's new and exciting mobile phone while gesticulating during a story about their work nemesis Jackie 'The Jackdaw'. 'Have a shower, you'll feel better,' she said.

'*Argh*, I just feel so ashamed,' Clare said, getting up. Fran handed her the one spare towel. 'All that time, I was going on about him, and thinking it was for real . . . and he was still seeing his girlfriend! And now I have to go into work and see him. Oh Jesus.'

Fran watched her, frowning. 'Hey,' Clare continued, after a moment's thought. 'Can I borrow some pants?'

'God, nearly all mine are in the wash,' Fran said. 'Let's see what I can find.'

Clare followed Fran into her chaotic bedroom, and stood feeling bemused as Fran pulled her underwear drawer out and deposited its contents on her unmade bed. 'Right,' Fran said, sifting through the pile in front of her. 'Socks. Bra. No, that's no good. Ah. How about these?'

She held up a pink satin G-string, threaded through with red plastic ribbons. It was crotchless and had a plastic red heart at its centre. Fran was a bit saucy.

'Are you having a laugh?' Clare said.

'Oh,' Fran said. 'Fine then. Gavin bought them for me. But . . . ok, what about these? Oh no, that's another pair he bought me.' She blushed and buried her head in the pile.

'You must have *one* non-hooker pair of pants,' said Clare after a minute, feeling slightly desperate.

'You'd think, wouldn't you?' said Fran. 'They must all be in the wash. Or in the laundry basket.' She pointed to a huge wicker basket overflowing with clothes.

'I'll go without,' Clare said. 'God, I deserve it for being so drunk and awful.'

'Don't be stupid,' Fran said, almost crossly. She grabbed Clare's arm, still holding the crotchless G-string. 'Andy was a wanker, you weren't good enough for him, and you're going to march into work with your head held high and in clean pants, even if I have to find some and wash them myself. OK?'

'OK,' said Clare in a wobbly voice. 'Tha–'

'Bingo!' Fran yelled suddenly. 'I knew we'd find some. Oh god, they're a bit . . . naff. But they'll do.'

'I'll wear them,' said Clare. She held up the black lurex pants and looked at them doubtfully. 'What's that on the front, for Christ's sake?'

'A teddy bear,' said Fran. 'Holding a rose.'

'God,' said Clare. 'These truly are pants of shame. Look at them.'

They stared at them and then both burst out laughing.

'Never mind,' said Fran firmly. She pushed Clare out of the room, towards the bathroom. 'Have a shower, get dressed, cane it on the lipgloss front. And then we're going to stride into that office and show Andy what he's missing, even if you do still smell of booze and you're wearing shiny black pants with a cartoon teddy on them. Go!'

1998, Jane: feeling depressed. Just because.

'I don't know,' said Jane, knocking back the last of her mojito and wiping her mouth with a cocktail napkin. She was already a little worse for wear. 'Honestly, Clare, I feel like I go on date after date, truss myself up for these blokes when most of the time *I don't even like them that much*, and still nothing happens. I don't know why I bother.'

'Well, that's because you haven't met someone you like yet, have you?' Clare said. She looked at her watch. 'Shall we go? You don't want another one, do you?'

'Yes, I do,' Jane said firmly. She looked outside, onto Clapham High Street, which was buzzing already even though it was only a Wednesday. She swallowed, and said pathetically, 'I'm sorry to moan on.'

'Don't be,' Clare said. 'You never do.'

'You know me,' Jane said, smiling slightly. 'Better in than out. I just feel . . . God, I know it's pathetic but I'm just so *lonely*. Look at you. You've just met that new bloke . . . Dorcas?'

'Marcus,' Clare said, as always revelling at the sound of his name on her tongue.

'Exactly. Look how happy you are . . . and since Helen got engaged to Tony, I hardly see her anymore . . .' Tears welled in her eyes, and Clare tensed, it was so unexpected. Not Jane, cool, calm, together Jane.

'Oh love,' she said, rubbing her friend's back. 'You've just had a hard day, that's all. The Jackdaw's a bitch, don't let her get you down.'

'It's not Jackie this time, honestly. It's . . . ever since Ed, really. I can't seem to get over him.'

'I know, love,' Clare said, squeezing Jane's hand. 'I know you miss him.'

'All I want is someone to love me and take care of me and – oh god, I'm such a cliché. I'm going to move to a cottage and buy some cats and just accept I'm a sad old spinster.'

She lurched forward on the bar stool, suddenly, and lurched back. 'Perhaps I'd better not have that drink,' she whispered. 'I feel . . . drunk.'

Clare helped her up. 'I can't go back to the flat like this,' said Jane. 'Charlotte'll just be vile and her new boyfriend's staying all this week. I can't bear it. Can I . . . stay with you?'

'You should buy your own place, you know.' Clare said. Jane nodded. 'You really should. Come on,' she continued. 'We'll get you back to mine. Bethan's away, you can sleep in her room, she won't mind.'

In the warm May night they staggered around the corner to Clare's tiny flatshare, arms linked, singing *I Know Him So Well*.

'I need some pants for tomorrow,' were Jane's last words as Clare upended her into Bethan's bed. 'Got any spare I can wear?'

'Yes, of course,' Clare said, smiling into the darkness. 'Night night.'

1999, Helen: made redundant after six months in her new job.

Jane was in love with her new flat, but as her work bezzies sat round her new IKEA table, wine glasses in hand, she thought they could be anywhere. They were all watching Helen, open-mouthed with horror. Helen was the most beautiful girl she knew, but at this moment she wasn't looking her best. Her hair hung in straggles on either side of her mascara-stained face and she looked so, so tired, Jane wanted to lock her in a room and drug her so she'd sleep for two days.

'So they said it was last in, first out, and they were really sorry, but they'd have to let me go,' she finished, her voice tight with the strain of trying not to cry.

The others were silent.

'It could be worse,' she said. 'I get four months' salary. It's just . . . we've just bought the flat, and Mum hasn't been well, and stuff. I wanted to take her on holiday . . .' She put her head on her arms and began to cry silently, her shoulders heaving.

'Oh, love,' Jane said, putting her arms round her best friend and hugging her.

'I just feel so stupid,' Helen said, sitting upright. 'I just can't help thinking . . . if I'd been any good, they'd have kept me on. I just think I didn't fit in. I didn't like it there. I should never have left Faraday . . .' She started crying again.

Jane said, 'I'm going to talk to Jackie tomorrow. They're looking for freelancers.'

Jane was scarier than the other three put together, much more so these days. And more senior at Faraday. The others nodded, mute.

'I can't do freelance, though,' said Helen, wiping her cheeks and her chin and sniffing. 'It's got to be full time, otherwise I'm fucked. We're stretched so tight. I don't know what to do . . .'

She stopped, her voice rising at the end of this speech. As

if realising it was all too dramatic and awful, she said, 'The salad was lovely, Clare. I'm going to miss my train. I'd better go.'

'It's really late,' Fran said. 'The last train left about forty minutes ago.'

Helen looked at her watch. 'Shit. You're right. How am I going to get home?'

'Stay here,' said Jane. 'That's a sofa-bed. I can lend you some stuff tomorrow. Call Tony and tell him. Have some more wine.'

'Yeah,' said Jane, pouring the wine out. 'You can borrow The Pants of Shame.'

'The what?' Helen said.

Fran and Clare cackled, while Helen looked blank.

'I'll explain later,' said Jane. 'It's going to be fine, my love. Have some more wine.'

Helen smiled, for the first time that night. 'OK,' she said.

2001, Clare: off to visit Helen.

Fran looked round Helen's new kitchen doubtfully. 'It's . . . it's just lovely,' she said, sipping her tea and burning the roof of her mouth. 'God. Le Creuset pans on hooks hanging from the walls. In *Wimbledon*. It's so *grown-up*.'

'Well, we are grown-up,' Helen pointed out. 'I'm married and I've got a baby. When else am I going to have le Creuset pans on hooks?'

'I know,' Fran said. She couldn't think how to say it. 'It's just . . . you know. Two years ago – you'd lost your job, you had no money, Tony and you – well, you know. And now you're practically a millionairess. It's just weird.'

'I'm not a bloody millionairess!' Helen said in exasperation. She shifted the tiny baby on her lap. 'Mum just left more money than I'd realised. And Tony got that new job. Believe me, I'd rather it hadn't happened that way.' She looked out of the window.

'I know,' Fran said. She felt bad. But it was something else, she couldn't say what. Helen felt distant from her, all of a sudden.

'So,' Helen said. 'How is everyone at Faradays? What's the news?'

'Nothing much,' said Fran. 'Since Clare left, it's boring as hell. Jane's practically running the place, she gets more and more like a dictator every day.'

'Well, you know Jane,' Helen said, carefully depositing baby Catherine in her carrycot. 'Ever since Ed finished with her, she's obviously decided to be a career woman. I haven't seen her for ages, actually. It's a shame, we used to be so close. But, you know. Her life's so different from mine now.' She wiped her hand across her brow.

'She's OK,' said Fran uncomfortably.

'Have you heard from Clare recently?' Helen asked.

Clare had jacked in her job and gone travelling for six months with Marcus. They were in India at the moment.

'Not for a month or so, but we're having a proper leaving party for her when she comes back,' Fran said. 'You should try and come, Helen. It'd be great to have all four of us together again.'

'That'd be nice,' Helen said distractedly. 'That reminds me,' she said, jumping off the kitchen stool. 'I've got something for you. Stay there.'

She reappeared a couple of minutes later with a plastic bag. 'There,' she said, slightly awkwardly. 'I've been clearing

170

out my drawers and I found these. Thought you should have them back, since you were the original owner.'

Fran pulled the Pants of Shame out of the bag. 'Oh my God! I'd totally forgotten about them!'

'Those really were the days, weren't they?' Helen said, cracking a smile. She met Fran's eyes.

'They were,' said Fran, smiling back at her.

Helen bit her lip. 'I should come to that party, you know. It wouldn't hurt me to get out of the house once in a while.' She clapped her hands together suddenly. 'And you know what we should do, for Clare? As a leaving present. Kind of from the three of us.'

'What?' said Fran.

'These.' Helen waved them around, and Fran remembered Clare back in her flat on the first morning of the Pants of Shame. 'Get them framed. As a memento.'

'Frame some pants?' Fran said. '*These* pants?'

'They're clean,' Helen said indignantly. 'I ironed them as well.'

'Of course they are,' said Fran hurriedly. 'I just meant – well, it's a bonkers thing to do.'

'I know!' said Helen. Her eyes were shining. 'But – it's perfect, isn't it? We can't just have them moulder away in your drawer, can we? What better way . . . we used to know each other so well, and now all that's changed. Wouldn't it be nice to know they were on Clare's wall, always there?'

'I suppose so,' said Fran. 'Yes, I suppose it would.'

The day after the move, Marcus came into the downstairs loo to find Clare wobbling on a chair, a hammer in her hand.

'Help,' she said.

He lifted her down, and she stood back and looked at her handiwork.

'They look good, don't they?' she said.

'Er . . . lovely,' said Marcus. 'They're the nicest pair of framed pants I've ever seen.'

Clare nudged him. 'Shut up. Hurrah. They're up now.' Her mobile phone rang in her pocket and she picked it up.

'Hello? Hi, Jane. How are you? Good, good. You can come? That's brill.' She walked out of the room, swinging the hammer, and Marcus watched her go, his heart full of love for her. 'I'm so glad. No of course, it doesn't matter if you're a bit late. Helen's coming from Wimbledon and she has to wait for the babysitter, so she'll be late too. Oh, you spoke to her? Fantastic. It's just so great you can all come. I know! I know . . . I can't wait either. The Pants of Shame? Yep, they're up. In the loo. I know, just in case Fat Spotty Postroom Boy's on his way over so I've got somewhere to hide from him . . . I know . . . I did not fancy him! You lying witch!'

For the real Pants of Shame girls and honorary member Jean Michel.

Mike Gayle was born in 1970 in Birmingham. In that time he has (although not necessarily in this order): gained and lost several girlfriends; freelanced for the *Guardian, The Sunday Times, FHM* and *Cosmopolitan*; made a phone call from the loos at 11 Downing Street; been employed as an agony uncle for *Bliss* magazine; learned to walk; dyed his hair red for *Just Seventeen*; grown taller; gained 'O' levels, 'A' levels, a BSc in Sociology, and a post-graduate diploma in magazine journalism; been a false answer on a question on *Who Wants To Be a Millionaire*; got married; broken his leg playing football; and written five bestsellers – *My Legendary Girlfriend, Mr Commitment, Turning Thirty, Dinner For Two* and *His 'n' Hers*. His new novel, *Brand New Friend* is out now and he can be contacted via his website: www.mikegayle.co.uk

VICTORIA'S SECRET

Mike Gayle

'Dan?' says my girlfriend, Liz, as we sit down to eat dinner round at her place.

'*Mmmm*,' I reply, with a fork full of pasta in Lloyd Grossman's tomato and chilli sauce hovering just inches from my lips.

'Do you know what it is the day after tomorrow?'

'*Mmmmm*.' The pasta is now mere millimetres from its destination.

'So what day is it?'

'It's Saturday,' I tell her as the tip of my tongue flicks against the end of the fork, sending my taste buds into a paroxysm of delight. 'The weekend.'

'But it's not just any Saturday is it?'

'Isn't it?' I move the fork away from my mouth. I need to concentrate.

Liz punches me playfully but firmly on the shoulder – as if to say 'I know you're only joking but you can take a joke too far'.

'It's my birthday,' says Liz.

'I know.' Relieved, I reposition the forkful of pasta again. 'I'm just checking that you hadn't forgotten.'

'That,' I say smiling at both Liz and my pasta, 'would be impossible.' And with that I open my mouth and shovel in the forkful of pasta.

In the ten months that Liz and I have been together she has reminded me of the date of her birthday on an almost weekly basis. Any chance at all to shoehorn it into the conversation and she practically leaps at the opportunity. I don't mind too much because in the time that we have been together I have come to the conclusion that I love her a great deal. The problem I have, however, isn't about remembering when her birthday is, it's this: what do I get her? In the last ten months I'm pretty sure that I've thought about every single present under the sun. Small presents, big presents, homemade presents, sexy presents, edible presents, and even presents that will last a lifetime. And while all of these presents seem fine on the surface, I know deep down that Liz will somehow manage to find fault with all of them, because she's like that. To Liz, an innocent box of chocolates isn't just a box of chocolates, it's '. . . a cellulite time bomb waiting to be released on my thighs'. For most normal people vouchers for treatments at a beauty spa might be a way of saying: 'you deserve a bit of pampering', but when they're a gift from me to Liz apparently they mean, 'you look hideous! Get some work done!' And quite how a promise of a weekend in Barcelona could be interpreted as 'an excuse to ogle women with a better tan than me', I'll never understand.

Thanks to the little Liz-voice that now lives in my head, over the past few months I've managed to reject parachuting lessons: 'What, are you trying to kill me?'; posh new shoes: 'Why don't you just come out with it and tell me how much you hate all the rest of my footwear?'; perfume: 'What made you buy that particular brand? Is it one your ex-girlfriend used to wear?' and a whole multitude of gifts that any normal woman would've been grateful for. But of course, Liz *isn't* normal. She's the very definition of the word 'neurotic'. And 'mad', and 'slightly unhinged'.

With less than a month to go until her birthday I realised I was all out of ideas, so one night when she was round at mine watching telly I asked her outright: 'Liz, this is driving me mad trying to work out what to get you. So, just tell me, what do you want for your birthday?'

With a smile on her face, the like of which I'd never seen before, she turned to me and whispered in my ear, 'Underwear. Because it reminds me of . . . you know . . .'

'Of course,' I'd replied sadly. 'But are you sure?'

'Yes,' she'd smiled. 'I'm one hundred per cent sure.'

On the face of it Liz's request made perfect sense. Why? Because Liz loves underwear. Sometimes I think she loves it more than life itself. She's always said that good underwear can make her feel special. How could I not want to buy her something that made her feel special? I wanted her to feel special all the time. But if there was one thing I really did not want to do, buy Liz underwear was it. I didn't want to do it. Not if I could help it. Why? Because the last few times I've bought girlfriends underwear have resulted in a whole lot of trouble. The kind of trouble that can turn a man's world upside down.

This time, I told myself, *I can't just crumble. I have to be strong-willed.*

It's late the following evening and all I want to do is go home, have something to eat and fall asleep in front of the

TV. My knees are killing me, I've had a terrible day at work and rather than being in the car on the way home I'm in a high street department store, skulking around the women's lingerie department in search of the perfect bra and matching knickers. To say I was scared would be something of an understatement. I was terrified. To a man, the lingerie section of a department store is a bit like the moon. While we know it exists we're also aware that it's best not to go there without the aid of breathing apparatus. And yet here I am, the only man on the moon, and I'm in desperate need of oxygen.

It's hard to concentrate around all this underwear. It's as if I'm drowning in a sea of B cups and C cups and Double-D cups. And what a way to go! Engulfed in a deluge of frills and lace. *How do women concentrate in a place like this?* I ask myself. And then the answer comes back: *they concentrate by not being men.* I have to stop and touch the corners of my mouth several times to make sure that I'm not drooling. I feeling like I'm sticking out like the proverbial sore thumb but all the women around barely notice me. Thankfully it's as if I'm invisible. They all have a look of extreme determination about them. They are in Bra and Pants World – a dimension of the universe where men don't exist and where underwear isn't merely about base seduction, but rather about celebrating the feminine form in all its glory. And so as they pick up bras and scrutinise them carefully with all the analytical skills of a scientist in a laboratory they ask themselves the question: will this be the underwear that finally makes me feel like the woman I want to be?

Following the women's lead, I gingerly pick up a black lacy uplift bra with matching thong and hold it up to the light. As women's underwear goes it looks nice. I could easily imagine Liz in it. But then again as a man I could easily imagine Liz in any of the underwear in this store. I'm not that fussy. And so it soon becomes clear as I continue to hold the underwear aloft that I have no idea what it is that I'm looking for – I am just a man, alone, standing in the lingerie department of a high street department store staring at women's underwear. Surely, I think to myself, it must be just a matter of moments before someone calls the store's security guards to have me escorted off the premises.

Just as I'm about to throw down the underwear and run for my life a woman enters my line of vision and approaches me. She's wearing the department store's pale grey uniform. Her name badge reads: Victoria. She has jet black hair, a clear complexion, and smiling eyes. She is also very attractive.

Not again, I tell myself. *I knew this was a bad idea. I knew it. I can't let it happen again.*

But before I can do anything this monster in Mac eyeliner is upon me.

'Hello,' she says. 'I'm Victoria. I was just wondering if I could help you at all. You seem a little bit bewildered.'

'I'm looking for a bra,' I tell her and then after a moment I add: 'And some pants,' and then after that I add: 'They're not for me. They're for a woman.'

'Your partner?' she asks.

I nod as though I have momentarily lost the power of speech.

'Well, she's more of a girlfriend than a partner,' I say eventually.

'And what kind of thing does your girlfriend like?'

I take a moment to mentally scan through Liz's underwear drawer.

'Not red,' I reply. 'It's too tarty apparently. Not white or cream because it's too boring. And nothing with a pattern because she doesn't like patterns.'

'So that's all the things she doesn't like,' says Victoria, smiling gently. 'What about the things that she does like?'

'Well she likes lacy type stuff I think . . . you know, stuff that looks pretty . . . oh and she loves stuff that utilises new technology . . . you know the type of thing . . . materials that stretch or breathe . . . oh, and she likes underwear in black . . . of course . . . oh, and pastelly colours too.'

'Right, then,' says Victoria, grinning. 'Let's go and find your girlfriend some underwear.'

Together Victoria and I roam the rails of underwear. Some things I dismiss because they're not right, some things she dismisses because she thinks they're not right, but then finally we come across what we both agree is the perfect set of underwear. It's a lilac bra (with lacy detailing and excellent support both front and rear) and matching knickers (high cut on the leg which apparently is more flattering, yet more lacy detailing and extra support in the form of a new elastic fabric first designed for use by the crew members of an early US space shuttle mission).

'These are perfect,' I tell her. 'How much are they?'

Victoria repeats a figure large enough to make my eyes water.

'Is that too much?'

'No,' I reply, trying to steady my voice. 'Liz is worth it. I'll take them now shall I?'

Victoria laughed. 'Well you haven't actually told me what size your girlfriend is.'

'I have no idea,' I reply.

'None at all?'

I shake my head.

'Maybe you should leave buying them until you do know,' says Victoria.

I feel woozy at the thought of having to come back here.

'Well . . .' I begin holding the bra and pants set up to Victoria, '. . . if the truth be told she's probably about your size.'

Victoria laughs sweetly – it sounds like summer – and then flicks through the rail skilfully. 'Well that'll be size 10 knickers and a 32C bra then.'

I swallow hard and nod. 'I suppose it must be.'

'Right then,' says Victoria, 'let's get these paid for.'

At the till I hand over my credit card and Victoria says casually: 'She's a lucky woman, your girlfriend. What did she do to get a nice guy like you?'

I pause, lost in my own thoughts until the silence is broken by the sound of the credit card receipt churning out of the machine.

'Could you just check the amount and sign there?' asks Victoria.

As I sign I say: 'It's a long story.'

'What is?' says Victoria.

'How Liz and I got together.'

Victoria smiles warmly. 'Well I get off work in ten minutes, so perhaps you can explain it to me then over a drink or two?'

'I'd love to go for a drink,' I tell her. 'But I'd prefer to keep the story of Liz and me a secret for just a little longer if you don't mind.'

'Fine,' says Victoria softly. 'I like a man with a little bit of mystery.'

It's a Saturday morning and today is Liz's 31st birthday. The two of us are sitting on the sofa round at her house while she opens all the presents she received from her friends and family last night when we all went for a drink. So far she has had chocolates from her friend Kate, vouchers for a beauty spa from her brother Ben and a weekend break in Barcelona for two from her mum and dad. She tells me she loves every single one of her presents and right there and then I come to the conclusion that I will never understand her.

'I've saved the best till last,' says Liz picking up my present. 'Can I guess what it is?'

'Liz, you don't need to guess,' I tell her. 'You know what it is because you told me what to buy.'

'But you did ask,' she sniffs.

'Okay . . .' I say sarcastically, '. . . well guess away then, Sherlock.'

There's a brief pause while we teeter on the brink of a fully-blown argument. It could go either way, but I can see in her eyes that she's deciding against it and her annoyance soon dissipates.

'I'm guessing it's underwear,' says Liz, laughing.

'I'm guessing you're right,' I reply and with that she starts tearing at the wrapping paper.

'Oh Dan!' says Liz excitedly, as she holds up the under-wear in the air. 'They're wonderful . . .' she pauses and looks at the label, '. . . and they must have cost you a fortune. Did you choose them yourself?'

I swallowed hard. 'Not exactly.'

'What do you mean "not exactly"?'

'I had some help.'

'You had some help choosing *my* underwear? Who from?'

'Victoria,' I reply.

'Who is Victoria?'

'She's the assistant in the lingerie department who helped me choose your underwear.'

Liz's face falls.

'And the thing is Liz, Victoria and I have kind of fallen in love.'

It's six months later and I'm sitting on the sofa round at my new girlfriend Victoria's house.

'Dan?' says Victoria.

'Mmmm,' I reply.

'Do you know what day it is the day after tomorrow?'

'Mmmmm.'

'So what day is it?'

It's Saturday,' I tell her. 'The weekend.'

'But it's not just any Saturday is it?'

'Isn't it?'

Victoria punches me playfully but firmly on the shoulder – as if to say 'I know you're only joking but you can take a joke too far'.

'It's my birthday,' says Victoria.

'I know.'

'I'm just checking that you hadn't forgotten.'

'That,' I say smiling, 'would be impossible.' I pause and then ask her the big question – the same big question that I'd asked all my recent ex-girlfriends (Stephanie from Knickerbox, Eliza from Anne Summers, Tracy from Rigby and Peller, Shannon from Agent Provocateur and Belinda from the Calvin Klein underwear counter at Selfridges): 'What would you like for your birthday?'

She turns and whispers in my ear: 'Underwear. It reminds me of . . . you know . . .'

'I know . . .' I reply. 'I know. But you work in an under-wear shop. Why do you lot always need me to buy it for you? That's what I'd like to know.'

Victoria laughs and smiles to herself and then finally she says: 'I guess that's just my little secret.'

Kristin Gore was born in 1977. While attending Harvard University, she was a writer and editor for the *Harvard Lampoon*. She went on to work as a comedy writer for several television shows, including *Futurama* and *Saturday Night Live*, for which she received an Emmy nomination. Her first novel, *Sammy's Hill*, was published in 2004 and quickly became a bestseller. Kristin lives with her husband in Los Angeles, where she is writing the screenplay of *Sammy's Hill* for Columbia Pictures and working on her second novel.

STRAY

Kristin Gore

I've never been on a plane I didn't assume was going to crash. Even on the smoothest flights, I still manage at least one moment of sheer, liver-gripping terror – one moment of complete certainty of imminent doom. I have yet to be in an actual plane crash, though I generally average a couple of flights a day. I'm a flight attendant, or stewardess if you prefer, which I do. Few join me in this preference. Most people consider it a politically incorrect term. I consider it a spiritually satisfying one. The Bible instructs us to be good stewards of the earth, in a passage that's particularly popular with environmental groups. The Bible talks a lot about mankind, and makes it clear that my gender came from a rib, so when it talks about stewards, I can't help but think it's addressing men. And if I were a man, I'd be a steward of the earth. And probably gay. As things stand, I'm a stewardess. A stewardess with a fear of flying.

I realize I'm a throwback, but I'm a sucker for the 'ess' suffix in general. To me, Meryl Streep is not a phenomenal actor, she's a stunningly talented actress. Similarly, Audrey

Niffenegger is an engaging authoress. And the fact that I stole a pack of Big League Bubblegum Chew from the Rite-Aid when I was eleven didn't make me a burglar, but a burglaress. I suppose I'm still a burglaress, though I'm no longer practising.

I'm non-practising when it comes to a lot of things, actually. I'm a non-practising exerciser, a non-practising inventor, a non-practising genius. When I was younger, I was a non-practising child prodigy. The brilliance of the 'non-practising' adjective impressed me from the moment I first came across it. It allowed one to declare oneself something and then never have to actually back it up, since that would be against one's beliefs. I *am* this, but I choose not to demonstrate it, so you'll just have to take my word for it. Genius. Like me. Non-practising.

One might think a non-practising genius like myself would find another job that didn't panic me several times a day, but I don't feel qualified for anything else. I got into steward-essing because of a fascination with the tiny little liquor bottles available on planes and in hotel minibars. These perfect little vessels never fail to soothe me. I stare at them and feel happy that not everything is forced to grow up. I decided early on that I wanted to be near them.

The hotel industry was slow to respond to my overtures, but the airline snatched me and my largely fictional resumé right up. I soon realized I was a naturally talented stewardess and felt less guilty that I may have been hired thanks to false claims of extensive hot air balloon work. I am disturbingly good at fake-smiling when I feel like crap, which is the single most important skill a stewardess can possess. That, and the self-restraint not to ram the knees of obnoxious passengers with the beverage cart. So far I've made the cart assaults seem like lawsuit-proof accidents. Micro-turbulence is a trusty alibi.

One of the perks of being a professional stewardess for a major airline is that I get to fly for free whenever I want. I appreciate this benefit, though I've never taken advantage of it. I won't set foot on a plane unless contractually obligated to do so. No, flying is much, much too risky, which is why I'm presently driving the eighteen hours back to my hometown. I know the statistics about driving being more dangerous than flying, but I don't believe them. I think they're perpetuated by the airlines attempting to drum up more business, just like I suspect the movie *Attack of the Killer Tomatoes* might have been funded by the Pickle Lobby.

I've asked if I can cash in all the free flights I'm not taking for some other kind of perk, like use of the stair car during holiday decorating season or free massages at the Shiatsu Stall in terminal A, but my requests have thus far been denied. I plan to continue pestering HR, because those massages are worth fighting for.

I could certainly use one of them now. I sense the familiar stiffness in my neck settling in for a long stay as I pilot my banged-up Dodge Neon down the back roads I prefer to the highway. A learner's permit-driver sideswiped my car months ago, leaving me with a handicapped passenger door and a persistent case of whiplash.

I try to self-administer a quick neck rub and am suddenly reminded of a ghost story I heard when I was younger, back in the non-practising prodigy days. It was about a woman who always wore a ribbon around her neck. Her husband repeatedly asked her why but she refused to tell him. Finally, when she was a very old lady, she told him to go ahead and untie the ribbon. He did, and her head fell off. This story had haunted me when I was little and to this day, I'm very wary of women wearing chokers.

I glance over at the passenger seat to check on Grant. Or rather, to check on Grant's ashes, which are resting in a slightly-mangled plastic Elmo doll that used to be one of his favorite chew toys. It's made of some sort of canine teeth-cleaning material that he'd really flipped for. He'd loved holding it down with one paw and leveraging his lean torso into an optimal chewing position, turning his tail into a thumping metronome. If they made human dental products that exciting no one would ever have any cavities. Grant had been a large, happy, loyal dog and I never imagined he would be insubstantial enough to fit inside one of his little toys. He didn't even fill it all the way up.

I blink a few times and wonder what my aunt and uncle are doing. Most likely, my uncle is setting up one of his elaborate Dominos exhibits in the room that used to be my bedroom, before he and my aunt garage-sold all my childhood possessions to make more space for themselves. And when I say Dominos, I'm not referring to the small plastic rectangles people arrange to cascade in spotted waterfalls. I'm talking about the pizza boxes. My uncle eats a small Domino's pizza every day and then glues the empty boxes together to construct various sculptures.

He started doing this soon after I came to live with them. I've heard that the Domino's Corporation owners give tons of money to anti-choice groups and I've suspected my uncle's sculptures are more political than he lets on, but I've never had the energy to investigate.

My aunt, I feel sure, is asleep. That's what she does when she isn't taking pills. She hasn't always been like this. Just for the last twenty years. I sigh and remember the phone call that had led to an earlier eighteen-hour drive to pick Grant up in the first place.

'We're going to put him down. He's old and it's for the best.'

'Is he sick?'

'No. But we're sick of taking care of him.'

I'd got in the car half an hour later. Grant had lived three more years under my care before dying on his own terms.

Were there some meaningful place to scatter Grant's ashes that didn't involve a trip home, I gladly would have pounced on it the way he used to pounce on the mail the instant it slid through the slot. Wrestling it away from him before he managed to shred anything important was always an adrenaline-pumping project. But for better or for worse, there was only one place where Grant could rest in peace – the ravine behind my aunt and uncle's house.

Grant and I had escaped to the ravine every day of our lives together in that house, no matter what the weather. It was our refuge – our land of magic and intrigue. Anyone observing would have seen a sad little kid and a dog not fitting in together, but we saw ourselves as world-weary adventurers ever determined to plot one more mission. Grant was the co-pilot, my Chewbacca. I, obviously, was Han Solo. We were devastatingly significant, whether or not anyone else realized it at the time. Often the fate of the universe rested in our hands.

The summer I turned nine, my aunt and uncle toyed with the idea of clearing out the ravine and putting down Astroturf. When I heard about this scheme, I screamed for seventeen minutes and thirteen seconds. I knew the exact duration because I used my mom's old watch that I'd started wearing to measure it. After minute fourteen, my aunt and uncle just left the house. That's how they tended to deal with difficult things. But they never brought up Astroturf again.

Sometimes I feel like screaming for extended periods of time on plane flights. Not in response to obnoxious passengers – I handle them with cart rams and practiced ignoring – but in reaction to repetition. Instead of telling people the same useless lines about their seat buckles and flotation devices, I often feel like screaming. Or actually like high-pitched shrieking, a la Yoko Ono, but I never go through with it. I mentally add non-practising artist to my resumé.

The only part of the standard stewardess recitation that I attach any sort of significance to is the part about the emergency exits, because I think one of the instructions is philosophically profound. I infuse my voice with subtle but palpable reverence whenever I utter the line: 'Bear in mind that the nearest exit may be behind you.' How true. To me, the words are poetic and wise. And tragic, because in real life I can't go back to those exits.

Approximately every third flight, I fantasize about jumping out of the plane. My neighbour told me when I was younger that falling through clouds makes a person go blind. I'd been suspicious of this claim but never had the chance to prove it wrong. Doing so is one motivation for jumping, but the stronger one is the shock value. No one would ever expect it. People would be so surprised. I therefore find the prospect almost overwhelmingly tempting. If opening the door mid-flight and leaping out wouldn't endanger the lives of my fellow passengers, I might consider it. But I know that it would and therefore can't in good conscience seriously fantasize about it. Maybe jumping off a building would be a better bet, if I could ensure that no passers-by would be landed on. The building would need to be tall enough for clouds.

I don't consider myself suicidal, just fundamentally bored. But maybe that's occasionally the same thing.

And when I think about jumping, I think about my aunt and uncle. My guardians. I suspect they'd be surprised, and sad, and probably annoyed to have to deal with the aftermath. Would they even deal with it? Or might they just leave it to someone else?

I sneeze violently and wonder whether I'm allergic to Grant's ashes. Or to his absence. I've never had any problems with live dogs, but dead ones are a previously untested allergin. In general, they shouldn't be too difficult to avoid.

My aunt and uncle had never liked the idea of Grant. They warned me that I didn't know how hard it could be to take care of another living thing and did everything to dissuade me from adopting him, short of forbidding it. They told me I'd regret it, that I'd grow to resent him, that I'd be driven crazy by the demands of his simply existing. I listened to them, knowing they were really talking about me, and reminded them that my parents had promised me a puppy before their accident. They sighed and shut up.

As I think about these people who never chose to have me, it begins to rain regularly, then unreasonably. I have to pull over because I can't see anything except my windscreen wipers drowning. I'm annoyed, but also pleased that nature is still capable of such sabotage. I'm happy we haven't completely won, and I feel like this sentiment elevates me to the ranks of enlightened stewardesses.

When the river of rain finally slows and I can discern actual individual drops again, I hear barking. I look quickly at the Elmo urn, but Grant remains in ashes, which shouldn't surprise me but does. The barking is close and ostensibly part of the land of the living. I stretch myself up to look further over the steering wheel and see a three-legged dog engaged in a fierce face-off with my car's right tyre. My money's on the tyre. The dog must be a stray since I know from previous drives that there's no one and nothing around for miles. I purposely drive this stretch of back road *because* it's lonely and abandoned – I don't feel like either of us has to put on any airs.

But just as I've begun to empathize with the loner life this three-legged dog must lead, I spot a dishevelled man limping out of the trees towards my car. He whistles to the dog as he stares at me through the windscreen. He's completely soaked.

I stare back at him. He jerks a hitchhiker's thumb but doesn't smile or soften his expression in any way. I feel like he's double-daring me to be crazy enough to pick him up. I consider the options. He could either kill me or make the drive much more interesting. Or both. On the other hand, I could just drive away and stay alive and bored. I roll down the window.

'Where are you headed?'

'End of the rainbow.'

'Is that off Route 9?'

He glares at me for a moment before nudging his dog towards the passenger door. I open the glove compartment and carefully place the Elmo urn full of Grant inside. The man opens the door and climbs in, getting the seat wet and muddy. His dog takes care of the floor.

'What's your name?' I ask. I should at least know his name.

'Tall,' he answers.

He's not really that tall, but I notice he has enormous feet. Maybe he'd been born with them and his parents had made assumptions. I wonder if they feel mistaken. I wonder if they're still alive, worrying about him. I put the car in gear and ease back onto the bumpy road.

'And that guy?' I nod to the dog.

'L. Like the letter.'

L is pretty cute, in a mangy and wild sort of way. For the first time, I notice a bedraggled ribbon tied around his neck. It might have been red or blue once, but it looks as though it's been the color of damp, dirty fur for a long while. I wonder where this pair has been.

'How'd he lose his leg?' I ask.

'Accident,' Tall answers. 'Wrong place at the wrong time.'

'Mmmm. People say timing is everything.'

'What people?'

His tone is unmistakably challenging. And paranoid? I wonder if he battles imaginary enemies. I wonder if the metal flashlight in the pocket of my door could be an effective weapon.

'Um . . . I don't know. My mom. My mom always said timing is everything.'

I glance sideways at him to see how he takes this. His forehead appears deep in thought, though his eyes look dull and dead.

'What's your dad say?'

'I don't know. He agreed, I guess.'

Tall breathes in and out in loud, irregular gasps, before sneezing raucously. I feel the spray on my arm and grow nauseous. When Tall speaks again, he speaks slowly in a low voice, drawing out each word.

'Do you love your parents? Would you die for them?'

I continue steering with my right hand and close my left one around the flashlight, testing its weight. I'm left-handed, like my father.

'My parents passed away when I was young,' I reply, trying to keep my voice even. 'My aunt and uncle raised me. As much as they bothered to, at least,' I can't help but add.

'What's that mean? What'd they do to you?'

He's confrontational again. It's getting dark and the rain is still battering the windscreen. I wish it would stop so I could just see a little better. Maybe the back roads weren't such a fantastic plan.

'They didn't do anything to me. Which was the problem. They never seemed to want to deal with me.'

Tall bursts into gravelly laughter. I hold my breath, waiting to hear what's so funny. I wonder if it's the gleeful thought of my imminent strangling.

'Maybe *you* were bad timing.'

Lightning flashes overhead and I mentally review what I'm supposed to do if it strikes the car. We can survive it, as long as we don't touch anything metal. Grant's collar is metal, and I've strung it around my neck with even more metal. It felt better to put it against my skin than away in some box. The flashlight in my hand is metal too. I fake-smile at Tall.

'Maybe I was.'

He seems mollified. He slides his neck around in a reptilian stretch.

'Got anything to drink?'

I do. I have a backpack full of tiny liquor. I don't drink, but I'm always encouraging others to partake so I can have the empties. I like filling the little bottles up with things I think are better for them. Tall is having none of it.

'I meant water.'

He sounds angry. And offended? I don't have any water, which I tell him. Buying water depresses me. It should be free and available, like air and love.

'We'll have to stop then. L is dehydrated.'

Tall says this defiantly with a smack of his gums, like he's challenging me to argue with a toothless maniac. L doesn't look particularly dehydrated. He's curled up beneath the glove compartment, snoring the stuffy snores of flat-faced dogs.

'I'll find someplace when we make it back to the highway.'

I sneak a sideways glance at Tall and am alarmed to see that his face has twisted into a menacing sneer. Behind him, the side of the road drops off into a steep ravine.

'Stop now,' he hisses abruptly. 'You don't have a choice, YOU'RE GOING TO STOP NOW.'

He's reaching into his coat for something. I am instantly hot with the panic that comes with sheer, liver-gripping terror. I think about Grant in the glove compartment and wish he were in the passenger seat instead. I open my mouth to finally start screaming.

Suddenly, I remember that the passenger door is broken and can only be opened from the outside. Since I rarely have anyone along for my rides, I've put off getting it repaired. My panic flees. I feel calm, practically giddy. I break into a real smile as I curl my fingers tighter around the flashlight. It's all I can do to keep from giggling. I glance down at L and know I won't have to throw Grant's toys away after all. The ribbon's coming off though. I'll give him a nice collar instead.

I take a long, deep, free breath. As of right now, I'm a non-practising victim. Tall is the one who's trapped, not me. Though he hasn't been told yet, his only exit is behind him.

As the adrenaline courses through me, I catch a split second glimpse of his weapon: a soggy pack of cigarettes. The truth is, people have killed for less.

Lauren Henderson was born in London, where she worked as a journalist before moving to Tuscany and then to Manhattan. She has written seven books in her Sam Jones mystery series, which has been optioned for American TV, many short stories, and three romantic comedies – *My Lurid Past, Don't Even Think About It* and *Exes Anonymous*. Her latest book is *Jane Austen's Guide to Dating*, which has been optioned as a feature film and is published in the UK by Headline. Her books have been translated into over 20 languages. Together with Stella Duffy she has edited an anthology of women-behaving-badly crime stories, Tart Noir, and their joint website is www.tartcity.com.

DATING THE ENEMY

Lauren Henderson

We treat the people we want to love like adversaries.

'You can't trust what people say any more,' says my friend David. 'Everyone knows what people want to hear. We all know exactly how to show the socially acceptable sides of ourselves. Don't listen to what people say. Watch what they do. They can't disguise that.'

David gave me that advice when I first moved to New York. I thought he sounded as paranoid as a character from a horror film telling the others how to spot the aliens. But he was right. We're fighting for our emotional lives. Guides to dating rules might as well be called *Lao Tsu's Art Of War*. As soon as you let your guard down they knife you; then you crawl back to your friends to lick your wounds while they analyse where you went wrong and what was going through your attacker's head, with the finely-honed skills of thirty-somethings who have paid extortionate amounts to have their sensitive psyches probed by Upper East Side analysts.

We dress in grey and black and khaki. Combat trousers,

big sweaters, bags strapped across our chests so that our hands are free to defend ourselves. The bare minimum of makeup. Big, ugly, rubber-soled shoes, in which we can run away from trouble. Our one sign of frivolity is the occasional bright, lace-trimmed vest. And pretty underwear, seen, alas, mostly by ourselves. We are urban survivors, striding across concrete pavements, ducking and weaving to avoid being elbowed by passing strangers who think we're in their path, dodging cycle couriers riding the wrong way down one-way streets, navigating through subway systems and a network of late-night bars where we drink too many martinis and smoke too many cigarettes to forget the last person who looked like they could be The One, and turned out to be a liar on a quick break from their ex.

We spend a fortune on cabs.

CASE STUDY ONE:

Paola goes out for a drink with friends and bumps into a guy she nearly had a fling with at a work conference a few months ago. They fooled around but she didn't actually sleep with him because they're on the same work network. He's younger than she is and lower down the pecking order. She was nervous of the gossip. By not actually having sex with him, she could keep her options open.

All good excuses. Actually she was scared.

So now here he is again: keen, handsome, attentive, and making it clear that he still wants to sleep with her. A sure thing. And, from the fooling around, she assumes that the sex will be excellent. But she's out with a couple of people from work, and they know him. No way is she going to let her guard down, show that she wants to take him home, with the danger that it won't work out and that word will get around. It might make her vulnerable. What if he only wants her for sex? If they were both going in the same direction at the end of the night they could share a cab; but they're not. So she lets it go.

He asks her to ring him. She says she will. She won't. It's too close to home. Think of the risks.

We are perpetually sensitised to possibility. Phrases of cheap music run through our heads; we're always at the stage where they're meaningful. Even the most banal lyrics seem directly applicable to our current tortured situation.

> *'If only you were here tonight*
> *I know that we could make it right . . .'*

We would die rather than confess to liking the singers; our images demand that we be listening to the latest hip bootleg remix, not trashy sentimental pop.

'If you chase someone you like,' says Phil, 'then you can be the one to dump them after you have sex.'

'Go for the ugly guys,' says Paola. 'They're much more grateful.'

CASE STUDY TWO:

Laura's the only one of our fighting unit in a relationship. She loves Skip and he loves her. He keeps asking her to marry him. They met four years ago and spent the first few months fucking each other's brains out. Laura ate like a horse and lost five pounds. After a year they decided to move in together. Both of them were ecstatic. The first night they spent in their new apartment, Skip rolled over with his back to her and said that he was really tired. That was it. They've hardly had sex since. It's been over a year.

She tried to talk to him about it but every time he had a different excuse. He was stressed at work, he'd overdone it at the gym, now that they were living together they were going to have to get used to not having sex every single night. Gradually the excuses faded away, to be replaced by what turned out to be a manifesto. Why did sex matter that much anyway? Surely what mattered was how much they loved each other? Most people had much less sex than they boasted about, after all. They were just another normal couple. Laura shouldn't get so worked up about this. Hadn't she heard the story about the jar full of coins?

And every so often he would have sex with her, when he sensed that the strain of celibacy was becoming unbearable. The night before last had been one of those times.

'Pity fuck,' says Phil.

'Relationship-maintenance fuck,' I correct.

'Well, no. The trouble is,' Laura says helplessly, 'is that it was *good*. You know what I mean? It wasn't a let's-get-this-over-with-so-she-can't-complain-for-another-few-months fuck. It was like the old times. That's the thing. Nothing's changed. And that just makes it worse. I mean, he can still do it like that, so why doesn't he?'

'Would you have preferred it to be perfunctory and loveless?' David enquires.

'You're going through the motions but you don't really care,' Paola sings, a snippet of an old song that's just been covered and remixed within an inch of its life over the latest stripped-down, kicking dance beat, the original singer long forgotten.

'No, he did care, he does care,' Laura says miserably. 'And yeah, I would much rather the sex was crap. At least I could say, OK, that side of things is over, and deal with it. But when it's that good, it's like he's keeping me on a string. Doling out something from time to time just so I keep from starving completely.'

'You do have that I-had-good-sex-recently glow,' David observes.

'Yeah, what's your problem, bitch?' I say jokingly. 'You had great sex the night before last! That's probably more recent than anyone round this table!'

Laura shoots me a foul look. And so does everyone else.

'What's the jar full of coins thing?' Phil asks.

Three of us start to speak at once. David makes it through.

'That if you put a coin in a jar for each time you have sex the first year in a marriage, and take one out every time you have sex after that, the jar'll still have coins in it when you die.'

'*Whoah*,' Phil says. 'That's why I'm never getting married.'

This is a complete bluff, a moment of machismo. Phil would love more than anything to get married. We all know this so well that no-one bothers to call him on it.

'Look,' Paola says to Laura, her voice sober. Clearly she has decided to be the voice of reason. 'It'll never get much better. You've got two choices: leave him or have affairs. I think you should have affairs. Bet he never asks questions. Shit, he'll probably be grateful.'

'Well-concealed commitment issues,' says David, grave as a doctor diagnosing a fatal disease. 'That's a tough one.'

'Maybe he's depressed,' says Phil. 'That's the first thing to make a guy lose his woody. The trouble is, even the new anti-depressants don't exactly up your libido.'

We all look at Phil.

'Yeah,' he says. 'But you know the thing is, I don't care! I'm so happy on my Prozac right now I don't care if I ever get laid again!'

We all edge back in the booth like vampires who have just spotted a clove of garlic in the middle of the table.

'We'll do that one later,' Paola decides. 'Right now we're still on Laura.'

'I'm scared of rocking the boat,' Laura says. 'The rest of the time it's so perfect. And maybe if we get married it'll get better.'

We all laugh sardonically. Laura has talked about this problem so many times that we are allowed to find this amusing.

'What makes you think that?' David looks weary. We have all had this conversation with her, over and over again. 'If moving in together fucked up the sex, then marriage'll be ten times worse.'

'But it's so perfect in every other way,' Laura repeats hopelessly. 'I mean, I don't have to tell you guys that.'

We all know and love Skip. He's funny, sweet and dealt very well with the trial-by-fire of meeting Laura's friends. He has a good job which he enjoys, and is good-looking without being so unnecessarily handsome that other women hit on him all the time or are automatically hostile to his girlfriend. He's easy-going, not a slob, and obviously adores Laura. Your ideal man. As a gay best friend.

'What happens if I do leave him?' Laura is so scared by the thought she can barely get the words out. 'Back on the street again, out there in dating hell . . .' She shivers. 'No offence, you guys . . .'

We shrug to show that none has been taken.

'You all know what I went through before I met Skip. I honestly don't think I can do that again. My God, I'll be single for the rest of my life.'

Laura doesn't actually say it; she knows we'd shoot her down. But we can see her thinking it. Better a stable relationship with a guy who loves her, the social certainties of being in a couple, the end to loneliness, than our nocturnal, bar-crawling existence, our latest reports from the war front.

I can't blame her.

'Is he getting it anywhere else?' asks Phil. Prozac has not managed to suppress his cynicism.

This is the first time anyone has put this question to Laura. She looks shell-shocked.

We don't know how to advise Laura, or anyone with long-term relationship problems. No-one does, apart from our shrinks. Long-term relationships require patience, compromise and faith, and we are familiar with none of the above. Indeed, we see them all as signs of weakness.

'I hung on, hoping she'd change,' one of us will say feebly, and the others will expel their breath in tight hisses through clenched teeth, like the last puffs of a milk frother making cappuccino. In our world, you never hang on. You explain that the person's behaviour is unacceptable, that they have breached your tolerance limit, that you value yourself too much to put up with their latest sin of omission or commission, and you move on, head held high. Your friends applaud: you have done the right thing.

We are terrified of being like our parents, either trapped in unhappy marriages or undergoing bloody, prolonged divorces. We all remember what those felt like, our limbs strapped to four horses all running in different directions. Even now we are barely managing to put the pieces together again, with the help of the aforementioned expensive therapists. No way are any of us getting into that kind of mess ourselves. Our parents' pathetic excuses for the misery we went through are still vivid to us. The lesson we have learned is never to put up with anything: any signs of trouble and we're out of there.

We are all desperate to be in love. But we are still more desperate to hide it. So for pride's sake, we pretend, to ourselves and others, that it's all about sex instead.

I'm waiting for Ivan to call. It's been a week now and my stomach is processing food faster than I can eat it. I'm chainsmoking and ringing my friends constantly to discuss what might have gone wrong on the date that would mean he wouldn't want to see me again.

'Go to bed with someone else,' says David. 'It's perfect. You distract yourself and then, when he does call, you can be really cool.'

'What, just go and pick some guy up in the bar on the corner?' I say sarcastically.

'You must know someone. What about that guy you were seeing a couple of months ago?'

'Seamus?'

'He was really into you, wasn't he?'

'Yeah,' I say smugly. 'Took him ages to stop calling.'

'And the sex was good, wasn't it?'

'Great,' I confirm. 'It was the conversation that was the problem.'

'Well, that's perfect!' David says enthusiastically. 'Call him up right now and tell him to come over because you need to get laid. If a woman I'd been seeing gave me a call like that I'd be ecstatic. Even if I was busy, or dating someone else, I'd be ecstatic.'

'Wouldn't you think I was a slut?' I ask.

David is my, and many other women's, Official Man. We touch base with him to see what men are really thinking. The trouble is that he tells us.

'No way. I'd be hugely flattered and I wouldn't be able to stop thinking about you. So ring him.'

'Oh David,' I whine, 'I can't. He's only just stopped calling. It would be cruel. It would give him false hope.'

I am very nervous at the thought of seeing Seamus again, reading that happiness in his eyes, his pleasure at seeing me. It makes me feel horribly guilty.

'Bullshit. Just be straight with him. Tell him you don't want to date him but the sex was fabulous and you want to get laid.'

'You'd never do something like that yourself,' I say. 'It's all very well advising other people to do it.'

Silence. My phone beeps.

'David, I have another call, hold on . . .'

I switch over. It's Paola. I tell her I'll call back.

'Was it Ivan?' David says.

'No,' I say miserably.

We observe a moment's silence, as if in mourning.

'Anyway, I feel really bad about the way I treated Seamus,' I say. I do feel bad. But also, shameful though it is to admit it, I am cheered up just a little by the knowledge that, while I am pining for Ivan, someone else is doing the same for me. 'Here I am complaining about Ivan not ringing, just disappearing like this –'

'You don't know that,' says David, automatically reassuring. 'He might just be busy at work. You know girl time is very different from boy time.'

'– and that's exactly what I did to Seamus.'

'You haven't had sex with Ivan yet.'

'Well, that makes what I did to Seamus even worse. I never returned his calls. I was a real bitch. And now I'm whining about someone doing that to me. I don't deserve Ivan to ring me back.'

'Hey.' David's voice sharpens. 'It's all tactics. Remember that. You didn't promise Seamus anything, did you?'

It's a rhetorical question: he knows the answer already.

'So there's no guilt,' he continues. 'You didn't break any promises.'

'I could at least have told him what was going on.'

David sounds very weary now. 'Forget the conscience,' he says. 'That isn't how it works. You know that.'

Our pockets are full of matchboxes from bars we can't even remember, hangouts we have been swept along to at three in the morning by groups of people we don't know that well. It's not so much that we think if we stay out till dawn we might finally stumble across The One, bleary-eyed and blinking, like us, in the daylight; no, we want to postpone the moment of going home alone to our single-bedroomed apartments until we're too drunk or tired, or both, to be anything but grateful that there are no witnesses waiting up to see the state in which we stagger through the front door, throwing our keys clumsily at the hall table and missing.

We are in our thirties. We all earn plenty of money and have only ourselves to spend it on. We are very spoilt. We know we're spoilt, but it doesn't make us feel any better.

Paola's on a radical diet. She's decided that she needs to lose ten pounds. Paola probably *does* need to lose ten pounds, but we're worried about her reasons – she's frantic to get a steady boyfriend – and her methods, which are frighteningly drastic. All she's eaten for the last three weeks are meal-substitute bars and the occasional piece of fruit. And she's taken up circuit training.

'Her body is just not up to this,' Laura says. 'I mean, think of the shock to the system!'

'Not as much of a shock as it would be if she gave up drinking,' I say.

We exchange a glance. This is the trouble. The one vice Paola is allowing herself is alcohol. She's drinking as much as ever, only now with much less in her stomach to soak it up. As if to compensate for the deprivation through which she's putting herself, she eats her meal bar and then comes out with us to consume the same amount of cocktails that she did when she was still packing away heaped platefuls of comfort food. Every night we have to practically mop her up off the floor and pour her into a cab.

The reason Paola doesn't have a boyfriend is that she gets off with men practically as soon as she meets them. She hasn't been on a first date in the last couple of years which didn't end, at least, with a tongue sandwich and a fumble in the back of a cab. Mostly, this city being a brutal arena in which women who give away too much too soon are seen as weak, the men never call her again. But sometimes they do. In which case she decides that they must be desperate. Why would they want a fat girl otherwise?

Paola isn't fat by any standards but the near-anorexic ones of this city. One would think that the legions of men who keep asking her out would eventually convince her that she's attractive, but it doesn't seem to work that way. Instead the way she behaves towards them creates a self-fulfilling prophecy.

'She blames everything on her weight because it's easier that way,' Laura says.

I agree. 'But if she loses it, what's her excuse going to be?'

'That's the problem,' Laura says darkly. 'I'm sure that's why she's getting so drunk.'

'Fear of not having anything to hide behind.'

'Exactly.'

'Oh, fuck,' I say selfishly. I have enough to deal with right now without the prospect of a hundred and twenty pound Paola in deep existential crisis.

CASE STUDY THREE:

Ivan seemed perfect. A friend of a friend, highly recommended. Attentive, funny, sweet, caring, good job, nice apartment. Someone older than me, stable, a rock in high seas. For every question I ask about him he asks ten about me. We go to bed, and it's wonderful. He rings me the next day. We're making plans for the next few weeks. Then nothing. Two weeks later, I finally get a phone call, telling me that he's hooked up with an ex-girlfriend; they'd had problems that they've now resolved. And – the clincher – she's madly in love with him.

'He's trying to set up a competition between the two of you,' says David.

'What's this madly in love thing?' says Laura. 'What are you supposed to say – I love you more? You've only known him a few weeks!'

'You should have said: *What are you really telling me?*' says my therapist. 'Think more about your own emotions and less about his.'

'What's his emotional history?' says Paola. 'Has he been married? Lived with anyone? For how long? What do you mean, you didn't ask him? You've always got to find that out! If a guy's hitting forty and he's never been married or lived with anyone, he has serious issues to resolve.'

I realise that I am very, very tired. I go to bed instead of hitting the bars with my posse and I sleep for twelve hours straight. I don't feel that much better in the morning but at least I don't have a hangover. Maybe this is a new start.

Yesterday I was walking down Fifth Avenue, listening to my iPod, when a wash of peace flooded through me. I felt invisible, or at least transparent. I wanted to open my arms wide and stand there, letting people walk through me as if I were a ghost. It was wonderful. Does that mean I don't care any more? That would be such a relief.

'Typical of you to have a Zen breakthrough in the middle of Fifth Avenue,' Laura says.

'I know!' I say. 'And I wasn't even outside Gucci!'

'What does your shrink think about it?' she says curiously.

'I haven't told her yet,' I admit. 'I'm keeping it to myself.'

And as I say this, I realise how good it feels. Maybe I shouldn't even have told Laura. For three years I've had this tight little support group – David, Laura, Paola, Phil; we recount every last detail about our lives, we play back crucial scenes to each other as easily as we hit the instant-replay button on our TiVOs. We're the safety net, and everyone outside is the enemy. And now I wonder how much it's actually helping. Perhaps I should start keeping more things to myself. I don't know if it would help, but it might be worth trying.

Something has to change, after all. Maybe I'll start with this.

Wendy Holden was a journalist for fourteen years before becoming a full-time writer. She has written six novels, all top ten best-sellers. She lives in Derbyshire with her husband and two children.

HELLO SAILOR

Wendy Holden

He was loud and red-faced with small, suspicious eyes. He looked boorish – the sort who farted in bed and routinely belittled women. He had an unattractive body – that solid, thicknecked, wide-calfed build of a man predisposed to fat but who keeps it off with sweaty and straining exercise. It was horribly easy to imagine him in a pair of smelly black Lycra cycling shorts.

Nevertheless, I looked at him and knew that he was everything I had been searching for. He was The One. The One I would marry. My husband. And the reason I knew this was because he had the perfect wife.

It had taken me a while to spot her. I have to admit that, by the time I did, I was close to despair. The whole exercise seemed about to prove fruitless. The night I sat down to the right of the captain at his table, I was convinced I'd wasted thousands of pounds of my savings for no return at all.

The captain chattered merrily away, doing his 'cheer up the poor single woman on board' routine. Which was understandable, given how miserable I must have looked. Though the captain may well have been interested for other reasons – I keep myself in pretty good order and manage to turn heads in the street a good decade after most women my age have bid their last building-site wolf-whistle a long-distant goodbye. Not that builders are my target audience exactly. Or ships' captains, come to that. What I'm after is serious money, and while there was obviously plenty of it on board, it was being guarded by the most ferocious set of spouses I'd yet come across.

'. . . and of course tomorrow we arrive at Buenos Aires which is great fun, a simply marvellous place . . .' As he banged on in a well-practised undertone, the captain was eyeing up the point at which the two sides of my Diane von Furstenberg wrap parted over my upper thigh. I've always had good legs, thanks to being a dancer all those years. And it was also thanks to being a dancer that I got involved in all this in the first place.

I almost didn't, mind you. I was desperate not to do the cruise ship job when my agent first suggested it. Dancing on cruise ships was the naff lowest of the low – at that time I still entertained hopes of *Swan Lake* at Covent Garden, or, failing that, *Chicago* in the West End at the very least. When I told this to my agent, Moira, a no-nonsense Cockney, she clearly decided she had had enough of my fancy ways. 'Darlin', there ain't no nice way to say this, but you ain't no Margot Fonteyn. I'm not even sure you're *Strictly Come Dancing*.' Being told that, despite being a professional dancer of many years' standing, I didn't even come up to television amateur standards was a sobering moment. I took the cruise ship job. It was on a vessel labouring under the moniker *Cornucopia II* (wasn't ruining one ship with a name like that enough?) which was going along the coastline of the South of France.

I hate sailing, it makes me feel sick, and cruises are particularly grim. All that trapped humanity endlessly milling about low-ceilinged lounges carpeted in swirling orange and edged with trestle tables bearing platters of poached salmon. There seemed to be the most amazing quantity of said fish on board this ship. It was obviously meant to be a symbol of luxury, but it made me feel ill every time I passed it.

The gig, if anything, made me feel worse. It was an excruciating Twenties-style variety show with the toe-curling title *What Ho!* The purpose of it was to encourage the saddoes on board to persist in the fantasy that they were Bright Young Things from the great days of luxury cruising. What they in fact were was lumpy businessmen from the East Midlands and their dim wives. It would have been funny were it not so pathetic – the sight, night after night, of large-tummied natives of Nottingham turning out in sequinned headbands and white tie and tails and waving fat legs around to the Charleston. And that was just the blokes.

Afterwards, I chatted to some of the punters in the bar. I can't say I particularly wanted to, but there was sod-all else going on. One chap, whose name was David, was actually rather nice. It turned out he hated cruises as much as I did and had only agreed to this one after a year-long lobbying campaign by his wife, Rita. 'That's her over there,' he said without enthusiasm, pointing to a generously-proportioned woman whose tight silver sequinned dress only increased her resemblance to a vast and over-made-up herring.

David and I ordered a few more drinks and found we got on increasingly well. For example, we both liked Indian food, Agatha Christie novels and going to Italy on holiday. After that first meeting, we rather got into the habit of a chat in the bar after the show. There was no agenda, at least not from my point of view. I knew that David was rich – he owned some massive DIY business that was apparently going great guns. But I can't say I cared. I feel about Destroy It Yourself much the same as I feel about poached salmon and dancing in Twenties spectaculars called *What Ho!*

Then, one day, something quite bizarre happened. The *Cornucopia II* dropped anchor at Beaulieu-sur-Mer where, apparently as a result of the intense heat, Rita had a heart attack and dropped dead.

Naturally we were all terribly shocked. There was no show that night as a mark of respect, and of course no David in the bar. I can't say I was expecting ever to see him again when, two days after Rita snuffed it, I was called to the ship's telephone. It was David on the line.

Of course, I expressed my sincere condolences. And I did feel sympathetic, I really did, especially to the sequin industry of the East Midlands, who probably didn't get an acreage like that to cover every day of the week. 'Well it's very kind of you to say so,' David said. 'And I do appreciate it. But the truth is that Rita and I, well, we were friends and all that, but to be honest, some of the zing had gone out of our marriage.' He went on in this vein for a while until I realised what he was getting at. He wanted to ask me out just as soon as I got back on dry land.

Reader, I married him. A couple of dates on terra firma made me realise that, while DIY bored me to tears, I could get very interested in the money it made. David lived in a vast nouveau mansion with a butler and three Rollers in the garage, and was quite obviously stinking rich. We had a luxury honeymoon in Porto Ercole, eating Indian takeaways and reading Agatha Christie until our eyes popped out. And for a couple of years all was well, until I realised the age gap – twenty-six years – was about to become more of an issue. I decided to bail out before the Parkinson's started. I divorced him for unreasonable behaviour (his obsession with Derby County football club came in very handy here) and, thanks to the toughest lawyer I could lay my wallet on, walked off with a good portion of David's dosh.

The thing was, as I realised shortly afterwards, it wasn't enough. I was rich, but not super-rich. I'd been used to limos taking me everywhere, or the company helicopter. Once or twice I'd even been on private jets. Admittedly I had a flat in London and an Old Rectory crawling with wisteria as part of the divorce deal. But it wasn't the same. What I needed, I decided, was another rich husband.

As I had no idea where else to look for one, I went back to where I had struck lucky before. A cruise.

Unfortunately, in the years since we'd last met, the good ship *Cornucopia II* had run into some bad luck – and a ferry – in the Bay of Biscay. She had been so badly damaged, she'd had to be scrapped. I shed a sentimental tear for those swirly-carpeted lounges and cast around for a replacement. Eventually, leafing through some Saturday supplement, I noticed a double-page ad for a cruise of the Dalmation Coast on board the *Princess Persephone*. Bingo! The Dalmation Coast, I knew, was the new Riviera. Everyone who thought they were anyone, which admittedly usually meant that they were not, would be down there this summer.

Within minutes I had booked my stateroom and hoped there would be a footloose millionaire or two on board.

* * *

When, at the appointed hour, I rocked on board with the old Louis Vuitton, I could see that there were plenty. Thanks to my marriage to David, I'd spent enough time with rich men bored with their wives to be able to spot the breed a mile off. The problem was the wives. Obviously sensing the possibility that their husbands might hare off at any moment, they were all but sitting on them. No doubt that was why they had chosen a cruise holiday; there was nowhere for their menfolk to run. Nowhere for any of us to run, which was a shame. The *Princess Persephone* made the *Cornucopia II* look elegantly understated. The lounges were vaster, the carpets even more whirly. There were even more platters of poached salmon, and after dinner the staff handed round small plates containing huge and sickly Belgian chocolates. To cap it all, the on-board show was rock-and-roll themed and called *Gee Whizz!*

I decided to bide my time. I made the corner stool at the copper-lined cocktail bar my headquarters and sat there sipping Martinis and reading Agatha Christie. Eventually, as I had hoped, a fish slipped enquiringly into my net.

And a pretty big fish, too. His name was Nigel, he was from Aylesbury, and he was neither the most handsome nor the ugliest on board. But he was the richest. I'd worked this out already by observing that he and his wife had dined with the captain more than anyone else, and had noted from the passenger list that they had the biggest stateroom of all, some sort of duplex penthouse somewhere up front. Nigel told me, with marked lack of enthusiasm, that it even had its own swimming pool.

We got on well. I was slightly disappointed to learn he was even keener on football than David had been, but as he was obviously considerably richer (his company was one of those faceless mega ones owning several household names),

I was prepared to make allowances. David's Derby obsession even came in useful – I was able to trot out some of the terminology I'd picked up. This electrified Nigel, who swiftly became smitten. 'My wife hates football,' he lamented. 'It bores her to tears.'

I had initially been encouraged by Nigel's much-aired dislike of his wife. The problem was that she was unlikely to remove herself from the scene. Maureen, for that was her name, not only looked like an ox, but was apparently as strong as one. I questioned her husband carefully about her health and was disappointed to learn that the only way she might drop dead in the street was if somebody shot her. And tempting though that was, subtle it wasn't.

'I'm not sure my wife understands me,' Nigel moodily shovelled peanuts into his mouth. 'I wish she'd stop eating and lose some weight. The way she stuffs those chocolates down every night, even after she's had cheese and pudding . . .' Blah blah blah, it went on.

I yawned and sipped my Martini. This would be music to my ears, except that it had by now become obvious that Nigel would not be leaving his wife unless his wife left him first. He was quite clearly terrified of her, which was under-standable. So I was hardly listening to what he was saying when something, I'm not sure what, made me tune in. 'Tell you what, though,' Nigel was gesturing at the peanuts. 'These are about the only things she doesn't eat. Kill her if she did, they would.'

I spluttered into my Martini, but managed to regain my composure. It was vital not to seem too interested. So I pretended to be only half listening as I hung on to Nigel's every word while he described Maureen's vulnerability to anaphylactic shock.

I lay in my stateroom that night plotting. By morning, I had come up with the answer. The simplest and most effective thing to do would be to slip a peanut into the base of one of the big white after-dinner chocolates I'd noticed Maureen was particularly fond of guzzling. It was so simple it was like something out of an Agatha Christie novel, which perhaps it was. I'd read enough of them, after all.

The plot went like clockwork. I saved a white chocolate the night before (no mean feat considering how popular they were), and spiked it in my stateroom during the afternoon. 'There you go, my little friend,' I told the tiny piece of peanut as I poked it into the bottom of the chocolate. After dinner, I joined Maureen and Nigel's group. The women all looked at me suspiciously, which was quite right, except it was because I was half their size rather than because they thought I was about to bump one of them off. I pretended to knock over the plate of chocolates and slipped the adulterated one out of my bag as I gathered the rest up from the floor. I handed the plate to Maureen, waited until I saw her fat, shiny, bejewelled fingers hovering over it, then quickly slipped away.

I was glad I missed the crucial moment. According to witnesses it was not a pretty sight. And unfortunately Maureen was not the only victim; the ship's patissier, who had, for Maureen's benefit, been making all his chocolates nut-free, was arrested on manslaughter charges. But these things happen; collateral damage, as they said during the first Gulf War. And it worked, anyway. After a suitable pause, Nigel and I were married and no one, least of all my new husband, suspected a thing.

Unfortunately, as with David, I got fed up with him pretty fast. Nigel didn't even have David's interest in reading; all the books in his nouveau mansions (two in all) were bought by the yard and, when opened, contained blank pages. He evidently didn't expect anyone else he knew to read either. So we divorced and I got another good settlement, but not as good as the first, because Nigel was wilier with money and had hired a lawyer so sharp you could cut yourself just passing him. So, moneywise, I was back to square two again. And as I obviously needed more, it was back to high-seas piracy.

Which is where you find me now. On a cruise of the Baltic States with what seemed like the entire population of Glasgow. Posh end, obviously.

He was loud and red-faced with small, suspicious eyes. He looked boorish – the sort who might fart in bed and who routinely belittled women. He had an unattractive body – that solid, thick-necked, wide-calfed build of a man predisposed to fat but who keeps it off with sweaty and straining exercise. It was horribly easy to imagine him in a pair of smelly black Lycra cycling shorts.

Nevertheless, I looked at him and knew that he was everything I had been searching for. He was The One. The One I would marry. My husband. And the reason I knew this was because he had the perfect wife.

Well, that and the fact he'd been giving me the glad-eye in the bar as well. We'd even exchanged a few words and I was able to trot out my football knowledge again – he was a Rangers fan. We also, it turned out, had a mutual passion for *Dalziel and Pascoe* – well, he did. I had no idea if it was a department store or a brand of brown sauce, but I played along until I learned it was a TV programme; one, moreover, that the ship's DVD library had copies of. Obviously *D & P* fans were a well-established part of the customer base.

But if the conditions were ripe, the wife was even more so. We'd slipped into conversation earlier – side by side on the loungers with aspirational striped cushions that lined the ship's swimming pool. She was, as usual, a whale in human clothes, like those pictures of dogs playing snooker in tail-coats that one of my husbands – I forget which – used to be so fond of. I'd asked her what she liked about being on board and she'd stretched in a wobbly sort of way and said it was the sky at night.

'The sky at night?' I'd echoed. All that suggested to me was Patrick Moore.

'Ooh yes,' crooned Susie, as I'd learnt she was called. 'I'm the romantic type, I am.'

Aren't you just, I thought, taking in the size million navy swimming costume under her bathrobe. It looked as if it had been constructed in the same place as the boat.

'Not that Fergus understands that of course,' she sighed, referring to the husband. 'He's not very romantic. He never wanders around the deck alone in the middle of the night like I do.'

It was as if someone had plugged me straight into the National Grid. I forced myself with all my might not to sit bolt upright and yell '*Eureka!*'

But I didn't, of course. I lay back and listened as Susie described how she plodded alone, at two or three in the morning, around the dark, deserted and potentially very dangerous deck. Her favourite place for star-watching was where they stored the buoys at the front of the ship. 'Pitch black and empty. No one can even hear you if you yell,' she smiled at me.

And no-one will, I thought, as I smiled back at her.

224

Belinda Jones is the author of four novels – *The Paradise Room*, *The California Club*, *I Love Capri* and *Divas Las Vegas* – and one real-life romp across America called *On the Road to Mr Right*, which made it onto the *Sunday Times* non-fiction Top 10 list in 2004. Belinda grew up in Oxford and Devon, dreams of owning an Italian villa and is currently renting an apartment in a mock southern plantation mansion in Los Angeles, California.

For more information visit www.belindajones.com.

ONE MOTHER OF A HANGOVER

Belinda Jones

I don't know how often you get drunk with your mother, but last night was a first for me. I wouldn't say we were three sheets to the wind but we were at least two and a pillowcase.

The occasion was her 60th birthday and though I expected tears, I didn't expect them to be great chugging, puffy-eyed, snotty-nosed affairs. I also didn't expect them to be mine.

Originally we'd planned for her to escape the gusty chills of cliff-side Devon and enjoy a week of winter sun at my pad in Los Angeles, but as her arrival approached it dawned on me that, with the possible exception of Copacabana beach in Brazil, there could be no worse place on earth to embrace becoming a senior citizen. It's no myth that LA is over-run with flawless twentysomethings gussied to the max even at the mall just in case today is the day they get discovered; and what kind of message would it send her that everyone over forty is Botoxed to robotic blankness and fifty-pluses look like they're pushing their faces through a sheet of cellophane? Hardly the poster city for growing old gracefully. I decided there must be a neighbouring locale that could offer an OAP a little TLC and consulted my road atlas. We'd already exhausted the coastal communities on previous visits, and I wasn't sure either of us were street-savvy enough for Compton. And then I spied Palm Springs.

I'd only visited fleetingly a few years back but I recalled it being rife with liver-spotted wrinklies and boutiques selling those sequinned baseball hats favoured by eccentrics *vrooming* around on motorized wheelchairs. Surely my mum would feel like a young, sleek gazelle by comparison? I checked the logistics – just two hours' drive, easily navigable (bomb along the 10 freeway then wiggle a bit on the 111) and a whole ten degrees hotter than Hollywood – we had a winner!

As we pelted along the freeway ignoring the lure of the outlet stores I casually peppered my conversation with mentions of Marcus. It was such a novelty for me to have a boyfriend I couldn't help but show off a little. Now she could yap about Greg all she liked and I wouldn't feel left-out and unloved like I'd always done before. (Greg is mum's boyfriend of ten years. I definitely consider it a blessing that I've been out of the country for the majority of their relationship because that man gets on my very last nerve – he always hums when I talk as if to say, 'Not interested in anything you have to say! You don't exist! *Na-na-na!*' And though he's sickeningly attentive to my mum, he's never once asked about my video production company or what it's like to live in a country without Marmite. I pretend to be interested in his world, couldn't he at least extend the same courtesy to me?) So there I was, primed to match her slushy anecdote for slushy anecdote but she just didn't give me the opportunity. Just once I want to be able to say, '*Oh I know, Marcus does that!*' But no . . .

As we joined the privileged few in the car pool lane, I wondered if maybe she was uncomfortable with the fact that I've finally found myself a man. I've heard that those closest to you are often resistant to change, even when it's for the best. People get so used to you being one way – in my case pitifully single – that when you can no longer be labelled as such they are almost at a loss for how to view you. There certainly seemed to be an unfamiliar awkwardness, as if she didn't quite know how to respond to me as half of a couple. Not that we'd ever talked much about relationships prior to this, mostly because I'm never in one. I told myself it could just be jetlag making her seem distant and vague. Or maybe she was a little uneasy at the prospect of saying farewell to her 50s? That was probably it.

'Look ma, we're nearly there – see the wind turbines?' I tried to bring her glazed expression into focus by pointing out row upon row of rotating white blades on mile-high poles.

'We've got those in Devon now,' she observed as I wrestled to steady the car against the sudden buffeting breeze. 'But the locals say they ruin the aesthetics of the landscape and want them removed.'

I understand their concern, but to me they are so starkly graceful they actually enhance the view, at least set against this desert mountain range.

'So, this is Palm Springs,' Mum chivvied herself into a state of interest as we merged onto the main drag of Palm Canyon Drive. 'I've heard of it like I've heard of Key West but I don't really know anything about it. What's it most famous for?'

I censored my 'Rich retirees!' response and instead said, 'Let me see – Sonny Bono was once mayor, and Bob Hope,

Howard Keel and Frank Sinatra were all former residents. Basically it's considered a chi-chi resort oasis though I'd say its heyday was in the Fifties . . .'

Right on cue, we're cruised by a silver-finned convertible Imperial and a cream '56 Chevy with a gleaming copper dashboard.

'I feel like we're in *Grease*!' she giggles, looking, if not like a teenager, at the very least like Olivia Newton-John playing one.

So far so good!

We continued on past innumerable restaurants offering patio dining and a gift shop selling comical granny statuettes including one drawer-dropper quipping 'You're never too old for a booty call!' and then we came to a halt at the lights. There a man shuffled in front of us leaning heavily on his walker and breathing wheezily through a nose clip of plastic tubing which dangled for yards about his person. I joked that this was Palm Springs' version of iPod wires but judging from the mortified look on my mum's face I'd gone too far, inadvertently scaring her with what might lie ahead for her. Mercifully our hotel was definitely more hip than hip-replacement – The Viceroy bills itself as 'dramatic glamour under the sun' and the lobby alone provided a visual spritzing with its striking black and white décor zapped with acid-yellow accents. I snuck a look back at my mother reclining on the pinstripe chaise while I checked in, and was delighted to see her eyes widen as she took in the zebra skin rug on the marble floor, the lacquered white of the bar beyond and the skinny plaster greyhounds guarding each balcony.

Minutes later we were gasping in unison as we stepped into the living room of Suite 304: wall-to-wall striped carpet in ridges of charcoal and ivory, a chequered sofa you could stretch out on in stilts, white walls stencilled with black panels, a vast yellow enamel chandelier, a white gloss urn, a laminated TV cabinet, a wall of mirrors . . .

Mum sat in one of the high-backed canary-yellow Regency chairs and told me she felt like Alice in Wonderland.

I felt triumphant! Alice was, what, twelve? That was forty-eight years lopped off and we hadn't even unpacked yet!

Having admired the theatrical curtains framing the bath and twisted our necks at the off-kilter bedroom (ornate ceiling rose at the head of the bed and black and white potato-print wallpaper on the ceiling), we had planned to while away the afternoon lolling beside one of the three pools before getting dolled up for a night on the town. But then it started to rain.

'Oh no!' We were both appalled. There's something about rain and our family – it just seems so conducive to tears. I chose to distract her with her birthday card. (Well the clock had just struck four, which meant it was midnight in England.)

'Happy 60th Ma! You're finally grown-up!' I teased as I handed her the hot pink envelope.

'That I am,' she said sounding serious for a second, before perking up as she read the words I'd transcribed from a recent round-robin email and surrounded in glitter.

'Life should not be a journey to the grave with the intention of arriving safely in an attractive and well-preserved body, but rather to skid in sideways, margarita in one hand, chocolate in the other, body thoroughly used up, totally worn out and screaming 'WOO HOO! – What a Ride!'

She gave me a big hug and whooped, 'The cocktails are on me!'

Now that was unexpected. Not her offer to pay, but her eagerness to imbibe before dark. I'd only ever seen my mum a teeny bit tipsy at Christmas but here she was downing a Frozen Bikini so fast she was in danger of getting brain freeze. I told myself this was celebratory abandon but as her second empty glass hit the mirrored surface of the side table I realized it was Dutch courage.

'I've left Greg,' she blurted, wiping a stray dribble of peach vodka from her chin.

'*What?* I balked. 'When?'

'Six weeks ago. Six weeks today in fact. Let's have another drink!'

I was totally thrown. I'd wanted to match her in the man department, not better her. Suddenly I felt extremely unbalanced.

'Why didn't you tell me before?' I wavered uncertainly as she reached for the cocktail menu.

'I didn't want you worrying about me coping on my own. And besides, you were so happy with Marcus. No one wants to hear of a break-up when you're in the honeymoon period of a new relationship.'

The honeymoon period? I wanted to query that sentiment straight off but I was distracted by further questions.

'Why? What happened?'

'Oh you know how relationships are . . .'

'Not really,' I confessed. 'It seems awfully out-of-the-blue. When did you realise it was going wrong?'

'About four years ago.'

'*Four years?*' I squawked. 'You've been miserable for four years?' Amidst the shock I also felt shame – I couldn't believe I didn't even notice anything was wrong. 'Why didn't you say something before?' I complained.

'Well, you've never liked him, I didn't think you'd want to hear it.'

'Are you kidding? I would have loved to have heard all the bad stuff!'

She laughed and took my hand. 'It's okay. It's all in the past now.'

She was clearly keen to proceed with dialling room service but I wasn't finding it so easy to move on. 'So what was it specifically?' I persisted.

She set down the phone and sighed. 'You really want to know?'

I nodded.

'Where to begin? The constant nit-picking and critiquing he tried to pass off as friendly teasing. The running commentary on everything I ate, his constant reminding that he didn't want "a fat woman on his arm". The way his frustrations at his own shortcomings spilled over into impatience with me. His unpredictable mood changes. How off-hand he was to my friends. I think he wanted them to feel unwelcome so they'd stop visiting. And they did. I'd visit them but then he'd ask me so many questions it felt like an interrogation . . .'

As she spoke all I could think was: *Marcus does that*. And that. And that.

The horrible sinking feeling got worse as I listened to her saying how often she felt judged or controlled or simply wrong and a small, long-ignored voice inside me said, 'That's just how I feel.'

'But enough of my wallowing!' she jumped to her feet. 'I think we may as well order dinner while we're at it. I know we said we'd paint the town scarlet but it's bucketing out there. Wouldn't it be cosier if we had a nice girls' night in?'

I was so dazed listening to her place the order for monk-fish with picholine olive, saffron seafood risotto with manchego cheese and a dessert of Valrohna chocolate soufflé (whatever would Greg say?!) that when my phone rang I answered without thinking.

'Baby?'

Oh no. I closed my eyes in dismay. It was Marcus.

'I've been waiting for your call.' He sounded instantly petulant. 'You said you were going to ring to let me know you'd arrived safely.'

'Sorry about that. Mum and I got chatting and –' I curbed what was about to become a rambling apology. 'We are here and we are safe.'

'Do you miss me?'

'Yes, of course,' I replied, checking myself too late. Did I even have a say in what I felt any more, or was I merely programmed to respond in the appropriate way?

'You know if I left now I could be there in time to join you for dinner.'

'Actually we've already ordered something, we didn't stop for lunch so –'

'You realize your mum will probably be asleep by 7pm after that long flight, what will you do then?'

Was he worried I wouldn't be able to amuse myself, or worried I'd go out and pick myself up a sugar grand-daddy?

'I'll be fine,' I told him.

'Okay, well then in that case I'll probably go out with Grant.'

He waited for my reaction but I gave none.

'I don't know though, you know he's on a bit of a pick-up binge at the moment, ever since he broke up with Carly, he'll probably want to go to the Saddle Ranch . . .'

Was this a threat of some kind? Was he trying to provoke me with the prospect of loose women astride a mechanical bull? For some reason I simply didn't care.

'Well you have fun! Don't you go leading him astray!'

'A-alright,' he faltered. 'Well, call me before you go to sleep. Let me know everything is okay.'

'Right.' I wanted to say, 'I'll let you know if the air con is too cold or the water is too hot or the towels are too rough or the bed is too firm or the alarm is too loud so you can make it alright for me cos I'm so helpless and incapable myself.' But I didn't.

'Okay baby, I love you.'

'Speak to you later!' I tried to hurry my goodbye out but he was too swift, whining, 'Aren't you going to say you love me too?'

I squirmed inside and out. I'd parroted the phrase enough times, why was it sticking in my throat now? Was it because I didn't want my mother to hear me lying?

'Sorry, the reception isn't good in here, let me try out outside . . .' I slid open the patio door and stepped onto the terrace. 'That's better,' I faked as my insides contorted. 'I love you!'

'I love you more!'

I wasn't going to argue with that. As I closed the phone I came to the sick realisation that every conversation with Marcus left me feeling peeved or patronized or simply awry in some way. Was I really so desperate to have a boyfriend that I'd convinced myself I was happy with him? For a few minutes I stood and watched the rain. And a couple braving the downpour to get to the jacuzzi. They were laughing as they sank into the steaming water and I thought, '*I don't remember the last time I laughed with Marcus*.' I knew if he was here now he'd be too concerned about the bacteria in the bubbles or getting concussion from a falling grapefruit off the overhanging tree to enjoy himself.

I returned to the room to find my mother holding up two bottles of wine – a Lapis Luna Chardonnay for me and a Dynamite Merlot for her. 'Well, a glass wasn't going to be enough . . .' She patted the sofa cushion next to her. 'Are you alright, darling?' she asked as she poured, then tutted: 'This is exactly why I didn't tell you before. I knew you'd get upset . . .'

'It's not just that –'

Again my phone rang.

What now? I was ready to cut the power but the display read Out of Area and I was waiting for a business call from New York so I answered.

'Hello?'

'Charlotte?'

Oh my god, it's Greg! I mouthed frantically at my mum.

It was very clear from her responding mime that there was no way she's going to talk to him.

'*Um*, she's busy right now Greg, can I take a message?' What is it about being English that makes you carry on being polite long after it's ceased to be necessary?

'I just wanted to wish her a happy birthday –'

'Okay, lovely, will do.'

'Look, just put her on.'

'What?'

'I know you girls are up to your usual conspiracy shit,' he spat. 'Put Anna on the phone now.'

He had me reeling, amazed that he thought bullying would be an effective tactic. 'No!' I scoffed. The cheek of the man!

'Charlotte!' he growled.

'*Grrreg!*' I mirrored his threatening tone.

My mother started to look vexed. I may not be able to be strong for myself but I can be for her.

'Look,' I began, before he could say another word. 'My mother has already said everything to you that needs to be said. Now she's here with me. Please respect our time together.' I took a breath. 'And don't call her again. Ever.'

With that I clicked the phone closed.

'Oh my god, you were brilliant!' Mum leapt to her feet, spinning me around in a giddy dance.

I couldn't believe it either. Where did that steel come from? For the past six months I'd been feeling so weak and ineffectual . . .

'Bloody idiot's been badgering me every five minutes. Let's see if you did the trick and I can finally get some peace!'

The pair of us sat down and stared at the little silver Sony Eriksson. Two women, desperate for the phone not to ring. Now there's a turnaround.

'Oh, put the telly on!' Mum finally broke the silence. 'Let's think about something else until the food arrives!'

I snuggled beside her as we watched Oscar-winner Jamie Foxx being quizzed about his bachelor status, the interviewer implying that perhaps, at thirty-seven, he should be settling down.

'You are currently single, are you not?'

He smiled, didn't look in the least bit concerned or apologetic and whispered, '*Single deluxe!*'

Was that a pang of envy I just experienced?

'I don't think he's going to ring,' I ventured as my mum began to channel hop.

'Neither do I,' she confirmed happily.

'Ma, will you do the same for me?' I scrabbled up onto my haunches and turned to face her. 'Will you tell Marcus I don't want to speak to him again. *Ever!*'

'What?' she looked stunned.

'*Please!*'

'What's going on? I thought you were happy?'

'I was just pretending. I mean, I've tried so hard but it just doesn't feel right. Hearing you talk about Greg . . . I don't want to wait another god knows how many years before I get the chance to escape!'

'*Escape?* Is it that bad?'

I nodded.

'Then you should definitely talk to him.'

'I can't!' I wailed. 'I've tried so many times . . .' Suddenly I was blubbering and I couldn't seem to stop. My body was shuddering as the tears of frustration and disappointment and sadness flooded out of me.

'Oh Charlotte darling, why didn't you tell me this is how you were feeling?'

I heaved a juddery sigh. 'Same reason as you I suppose – I didn't want you to worry. Didn't want you thinking I wasn't capable of having a relationship.' I oozed and sniffed some more. 'When I first told you about Marcus you sounded so relieved that I finally had someone of my own . . .'

'Oh gosh, if there's one thing looking sixty in the eye has taught me, it's that life's too short to waste a single heartbeat on the wrong man.' She took my chin in her palm. 'If I had a single birthday wish it would be that you don't have to wait 'til you're claiming your pension to get wise to that fact.'

'I just don't want to be thirty-five and single again!' My fears elbowed their way to the fore.

'Try being single at sixty!' my mother countered.

'Actually in this town I think you've got the edge!'

My mother laughed. 'You could be right there!'

I sighed again. 'Coming here has made me realise Marcus is not a man I want to grow old with.'

'Then don't put it off any longer.'

As mum slid the phone over to me I experienced a surge of nerves. 'Can't you do it for me, please?' I implored her.

'He's got to hear it from you first or he'll never accept it.'

'What if you pretended to be me?' I blustered, grasping at straws. 'Everyone says we sound so alike on the phone . . .'

I looked pleadingly into her eyes until she succumbed with a brow-beaten sigh. 'What's his number?'

I was shaking as I waited for him to pick up. I couldn't believe the time had finally come, that within minutes I might actually be free!

'Marcus?' My mum held the phone so I could hear.

'Baby! Heyyy, I knew you'd call. Are you feeling a little needy? Are you missing your boy?' His voice was so condescending, almost like he was willing me to be weak and dependent.

'Listen,' my mum began. But before she could get to word two I grabbed the phone.

'Marcus, it's Charlotte,' I tried to stop my voice from quavering as I blurted, 'I'm sorry to have to do this on the phone but I no longer want to be in a relationship with you.'

There, I said it! I didn't think I had it in me, but I did it anyway!

First there was incredulity. Then anger. Then begging.

'I don't want to lose you!' he whimpered.

'I don't want to lose me either, that's why I have to do this.' I stood strong.

Then came the abuse, which just confirmed my decision. And then tears, which came too late. And then the calm after the storm . . .

*   *   *

The next morning, after my first full night's sleep in months, we awoke to blinding sunshine. The promise of a poolside breakfast had me pogoing out of bed and into the shower where I tried to soap my armpits with a bar of white chocolate. Turns out ma had been getting up to drunken mischief after I'd conked out, switching the toiletries for items from the minibar. *Ahhh*, so the reason the shampoo wasn't frothing was that it was, in fact, vodka.

'If you'd used beer that actually might have done my hair some good!' I yelled from the tub.

'I was going to swap the crème de menthe and the mouthwash but I don't suppose anyone would notice the difference!' she stuck her head around the door. 'You nearly ready? I'm starving!'

You've got to love a hotel that sneaks a spirit onto the breakfast menu – there can be no more discreet and yet decadent way to garner a little hair of the dog for your hangover than ordering a platter of buttermilk pancakes soaked in raspberry cognac. I tucked in with vigour – all this time I was so dreading finishing with Marcus, but I think I must have used up all my anxiety prior to doing the deed. Now I just felt relieved. Detoxified even. There's something about telling the truth that is so purifying. Not to mention rejuvenating – Mum looked easily ten years younger as she stretched out on one of the yellow and white candy-striped sunloungers set with matching towel scrolls.

I reclined beside her, counting three types of palm tree around us – one spindly skyscraper resembling one of those dusters with extendable handles, one twelve-footer with what looked like a soft green scarf wound around its giraffe-like neck, and another stumpier variety with ruffs of brown bark.

All set against a forever blue of sky. I inhaled deeply and smiled to myself.

I mean look at us – the pool is all ours. We've got no schedule to meet and only ourselves to please and we're sipping on crushed ice doused with citrus and mint, freshly plucked from the hotel gardens.

Now if this ain't the definition of single deluxe, I don't know what is!

Louise Kean was born in 1974 and works as a marketing consultant for the film industry in Soho. A graduate of UEA, she is the author of three books: *Toasting Eros, Boyfriend in a Dress* and *The Perfect Ten*. She lives in Richmond, Surrey.

THE NIGHT BEFORE CHRISTMAS

Louise Kean

She throws two ice cubes into a long glass: they scratch its sides before fizzing and sinking into a gin river, whose tides have risen and fallen several times already this evening. You wouldn't know to look at her. Or maybe you would, but only because of the two tiny red capillaries squirming in the furthest reaches of her eyes. Even then, you'd have to be inches from her face to spot them, to know that she is on the gloriously dangerous road to drunk.

Alexandra walks towards the window, but stops and lingers two feet away. At least one hundred, perhaps one thousand cameras flash simultaneously twelve floors below. A pack of paparazzi dance around like Goofy and Donald Duck in *Disney on Ice*, as they playfight with a choreographed ridiculousness, jostling for a foot of the next guy's pavement. Every warm breath exhaled becomes a tiny, boozy fog that circulates above their heads, clouding their judgment but not their vision. The air is routinely splintered with careless sprays of profanity as they lose their footing in the slush and snow. The violent scream of light from cameras clicking cuts like a blackout the second that she turns away from the window. Only the most inexperienced snap at her shadow on the thin voile curtain as it glides off, frames behind her.

As Alexandra walks away she can still hear her name being hollered on the street by different voices, pleading in foreign accents but constricted by the bright, tight scarves bound around their throats. Suede and sheepskin gloves pad hard against each other as the night settles in, and the temperature dips spitefully below freezing again. She hears them call Thomas's name too, quite clearly, but not as often. He started on the stage, she has always been film. His star is still ascending, shooting furiously towards hers; she's only a thousand feet above and beyond him now. He is closer than anybody, well on his way so that they might burn together, above everybody else. The snow started falling last night, at dusk. They shut themselves away then. It's Christmas Eve.

With one lazy elegant movement – glass to lips, an arched neck – her drink is all but gone. The thud of her gulp bangs on his eardrums; it is so loud that he winces. He sighs. His sighs replace his words when he runs out of steam, and his thoughts begin to squabble with each other. His legs stretch out before him, crossed at the ankle. His body is at a forty-five degree angle with the floor, straight like a slide for children to plummet down, laughing. He has balanced in this position for the last hour. His legs seized up at some point, although he isn't sure when. With a mammoth effort, he hoists his large feet onto a perspex coffee table. The table doesn't smash as his careless Scottish boots fall onto it, landing on a script that got there first, its bindings clumsily dragged back and breaking, the words already stained from hastily poured wine; black rings like precise circles of dried blood on the pages.

'So?' Her eyebrows rise dramatically together like a curtain going up at the theatre.

'So . . .' he says, still blowing the 'o' out moments later, swilling the ice in his gin round and round as he does, waiting for it to dissolve and water down his drink. Then, when he throws it back, it might take a diversion from his throat to his soul and water down his feelings as well. He needs to dull the bloody obstinate thumping in his chest and his head, like a bell tolling in some distant kirk, signalling the end of a day, or the start of a new one.

Thomas sighs again, and with a wide pleading mouth, accepts half a glass of gin.

'Here come the sighs,' she says, quietly. 'You know I hate the sighs, Thomas.'

As he closes his eyes his head falls heavily back against the bruised sofa cushion. He sighs again. Bright but dimmed light seeps from beneath oversized heavy purple shades, like vast poisonous belladonnas. A diamante orb hanging in the adjoining bedroom sparkles above a queen-sized bed, turned down for the night, fresh and clean, an easy invitation not to talk any more. Some maid must have sneaked in unnoticed, while they fought or sulked or screamed, and gently tugged away last night's torn and tired sheets with the image of their sweaty torsos burnt into them. *Like a modern day Turin Shroud* he thinks. Those sheets would be the ultimate eBay prize, prompting a deafening *tap tap tap* across the world: frenzied fingers desperate for a piece of him and her, if the maid had the sense and the guile to sell them without getting caught and fired. He should have thought to burn those sheets this morning.

'I hate the sighs!' she screams suddenly, hurling her glass at the wall for punctuation. It shatters on impact, above an elegant Norwegian fir that is bursting with coloured balls and glistening stars by the wall. Shards of glass fall and dust the tips of the branches like evil fairy lights. Thomas springs forward on the couch, his eyes flying wildly open to dart from Alexandra to the wall and back again. She is crazy! She is mad and unstable, ridiculous, a child, spoilt and awful. And that's the third shattered glass tonight.

'Pull yourself together, Alexandra.' His low, booming voice carries to a gaggle of guests waiting by the lift in the hallway, who look around for a TV screen, perplexed.

'I hate it when you sigh at me! In your lonely voice, like I exhaust you or something. Thomas? As if you might get up and just leave at any minute, as if you are just summoning up the effort to go! And you know that it keeps me desperate. You say *'you know you're beautiful'* like it's a reason that you'll always stay, but it's not as important as you make it sound, it's nothing. Nothing really. Nothing at all. It's never meant anything to anybody that counts. You know that.'

'I'm sorry,' he says quietly, closing his eyes again, leaning forwards over his knees, cradling his drink in his hands, the craziness passed, the fatigue kicking in again. She falls onto her knees, on the floor in front of him. The tops of her ears are flushed pink, and a small patch of her neck is turning red, like a rash, an adverse reaction to him and his sighs. Her cheeks burn furiously in two small circles like a painted wooden doll, but her bright blue eyes are full of life as they scramble around his face, searching for a way in. Her dark hair, still pinned up from yesterday afternoon's filming, is flying and tumbling around her face. Is it this grand, urgent face, so desperate with fury, that will be his ruin?

'Won't you even say something to me, Thomas, to make me feel better? Please?'

Her words are small now, she speaks in childish tones. Thomas smiles somewhere inside of himself, in spite of himself. They are the world's most adored actors, who really knows what of this is real?

'Won't you even say how you feel? Don't you want me to feel better?' Alexandra twists a lock of her hair over her shoulder, and engages him with her wide eyes.

'Haven't I said everything already?' he pleads, exhausted.

'You damn well know you haven't!' she pushes herself to her feet and takes two steps away from the couch, before turning back to face him, composed. 'Do you want to know how it feels? It's as if some time ago, five years ago maybe, you decided to allocate all of your feelings to a certain finite list of things, and now all that feeling is allocated, and you have none left for me. And you won't even try and squeeze me in, or redistribute those feelings. And I'm not just talking about Sybil, and the girls. I'm talking about acting, your 'craft', skiing for Christ's sake! I think you feel more for a mountain than you do for me. You talk about Mont Blanc with more affection than I have ever glimpsed when you talk about me, the woman who holds you every night, who lets you climb into her, who is letting you make a mockery of her in front of the whole goddamn world, every time you go running back to your wife! And why Thomas? Just because I was too late, and you're stubborn? All your feelings have been distributed, and you've locked up your soul, and thrown away the key? Well I am not going to get down on my hands and knees and go scrubbing around in the dirt to find it, Thomas. Don't forget who I am.'

She turns, and the air cracks around her as she walks back towards the bar in their suite. It has gradually been restocked throughout the night and then today by a procession of bellboys and maids, answering urgent calls for fresh gin, fresh soda, fresh ice . . . fresh gin. Every time she opens the door of the suite she is greeted by *Good King Wenceslas* or *The Holly and the Ivy*, like soft slaps in the face. And even though her final words are arrogant, lest Thomas forget for a moment that by ill luck or fortuitous timing he has captured the heart of the most celebrated woman in the world, there is an encroaching desperation in her voice when she speaks. He knows that he is guilty, that he still refuses her entry, even now as he makes up his mind about tomorrow, and one measly turkey-spattered, tinsel-covered, flashy, rotten Christmas day . . . that will shape the rest of his life.

'We can't stay holed up in here forever, in this box of a room, playing at being together, ignoring everything else.' She gestures with her thumb over her shoulder at the hordes outside; it's a hard look, like a lorry driver gesturing to his cab. She never fails to surprise him.

'I need to know where you're going tomorrow, Tom. I need to know if I'll be on my own.'

Paul, the Assistant Director, and then Buffy, the Director, and then Hector, the Producer, all called that morning, begging them to come to the set for the last day of shooting before the Christmas break. But Thomas, then Alexandra, hung up and stayed where they were. The two stars, absent without leave, shut the set down. It's a love story, but they are both free in the script. She was meant to die tragically young in the end, but in discussions with the producers and director she thought it best that she live, after all. It's a positive message, she's a fighter, it's the image she wants to reflect. So now they find a cure for cancer.

When the courier arrived with the revised script two days before read-throughs were due to begin, and he read the proposed changes with incredulity, Thomas flew into a fury.

He sat up late, watching over and over again the tapes of her that Marty had sent him: rewind, rewind, rewind. And the prospect of Alexandra West filled him with fury, knowing as he did that she would be spoilt, and demanding, late and difficult. *A cure for cancer . . .*

Thomas arrived at the office at Pinewood on a late August morning, half an hour early, dripping in the black mood that had woken him, hungover from the week before. He hadn't been back to Scotland for over a year. She arrived five minutes late. He sat at one end of a long wooden table, and she at the other, with Buffy somewhere in the middle on a raised stool like a weak Wimbledon umpire. Thomas immediately served the table with the deadpan suggestion that, on reading the revised script the day before, it had struck him as particularly appropriate that Alexandra's character might actually find the cure for cancer herself, from her sickbed, via the web. Her eyes glistened with delight as he spoke. He smiled smugly at her from the other end of the table, to a soundtrack of suppressed sniggers from the crew, thinking finally, finally, she's met her match. Alexandra had raised her eyebrows and smiled, placing her palms flat on the table, examining the diamonds on her fingers, and said simply, 'Well . . .'

The room held its breath.

She looked up, after a dramatic pause, and stared at Thomas, who stared back. She closed her eyes, turning her head instead to face Paul Benetto, the scriptwriter, a bleary-eyed boy on the point of collapse from weeks of script revisions and no sleep. Her eyes snapped open. 'Paul, could you script up Thomas's ideas for first thing tomorrow morning? Let's see if they work. Mr Gregory,' Alexandra turned back to Thomas. 'Shall we get on?'

Thomas needs to decide about tomorrow. Maybe he will be

with his wife and children in their sprawling rented house in Greenwich, with a vast tree, its underbelly littered with presents, and his brothers and their families all down from Scotland, and a piano, and a feast, singing and drinking and smoking, and ignoring the life he has led for the last four months. His wife, only a month younger than he to the day, her serene face faintly lined like a map of the Scottish seaside town they grew up in. It is lined from raising their children, and supporting his life. She will stroke his hair, and look at him with twenty-two years of love, and whisper that it will never matter that his indiscretions have been splashed all over the tabloids with a sadistic joy by puritanical hacks revelling in his midlife madness. She understands. Or maybe he will spend Christmas here, in this suite with Alexandra, his co-star, his mistress, in their borrowed bed. She is the only equal he has ever known.

'I'm so drunk,' he says evenly, staring at the wall.

'So stop drinking,' she says, her hands on her hips. Her black dress plunges at her chest in a violent V.

'I feel better drunk on gin than drunk on you. At least it's my hand on the bottle.'

Alexandra ignores him. She studies her face and her neck and her breasts in a huge mirror. She raises her chin in the air, and casts her eyes down to appraise something that the rest of the world doesn't notice.

'I'm booked into the clinic again over New Year,' she says, her eyes fixed on the thing that needs fixing, that nobody else can see.

'What now?' Thomas asks.

'Just tidying up, from before. I'm not a teenager anymore. Will you come with me Thomas, and hold my hand?'

'Whichever way I turn to hold a hand, I break a heart.'

A frightened fist knocks at the door.

Alexandra walks slowly across the room and swings it open. A tall, blond bellboy stands in front of her, caught in her gaze, barely remembering the bottle of Bombay Sapphire in his hand. She seems to be smiling even when she isn't.

'Thanks,' she whispers, taking it from him. She flashes her candyfloss smile then, the real thing, and widens her eyes for him to fall into. Thomas looks over her shoulder at the bellboy, who is mesmerized.

That boy envies me, he thinks. *He wants her totally, utterly.* As she swings the door closed to shut them in again, Alexandra turns to face Thomas. A tidal wave of doubt and insecurity smashes across her face and wipes away her smile. That's the face that the world doesn't get to see. He wonders if it would love her quite so much if it did.

'Why do I want you?' she says quietly as she leans against the door, a bottle of gin in her hand, Thomas laid in front of her on the couch. But nobody hears. His eyes don't register whether he does. They are speckled with arrogance, lined by bursts of laughter and late-night boozing. His voice, the first time that she heard it, made her turn and face the television and seek it out. Its distance and dominance demanded to be conquered. His brown leather jacket looks lazy at the elbows. The soles of his boots are worn. They still wear them at the factory, he told her; his brothers still wear the same boots. The flats of his soles face her accusingly.

She moves quietly to his side, sitting down next to him on the couch. A group of carol singers chant her name and then his to a familiar Christmas tune. She strokes the side of his face, the hair from his forehead, and the sideburns streaked with grey, and he opens his eyes, his pupils slowly edging to the right. Their gaze locks. Their sparks could light the lights on Oxford Street, and Regent Street, and Piccadilly.

She pulls long strands of her dark hair over one shoulder, and leans over his mouth. Her painted lips hover above his Scottish frown. His eyes drag themselves open again.

'Your brother hates me,' she says quietly, and kisses him.

He holds her face in front of him for a moment, '*And the sunlight clasps the earth, and the moonbeams kiss the sea: what are all these kissings worth, If thou kiss not me?*'

'Say it Thomas. Say that he hates me,' she says between kisses.

He sighs. 'It's not about you, it's about me. He thinks if I go to Spain next, do the Gladiator thing, take the family, we'll get through it . . .'

'Is that what you want? Spain? I'll be in Argentina!'

'I don't know. I don't know what I want.' He turns and takes her face in his hands. 'But don't you care that I still love them, baby? That it's tearing me apart to leave them, to not be with them tomorrow, or next week, or next year? I won't be this man anymore, if I leave them. I'll carry that with me. Don't you care?'

Alexandra smiles at him softly. 'I'm not a child, Thomas. I'm thirty-six years old. I've been married before. I don't care who you loved last year or even last month. I don't care who's meant the world to you, consumed you, and swept you along for the ride. I don't care as long as you say it's me you love now.' She whispers it convincingly, in case he has any doubts, and strokes the side of his face gently with a long finger, trimmed with a carnival-pink nail. She has a scarf around her forehead, knotted on one side, multicoloured with spots and stripes and flowers. Was it there, a second ago? Maybe it was . . .

When Thomas doesn't answer, she pulls away from him,

and quickly changes the subject. 'Buffy says I need to cut down on the gin.'

'Why?'

'The hangovers, the lateness. He says you can see my weight going up and down in the dailies, like an inflatable doll with a puncture that keeps getting mended every couple of days.'

There is another knock at the door.

'Will you get it, baby?' he asks her, his eyes closing again.

'Aren't you moving this evening?' she asks him coolly, pushing herself to her feet to answer it nonetheless.

Another bellboy, a redhead this time, stands at the door. He stares at them, at the two most famous and hunted people in the whole world: Thomas slumped on a sofa, Alexandra standing expectantly at the door, as the snow falls outside and the cameras flash at their window, and the crowds chant their names.

'Well, what do you want for Christ's sake?' Thomas asks, his voice rising, his eyes popping open.

'A package came for you,' the bellboy manages to say.

'Taking it in turns are you? Come to see the freaks?' he booms from the back of the stage to the upper circle, as Alexandra offers out her hand, and mouths 'I'll take it.'

'You or me?' he asks, as she closes the door.

She eyes it coolly. 'Me,' she says.

'I'll have another' he says, a low-lying rage in his voice.

Alexandra drops the script on the bar, and lazily picks up the ice bucket. Rocking it gently like a baby finally falling asleep, she hears the ice cubes shift uneasily from side to side.

'Go to Sybil on Boxing Day and tell her you want a divorce.'

'I can't just leave. I'm tired of spreading havoc, ruining lives.'

Alexandra flings the bucket forwards, flipping rocks of ice all over him.

'Jesus Christ! Have you lost your mind?' he jumps up,

fuelled by an old rage that reminds him of walking from audition to audition in Glasgow, cold and damp and desperate. And here she stands in front of him, perfumed and privileged, everything he always hated and wanted. Together they can conquer the world. If that's what he wants.

'Why can't you say that you love me?' she says, standing opposite him in their suite, lit badly from behind by a lamp and a chandelier, and yet still illuminated.

'I want to be with you, Alexandra. You captivate me. You're glorious.'

'Then say you love me!'

'I can't.' He twists the top of the gin bottle she has placed on the sideboard. He manages to unscrew it on his second attempt, and leaves it on the floor where it falls. He pulls at his damp jacket pocket where an ice cube has lodged itself, swipes a drip off his chin, pushing his wet fringe from his face.

'You won't let yourself feel it, that's all! You love me heart and soul, body and mind. Just say it.'

The fight drips from him as well as he sighs again, slumping back down onto the sofa.

'You sigh instead of speaking these days. I wonder if you even realise that you do it. It's laughable when you think that you communicate for a living, you convince people of your sensitivity and your passion, and you're the king of the stage, of Shakespeare, of Arthur Miller. But you can't tell me what you feel. You're fearless on stage, and yet you're terrified tonight. Say that I'm everything you want, more than anything you've got. Admit it Thomas, for both our sakes.'

'Why? Why do you need to hear me say it? You can see I adore you, woman! You can see that you're tearing my life apart. You stand there and watch while I rip it to shreds with my own hands.'

'Don't compartmentalize me, Thomas, into the woman you sleep with, the woman you touch, the woman you hold, while your wife sits at home and reads to your children in the real world. This is real too, this could be your life. It's just different, that's all. Why does she even want you, still? The whole world knows!' Alexandra grabs a newspaper and throws it at him.

He ducks, but his reactions have been dulled by thirty-six hours worth of gin, and it strikes his right ear. She grabs another one and throws it, and it catches him on the cheek.

'Jesus, will you stop!'

'I'm going mad in here. I didn't choose this. I never chose this!'

He runs across the room and grabs her arms, holding them tightly by her sides. His breath is heavy.

'Why do I want you?' she says again, and Thomas flinches.

Chunks of diamonds, the earrings that he bought her last week, sit lazily on the coffee table. Alexandra shakes him off, leaning back on the sideboard for support. She picks up the script and rips it open. Her experienced eyes dart over the top sheet, before she begins flipping pages every thirty seconds.

'Who's in it?' Thomas asks. Otherwise she would have thought him asleep, standing up.

'Chad,' she says truthfully. She bites her lip.

'No!' Thomas screams, grabbing a glass from the bar, flinging it at the damp target they have set themselves above the Norwegian fir. It smashes into large, loud chunks that fall heavily through the branches to the lower levels of the tree.

'I just won't do it,' she says evenly.

'Why has Marty even sent it to you? Does he think he's interfering?'

'He probably thinks that he's helping. He probably thinks

that you're nothing but a large dose of northern trouble. I may as well read it,' Alexandra licks her fingers and turns another page.

'Throw it on the fire,' His eyes are furious and black.

'No,' she replies, without doubt or question.

'Throw it on the fire!' He steps forward to grab the script, but changes his mind. His fists clench in rage, and he tears off his jacket. There are sweat patches on his shirt, sweetly sticking to his chest. The phone rings.

'Don't answer it,' Alexandra says, shaking her head. All of a sudden it is she who is pleading. Thomas picks up the receiver and says, 'this is Mickey Mouse.' He listens for a minute. 'I can't tonight. I don't know, I don't know. Tomorrow, we'll speak tomorrow.' He hangs up and slowly wipes his eyes.

'Don't cry for her! Don't sit here in front of me and cry for her!'

'What do you want from me, Alexandra? She is the mother of my children. She is my wife! What do you want from me?'

'I want not to want you. I want to go back to the way we were, before I met you, before you walked onto the set. I always thought, if I met my soulmate, it would be wonderful. But this is almost terrible, almost awful.' She lowers her chin and her eyes, and the corners of her mouth dip. They have turned each other's worlds upside down.

'What if you leave me?' she looks up at him.

'I could drown in those eyes' he says.

'So drown.' She strokes his hair. He moans in approval.

'So, will you tell her tomorrow?'

He stares at her sadly. 'Yes.'

'You understand, don't you Thomas? She got to you first, by mistake. It's just a twenty year mistake. You understand, don't you?' She strokes his face as he stares at her.

'I do understand. I do. I need you. You consume me.'

'Then tell me you love me.'

'I won't.'

'Why not?'

'Because it's all I have left.' All the bottles are empty. They slur their words but don't notice. The noise outside continues, the cameras flash intermittently at nothing, desperate and relentless. Alexandra walks to the window and pulls back the voile to look at the snow, and immediately the noise from outside rises, as if the air itself has become swollen and saturated with their names. The bulbs sparkle brightly like fairy lights spun around and around on the pavement below.

'It's still snowing. Do you think it will be done by tomorrow?' Alexandra places her open palms on either side of her face as she presses her nose to the window, staring at the snowflakes as they fall, almost oblivious to the crowds.

'Maybe.'

She glances down, as if spotting the sea of faces below her for the first time, and waves. 'Come and wave Thomas. They've been out there all night.'

'I don't want them there. I want them to go home, or die of frostbite.'

'Still. Come and wave. They're the butter on our bread.' She turns to face him and smiles, and it is like a needle in his arm.

'We'll be happy, Thomas, if you tell me that you love me.'

'Never,' he says, as he reaches her side and puts an arm around her waist. They wave, eyes glassy, both drunk. Thomas glances sideways at her, her eyes red from drink and tears. He pulls her to him, kissing the top of her ear, and the crowds cheer, as he whispers, 'It's all I have left.'

Cathy Kelly is the author of eight novels – *Woman to Woman*, *Never Too Late*, *She's The One*, *Someone Like You*, *What She Wants*, *Just Between Us*, *Best of Friends* and *Always and Forever*. She is a number one bestseller in the UK and Ireland, and a top ten bestseller internationally. *Someone Like You* was the Parker RNA Romantic Novel of the Year. Cathy Kelly lives in Wicklow with her partner and their twin sons. She is currently working on her next novel. *Always and Forever* is available now in paperback.

For more information about Cathy Kelly, visit her website at www.cathykelly.com

INTERESTING TIMES

Cathy Kelly

The night of the Ryans' twentieth wedding anniversary was the first time Ruby Anderson ever felt really old.

The first blow came when she discovered that she couldn't fit into her black fat trousers, the emergency ones with the forgiving waist.

'It's official: I am thirty-nine-and-three-quarters and a frump,' she told her reflection gloomily, ignoring the screams of delight from downstairs as the babysitter produced the evening's dual bribes of a deep-pan pizza and the DVD of *Shrek 2*. Shrek was a cultural icon for Elsie, nine, and Lewis, seven.

'Whadidyasay?' roared Jake from the bathroom, where he was clearly doing things with that horrible nose-hair trimming machine his mother had given him for his birthday. Even its buzz sounded nasal.

'I can't fit into my clothes,' Ruby roared back, delving into the wardrobe again at high speed. They were late already. 'My black trousers are too tight.'

Saying the words was a mini defeat in itself. She was finally on the road to having no waist. And she didn't have fabulous legs to compensate, like her mother.

'Wear jeans,' Jake said over the drone of his nose machine. 'It's a barbecue. That's pretty casual, isn't it?'

Fury flared briefly in Ruby's eyes. If she couldn't fit into her ordinary clothes, she was not going to metamorphose into Angelina Jolie in her jeans, now was she?

The brown hip-skimming jersey tunic and matching elastic-waisted trousers – bought in a panic when Lewis was three months old and she'd still looked heavily pregnant – were the only decent, non-sweatshirt items of clothing that actually went over her hips. It was a sexless outfit, Ruby admitted miserably to herself. She resembled nothing more than a large dark chocolate: solid, firm-bodied and definitely a little bitter on the inside. Her night out was not shaping up well.

The second shock came courtesy of the Ryans themselves. There had been wine, food (wonderful Chinese dishes from a proper catering company, a step up from the normal fare at barbecues on their road), plus a jazz band and real waiters with a seemingly endless supply of booze. And just when everybody thought it couldn't all get any better, Lorraine and Brian Ryan delivered their news.

'We're emigrating to Australia,' Brian announced. Lorraine was grinning so much that her fillings were visible. 'The house is sold. We're off next month. To Melbourne.'

Expecting fifteen minutes of anodyne *'thank you all for coming and we would like to thank our families'* speeches, Ruby thought this must be Brian's idea of a joke. 'Australia? Lorraine and Brian?'

'Fair play to them,' said Jake beside her. He'd availed himself freely of the waiter service and his world was now a happier place. Even better, the Ryans lived four houses away from him and Ruby. They could stroll home whenever it suited them without the palaver of looking for a taxi. Happy days. Her husband was easily pleased.

'But I'd have never thought . . .' stammered Ruby. The Ryans, of all people, to do something so exciting! Lorraine Ryan was so indecisive she could spend a month deliberating over whether or not to have her hair layered. What fit of wildness had prompted her and her husband to up sticks and emigrate?

'It's such a big step,' Ruby went on, thinking of what she'd read about beautiful Australian homes, with their year-round sunshine and pools in the back yards.

'Wait till I show you photographs of the house in Melbourne,' Brian Ryan was proudly telling everyone about their fabulous new life-to-be. He talked animatedly about a half-acre site with a verandah around the house, a championship-quality golf course just up the road, the wonderful school the kids would go to. 'Sasha wasn't sure at first. She's nearly seventeen, so it's harder for her to leave her friends, but when we told her about what life will be like out there, she was hooked like the rest of us.'

Brian looked different now, Ruby thought, as if the news had given him a new glow. He and Lorraine were doing something with their lives, not just stagnating like so many people did. Like her and Jake, Ruby realised in horror, conscious of the promise of youth drifting away.

It was the last surprise that completely floored Ruby. She'd decided that tomorrow was the day to start the Diet To End All Diets, and was dickering over the strawberry pavlova or the lemon cheesecake when she found herself beside Fiona, the woman from eight doors down who had a daughter in Elsie's class.

Normally the sort of mum who rolled up in old jeans and a T-shirt to pick up the kids, today Fiona was wildly glamorous in a striking pink chiffon kaftan and cream linen trousers.

Fiona had a man in tow and she introduced him gleefully: 'Hi, Ruby. Lovely to see you. Meet my date, Paul.'

As Fiona already had a husband named Mike, theoretically rendering the whole date thing obsolete, Ruby was momentarily speechless. Fiona and Mike must have split up and nobody had told her. Should she say something about how awful that was, or just forget it and act delighted to meet this new guy?

'Hello, how are you?' said Paul cheerfully, holding out a hand.

He was much better looking than Mike, Ruby thought. Mike was quiet and sturdy. This guy had an open-necked shirt, leather rockstar necklaces round his throat, and Raybans stuck in his shirt pocket. He was cool, or whatever young, hip people said nowadays.

'Nice to meet you too,' mumbled Ruby.

'Great party,' said Fiona chattily. 'The food's lovely. And isn't it gas about them going to Australia? Might as well grab life while you can, right?'

'*Er* . . . yes,' said Ruby.

Fiona might think she was very cold if she didn't mention Mike and commiserate over the breakup of the marriage. Surely Fiona should have whispered that in her intro, like: '*This is Paul. Mike and I are separated. It was awful, but I got over it, and wayhey, I've got a new man!*'

Ruby felt the pressure build to say The Right Thing.

'Sorry about you and Mike,' she whispered so that Paul wouldn't hear.

'Oh we haven't split up,' said Fiona loudly. 'Paul's just a bit of fun.'

'He'll hear you!' Ruby went puce with mortification.

'Oh, he's deaf unless we're talking about sex, aren't you, honey?' She put an arm around her date's waist. 'Better go,' she added. 'Places to go, people to see.' And she winked at Ruby.

Ruby had pavlova *and* lemon cheesecake, to restore herself after the shock. What was happening to the world? Was she the only sane one in it?

'Did you meet Fiona's date?' asked Sheena, another neighbour. The party was winding up and the waiters were distributing tea, coffee and fortune cookies.

'God, yes,' said Ruby, dying to discuss it. 'She introduced him to me and I honestly didn't know what to say.'

'He's fabulous looking,' Sheena said, as if that was explanation enough. 'She's introducing him to *everyone*! Wouldn't you?' Sheena was an elegant fifty-something who had two grown-up kids and a recent divorce.

'But what about Mike?'

'What about him?' shrugged Sheena. 'If Fiona wants a bit of passion, who are we to stop her? That's where I went wrong with Bill, you know. We stuck it out like two squares for years, clinging to marriage because that's what people did. If I'd had an affair, I might have realised what I was missing and got out when I was still young, instead of sticking to Bill until it was too late for us both.'

Ruby was used to straight-talking from Sheena, but this was intense stuff.

'They say that when you die, you think about all the things you didn't do,' Sheena added thoughtfully, 'not all the things you did.'

'Fortune cookie, madam?' asked a waiter, interrupting them.

'Thank you.' Ruby took one and cracked it open absently.

'*The dawn brings wealth tomorrow*,' Sheena read hers out. 'Remind me to buy a lottery ticket. What's yours say?'

Ruby unfurled it. '*May you live in interesting times*. Some hope of that,' Ruby muttered. 'My life's totally uninteresting.' Compared with everyone else's, it was. She must be dull as dishwater and conservative to boot to be shocked by Fiona's affair, when even Sheena, who was at least fifteen years older than Ruby, thought married women having lovers was a good thing.

'I don't think that's a good fortune,' Sheena said thoughtfully. 'I think it's a curse, actually. I'm surprised they put that in a cookie.'

Ruby put the fortune in her handbag. How could interesting times be a curse? Boring, dull times: now that was a curse, all right.

That night, Ruby lay in bed and thought about it all. When she and Jake first got married, they'd had such hopes and dreams. They were going to change the world, be different from their parents, never own a gravy boat or tell their children that modern music had awful lyrics and no tunes. Now, she read about other people's hopes and dreams in *Hello!*, shuffled along with her life and watched her neighbours do interesting things. Like emigrate to stunning countries, or have wild, sexually-charged affairs with men other than their husbands, and fit into their clothes without leaving the waistband buttons open.

Nobody wanted to have wild sex with her, and she would never have considered the possibility of such a thing, although it seemed she was the only one in the area who didn't.

She couldn't fit into most of her wardrobe and she could suddenly see herself in ten years' time, looking in the mirror at a woman wearing sensible mumsy clothes, and wondering where the slim-hipped girl she'd been had gone. Even the most boring neighbours on their road had a more exciting life than her and Jake.

Ruby was a part-time digital typist in a secretarial firm and the most thrilling part of her day was wondering whether to have a latte or a cappuccino for elevenses. While the Ryans were emigrating to the other side of the world. The flirtations with punk music, trips in a beat-up camper van to wallow in the mud at Glastonbury, and her pilates classes had all been in vain: she and Jake had become their parents. They were old. *She* was old.

Ruby sat bolt upright in the bed. Life was passing her by. Hadn't her fortune told her she could have interesting times? She was damn well going to jumpstart the process herself. Beside her, sleeping off the barbecue wine, Jake snored contentedly.

'Do lots of people have affairs, do you think?' Ruby asked her sister, Cat, the following Monday. Cat worked in television, knew everything, and if by some miracle didn't know what you asked her, had the mobile number of someone who would.

'They're all at it at work,' Cat said dismissively. 'Long boozy media lunches are supposed to be a thing of the past, but they're not. There are hotels around here where you can definitely rent rooms by the hour. Most people meet lovers in the office, you know. It's the new sexual hunting ground.'

Not in Carrickmines Secretarial Services, Ruby thought. The staff were all female, so unless she became a lesbian or went bi, it was not a suitable sexual hunting ground for her.

'Hey, do you fancy going out on a girls' night the week after next? Annie, remember, my old pal from college? She's back in Ireland for a month from New York and a few of us are taking her clubbing. She'd love to see you.'

Normally, Ruby said no to Cat's rare invitations for nights out. Cat was five years younger than her, lived a totally different lifestyle and went out five nights a week. She often goodhumouredly teased her older sister about being middle aged.

'You're on,' said Ruby firmly. 'I could do with a bit of partying.' Annie was a high flier in journalism in Manhattan with a lifestyle that was envied by all and sundry. Any party involving her would be fun.

'Great. It's the Thursday night. Cocktails at my place at nine, then we'll hit the clubs.'

Ruby hung up. Starting at nine? What time would she be home at, she fretted? Then stopped. You didn't get to live in interesting times by worrying over a late night.

At the school gates that afternoon, Fiona arrived late and rushed off without saying hello to Ruby. She looked amazing, Ruby thought gloomily, feeling lard-like by comparison in her pink striped sweatshirt. It wouldn't be hard to get a lover if you looked like that. Not that Ruby wanted a lover, she told herself. But it would be quite nice to have someone flirt with her, as if they desperately wanted to drag her off to a hotel for some room-by-the-hour sex. She could always say no. But being asked would be nice. It would make you feel better about your marriage if you knew someone else wanted you, wouldn't it?

'I think Fiona Timmons is having an affair,' she told Jake when she was taking the lasagne out of the oven that evening.

'Really,' murmured Jake, stuck on nine across.

'Well, I know she is,' Ruby amended.

'Yeah.'

She slammed the pasta pan down on the counter with a bang. Jake didn't even look up from his crossword.

'Brian and Lorraine are going to be off to Australia soon. It sounds amazing out there. Have you ever thought about us emigrating?' she asked.

'What?' Jake dropped his pen. 'When my team's doing so well in the Champions' League?'

Ruby borrowed a whole pile of diet books from Cilla at work. Cilla had been at Carrickmines Secretarial Services nearly as long as Ruby, and she'd tried every diet going: Atkins, South Beach, GI. As the GI didn't involve eating eggs morning, noon and night, Ruby plumped for that. Fired up by her new determination, she found it was easy enough, and after a couple of weeks she was able to sit down in her jeans without feeling as if someone had tied a tourniquet around her waist. The shedding of six pounds made Ruby feel a whole lot better. Still not young, but better. Able to flirt, anyhow. She was already planning what she'd wear to Cat's clubbing night out. Maybe she'd buy something fashionable and trendy. She didn't want to look like Mary Hick beside the likes of Annie.

On the Saturday morning three weeks after the Ryans' bash, she drove Lewis to swimming and then dropped Elsie at ballet. She had a whole hour and a half off. Most weekends she wheeled a trolley up and down the supermarket aisles. Today, a different sort of woman was going to buy the family's food, a woman who refused to give in to old age and who'd spent ages with the eyeliner trying to perfect that little Audrey Hepburn-esque flick up at the corners. Her dark hair was shiny, she was drenched in *Eternity*, and she was ready for some interesting times.

The man behind the counter in the deli on Market Street was pretty gorgeous. Greek, she thought, with olive skin, lips made for kissing and a flirtatious way of looking at his female customers.

'Hi.' Ruby leaned against the counter, twirled a bit of hair with one finger and tried to look sexy.

'Hello, can I help?' Adonis asked.

'Well, I'd like some Parma ham, twenty slices, and a piece of that brie. Four euros' worth.'

'No problemo.'

He hefted the wheel of brie up and began to cut it, without looking at Ruby. She tried to stand provocatively, balancing a hand on one hip, making sure her glossed lips were still moist. His eyes stayed on the brie. She twirled some more hair. Honestly, would he ever look at her.

Finally, he handed her the package of brie. It was now or never.

'How are you?' Ruby tried a bit of glinting eye technique and followed it up with some eyelash flickering. 'I haven't seen you for ages.' *Flicker, flicker.*

Adonis angled his handsome head in concern.

'Have you got something in your eye?' he asked helpfully. 'A speck of dust? Do you need a mirror?'

'No, it's fine,' Ruby murmured and looked down at her

feet. 'I'm fine. Do you know, I'm in a rush. Forget about the ham. I'll just pay you for the cheese.'

A huge moving truck was parked in the Ryans' driveway when she arrived back home with the kids. The house must have sold as soon as the estate agent got the details because no For Sale sign had ever appeared in the garden. Ruby thought of her own house and what sort of frantic hard work would be required to make anyone want to buy it before a sign had been put up. There were scuff marks all over the magnolia-coloured walls. Her parents' house was magnolia too. What had she been thinking?.

'We need to redecorate,' she announced to Jake when he got home. 'This place is a pit and it's so old-fashioned. We need to liven it up!'

'Painting?' asked Lewis, happily. He loved painting, especially when the teacher let them put paint on their hands and do handprints. 'I can help.'

'And me. Can I have a purple bedroom instead of pale pink?' asked Elsie. 'I don't like pink anymore.'

'You can have whatever colour you want,' Ruby said, kissing her daughter. 'The whole house is going to be brightly coloured from now on. It'll be fun! We're going off to buy paint after lunch.'

'This afternoon?' asked Jake, who'd had a hard week at work.

'No time like the present.' Ruby wondered why she hadn't thought of this before. Once the house was a vibrant family home, instead of a shrine to magnolia, she could get a book on Feng Shui and put everything in its proper place. Then lots of interesting things would happen and life would be exciting. 'We could paint the hall plain white, like a gallery, and put pictures everywhere. And have the kitchen crimson or dark blue, and have a mural in the bathroom, with a jungle theme. Wouldn't that be gorgeous?'

The hall was bigger than it looked and it was only half-painted by nine that night. Ruby was quite weary at the thought of having to start again in the morning, but they couldn't leave it now. One half was a shabby cream and the other half was blindingly white. Plus, she was tired and had belatedly realised that decorating was only bearable if you could stop for lots of cups of sugary tea and chocolate biscuits. But she was going to carry on being good if it killed her. She couldn't allow herself to slump back into the torpor of early middle age.

'Are you in the mood for love?' asked Jake hopefully when they slumped into bed, still with spatterings of white paint on their skin. He nuzzled her neck gently.

'I'm on the GI diet,' Ruby shrieked, with the full force of a woman deprived of Kit-Kats. 'If I'm not allowed anything nice, neither are you!'

On Sunday, they ran out of paint. To get everyone out of the house, where both tension and the scent of paint were high, they all went to buy some more. In the DIY store car park, they spotted Mike Timmons, Fiona's husband, parking his car.

'Hide!' shouted Ruby, crouching low in her seat.

'Why?' asked Jake.

'I told you,' she hissed.

Lewis and Elsie both had their faces pressed against the car window.

Inside the store, Ruby told Jake about Fiona for the

second time. Further proof that he hadn't been listening the first time was the look of pity on Jake's face as he heard the story.

'That's just so sad,' Jake said, taking Ruby's hand in his and squeezing it tightly. 'Six months down the line, they'll be splitting up. And look at what they're going to lose.'

Ahead of them, the children were picking wild colours for their bedrooms, Lewis giggling as he produced dung-coloured paints for Elsie, who retaliated with Barbie-pinks for him.

'I always thought Fiona was a stupid cow. She must be mad to risk her family for a meaningless shag.'

Ruby squeezed her husband's hand back. 'So you don't think variety is the spice of life?' she asked.

'No,' he said firmly. 'Do you?'

'No,' she answered hesitantly, and was rewarded with a surprised look from Jake. 'It's just that Sheena and I were talking that night, and she said she wished she'd had an affair when she was married so she'd have known straight off that she and Bill weren't suited. And I was shocked, and then I thought . . .' Ruby paused. It sounded stupid now. 'I thought I'd turned into my mother and that I was getting old, because my mother would have been shocked, too.'

Jake laughed so loud that Lewis and Elsie stopped messing with paint for a moment to cast quizzical glances at their parents.

'What's so funny?' Ruby demanded.

'I like your mother.'

'But you don't want to be married to her, do you?' She felt annoyed by Jake's lack of understanding.

'Ruby, you're unique, do you know that?' He gave her a hug.

'Unique in a good way?' she asked grumpily.

Lewis and Elsie made yeuching noises at the sight of their parents kissing.

'Unique in a fabulous way.'

'Not old?'

'Not old,' Jake agreed. 'Now can we buy paint and go home, so we can start on the second phase of changing the house?'

The Thursday of the clubbing night arrived and Ruby, wearing her new, funkier clothes, sat in Cat's tiny apartment and drank a lethal pale pink cocktail out of a pretty Moroccan glass. Cat's friends arrived in a laughing, sparkly gang: three gorgeous women, and Annie, looking almost as young as she had in college, and exquisitely groomed in a very Uptown way.

'Ruby, how lovely to see you!' cried Annie, hugging her. 'Cat's been telling me about your adorable children. Have you pictures?'

After another enlivening cocktail and some gossip, they headed out to a club with ambient music, supermodel-type bar staff and far too many mirrors for Ruby's liking.

She wanted to dance. The others wanted to sit and talk about men or the lack of men.

'We were engaged, you know,' Annie mournfully told Ruby, towards the end of the night. She stretched out her exquisitely manicured New York fingers. 'He dumped me. I 'spect Cat's told you all about it. I thought we were going to have it all: the Volvo and 2.4 children. The dream. And now look at me. Dumped.'

'Oh Annie,' sighed Ruby, thinking how utterly bizarre it was that Annie, of all people, could envy what Ruby had. 'The grass is always greener on the other side.'

And as she said it, Ruby suddenly knew it was true. It had taken other people valuing her life to let her see how wonderful it was.

'There's no rule book for life.' She was saying it as much for her own benefit as for Annie's. 'You're a wonderful person, it'll come right in the end. And there are times when you want to kill the husband and the 2.4 children,' she joked.

Annie nodded. 'I suppose you're right, Ruby,' she said. 'You always were a wise one, weren't you?'

Ruby grinned. 'I wish,' she said.

On Tuesday, Ruby was shopping when spotted Lorraine Ryan across the floor of Brown Thomas. Surely she should be in Melbourne by now, lying by her pool or admiring the garden from her verandah?

'Hi Lorraine,' Ruby hesitated as she got closer. Lorraine looked utterly miserable. 'Everything all right?'

'Oh Ruby, no it's not,' wailed Lorraine. And in the middle of the second floor her face crumpled and she began to cry great heaving sobs.

With Ruby comforting her, it emerged that Sasha, their seventeen year old daughter, had not been pleased about upping sticks and moving to Melbourne after all.

'She has a boyfriend,' sobbed Lorraine. 'She doesn't want to leave him. She says we can shove off if we want, but she's not coming with us. She says she'll be an orphan if that's what we want: she doesn't care.'

Ruby winced. What a horrible scenario. 'I'm so sorry, Lorraine,' she said. 'What are you going to do?'

'I don't know. It's all a mess,' Lorraine muttered. 'I told Brian you can't up sticks at the drop of a hat but he convinced me. He said we've only got one shot at life – he says that

273

all the time since his heart attack – and we should go for it. And now look! My daughter refuses to move and my husband insists we're going!'

'Sasha might change her mind,' volunteered Ruby. 'Here, let's go for a cup of tea.'

After a coffee and a bun, Lorraine felt well enough to say goodbye to Ruby. But her face was still tear-stained. Interesting times, Ruby thought sadly. Poor Lorraine. Somehow she wasn't in the mood for buying all the clothes she'd picked out. They looked suspiciously like Fiona's latest outfits. She went home with just one bag.

'What did you buy?' asked Jake that evening, as he looked at the tissue-wrapped package on the kitchen table. 'Some feng shui thing, I bet.'

Ruby smiled and added a big dollop of cream to the soup. She'd had enough of dieting.

'No,' she said. 'It's a present for you.'

Jake unwrapped the tissue and looked up with a smile. 'I thought you hated this sort of thing.' It was a plain white gravy boat.

'So did I,' Ruby agreed. 'Then I came to see that some home comforts are meant to be just that – comforting.'

She smiled at her husband.

Helen Lederer is known for her appearances in many top comedy television programmes, including *Absolutely Fabulous, The French and Saunders Show* and *One Foot in the Grave*. Having established herself as one of Britain's best-known comediennes in the 80s, Helen was commissioned by Hodder to write *Single Minding*. This book followed *Coping with Helen Lederer*, which was ahead of the game in a parody of self-help blockbusters – without the block or the bust, it has to be said. Helen is currently writing a sitcom which sits well with her articles for the *Independent, Mail on Sunday, Daily Telegraph* and her regular column for *Woman and Home* magazine. Her short stories have been published in the *Saturday Express, Girls' Night In* and the *New Erotica*. She is currently at work on a novel.

NEEDS MUST

Helen Lederer

Carey was fat. Really fat. There was now a distinct fold of
fat in her side which hadn't been there before. It looked
like a Labrador puppy fold, but without in any way being
cute. A dimpled wedge of white dough had landed on her
torso.

Special perfume then. Her lucky perfume, the cheap one
that always got the boys going when she was at the poly-
technic. Yardley's *Chic*. It was so old you'd think it would
have atrophied. She sniffed it. It had, but it was still lucky,
and with the recent fat increase she could do with a coun-
terbalance of fortune.

The whole point about auditions, Carey reminded herself,
was that they were only a ritual. In fact you might as well
not turn up, really. They knew who they wanted before they
started, but auditioning people was a way for directors and
casting ladies (women in their twenties in white trousers and
clipboards, mostly) to think they had an important job. So
one had to play along, especially if one was to make an
attempt to pay off one's debts, or avoid confronting a nasty

bank manager's letter which had threatened something so hideous Carey had sensibly hidden it behind some paper napkins.

An assistant (who was assistant to her agent's assistant) had phoned Carey the day before in great excitement to tell her she was 'up' for a 'casting'.

Carey knew better than to ask Tracey (her real name) too many detailed questions. It seemed cruel. She plumped for a general inquiry.

'And what's the casting for, Tracey?'

There was a pause and a rustle of paper 'Can you hold on for me?'

Why should Carey hold on for Tracey? Holding on for her flat, her MasterCard and her integrity was her current concern, but holding on for Tracey – she didn't think so. Mind you, needs must.

'Me again!'

'Yes,' Carey agreed.

'It's just for Europe.'

'Yes,' Carey waited for slightly more information.

'Yes?' Tracey was confused now.

Carey didn't enjoy the feeling of superiority that talking to Tracey gave her. It made her feel guilty that there should be someone so very simple shuffling papers about in an actors' agency when really she should be in a supported unit, making collages of her family and receiving appropriate help.

'And is there, you know, any description about the story-line? Character? Any dialogue? A script perhaps?'

'No,' said Tracey, firmly. This was one of her favourite words. She co-opted it from the other agents in the office to make sure she kept up to speed with theatrical and TV parlance.

'Oh hang on, it says a middle-aged fat person is running on a treadmill, a one hander, so that must be you do you think? Or do you think they mean a one-handed middle-aged fat person?'

'Any script to go with?'

'No. It just says a fat person is on a –'

'Got that – great!'

'Good luck then. I'm sure you'll get it if your recent *Spotlight* photo is anything to go by . . .' Carey found a meter which not only was free but fully functioning. She looked around to see if it was a wind-up. No immediate sign of Jimmy Carr, but a traffic warden aged about nine was peering at cars close by. As Carey passed him she tutted and gave him a half mast V sign. He beamed back at her. He must have been on a training course. Bastard.

She was just reapplying her lip gloss and a second *squish* of perfume around her uplifted décolleté region when she saw a very large woman with an A-Z coming towards her. She'd just follow her then.

Sure enough, the large lady led her to a basement studio beneath a sandwich shop. Castings normally took place in damp basements, annexed beneath seedy sandwich shops with limited loo paper and free property magazines.

This one had a tiny vestibule with an even tinier receptionist's desk squeezed into it, to make it look official.

'Sign here,' spat a butch woman who was mid-bite of a three-tiered McDonald's arrangement. Some gherkin escaped.

'Gosh, I didn't think they still did those!' said Carey pleasantly.

The butch returned to her *Nuts* magazine, oblivious to the gherkin, which was now attached to her chin.

Carey followed her new friend with the A-Z into a

waiting room and found herself staring at sixteen other large, middle-aged ladies in an assortment of primary-coloured tracksuits and leisure wear.

No one spoke, but there were a few sighs and furtive looks in case another fat person might want to start an exchange.

Carey was used to these situations. People were either silent or became buddies in that false way you do when you all want the same thing. Both systems were equally alienating. She found a seat and sat quietly. What could she do that was useful? It was too quiet to phone a friend and anyway, what would she say? 'I'm sitting in silence with sixteen fat people. We're all in tracksuits. You should be here.'

Some women were mouthing the words of the script as if they were learning it. '*A large woman is on the treadmill. The treadmill gets out of control. She attempts to gain control of it, to great comic effect. (This was in bold.) End shot. She eats an apple. She is happy.*'

One woman with a crewcut, a pink day-glow hoodie and incongruous platform shoes was fanning herself with the pink pages of an *Evening Standard*. She was bound to get it, thought Carey bitterly. Oddballs always had the edge over the needy.

Names were being called out in no particular order, but people were too desperate to complain. Carey was about to address the butch receptionist with the gherkin when her own name was called.

Fair play was forgotten as Carey's mounting debts came into focus again.

She stuck out her midriff and tried to look dignified at the same time. She was more used to sucking in that part for grand entrance purposes, but needs must.

Five men were seated behind a desk, looking bored. A casting lady with the predictable clipboard and crotch-splitting trousers teetered forward with a form for her to sign.

'Hello Carey! Can you sign here and then say your name, age and if you've done anything before.'

'What kind of thing?' Carey asked, smiling brightly. She was preparing a joke to make herself stand out. When she looked at the men behind the desk, she changed her mind.

'Adverts,' replied White Trousers crisply, before sashaying back to her seat. Wedge shoes were just the job for de-stabilising – if that was the look she was after.

The director (she assumed, since he was wearing fake tan and smelt of red wine) came over and stared at Carey's body intently. He paid particular attention to her breasts and sniffed the surrounding air.

He might have modelled himself on Patrick Litchfield, but Carey couldn't be sure. He had very thin legs with surprisingly tight trousers (which clearly seemed to be favoured in the world of low-budget commercialettes) and the kind of veneers which wouldn't be out of place as a gumshield.

'Hi Carey. I'm Torquil.' Perhaps the posh name explained why he felt entitled to take her shoulders and walk her over to a spot on the stained carpet. She could feel him smelling her Yardley again. Fingers crossed she'd put enough on.

'This is the treadmill.'

'Where?'

'Here.'

Carey spotted a bit of masking tape on the floor.

'Oh, sorry. Long time since I left drama school. I only did a post-grad, actually, so –' Another opportunity to refer to her marginally superior intelligence perhaps? Although a minor degree in humanities might not cut the mustard with Torquil and his gumshield.

'What I want you to do,' Torquil interrupted before glancing at his sheet, 'Carey,' – she could now smell egg and toast on his breath – 'is really run and run and run like this.'

To Carey's surprise, Torquil proceeded to run very fast on the spot like a hamster on a wheel, which wasn't altogether flattering in his tight trouser section. Not that she was looking.

The men behind the desk didn't bat an eyelid. The white trouser girl was busy retying her huge wedge shoes. He'd done this before.

'Brilliant,' said Carey. Praise where praise was due. Torquil could run on the spot.

'And then,' A second man stood up from behind the desk and walked towards her. 'For the funny bit . . .' He grinned.

'Are you the funny bit?' asked Carey.

'No, you are,' replied the second man crossly. The Creatives didn't like to be talked to directly. She could see that now. It must be a case of be fat, run and then be funny.

'So, when the treadmill gets out of control, you sort of grimace in a funny way and look around for help.'

'And will there be any help forthcoming?' Carey asked brightly. The funny man clearly didn't do answering.

'And then you finally – but only when you feel you've been really funny, though – get off the treadmill to eat an apple. Candida, have we got an apple please for Carey?'

Candida hobbled over on one shoe and presented a browned segment of apple. Carey was sure she could see teeth marks.

'We're pushing apples in Germany,' explained Torquil.

'Do they have an apple shortage over there?'

'Right, in your own time. ACTION!' Torquil shouted in a high-pitched voice, clapping his hands excitedly for emphasis.

Carey ran and ran. She ran for her debts. She ran for her second mortgage repayments. She ran to exorcise the bank manager's upsetting letter and she ran for her £750 fee. Possibly.

She tried to gauge how her running was going down. No one was giving much away. Time to be funny, then. She made huge, wide-eyed contact with an imaginary fellow runner on the next door treadmill. Then she pretended to make an urgent call on an imaginary mobile phone. In her excitement, Carey slightly broke wind which rang through the dank base-ment air like a mild party popper. No one said anything but it was hard to see how to salvage the situation. Then Carey had the brainwave of turning the release into a deliberate move and accused her imaginary neighbour of the crime. She then busily dismounted to eat the apple with as much pleasure as she could muster under the circs.

Silence.

Torquil came up very close to her. He smelt the air around her again.

'Did you do that on purpose?'

'Which bit?' When socially challenged, Carey had been brought up to ask a question.

Torquil put his hand on her metallic lilac sports top (hurriedly purchased from Oxfam the day before to 'big up' the fat aspect) and imperceptibly tweaked her nipple as he retrieved a piece of apple that had landed between her breasts.

'You dropped this.'

'Thank you.'

Was she supposed to pocket it? Before she could decide,

the man responsible for humour came over to take charge of his section.

'Can you do it again Carey, but less running, more on the phone and, oh, can you lose the, er, poop this time?'

Carey was mortified on two counts. One, that she had lost control of her sphincter valve so publicly and two, that her nipple might have been involuntarily aroused by Torquil fishing about for a bit of apple.

'Who would you like me to talk to on the phone?' Carey asked the humour man, more to reclaim authority than because she cared.

'Anyone you like!' He made this sound as if he were doing her a huge favour.

Carey duly ran on her treadmill for less time, exaggerated the imaginary phone call until her cheeks ached and finished off with a rapturous consumption of the apple segment.

They all clapped. This, she assumed, was a clue that she wouldn't have to do it a third time. Please God.

'That was great, thank you. We'll call you.'

'We'll call you,' said Candida

Torquil walked to the door with her

'Have you got a card?'

'Damn, I've run out,' Carey couldn't afford cards.

'I've got her details,' said Candida, adding in a surprised voice, 'If you really need them.'

'I've had fun. Really.' Carey skipped out gaily as if farting, running and nipple showing in public had been a romp and a hoot, if not a privilege.

She put her head round the door of the waiting room

'It's a doddle!' she lied to them. 'Good luck!'

'You too!' the women gushed automatically.

* * *

That night Carey was staring at the pile of paper napkins when the phone rang. She answered it because she needed a distraction from the thing that sat under the napkins.

'Hi, it's Torquil.'

'Hi!'

Carey's heart raced. She would be able to pay this month's mortgage repayment.

'You didn't get it.'

'Right.'

'But I loved your perfume! What was it?'

'It's from Paris. Who got it then?'

'The lady with a crewcut.'

Carey was depressed at the predictability of life.

'We decided to cut out the running and just go with her and the apple. But I wondered if you wanted to meet? To talk over some other possibilities. I'm starting my own production company . . .'

Weren't they all.

'I don't do possibilities, sorry.' She slammed the phone down.

She walked over to the napkin. Maybe she should just re-read it. Instead, she moved to the fridge for a major leftovers pork out. It was always best to sleep on a full stomach. That way, you couldn't see it.

The next day Carey made the phone call.

'Could I speak to Mr Fincham please?'

'And what is it regarding?'

Carey was unprepared. She decided to go for it.

'Shaking hands with the devil?'

'Putting you through.'

A seamless click and he was on the line.

'Hello?'

'You called.'

'Correct.'

'Any news?'

'Well I was thinking I could maybe comply with the first clause of your terms.'

'The weekend in Paris clause?'

'Yes.'

'I'll pick you up on Friday.'

She'd never pushed the boundaries this far before, but needs must.

The phone went again. If it was Torquil he could go and . . .

'Fantastic news, Carey! This is the one!'

'Hello Tracey. Which is the one?'

'Can you hold for me?'

Carey felt defeated. She was having to hold for Mr Fincham as well now, until she was solvent.

'Yes! A company called . . . hang on . . . *Flair for Living TV* want you! You have to host a TV quiz for older women about health. It says you'll be non-threatening, being on the large side.'

'Me?'

'Don't lie to me Carey, I know you're large. I've seen your *Spotlight*–'

'Me?'

'You. It starts next Monday. Eighty pounds an episode'

'Eighty?'

'Eight hundred. In Nantwich. Norwich.'

'Does it go out nationally?'

'Abroad?'

'UK.'

'Can you hold for me?' It was all getting too much for Tracey.

'Never mind. I'll do it.'

On Friday evening the doorbell went. She was going to have to deal with Mr Fincham in person. She took a deep breath and braced herself. Torquil was standing on the doorstep, joined seconds later by Mr Fincham.

Mr Fincham looked a little put out at having to share.

'I just came round with the loan details,' He enunciated the word 'loan'.

'Oh, this is my bank manager, Torquil.'

'Peter Fincham, actually,' corrected Mr Fincham.

'I didn't know bank managers did home visits?' said Torquil politely.

'It's a pilot scheme.'

'Actually Mr Fincham, I won't need the loan after all because I've got quite a well-paid job for large people now and–'

Torquil couldn't help himself. He had to interrupt.

'Candida gave me your address. I hope you don't mind, but I've been so obsessed about your perfume! It was such a Proustian moment for me when I smelt it and I just wondered if you wanted to go to Paris for a dirty weekend to track it down? I feel I could get rid of a lot of inner demons and–'

Carey rushed back into the house, leaving the two men on her doorstep.

Torquil called after her: 'Sorry, have I shocked you? Did you think I wanted to have sex?'

'God no, I was just packing. Mr Fincham, can we use your tickets? Needs must.'

Kathy Lette is the author of seven bestselling novels: *Puberty Blues, Girls' Night Out, The Llama Parlour, Foetal Attraction, Mad Cows, Altar Ego* and *Nip 'n' Tuck*. Kathy is published in over eighteen languages, in more than 120 countries. She lives in London with her husband and their two children.

For more information about Kathy and her books, please visit her website: www.kathylette.com

THE ART OF
GENITAL PERSUASION

Kathy Lette

When judging penises, it's probably not the most appropriate time to make small talk. That's the only bit of advice I can pass on if you are unsuspectingly called upon to undertake such a task – as was I, one bleak London day when I was abducted to a theatre in Shaftesbury Avenue and told by my best friend that now, once and for all, I would be cured of my 'irrational fear of the phallus'.

Phobias are as common as freckles. Heights, snakes, spiders, commitment, crowds, work . . . Well, I suffered from a phobia which was a little harder to explain away, especially to prospective boyfriends. I was penis-phobic. Successfully brain-washed by the nuns at Our Lady of Mercy All Girls School not to be a 'fallen woman' (the nuns failed to point out that women didn't actually 'fall', but were invariably *pushed*) – I'd only seen one or two male appendages in my entire life. And they'd terrified me. Especially during my late teens, when they'd been unsuccessfully prodding and pushing at me in a cold car on some dingy back road accompanied by male cries of 'Is it bloody IN yet?' or 'What are ya? Frigid?' (When will sexologists realise that the problem is not women faking orgasms, but men faking foreplay?)

Did this penis-phobia cramp my style in later life? Well, put it this way – the Pope took to ringing me up for tips on celibacy.

My best friend since kindergarten, Collette Kennedy on the other hand, was a penisaholic. If there were a 12 step programme for such cravings she'd be a regular. 'My name is Collette Kennedy and I am addicted to dick. I'm ad-dick-ted!' It was a love of word play which cemented our friendship from day one in kindergarten when she asked me which reptiles were good at maths? I looked at her blankly and kept chewing my braid. 'Adders,' she'd replied.

But it was the reptilian species known as the 'trouser snake' which now sparked her interest. A run-in with a lousy boss, a bad hair day, a hangover, a rejection by a casting director . . . all could be alleviated by taking the Phallic Cure.

Collette had thespian tendencies. Lesbian tendencies would have been preferable to her rather formal family, but um, sorry, absolutely no chance there. Collette giving up men was as likely as Michael Jackson getting a job in a day nursery. Her main stage roles had been limited to those of 'Buxom Wench Number Two', but she'd been murdered once or twice on *The Bill*, so had already written her Oscar acceptance speech.

My career choice was the antithesis of Collette's. I, Judith Jenkins, was studying to become a lawyer. Although all I'd experienced so far in my pupillage was subpoena envy. The barrister I worked for gave me nothing more intellectually arduous than menial filing. And he seemed to require an awful lot of papers to be put away under 'x', 'y' and 'z'. Which meant a *lot* of bending over.

'What pins Jenkins! Let's make the word of the day 'legs'. Why don't you come back to my pad tonight and we'll spread the word!' had been Friday's sexist comment du jour. Which is why I'd agreed with such alacrity to join Collette for lunch while she judged some competition or another at a theatre in Soho.

Collette was forever telling me to stand up to Rupert Botherington, Q.C. She maintained that the reason I found men intimidating was because of my penis-phobia. Demystification of the male was her mission. I just hadn't realised it would begin today.

'Oh goody. I love judging competitions. What sort? Scones? Flowers? Pumpkin carving . . . ?' I chirped as the mini-cab belched its way through Covent Garden.

It wasn't until we strolled onto the stage that the horror hit me.

'Penises!' I read the promotional poster. 'You want me to judge penises! Are you mad?'

'*Puppetry of the Penis* auditions. It's the cure, Judith. To your phobia. Surely you've heard of these Aussie guys? They perform a kind of genital calisthenics. Anyway, the show is so successful the producers urgently need more puppeteers. And as the producers are all gay, they booked me and some other actresses to judge the boys' performances from a hetero-sexual point of view. And I took the liberty of signing you up as well.'

'I know I'm training to be a cut-throat lawyer, but this is taking the term 'naked ambition' a little too literally Collette . . . I mean, saints preserve us!'

'And don't give me any of that shy convent shit. You know how I loathe that miserable God with his white beard and wagging finger.'

As Collette dragged me towards the other four female 'judges' already sitting on the panel, my shoes left skid marks visible from outer space. I tried to calm myself. It was all a bit of frivolous fun.

> **WARNING:** *these craft ideas are for amateurs.*
> *Do try this in your own home . . .*

I also made another mental note – kill Collette and sell her internal organs on the internet.

You see, unlike my best galpal, I'm not all that comfortable with public nudity. I've been to a nudist beach only once, in Greece. Gritting my teeth, I tried to shed my swimsuit and dive-bomb face down onto the towel in one deft movement – which merely resulted in a grazed chin, a cracked rib and a bit of seaweed up my freckle. Mortified, I lay rigid on the sand, fantasizing about putting my clothes back *on*. Then, just to be really kinky, I fantasized about other people putting their clothes back on as well! So you can imagine how I felt about an UNDRESS rehearsal.

Clipboard in hand, I perched one bottom cheek precariously onto my swivel chair. As the twenty or so male job applicants trooped on stage in jeans and t-shirts, I tried to put a positive spin on things. There are, after all, some good things about being nude. First off, you never have to buy anyone a drink – *'I'm sorry. But my money's in my jeans pocket'*. Nor is it likely anyone will ever steal your barstool. Having a dress code which reads 'clothing optional', also does away with all that boring *'I've got nothing to wear!'* angst.

But then the contenders started to disrobe. Shirts. Shoes. Jeans. As their undergarments came off, I wasn't quite sure where to look. I glanced at my clipboard for help. The score sheet comprised a list of boxes to be ticked.

Facial looks:	/10
Body:	/10
Appendage:	/10
Comedy skills:	/10

It was not unlike the kind of questionnaire Collette would hand out to a prospective boyfriend, really. Until I came to the last category which read, more worryingly:

Tattoos/Piercings/Other:	/10

'Other?' I gasped in a piercing whisper. 'What could they possibly mean by *other*?'

What was left of my mind boggled and my heart beat out a drum solo against my Wonderbra. Overcome with timidity, I decided to concentrate on **Personality** and made eye contact only. But eventually, having exhausted questions on stamp collecting and star signs, I had no choice but to slide my eyes slightly southwards . . .

All the applicants had serious 'pecs' appeal. Judging by their muscled physiques, these were the kind of '*excuse me while I do the six-hundred metre butterfly, climb two alps and abseil back down for some dressage and parachute formation before lunch*' types. Next to the boxes marked

Bodies, the all-female judging panel enthusiastically scribbled their 10/10 scores.

I would have given the candidates a high mark also, except that my hand was shaking so badly I couldn't write. It was palsied with terror, because the time had come to look at the mens' actual appendages. I'd heard of clubs for 'Members Only' but auditions for *Puppetry of the Penis* seemed to be taking this motto too seriously. Besides which, it was my lunch hour and I was decidedly worried that what I was about to see might put me right off my baguette. Anxiously and with great hesitation, I lowered my gaze even further.

If *I* was nervous, the candidates were more so. As the female collective gaze lingered on their groins, the men before me deflated faster than pump-up plastic lilos at the end of a beachside holiday.

'At least we know that the art of shrivelry is not dead!' Collette whispered to me. But as the director put the trainee puppeteers through their paces, they all rose heroically to the challenge.

In the next five minutes, the 'wow' factor of party balloons definitely paled into insignificance. The best way to describe the puppetry is to imagine party balloon tricks performed using the penis, testicles and scrotum. The fleshy creations I witnessed included *The Atomic Mushroom*, the *Hamburger*, the *Loch Ness Monster*, the *Windsurfer*, the *Baby Bird*, the *Boomerang* and the *Eiffel Tower*.

'Well, what do you think?' Collette dug her elbow into my ribs.

'The only apt word for such a spectacular performance is "outstanding", really,' I told her, breathlessly.

Collette giggled. As did I. Only I couldn't stop. The

laughter started to effervesce up in me like champagne. Nervous laughter I suppose, mixed with relief that the 'trouser snake' wasn't the carnivorous, venomous, aggressive creature I'd feared it would be, after all. And my laughter proved contagious. Soon we were all guffawing, judges and job applicants alike.

The barrister I worked for had inveigled me into a drink after work on my first day, only to dragoon me into a lap-dancing club. The atmosphere had been predatory and sinister. Men watched from the shadows in eerie silence as scrawny young women acted out their ersatz sexuality. But this experience was the opposite. With cheery rascality and matter-of-fact humour, the heterosexual men before me were happy to satirise their own sexuality. With not a whiff of baby oil.

'You see?' Collette prodded me again. 'It's nothing more than fear of the unknown. Blokes get to ogle naked women on a daily basis – page three girls in the tabloids, magazine centrefolds, internet porn, advertising. Naked women are used to sell everything from toothpicks to tractors.'

'The true meaning of "ad nauseum,"' I interrupted.

'Exactly! But when it comes to the male appendage, women don't often get to look it in its eye. I figured once you got to scrutinise a few scrotums they'd no longer threaten you. So, what have you gleaned?'

I glanced back at the performers. What I'd gleaned is that penises, like snow flakes, are all different. There's the lean, slinky, kinky ones. The thick, succulent types. The low-slung gunslinger sort. The stubby button mushrooms. The round-heads. The hooded eyes. The meat and two veg, packed-lunch variety. And women like them all. We judges admired every different shape and size. All this male angst over size. It's attitude women are really interested in. Women like a male member which says 'G'day! God, am I glad to see YOU!' And we certainly appreciate one which has been trained to do theatrical tricks for our entertainment. At the end of the auditions we applauded heartily. And the men on stage also looked pretty pleased with the way things had gone.

'Now *that's* what I call a standing ovation,' I told Collette as we left the theatre, hooting with laughter.

That afternoon I strode back into chambers. Rupert Botherington, Q.C.'s reprimand for being late was compounded by a threat to report me to our Head of Chambers. Except that this warning was followed by a salacious wink and a suggestive purr. 'Of course, you could always calm me down by letting me know just where those legs of yours end . . .'

Instead of wilting, I found myself imagining him naked, his scrotum comically stretched into a windsurfing sail. I then told him that these legs he so admired were now going to walk me to his Head of Chambers and report him for sexual harassment.

Puppetry of the Penis is referred to by the puppeteers as 'the Ancient Australian Art of Genital Origami'. But I prefer to think of it as the Art of Genital Persuasion.

PS: The names in this story have been changed to protect the guilty. The author would also like to add that no animals were harmed in the writing of this story, except for one misogynistic lawyer.

Gay Longworth was born in London in 1970. She lives there with her husband, a theatre producer, and their daughter. She has written four novels: *Bimba*, *Wicked Peace*, *Dead Alone* and *The Unquiet Dead* and should currently be at work on her fifth. She also wrote *Harvest* for *Big Night Out* and is delighted to have been asked to write for yet another impressive edition in the *Girls' Night* series. Thank you.

GIRLS' NIGHT IN

Gay Longworth

To: Carrie@hotmail.com; Val@aol.com
Subject: Girls' Night In
Hey,
Stocked up on wine and fags. See you at 8. When the kids are asleep.
Can't wait, LOTS OF GOSSIP!!!!
Love Joss

Reply: Joss@BTinternet.co.uk; Val@aol.com
Subject: Girls' Night In
Counting the minutes. Get me out of this hell hole . . .
Kisses and hugs
Carrie
PS still on detox, so I'm bringing vodka and edamame.

Reply: Joss@BTinternet.co.uk; Carrie@hotmail.com
Subject: Girls' Night In
Anything I can bring?
Val xx

Staying in is the new going out. There is no queuing. The chances of having your drink spiked are minimal. And you don't have to pay for a babysitter. Three friends of old decided they would try it on for size. The location was chosen between the ones who had offspring and then narrowed down to the one without the husband. That would be Joss. Joss had two children and had lived alone since her husband had yelled 'I want a divorce' at her in the middle of a drunken row. Sensing an opportunity, she'd kept him to his word. Joss stocked up the fridge with white wine and stomach lining taramasalata, put her children to bed and pulled out the first cork. Music to a mother's ears. She was in a great mood and looking forward to the evening. She'd lost five pounds, covered her grey and had met a man at work. She was longing to tell the other two about him.

Carrie was the first to ring the doorbell. She arrived carrying a bottle of vodka, some limes and soda. She'd read somewhere that vodka was a cleaner alcohol, and since she was still detoxing, she thought she'd bring her own. There were fewer calories per unit in vodka than wine. Carrie was a fashion and fads kind of girl. She had been blessed with exceptional good looks, but knew it. Her jeans were always skin-tight. Her make-up ever-present. She was that rare breed of blonde, bright and beautiful, with a razor sharp wit and buckets of sexuality. She was also single. Carrie could be described as a trifle on the high-maintenance side, and had on more than one occasion been referred to as neurotic. But to her friends she was always good value to have around.

Val was the last to arrive. She brought champagne. There was always something to celebrate in Val's life. Her husband's small business had become a slightly bigger business and had just been sold for a great deal of money. She and their twins were well looked after. Their house in Kensington appeared in magazines and they were currently in negotiations over a large yellow stone manor in Gloucestershire. Very quickly, Val had got used to turning left when she got on to an aeroplane, and no longer thought it strange that the nanny struggled alone in the back with the twins. Val had always been the fulcrum between Joss's moods and Carrie's overly dramatic take on life. She prided herself on her strength of character and her level-headed approach to life. As Joss and Carrie had been her friends since they'd been forced together in a hostile school environment, Val knew they didn't like her for her money.

Val walked in with a bag clinking with goodies from the off-licence. 'I am gagging for a drink,' she announced.

'Hi Val,' said Carrie. 'You look fabulous. You've lost weight?'

'No.'

'I'm sure you have.'

'You say that every time I see you. If you were right, I'd weigh two stone by now. You know I don't diet.'

'Get yourself a drink,' said Joss, kissing Val. 'The bottle is already open.'

Val looked in the fridge. 'I've decided since we're saving ourselves a fortune by staying in, we should have the best at a fraction of the price.' She pulled out a bottle of vintage Bollinger. 'There are two more in the bag. Throw that stuff away, and have this.' She popped the cork. 'I've been looking forward to this all day. The twins have been a nightmare. Ill and grizzly, which I know isn't their fault, but still . . .'

'Me too. I've had a bitch of a day at work,' said Carrie, turning back to the job of squeezing limes. 'You know that presentation I've been working on . . .'

'Yes,' said the other two in unison, anticipating the worst.

'They've only gone and shelved the entire project. Not enough funding, apparently.'

There were communal sighs of sympathy and hugs. The drinks were poured, and they moved out onto the small balcony, where smoking was permitted. Joss had enforced the rule on herself to try and cut her cigarette intake down to one pack a day. No one who knew her thought it odd that the telly was placed in the middle of the room, and angled towards the French window.

'What does that mean with regards to your job?' asked Joss, inhaling deeply and taking a large slug of champagne. Joss was effectively the sole breadwinner of her family. Her soon-to-be-ex-husband was one of those creative types. She had underwritten his lack of talent and vodka habit for years. She'd loyally backed up his stories of 'things in the pipeline', 'scripts being picked up', and 'interest from several parties'. It made her particularly sensitive to Carrie's irregular working patterns.

'They're bastards and don't know what they're talking about.'

Val and Joss looked at each other knowingly. Their beautiful friend would soon be looking for new employment. Her average stay at any one job was eighteen months. Six months of best behaviour. Six months of sliding productivity. Six months of scandal. Followed by the inevitable explosive walk out. Her love life followed much the same pattern, but could be measured in weeks, not months, and sometimes days.

'What about you?' Val asked Joss, coming in from the cold. She couldn't handle listening to Carrie blame the entire management of L'Oreal for the failure of her product. She also liked to deflect the attention away from Carrie, who

302

frankly got enough. Joss on the other hand had a tendency to melt into the background. Val thought of herself as the most stable of the three, and therefore could afford to be considerate. 'What's happening with the divorce?'

'Well he's drinking again, so things are getting worse.'

'Thank God you're out of it,' said Carrie, swigging back the booze.

'I know, but the kids don't see it like that. They want their daddy home.'

'Of course they do, Joss, he never disciplined them. You had to do all that by yourself and then he'd come in, break all the rules and undermine you completely by giving them the things you'd said they couldn't have,' said Val. 'You are very brave and I'm very proud of you.'

Carrie refilled everyone's glasses. Why did the first bottle always go down so quickly? Val went and fetched the second.

'You're not changing your mind are you?' asked Carrie. Carrie had very much enjoyed having Joss returned from the wasteland of marital life. Her partners in crime were waning and she'd been left having to make do with women she met on the treadmill.

'God no. Actually, I've met someone.'

'What?' asked Carrie. 'Where?'

'That's great,' said Val. 'Tell all.'

'At work. Bring the bottle and I'll tell you the gory details on the balcony.'

'You slaves to nicotine,' said Val, peeling back the foil.

'You'll get pissed and start smoking yourself,' said Joss.

'No I won't. I've stopped doing that.'

Joss and Carrie gave each other knowing looks as the second cork flew into the neighbour's garden.

Carrie couldn't be bothered to go and squeeze more limes

and anyway, after two, she was getting acid tummy. She poured the ice into the garden below and filled the tumbler with champagne. Most of Joss's belonging were still in storage and there weren't enough flutes anyway.

'He is younger than me,' said Joss. 'Twenty-six.'

There was simultaneous squealing.

'Lucky girl,' cried Val. 'I'm so jealous.'

'No you're not,' said Joss.

'Okay, I'm not. But I am happy for you.'

'So am I. It's fabulous, you deserve it. So when you say he's at work, like the same building, or the same office?' asked Carrie.

'Ten feet away.'

'Isn't that a bit dangerous?' asked Val.

'Not if you haven't had sex for ten months it isn't,' said Joss. 'And to be honest, things in that department weren't that great at the best of times. I'm like a bitch on heat and I'm powerless to stop it. And he's so star-struck, it's like child's play.'

'It is child's play,' said Val, and they all howled again. 'Have you slept with him yet?'

'No. We're still on a lot of eye contact and naughty sex-texting.'

'Now I am jealous.'

Joss grinned with delight.

'Honey, I've done what you're about to do, and it always, but always, ends in tears,' said Carrie.

'Doesn't stop you doing it again though,' said Val, coming to Carrie's defence.

'Bitch. It's not my fault, men just seem to like me.'

'Well they don't always fancy me, and it's nice to have some attention. The last thing I want is a relationship.'

'I'm just saying be careful,' said Carrie.

'Carrie has a point. You don't take rejection very well.'

They drank in silence for a while. Carrie broke it. 'Do you remember the man who owned the gallery I worked at?'

The three women started laughing again. It had been a disastrous affair from the outset. He was short, pale and ugly. But rich. He wooed Carrie with trips to Paris and expensive bags. After a stay in a posh hotel, Carrie felt a little guilty that she still hadn't put out. So she gave him a blow-job in the car on the way back. They got busted by a juggernaut, who gave them a blast of the horn. The boss panicked, accidentally slammed the Porsche into reverse gear and blew the engine. Carrie got the delightful reputation of having given the most expensive blow-job in history. When Carrie walked out on her contract, the company let her go. Val and Joss always thought it wasn't, as Carrie had said, because they were frightened of a lawsuit, but because they were so relieved she'd taken her dramatic antics elsewhere. But as always, those dramatic antics made up for the lack of any antics in the lives of the other two. Carrie coloured their lives and gave them something to talk about. When they weren't despairing of her, they were actively encouraging her. The three women laughed and drank and drank some more and talked about all the bad sex they'd ever had. When Joss opened the third bottle of champagne, Val mentioned it would be a good thing if they had something to eat. So the humous and taramasalata came out of the fridge and sat open, but untouched, on the table. It was way too late for food. Their appetites had been successfully drowned by then.

'Oh sod it,' said Val. 'Can I?' She pulled the pack of Marlboro Lights towards her. Joss and Carrie said nothing. 'It's just been such a stressful day.'

'Looking after the staff can be so tough,' said Carrie.

'Claws,' said Val.

'I'm only joking.'

'I wish I had a husband who paid for the nanny,' said Joss. 'Who am I kidding. I wish I had a husband who paid for a loaf of bread.'

'I wish I had a husband,' said Carrie.

'Then don't shag everyone at work,' said Val, laughing.

'I don't shag everyone at work,' said Carrie.

Joss joined in the tease. 'What about the pass you made at your boss's assistant?' said Joss.

'I didn't know he was gay.'

'He had a penis, that was enough of an incentive. And everyone else in your office is a woman,' said Val, finishing the story.

'At least I go to work,' Joss retorted. 'We can't all file our nails all day.'

'Now who's being bitchy?' said Val.

'You are.'

'No I'm not. You're just being over-sensitive,' said Val. 'We're only teasing. I have to go and have another pee.' Val turned too quickly, glanced off the door and tripped over the step. She lurched forward, but managed to right herself. She held up her glass triumphantly. 'Not a drop spilt.'

'Pisshead,' said Carrie.

'Make a sentence of the following words – Pot, kettle, black, calling.' Carrie prodded Joss in the ribs hard in retaliation as Val tottered off to the loo.

'Could the woman get any more patronizing? I don't sleep with that many men. My dreadful sister is a million times worse,' said Carrie, pouring out the remnants of the third bottle and swilling it down in one. 'And bring back a bottle you old tart,' shouted Carrie, as an afterthought.

'Takes one to know one,' shouted the disembodied voice of Val. Val and Carrie cackled, then Carrie turned back to Joss.

'She's such a bitch. Why should I say no, if these men want to take me out? You've said yes to the first bloke who's shown any interest.'

'One, the guy is on secondment and two, he is not my boss.'

'You really think I sleep around?'

That wasn't exactly what Joss was trying to say. 'Well . . .' It was a tricky subject. Carrie did seem to get herself into more situations than anyone she'd ever heard of, let alone met. If there was a drama, then Carrie was at the centre of it. Her 'scenes' always dented her prospects. She'd be back to temping any moment and she was one of the brightest people Joss and Val knew.

'Get off the fucking fence for once. Do you think I sleep with too many people?'

'Honestly?'

'Jesus Christ, spit it out . . .'

Joss inhaled deeply. This was dangerous territory. 'Perhaps it would make life easier if you didn't always sleep with someone at work. Then things wouldn't go wrong for you so much.'

'The people I work with are fucking idiots.'

'All of them? In every one of your twelve jobs? There's only one common denominator, hon, and it's you.'

'Christ, you're as bad as Val.'

'Are you still slagging me off?' asked Val, returning with Carrie's bottle of vodka, chopped lime and a glass of ice. 'We've run out of champagne. Vodka, lime and ice?'

'Perfect.'

Val poured the clear spirit unsteadily into the medley of glasses. 'So what were you witches saying I was bad at?'

'Nothing Val, you're practically perfect in every way,' Carrie was beginning to rock from side to side. It was only a small movement. But noticeable to those who knew which signs to look for.

'Anyway, let's change the subject before someone gets out of control.' Joss was trying to diffuse the tension, but like the others she was more pissed than she realised and failed to hear the condescending tone in her voice. Val heard it and decided to take over the job of defusing the bomb.

'I agree,' said Val, raising her glass and an eyebrow. 'Down in one ladies. To our girls' night in. Long may they continue.' They drank their vodka kamikaze-style.

Joss poured again. 'To finally getting laid,' said Joss. 'The ex has the kids for half term, I'm planning to put in a lot of extra hours at work . . .'

'Listen to you. One sniff of attention from a boy, and you get as worthy as Val.'

'I'm not worthy,' insisted Val.

'I am not like Val, and anyway, what's worthy about shagging?' Joss laughed.

'What does *I'm not like Val* mean?' asked Val turning to Joss. 'I've been supporting you all night.'

'Nothing, Carrie just didn't understand what I was saying as usual.'

'Superior as hell, is what Joss means Val,' said Carrie. 'And now you're doing it,' Carrie pointed a red nail at Joss. 'All because this little bus-boy who is probably after your job is pretending to fancy you.'

'That's not true.'

'You're only in a good mood when a boy fancies you, Joss, which sadly for us isn't very often.'

'Well it would be if I didn't have you throwing yourself at every male who walks in the room.'

'That's bollocks.'

'Calm down you two,' said Val.

'Fuck off,' snapped Joss. 'You're just as bad Val, pretending to be the loyal wife, but you draw everyone in. You can't have them, but you don't want anyone else to have them either. You wrap them round your little finger until every boy in the room is eating out of your hand. You've never left any for me.'

'Who is being over sensitive now?' said Carrie.

'Yes, you should have some water Joss,' said Val, as she poured more vodka for herself and Carrie. 'You don't drink that much anymore. You haven't got the stamina.'

'No, I was married to an alcoholic remember. Kind of put me off drunken antics.'

'Oooh, sorry we're so immature, madam,' said Carrie, pushing herself up from the sofa by leaning on Val.

'Exactly. If I can't let my hair down with my mates, who can I get drunk with?' said Val. 'I'm always with important people and have to be on my best behaviour.'

'I'm amazed you still condescend to see us,' said Joss. 'Did you hear that? She called us unimportant.' Carrie was zig-zagging her way to the bathroom.

'Don't be so ridiculous,' said Val. 'It was a compliment.'

'I don't like your compliments, they make me feel like shit.'

'That's more to do with you Joss, than me.'

'Bollocks it is. You love the fact that Carrie and I are all over the place, it makes you feel so much better about

309

yourself, doesn't it? God I bet you love going back to your stiff of a husband to tell him how utterly neurotic we both are and how very lucky he is that he got someone as rare as you.'

'It's not my fault that I don't have hang-ups like you do,' said Val.

'You're worse, you just pretend to be oh-so-level-headed, but you're as fucked as the rest of us. Where the hell is your emotion? You're like a zombie.'

'Just because I don't go around throwing wobblies, doesn't make me a zombie. Now who's trying to make themselves feel better? I refuse to engage with this nonsense.'

'Let's call your fancy boy,' said Carrie, returning from the loo.

'No.'

'Come on. It'll be funny. What's his number?'

'No.'

'Come on!' Carrie grabbed for Joss's phone, knocking over the bottle of vodka, but managing to grab it.

Val started valiantly mopping up the mess. 'Children, children.'

'I said no.'

'Uh-oh, she's going into one of her moods. Every one duck. Incoming!'

'Piss off,' Joss marched past Val and Carrie, and stormed off towards her bedroom.

'Don't start fucking crying, it's so boring.'

'Look you mad anorexic bitch,' said Joss turning wildly on Carrie, 'just because I don't want you to ruin yet another of my dates, doesn't make me boring.'

'I'm not anorexic any more!'

'Like fuck you aren't.'

'I'm not!'

'You are!'

'Come on you two.'

'*Piss off, Val!*' they screamed in unison.

'You're the only anorexic I know who got down to four stone and never gave up the booze. One stick of cucumber isn't eating. You're so fucking obsessed with yourself –'

'You can talk. You wish you were as thin as me, we both know you chuck up in secret. Bad breath kind of gives it away.'

Joss picked up the plastic tub of humous and threw it at Carrie. It missed.

'You stupid cow.' Carrie picked up the taramasalata and threw it at Joss. She darted sideways. The pink dip hit Val.

'What the hell are you two doing?'

'*Fuck off, Val!*' they shouted again in unison.

'I'm just trying to help.'

'We don't need your help!'

'I'm not staying here to be insulted,' said Carrie, picking up her coat.

'That's right, run! Run away, like you always do. God forbid you should see something through to the end.'

'At least I'm not desperate enough to marry a drunk midget!'

'At least I'm not a desperate old whore who fucks anything that moves!'

'Come on you two.'

'WILL YOU JUST FUCK OFF YOU POMPOUS COW!' shouted Carrie.

'Fine. I will.' Val picked up her coat and marched out. 'You two are absurd.'

'You can fuck off too,' Joss shouted at Carrie. 'Take your over-exercised arse out of here. Run off to some poor boy who hasn't wised up to how fucking *nuts* you are!'

'I wouldn't stay here if you paid me, you jealous freak,' shouted Carrie, who picked up her coat and stumbled out.

Joss had slammed the door of her bedroom before Carrie had reached the hall. After three bottles of champagne, one bottle of vodka and no food, silence ruled. The girls' night in was over.

To: Carrie@hotmail.com, Val@aol.com
Subject: The morning after the night before
Hey,
Hope you both got home alright? What the hell happened to the humous? I've got a stinking hangover, why the hell didn't we eat something?
Talk later, lots of love
Joss.

Reply: Val@aol.com; Joss@BTinternet.co.uk
Subject: The morning after the night before
Ouch. Can't remember getting home. But what a lovely evening. Same time next week at mine?
Kisses and hugs
Carrie

Reply: Joss@BTinternet.co.uk; Carrie@hotmail.com
Subject: The morning after the night before
Ouch indeed. Perhaps the bottle of vodka wasn't absolutely necessary . . .
Love you both.
Val xx

In 1995 Chris Manby met a New York psychic who told her she would write seven novels. She has just published her ninth, which means she probably won't marry that millionaire either! Raised in Gloucestershire, Chris now lives in London. Her hobbies include Pilates and finding creative excuses for avoiding it.

Chris Manby's novels: *Flatmates*, *Second Prize*, *Deep Heat*, *Lizzie Jordan's Secret Life*, *Running Away From Richard*, *Getting Personal*, *Seven Sunny Days*, *Girl Meets Ape* and *Ready Or Not* are all published by Hodder and Stoughton.

THE LAST MAN ON EARTH

Christine Manby

Newspapers all over the planet made front page news of the sorry story of the sudden deaths of Mimi and Leo, the last breeding pair of human beings in captivity. The brilliant scientists at the top research zoo in Outer Mercilon had been trying unsuccessfully for fifteen years to be the first to produce a real human baby. They had gone to great lengths to ensure that breeding conditions were perfect for their charges. They had provided the mating pair with everything they needed to be healthy and happy. The right food – no meat, pure soya for protein (though some geneticists argued that since a modified soya crisis had wiped out most of the earth's population in the late twenty-first century, Mimi and Leo might actually have adapted to need a contaminated food source).

The right environment was important too. A small part of the enclosure had been completely blocked off from the prying eye of the 24 hour CCTV camera, because it had quickly become clear that the human female in particular would absolutely not engage in even the affectionate preliminaries of mating if she felt she was being observed. The scientists even had to go so far as to replace the one-way mirror with a proper wall when it became clear that the unusually intelligent female had cottoned on to the trick and was subsequently still inhibited.

But the privacy room was to be the breeding project's downfall, for, while the scientists assumed that their subjects were getting down to creating the next generation, the grunts and cries they heard were not in fact the usual inelegant sounds that accompanied human mating, but the sound of the subjects killing each other with the candlesticks that some bright spark from the University of Mercilon had suggested would make mating inevitable and successful (he had picked up the tip about using candles for seductive lighting in an article on 'Perfect Seduction Techniques' in the *Cosmopolitan* book from the vast Earth archive).

Doctor Eugynon, the eminent professor who had been leading the breeding project, was distraught. His life's work, gone forever. They tried to rescue the female, who wasn't quite dead when the operative who fed the humans three times a day found her lying in a pool of blood upon the satin sheets of the mating platform. But she seemed to have lost the will to live. She refused food and medication until she too finally faded away. Not even the noxious brown substance the humans called 'Chock-let' could save her this time. Doctor Eugynon considered following the female to wherever it was that humans thought they went after death. He held the candlestick the woman had used to club her mate into unconsciousness in his own third hand and turned it over contemplatively. He went so far as to bash it against his own head a couple of times but it didn't even dent his radiation resistant silicon-based skin.

He was about to take more constructive suicidal measures with an atom dispersing gun when his assistant, the lovely Doctor Microgynon, with her fetching knee-length tentacles, raced into his office bursting with the news that a human ship had just been sighted outside the planet's atmosphere. A ship that contained at least two carbon-based life forms!

Eugynon shrugged his bony neck-plate. It was probably just another ghost ship infested with the spider-like parasites from Oooo-on Three that had finished off so many of the Earth Alliance Freedom Fighters during the Six-Hundred Years War. They gave a life-force reading very like that of a human child, those Oooo-on critters. The Oooo-on house at the zoo was about as popular as pigeons had been on the original Planet Earth. The last thing Eugynon needed was another pair of those, but he gave his permission for a hunt in any case. And within hours the ship (made of that primitive earth material that was actually affected by a simple magnet!) was dragged on.

And not only did the life forms inside survive the punishing entry into Outer Mercilon atmosphere, but when the flimsy hull of their vessels was opened, the travellers were revealed to be humans after all. Two perfect, tiny humans. All pink and shivering and covered with that disgusting silky hair that felt like entrails to the Mercilonian scientists lucky enough to handle the creatures. Eugynon was delighted.

The two humans (one of each sex, praise the moons!) were taken straight to the enclosure. The tiny room had been thoroughly cleaned since the death of Mimi and Leo but the new female one still wrinkled her nose in the way that female humans did.

'She can smell the previous female,' Doctor Microgynon

suggested. 'Do you think the remaining pheromones will encourage her to mate?'

'We can only hope so,' said Doctor Eugynon, as he crossed about sixteen of his fingers.

'There is blood on the sheets!' hissed Captain Melanie Eve to her First Officer Andrew Adams when he finally came round from his concussion on the rock-hard bed.

'Where are we?' he asked.

'Well, I don't think we're in the Earth embassy on Mars,' Eve commented sarcastically. 'What the hell were those things that brought us in here?'

'I don't want to know,' said Adams.

'Looked like some kind of cephalopod to me,' Eve mused. 'And it had to wear breathing apparatus to come inside here, which suggests that their atmosphere isn't friendly to humans and vice versa. We could be on one of the Outer Oooo-ons.'

First Officer Adams paled.

'I've got to speak to their leader,' Eve continued. 'Though I'm not entirely sure that the squid that brought us in here can speak.'

'Well, at least they haven't tried to kill us,' said Adams. 'Look at this food. They're trying to make us comfortable.'

'Or fatten us up!'

Captain Eve hammered on the glasslike substance that enclosed them. 'Nobody eats this soldier!' she shouted. 'I'm Captain Melanie Eve of Squadron Eleven of the Earth Alliance. I demand to speak to your leader at once!'

Professor Eugynon watched Eve closely from the observation deck. They weren't taking any chances with blind spots in the enclosure this time. Another ten cameras had been fitted.

The humans couldn't so much as sniff without him knowing about it.

'What's the female saying?' asked Microgynon. The only human dialect she knew fluently was Chinese – the most popular.

'I think that's a human display of physical strength,' said Eugynon as Captain Eve thumped the glass so hard she set off the breakout detector. 'She's signaling her genetic viability to mate.'

'Aren't they peculiar?' Microgynon mused. Human love-making was just so . . . rough. Once again she was glad that, as a Mercilonian, she merely had to flash a few lights along her bony head crest to signal her intentions. Not that Eugynon ever seemed to notice. Just that morning she had twisted her tentacles into a particularly complicated lattice in his honour. Professor Femodene had complimented her on her 'do' but Eugynon, as usual, only had eyes for the revolting sniffling creature he called 'the girl'.

'Are they a mating pair?' Microgynon asked her mentor when it was clear that he wasn't going to be distracted.

'I would say they are,' Eugynon nodded. 'Judging from the heated way in which they are communicating. See, Microgynon, she's touching him now.'

Captain Eve laid her First Officer out with a single punch.

'We're in the sodding Outer Mercilon research zoo, you idiot!' she screamed at him. 'See those two moons? The moons we never fly past??? How did we get here?'

'It's not my fault,' Adams whimpered.

'You were the fucking navigator! I told you to set the co-ordinates for home via the Oooo-ons, specifically avoiding here. Even a bloody first year grunt in the military knows that the magnetic forces around Outer Mercilon are irresistible. Even to our best fighter ships. You got us sucked down onto the most hostile planet known to humankind!'

'Hostile atmosphere?' Adams asked helplessly.

'Hostile bloody everything. The Mercilonians used to take package holidays to the earth colony on Venus to partake in their equivalent of fly-fishing – with the Japanese cosmonaut community taking the place of the rare Scottish sea-trout.'

'I didn't think that was true,' said Adams in horror.

'It was true,' shrieked Eve. 'They only stopped when the Intergalatic Community of The Dark Planets put a conservation order on the Japs. This is deep shit we're in now, lover-boy. Deep shit.'

'They're definitely a mating pair,' said Microgynon proudly, snatching on the one word of their dialect she did know. 'Did you hear her address him as "love"?'

'What's going to happen?' Adams asked nervously.

'We could be experimented on. We could be dissected. We could even be forced to mate.'

An uncontrollable spark of interest flashed in Andrew Adams' blue eyes.

'Dream on,' said Eve.

'But that wouldn't be so bad, would it? It's quite nice in here. Perhaps we're as precious as Giant Pandas.' Adams reached for an apple. Eve karate-chopped it from his hand before he could get it anywhere near his mouth.

'Are you mad?' she asked him. 'What if it's been drugged?'

'She's preventing him from taking sustenance,' Professor Eugynon observed. 'They're definitely about to mate.'

* * *

'How are we going to get out of here?' sighed Captain Eve.

'I don't know,' said Adams.

'Trust me, I didn't intend my question to be anything other than rhetorical,' Eve sighed. She paced the enclosure. 'Why did I let them palm me off with a man for a first officer?' she murmured to herself. 'Everyone knows a man couldn't navigate himself out of bed in the morning if his girlfriend wasn't pushing him.'

'Your sexist remarks aren't going to help us now,' Adams said petulantly.

'Just go back to thinking with your dick,' said Eve.

Adams' mouth dropped open.

'I mean the memory chip,' Eve clarified impatiently. 'The one implanted in your penis so that the Oooo-on fundamentalist rebels wouldn't find it. Don't you have maps of all the Dark Planets stored on that?'

'I do. But it won't work with my handheld info reader,' he told her. 'I have to insert my penis into the download port on board the ship to access it.'

'Brilliant!' Eve spat. 'Just my luck to get stuck with the one guy who *can't* just stick his prick into anything and get a result.'

'Blame the Defence Ministry,' he said, trying to raise a smile.

But Eve was not in the mood for joking. She pressed her nose against the wall of the compound and squinted out into the dusk. Outer Mercilon didn't have its own sun. The only light was the feeble glow of a distant star reflected by the two moons that orbited the planet three times every earth hour.

'See anything?' Adams asked.

'As a matter of fact, I can see our ship,' she told him.

'And there's nothing between us except these glass walls. It doesn't seem to be tethered. If we could just get out of this ridiculous pod. I don't think we sustained too much damage on entry. I loaded fuel to take us all the way back to Florida. We've done half the trip. We should have enough left to effect one more take-off . . .'

Adams looked at her doubtfully. 'If the Mercilonians have got us here as part of a breeding programme, there's bound to be heavy security. Wouldn't it be better just to lie back and think of Earth?'

Another slap from Captain Eve landed Adams on his backside in the fruit bowl. 'Send in more fruit!' barked Eugynon to his assistants. 'I don't want anything important to be missing when they finally start to make love.'

The feeding operative carrying the bananas didn't know what hit him. Mimi and Leo had never moved so fast. Captain Eve ran a swift circle around the confused Mercilonian with the bedclothes from the mating platform. The operative was blinded by a duvet cover. Adams finished the job off with a swift rugby tackle that took out all six of the operative's knees.

'Stop them!' Eugynon cried when the debacle was relayed to the viewing deck.

But it was too late. Captain Melanie Eve was not top of her class at Air Fleet Training School for nothing. She could get her ship ready for take-off in just under thirty seconds, which was ten seconds less than it would take the average Mercilonian to don breathing apparatus to enter the controlled atmosphere of the human compound. Even if he used all his arms.

As Eugynon slithered into the compound, followed by his

assistant Microgynon, Captain Eve put pedal to metal and the deceptively powerful earth ship blasted through the compound's fine silicon membrane roof. The roof shattered into a snowstorm of needle-sharp splinters that pierced Eugynon's earthling encounter suit and sent him scuttling back to the door.

'Foolish Earthlings!' Eugynon wailed. 'If they won't let us help them to regenerate, they'll be extinct within a year!'

Microgynon stole the opportunity to wrap one of her tentacles around his shoulder. 'There, there . . .'

It took almost all their fuel reserves to blast out of Mercilon's magnetic atmosphere. They didn't have the fuel to get back to Florida but there was just enough to get them to Van Halen. First Officer Adams was delighted. Van Halen was a small planet in the Pleiades that had been opened as a holiday resort by the legendary Paris Hilton's great-great-grandson.

'Think you can get us there?' Captain Eve asked her navigator.

'I'll need the maps in my . . .' Adams cast his eyes downwards.

'I won't look,' Eve lied.

Adams unzipped the front of his flight suit and sought out the info download port in the flight desk.

Meanwhile, Captain Eve took off her helmet and shook out her long dark curls. She was still a little breathless from the exertions of getting the ship safely out of Mercilon's orbit. She wondered if Adams really had any idea just how close they had come to disaster.

With the vital connection made between his body and fighter ship, First Officer Adams was busy at his console, tapping in the coordinates that would get them to the party planet in the Pleiades. Captain Eve looked sidelong at him. He had a rather attractive look of concentration on his handsome, if somewhat bovine, face.

Much as Eve wished she could suppress it, a primitive human reflex tugged at something deep inside her. It was just the adrenaline. She knew that much. And yet . . .

'Hey, Adams,' said Eve, kneading his shoulders with her long, strong fingers. 'Maybe I do fancy starting a breeding programme after all.'

Carole Matthews is the internationally bestselling author of eight outstandingly successful romantic comedy novels. Her unique sense of humour has won her legions of fans and critical acclaim all over the world. In the UK her books include *Sunday Times* bestsellers *A Compromising Position*, *A Minor Indiscretion*, *The Sweetest Taboo* and *With or Without You*. *For Better, For Worse* was selected by one of America's top TV book clubs sending it straight onto the *USA Today* bestseller list. *A Minor Indiscretion* is in development in Hollywood and her books are published in eighteen countries. Carole has also presented on television and is a regular radio guest. When she's not writing novels she manages to find time to trek in the Himalayas, rollerblade in Central Park, take tea in China and snooze in her garden shed in Milton Keynes . . .

To find out more about Carole and her books go to www.carolematthews.com

TRAVELLING LIGHT

Carole Matthews

The myth is that Americans don't like to travel. Yet wherever I've been in the world, they seem to get there – in droves, usually. Though I hadn't quite expected to see one here for some reason.

'Hi,' he says, looking up from his unpacking.

I just love how casual Americans are. We Brits are so much more self-conscious, reserved, uncomfortable with etiquette. Our brothers across the pond wade in affably, without preamble. 'Hello.'

'How are ya?'

'Fine, thank you.' I edge into the small compartment from the corridor of the carriage. Our train is travelling overnight from Gaungzhou to Guilin and I've booked 'soft' class, which means that I get a lovely comfy bunk bed, a little bathroom shared between fifty of us at the end of the carriage and a pair of fluffy blue complimentary slippers from the railway company, whose name is spelled out in Chinese characters, so I can't tell you what it is. It does mean, however, that I get to share with a complete stranger and it looks like this is him. I'd sort of expected to be sharing with another woman, but then I might have learned by this stage of my travels that I should always expect the unexpected. My roommate is already wearing his complimentary slippers and his are pink and fluffy. As they're intended for tiny Chinese feet, he's cut the toes out of them and is wearing them flip-flop style. I can't help but smile at them.

'Cool, right?' He holds up his peep-toes for my inspection.

'Very.'

Discordant Chinese musak plays, *plinky-plonking* over the intercom system. There's no way of turning it off.

'Do you want to be on top or on the bottom?' If only the other men in my life had been so direct! 'I'm easy,' he says.

'I'll take the top bunk if that's okay.' I reason that if he's planning to murder me during the night, then at least I have a chance of hearing him clambering up to my eyrie. If I keep one of my boots handy I could whack him on the head before he has the chance to do his dastardly deeds. These are the considerations of a lone, female traveller in today's society.

'I'm Kane,' he says. 'Kane Freeman.'

I have to say that he doesn't look much like a murderer. He look more like one of those surf-dudes. Anyway, he's wearing surf's-up type clothes, he's got shaggy blond hair that bears some witness to sun damage, a ridiculously golden tan, a freckly but otherwise perfect nose and clear blue eyes that, if I were up for being mesmerised, would be truly mesmerising.

'Alice.' I shake his hand formally.

He grins at me. 'Alice.'

I should point out that I don't feel like an Alice. It was my mother's idea of a sober name for a well-behaved, studious child. She thought that by calling me Alice, I wouldn't climb trees or fall off my bicycle, tie fireworks to my brother's head or torture frogs. And, for a while, she was probably right. I have gone through life with a name that I feel doesn't suit me.

'Well, Ali . . .' I'm taken aback at the familiarisation of my name. No one calls me Ali. And I suddenly wonder why not. '. . . shall we crack open a beer? It's going to be a hell of a long night.'

I don't normally drink. Stephen, my fiancé, doesn't like women who drink – or smoke, or wear revealing clothes, or say '*fuck*' in public.

Kane wiggles a bottle of beer in my direction.

'Yes, please.' My feet are killing me and my shoulders are aching from the weight of my backpack. I need something to help. 'Beer would be nice.'

My companion snaps off the cap and offers it to me. 'I also have a baguette and cheese.' His eyes flash with unspoken wickedness.

I barely stop myself from gasping. In mainland China, the rarity of these jewels can't be overstated. I have been travelling across the country here for three weeks now and have lived on nothing but noodles – prawn noodles, chicken noodles, occasionally beef noodles. Noodles, noodles, noodles and more bloody noodles. Dairy products and bread are as scarce as blue diamonds. He could ask me to perform any dastardly deed he jolly well liked for a quick bite of his baguette.

'Oh, my word.'

He gives a smug smile, knowing that he has me in his grasp. Kane starts to prepare our impromptu picnic while I heave my rucksack onto the top bunk and fuss with settling in for the journey. The small compartment is spick and span. We have a lacy tablecloth on a little shelf by the window which bears a plastic rose in a silver-coloured vase. There are lacy curtains at the window, obscuring the view of the seething mass of humanity at Gaungzhou station. I have never seen anywhere as crowded in my entire life. I inspect the bedding, which is spotless, starched within an inch of its life and embroidered with the same characters as our complimentary footwear.

I put on my slippers, position my boots in case I need them as a weapon and slide down to sit next to Kane on his bed. It feels terribly intimate to be in this situation with someone I've barely been introduced to. Stephen would pass out if he could see me now.

Kane carefully slices the cheese onto the bread. I can feel myself salivating and sink my teeth in gratefully the minute he hands it over. I can't help it, but I groan with ecstasy. Unless you've been there, you will never imagine how good this tastes.

Kane shows off his set of perfect pearly whites. 'Good, *huh*?'

'*Mmm*. Marvellous.'

The train whistle blows and we rattle out of the station, out of the town, leaving the squash of people behind, and head into the countryside.

'So?' he mutters through his bread. 'You're travelling alone?'

I like men who are keen-eyed and sharp witted. 'Yes.' It pains me to have to pause in my eating. 'I'm getting married in a few weeks.' I want him to be absolutely clear from the beginning that I'm not available. I would flash my gorgeous engagement ring – which is a whopper – but I left it at home in case I got mugged. 'This is my last chance to travel alone.'

Kane frowns. 'Should you want to travel alone if you're getting hitched?'

He isn't the first person to voice this concern. My parents were particularly vocal. As was Stephen.

'I just needed to get away,' I say. 'It was all getting too much. I had to escape. You know how it is.'

'No,' he says. 'I've never gotten close.'

'Oh,' I give a dismissive wave of my hands. 'There are so many things to organize. It's hell.'

'So why are you doing it?'

My French bread nearly falls out of my mouth. Why *am* I doing it? 'My fiancé. Stephen. We've been together for years. Many *happy* years. He felt it was time we settled down.'

'So you're here on a Chinese train with a stranger and he's at home ordering bridal corsages?'

I give a carefree laugh. 'You make it sound a lot worse than it is.'

Kane contemplates that while he chews. 'He must be an understanding man.'

'He's very . . . understanding.' Actually, I'm not sure that Stephen understands me at all.

Kane says nothing. We eat in silence. Try as I might, I can't recapture the joy of my cheese again.

'What about you?'

Kane shrugs. 'I like to see the world. I have no ties, no commitments, no permanent base. I go wherever the wind blows me.'

I can't even begin to imagine what that must feel like. My life is layer-upon-layer of commitment, confinement, duty. I live by timetables, schedules, appointments, mortgage payments. Doesn't everyone?

We finish our meal and the grinning guard comes and checks our tickets and gives us a thermos of hot water for tea. I reciprocate for the bread and cheese by supplying tea bags.

'Do you work?' Kane asks as he examines his brew suspiciously. Quite frankly, most Americans just don't understand the concept of decent tea so I don't wait for his approval.

'I did. As a radio producer.' I had to resign from my job to take this trip, as my employers at Let the Good Times Roll Radio also failed to 'understand' my need to get away – particularly when I've already got two weeks in the Bahamas booked as a honeymoon. Who could possibly want more than that? And yet I do. Is that greedy? Does it make me a bad person? 'I'm taking some time out.' Not necessarily voluntarily. 'I'll look for something else when all the fuss from the wedding has died down.'

'You're using a lot of negative images with reference to your forthcoming nuptials,' Kane observes.

'That sounds terribly Californian, if you don't mind my saying,' I observe back.

He smiles. 'I am from California. I'm allowed.'

At ten o'clock it's lights out on the train, which reminds me of my time at boarding school. The sudden plunge into darkness curtails our conversation and we scrabble to our bunks, clicking on the faint nightlights above our heads. I decide to stay clothed for modesty's sake, but Kane has no such inhibitions. He's wearing battered, baggy shorts and a sleeveless t-shirt which bears the faded remains of a logo, now too pale to discern. I'm used to a man who favours pressed chinos and striped shirts and who goes into the bathroom to change. In a moment, Kane is stripped down to his boxer shorts. He's clearly comfortable with his body and I suspect if I had a body like that, I would be too. I know that I should look away, but I'm afraid to say I can't. I just can't. He has a tattoo of a dragon high on the broad sweep of his shoulder. I wonder where he had it done and if it hurt him and I find myself thinking that I'd like to trace the outline with my finger.

He turns and smiles up at me. I do hope he's not a mind reader. 'Sleep tight,' he says and hops into the bunk below me.

I do no such thing. I lie awake looking at the air vent in the ceiling, occasionally peeping out of the lace curtain to the blackness of the paddy fields beyond and watching as, even through the dark hours, we stop at brightly-lit stations to let passengers come and go.

The train runs minute-perfect. Stephen would like that part of it. Stephen likes things to be regular. His habits, his meals, his bowels. Sorry, that's not nice of me. You don't need to know that. Even though it's true.

Stephen, on the other hand, wouldn't like the crowds, the smells, the squatty loos – apologies, back to toilet preferences again – the food, the heat, the pollution, the whole damn foreignness of the place. We'll be taking our holidays in the Caribbean from now on, with maybe the odd deviation to the Cote d'Azur. We'll stay in five-star hotels, with fluffy towels and spa facilities – somewhere we don't have to mix too closely with the locals. We won't even have to trouble ourselves to go to the bar for a drink, it will be brought to us on a tray at our sun-loungers by a smiling waiter. Is this what I want?

I close my eyes and try not to think of anything connected with the wedding. Have you ever felt like everything was crowding in on you? My whole world was becoming smaller and smaller, until I felt like my namesake after she'd drunk the potion and had shrunk to barely ten inches high. I felt I just didn't matter anymore, that I had become too tiny to be of consequence. My days were taken up with invitations and flowers and bell-ringers and wedding cars and who the hell was going to sit next to who? Everyone gets pre-wedding nerves, I was told – time after time. Is that all it is, this nagging feeling? I screw my eyes tighter shut but still sleep eludes me. The stations, towns, miles flash by. I hear the sound of my neighbour's soft snoring from the bunk below. Kane doesn't look like the sort of man who worries if he misses a poo.

Bang on time, the train pulls into Guilin station just after dawn. Kane and I haven't said much to each other this morning. Kane, because he's only just woken up after sleeping like a bear – his words, not mine. Me, because I'm not sure what I want to say.

We pack our rucksacks, bumping into each other in the tiny space as we prepare to leave the train. The doors open and the slow shuffle towards the exit starts. Kane and I join it.

'Thanks for the bread and cheese,' I say. 'It's been nice . . .'

'Where are you heading for?' Kane asks.

'Yangshuo.'

'I've been there before,' he informs me. 'It's a blast. I know a great hotel. Want to hang out together?'

I nod, mainly because my brain is urging my mouth to say no.

The Fawlty Towers hotel in Yangshuo is, indeed a great place. It has showers complete with hot water and clean sheets. And 'hanging out together' also seems to involve sharing a room. Single beds. I'm not that reckless. After spending a night together it seemed churlish to refuse. And it will help keep down the costs. I don't think I'll mention it to Stephen though. It's another thing he wouldn't understand.

Kane rents bicycles with dodgy brakes and we head out into the countryside, weaving our way through narrow valleys and straggly villages whose houses are still pasted with red and gold new year banners to bring good luck to those inside. Weather-worn mountains moulded by the rain into sugarloaf shapes tower over us. I can't remember when I was last on a bike and I'd forgotten how great the wind in your hair feels as it lifts the strands away from your neck to kiss the humid dampness away. We climb Moon Hill, Kane tugging me up the steep slope by the hand, until we look over the landscape that spawned a thousand paintings – soft, misty mountains, meandering rivers, the pink blush of cherry blossom. I return to Yangshuo feeling achy and strangely liberated – like a dog who's dared to stick its head out of a car window for the first time.

In the Hard Luck Internet Café, I pick up an email from Stephen. 'Hello Alice – the caterers have suggested these canapés.' There is a list of a dozen nibbly-bits, all of which sound perfectly acceptable. 'Shall I give them the go ahead? Stephen.'

I stare at a the picture of Bruce Lee on the wall and wonder if you should be addressing your future wife 'Hello Alice' – particularly when she's been away for nearly three weeks. Shouldn't the word 'love' appear in there somewhere? Perhaps Stephen is beginning to wonder why his future wife has been away for nearly three weeks. There has been a distinct lack of I'm-missing-you type emails. But then Stephen is very reserved with his emotions. It's one of the things I love about him. Really, it is. I've never been one for gushy stuff.

I type: 'Dear Stephen. Canapés sound fine.' And then in a rush of guilt or something, 'missing you. Love Alice.'

As I head back to the hotel, I see Kane sitting outside the Planet China restaurant drinking green tea and Yanjing beer with his feet up on a chair. I've never seen anyone look so laid-back. My stomach lurches when I approach him and it might not be due to the fact I'm back on the noodle diet. How old is Kane, I wonder? The same age as me? Not quite thirty. He is so loose and carefree with his life that it makes me feel older than time itself. I plonk myself down next to him and hear myself sigh wearily.

'You look stressed.'

'I am.'

'Wedding arrangements not going to plan?' Kane grins. I'm sure he doesn't believe that this wedding is ever going to go ahead.

'I've just agreed the canapés,' I say crisply. 'They're going to be wonderful.'

'Try this.' He hands me a cigarette.

'I didn't know you smoked.' But then there's a lot I don't know about Kane, even though I'm sharing a hotel room with him. I have no idea why I'm taking this as I don't smoke either. Stephen doesn't like women who . . . oh, you get the gist.

'It's herbal,' he says. 'It will relax you.'

I drag deeply on the cigarette and then the smell hits me. 'Oh good grief,' I say. 'Do you know what this is?'

Kane grins at me.

'Of course you do,' I take another tentative puff. I'm not a natural law-breaker. 'Is this legal here?' I suspect not. It's making me even less relaxed than I was. I can't do drugs, not even soft ones. Quickly, I hand it back. 'I could end up in prison for twenty-five years.'

Kane fixes me with a wily stare. 'Isn't that where you're headed anyway?'

'I need a drink.' In what sounds to me like passable Mandarin, Kane orders me a steaming glass of Jasmine tea and some rough Chinese vodka. I pick my way through the beautiful white blooms, inhaling the fragrance as I sip the tea, spoiling it with the raw cut of the alcohol as I chase it with swigs of vodka. I was going to have jasmine in my wedding bouquet, but now it will always remind me of Kane. And that might not be a good thing.

From Yangshuo we take a plane to Chengdu to see the giant pandas and I don't want you to read too much into this, but we're already acting like an old married couple. I can't believe how easily I've fallen into step with this man. At the airport Kane looks after the passports while I go and top up on 'western' snacks – crisps and boiled sweets rather than scorpions on sticks.

The next morning, we join the old grannies in the park doing tai chi, causing great hilarity as we heave our bulky frames alongside the delicate, bird-like movements of the elderly Chinese ladies. Kane causes a particular stir. He laughs as they cluck round him like mother hens and come to touch his spiky blond hair and his bulging biceps, which makes me flush, as it's something I've considered doing myself. The old men, some in ageing Maoist uniforms, promenade proudly with their song-birds in cages and a feeling of sadness and oppression settles over me. Without speaking, Kane takes my hand and squeezes. I can feel the edge of my engagement ring cutting into my finger even though I'm not wearing it, but I don't try to pull away.

Kane keeps holding my hand while we travel further into the country to visit the Terracotta Army at Xian. Beautiful, untouchable soldiers, frozen in time, unable to move forward. I cry at the sheer spectacle of it and at other things that I can't even begin to voice. He's still holding it a week later when we hike up to the mist-shrouded peak of Emei Shan and book a simple room in the extraordinary peace of a Buddhist monastery that looks like something out of a film set.

We have dinner in a local café with no windows and a tarpaulin roof, lit only by smoky kerosene lamps, the sound of monkeys chattering in the trees high above us. A group of local men play mahjong boisterously in the corner, each tile slapped down with a challenge and hotly contested. A scraggy cat sits hopefully at my feet. We're the only diners and the waif-like Chinese owner brings us dish after dish of succulent, stir-fried vegetables – aubergine, spring greens, beansprouts, water chestnuts.

Kane has been on the internet at the monastery. It makes you realise that there's nowhere in the world that can truly be classed as remote anymore. It also makes me realise that our time together is coming to an end. He's planning another leg of this trip which will eventually take him round the world. I had always dreamed of travelling the world and I feel a pang of envy that he'll be continuing the rest of his journey without me. He says the surf is good in Australia right now and that he'll probably head out that way. See? I knew my assessment of him was right all along. Do surfers attract groupies? I think they do. And I wonder will he hook up with someone else as easily? Someone less tied, less uptight, less duty-bound.

Kane is adept with his chopsticks, while I still handle them

338

like knitting needles. Give me a plate of chow mein and I could run you up a sweater, no problem. We finish our meal and bask in the warm night air with cups of jasmine tea. He plucks at the plaited friendship bracelet on his wrist and not for the first time, I contemplate when and how he acquired it. We both look so terribly mellow in this half-light and I wish I could capture this moment forever. Me and Kane cocooned in our own microcosm.

His fingers wander across the table and find mine. 'Just in case you were wondering,' he says gently. 'This brother-sister thing we're doing is taking its toll on me.'

I don't know what to say, so I say nothing.

Kane sighs, his eyes searching mine. 'What I really want is to make love to you.'

'Oh,' I say. 'OK.'

He looks at me for confirmation and I nod. 'Let's go.'

Kane wraps his arms around me and holds me tightly as we pay the bill and hurry back to the shelter of the monastery. Is it a sin to make love in a monastery? I don't know. I don't want to know. I'm too Catholic by half. I might burn in hell for this at some later stage, but I think it will be worth it. Can something so beautiful be punishable by fire and brimstone? I hope the monks don't mind – I wouldn't like to offend anyone. As I hold onto Kane in the dark, I don't consider that it might be a sin against Stephen. I don't consider anything but the curve of his spine, the strength of his arms and the look of love on his face. And it takes me by surprise, as no one has looked at me with such passion for a long, long time.

We take another overnight train to Beijing, to the Forbidden City. How appropriate. This time we squeeze together in one bunk, making love to the rhythm of the rattling rails, falling asleep in each other's arms.

The pollution in Beijing is worse in the spring, when the sands from the Gobi desert blend with the exhaust fumes of a million ozone-unfriendly cars. The mixture stings your eyes, strips your throat and makes it hard to see too far ahead. A grey veil blocks out the sun which tries hard to break through, but is generally thwarted.

When in China you must do as the Chinese do and we hire sit-up-and-beg bikes again to cycle through the jammed streets to the vast expanse of Tiananmen Square – the symbol of freedom to an oppressed world. We join the throng of Chinese tourists flying kites and are royally ripped off as we buy flimsy paper butterflies from a canny, bow-legged vendor. He could feed his family for a week on what we pay him for a moment's fleeting pleasure, but I begrudge him nothing as our lives are so easy compared with his. It makes me appreciate that I have very little to complain about.

We laugh as we run through the square, trailing our kites behind us, watching them as they duck and dive, playing with the erratic wind. But even then, I notice that my kite is not as exuberant in its swoops and soars as Kane's. It's more hesitant, fearful and it's tearing easily. I trail after him while he takes the lead, clearing a route through the crowd, leaving me to follow behind. And then he holds me close and I forget everything. I forget to hold tightly to my kite and it floats away, bobbing on the air, reaching for the hidden sun until it's quite out of sight. Free.

'I love you,' Kane says. But I watch my kite fly away from me.

Email from Stephen. 'Hello Alice – have ordered cars. Think you'll like them. Doctor and Mrs Smythe have said no. Shame. Missing you too. Stephen.' Is it a shame that two people who I don't even know aren't coming to my wedding? Do I really care what car will take me there? I stare at the screen, but can't make my fingers type a reply. Now what do I do?

That night we lie on the bed in our horrible Western-style hotel which has matching bedspreads and curtains, and shower gel and shampoo in tiny identical bottles. Already I can feel my other life calling me.

'Have you told him?' Kane asks.

'No,' I say.

'You can't go back,' my lover states. 'You know you can't.'

But I can. And I will. I can't explain this to Kane, but I love Stephen because he's anchored in reality. He understands about pensions, for heaven's sake. He polishes his shoes. He has chosen the wedding limousines. He may not make love to me as if it is the last thing he will ever do in his life. He may not chase life with an insatiable, unquenchable thirst. But Stephen is safe and solid and secure. We'll grow old together. We'll have a joint bank account. I will never feel the same about anyone in my entire life as I do about Kane – never. Not even Stephen. Kane is the sun, the moon and the stars. He is all the things I'm not, but that I would want to be. In a different life. I have never loved anyone more or as hopelessly. But Kane is as flighty as the paper butterfly kites, answering every tug of the breeze. How can you base a future, a whole lifetime, on something as unreliable as that? What would we do? Spend our lives wandering the earth, hand-in-hand, rucksacks slung on backs? Or would there come a time when I'd want to settle down, to pin the butterfly to the earth, stamp on it, crush it flat? Would I eventually become Kane's Stephen?

We make love and, this time, I feel that it *is* the last thing that I will ever do in my life. Every nerve, fibre, tissue, cell of my body zings with the prospect of life. Beneath him I lose myself, my reason, my mind. I'm part of Kane and he'll always be a part of me. But this excitement would die, wouldn't it? Could we always maintain this intensity, this intimacy? Isn't it better to have loved so hard and so briefly than to watch it sink and vanish from view like the setting sun?

I wake up and reach for Kane, but he's gone. The bed beside me is empty. There's nothing left of my lover but a crumpled imprint in the sheets. I pad to the bathroom and take a shower, concentrating on the chipped tiles so that I won't feel that my heart is having to force itself to keep beating. You can taste devastation – did you know that? I didn't until now. It coats your teeth, tongue and throat and no amount of spearmint mouthwash will get rid of it.

I decide to check out of the hotel, even though my home-ward flight isn't until tomorrow. I can't stay here alone. Not now. Slowly, methodically, I pack up my things and take the lift down to reception where I queue for an interminable amount of time behind a party of jocular Americans to pay my bill. I told you. They get everywhere. Inside your undies, inside your heart, inside your soul. Eventually, I reach the desk and hand over my credit card and my key. In return I get a receipt and a business card. The receptionist taps it.

'It was left for you,' he says.

I flip it over and my broken heart flips too. Somehow its jagged edges mesh back together. There's a caricature of a scruffy surfer and in big, bold type – Barney's Surf Shack, Bondi Beach. Kane has scribbled: *I'll wait there every day for two weeks.*

But I don't think he'll need to. I know now that there'll be no wedding. No hymns. No white dress. No bridesmaids. Not now. And maybe not ever. But I know that it's the right thing to do. I only hope that Stephen will understand. He deserves more. I shouldn't spend my life with someone I can live with; I should be with someone I can't live without. Wherever that may take me. My pension fund will just have to wait.

I hail a taxi and jump inside. I might just make it.

'Beijing Airport!' I say. 'As quick as you can!' My word, I've always wanted to say that! It doesn't matter that the driver can't even speak English. He must sense my haste as he careens out into the six lanes of traffic, horn blaring. I feel as if I'm swimming in champagne, bubbles rising inside me.

We pull up outside the terminal building and I race inside. There, standing by the check-in desk is an unmistakable figure. His rucksack is over his shoulder. He's head and shoulders above everyone else. One blond mop above a sea of black.

I run towards him as fast as I can. 'Kane!'

He turns. And when he sees me he smiles.

Anna Maxted is a freelance journalist and the author of the smash international bestsellers *Getting Over It, Running in Heels, Behaving Like Adults* and *Being Committed*. She lives in London with her husband, author Phil Robinson, and their two sons.

THE MARRYING KIND

Anna Maxted

For a short time, Michelle was a hippie. This aberration occurred during college. She wore gypsy skirts, skim-read left wing newspapers, and ate a lot of vegetarian food. Suddenly, it wasn't enough for her to be merely 'in love'. This limp inferior emotion had to be upgraded to 'loved-up'. A reference to ecstasy, which I found affected and irritating. Worse, she was suddenly *kooky*. 'Oh! I'm so ditsy!' was the message, even though her sharp eyes assessed you, black as currants. She proclaimed the wonders of alternative health.

I have to tell you, Michelle couldn't fool me. I'm no expert, but the deal on hippies is that they're *caring*. The entire point of them is that they boo war, they don't overspend on shoes, and they would eat dirt rather than use a Flash Wipe in their kitchen. A Flash Wipe (a disposable cloth, infused with a powerful bouquet of poisonous chemicals, to clean household surfaces, and sold, I'm ashamed to say, in packs of fifty) is just typical of this selfish, convenience, fast-food age. And Michelle *loved* Flash Wipes. So much more hygienic than an old germ-ridden rag.

Happily, the pose ended the minute she returned from college to her friends in North West London.

'Michelle!' said Helen. 'Where are your . . . clothes?'

Boom, that was it. Helen Bradshaw – less a fashionista than a fashion-missed-her, despite working for a womens' magazine – criticising *her* sense of style. It was important to Michelle to feel superior to Helen. It was how their friendship had survived. Embracing the New Age philosophy (peace, love, whales, *er*, couscous) was another excuse for Michelle to look down on Helen. Helen was a capitalist (her pay at *Girltime* was dreadful, her crime was she wanted to earn more), and she blew what little cash she had on six-inch heels instead of worthy causes, such as dolphins. But it was impossible, Michelle realised, to look down on someone when they were attired normally and you were wearing dungarees. Jesus, thought Michelle, I look like a freakin' baby.

I can't tell you what a relief it was for Michelle to revert to type (intensive grooming, fake leopardskin tops, big shiny car, Jackie Collins novels, spending money, money, money on little old *moi*). But it's only fair to explain why the ill-starred foray into floor cushions and plates of beans had occurred at all.

Men.

All Michelle had ever wanted, from the time she was a little girl, was to get married. Oh, I know. So very uncool. But true.

And, at college, even though it was 1991, it was considered – I do loathe this phrase – *right on* to be a hippie. (I think the only alternative was to be a young Margaret Thatcher, and Michelle wasn't interested in posh boys. She knew she wasn't their type. They'd only waste her time.

Meanwhile, she noted that both Aaron Levitt and Jonathan Kaplan had stopped shaving and said 'basically' a lot.)

The hippie pose worked at first.

Men gazed at her while she talked. They seemed *interested*. Though if in her as a person, or as a body she wasn't sure. Occasionally, it turned out, neither.

The man with whom Michelle professed herself to be 'loved up' was an astrologer named Josh. He had long shiny black hair (Michelle had a suspicion he washed it in lashings of hot water and luxury shampoo every other day, but this was denied) and asked Michelle her birthdate. She told him and he whispered, 'Now I can find out all about you. It's like you've given me the key to your house.'

Michelle didn't believe in all that shit, but found it pleasing that Josh wanted to find out all about her. Hence, the loved-up nonsense. Sadly, the day after they kissed, they met for lunch, and Michelle said to Josh, 'So, what have you been doing this morning?' Forty minutes later, he finished telling her. Then he sat back, sighed, and asked, 'Hmm. And what *else* have I been doing?' The louse didn't even try to put his hand up her skirt.

Michelle left college as she began it: single, and without a degree.

I'm sure you're judging her. Because, despite the fact that any sane person would prefer to live a life rich in love and affection – as opposed to one poor and starved of it – if a woman professes a desire to marry, she is regarded as somehow weak and pathetic. At least, she is in Britain. Strangely, if you live with a 'partner', that's okay. Why, only last week I found myself at a table with three authors, all of us cosily discussing our children. It emerged that they all lived with their 'partners'.

'Marriage!' scoffed one. 'I don't understand why anyone does that anymore!'

Another author thought to check, belatedly, if I was married. I imparted the bad news. And Big Mouth – too stupid to understand that marriage is not a wretched constant, but as good or bad as those within it – looked at me as if *I'd* made the faux pas.

Huf. So for obvious reasons, I'm a little touchy about people judging Michelle for wanting to marry.

You have to understand that from the second that she was born, and her mother murmured, 'My beautiful princess,' Michelle was expected to marry. In her parents' circles, it was what people did. And they were happy. If they *must* they had affairs, but had them discreetly. That way, no one got hurt. At least, not in public. Living together – note, these are the opinions of Mr and Mrs Goldblatt, not me, whatever works for you I say – living together was a nonsense, a nothing, there was no point to it. You lived with a man if you were a cheap girl and he was just using you for sex. (Here, I beg the feeble excuse, 'It's their generation'.)

I'm aware there are other options. There are.

One

Gayness. Fab as it is, homosexuality never occurred to Michelle, and thank goodness because life's tough enough without having to come out to your parents when they're Lewis and Maureen Goldblatt.

Two

Singledom. Michelle was forced to endure singledom in short bursts and she didn't love it. She had no plans to embrace it long term. She wanted a man to embrace, thanks.

You won't be surprised to hear that once Michelle stopped eating pulses and got a manicure, her wish was soon granted. She met Sammy. If I were being snide, I wouldn't totally define Sammy as a man. I happen to be quite close to Michelle's friend Helen Bradshaw, and I know that poor Helen spent a lifetime in dog years listening to Michelle whine about Sammy. Privately, Helen described Sammy as a 'namby-pamby bore'. If that sounds harsh, I promise you that Michelle described him in public as far worse. That boy wouldn't cut his hair without permission from Mummy. They ate at Mummy's on Friday nights where she decently refrained from cutting up her son's food for him. No girlfriend needs an opponent like *that*.

And yet, Michelle dated Sammy for over five years. Admittedly, dating Sammy had compensations for Michelle. She could do whatever the hell she liked. Her parents approved. Everyone presumed it would 'end in marriage.' (A dubious phrase if ever there was one). Also, Michelle liked to be the main attraction. She always made an entrance at parties, nails a-sparkle, cheeks red with blush, hair coiffed and teased till it *pouffed* just so, diamante black top hugging her food-deprived figure, beaming, gleaming, husking, 'Hello, sweetheart!' to people whose names she didn't know.

Sammy would arrive a second or two later, dragging his feet, hands deep in his pockets, eyes half closed, meekly resigned to his inferior status.

He followed her everywhere, and yet he was barely there. He even spoke like it didn't matter. His voice was quiet and nasal. I'd call it a drawl except 'drawl' is too go-getting for Sammy. I'd prefer to say, 'he talked very slowly'. Truth was, Sammy didn't have to go-get. He'd already got. His father was known in certain circles as The Big Bagel. Not because he was round and doughy with a hole where his heart should be – why do we always assume the sinister? – but because he was a sizeable part of the New York bagel business. And as he said at least three times a year, he planned on handing his entire bagel empire to Sammy.

In this, The Big Bagel might have been rash, but he wasn't stupid. He invited Sammy to come to New York, to learn about the business. There would be no trouble obtaining a Green Card. Anyone would have leapt at the chance. Sammy barely budged off the sofa. That boy certainly preferred to watch life from the side of the pool rather than jump in. He would have happily stayed in his ugly house in Temple Fortune, an indifferent London suburb, watching as much reality television as he could cram in between bed and work (telesales), letting a wife and a family come to him, allowing the world to rough and tumble and grow around him until he reached an untenable age and quietly left it.

However, Michelle was present – overseeing a new cleaner – when The Big Bagel rang, and overheard the conversation. To be honest, she heard the conversation as she had picked up the phone in the bedroom. (Sammy probably thought the click was wax in his ear.)

'OH My God, we're GOING TO NEW YORK!' she screamed, and threw her arms around him.

Sammy, used to taking the path of least resistance, let Michelle book the tickets on his credit card. Possibly, they had sex that night. Michelle – I trust you'll be discreet – wasn't mad on sex. She disliked men grabbing at her hair. Eleven lovers and (until Sammy, who'd been taught not to grab) not one exception. Also, she hated sweating off her make-up. She had this nasty sensation of the chemicals seeping into her pores, of bouncing up and down with a face like a melting clown. She always worked out in the gym bare-faced. But in the bedroom, there was scant regard for health or hygiene.

Michelle had a ball in New York. She loved the place, she loved the people. They weren't afraid to speak up. They had *energy*. There was so much to do and the shopping was glorious! Unlike in stodgy, whey-faced London, no one in New York called you 'boring' for going to the gym. Jesus, you could work out in a freakin' shop window, that was how progressive they were! And the food! So much choice in what not to eat!

Sammy loathed New York. He hated change. He had a horror of exploration. He didn't like speaking to people he hadn't known for at least a year. In London, people didn't expect him to speak because his girlfriend spoke for him. In London, people were used to Sammy. They didn't care that he had a dead-end job, it made them feel better about their own meandering career paths. They knew who his father was, they appreciated that Sammy never talked about him – in London we're strange like that, we don't like to be graphically reminded that our friends are richer than us, or will be.

Well. The good people of New York were agog at Sammy. The guy had, like, *nothing* to say for himself! His father was The BB, he didn't give a damn! What the hell was his problem? Didn't he want to succeed? It was all there, laid

351

out for him! Ah, but Michelle! Michelle was *so great*! What a fun girl! Why was she wasting her time with him?

Sammy stuck it out on the Upper East Side for just over two years. Then he fled back home to Mummy, who could at last stop sulking. Truth was, Sammy would always feel he was a disappointment to his father – he wasn't brainy, he wasn't sporty, he wasn't a businessman. And perhaps his father knew that he would always be a disappointment to Sammy for having divorced Sammy's mother. Michelle could hardly reside in The Big Bagel's rent-free apartment without Sammy so, furious and miserable, she followed him home. And then, shock, horror, she dumped him.

Incredible!

I was delighted for her. But from the way her family reacted, you'd have thought she'd turned down the king of England. I'll pause here to say what a pity that was. For Michelle, now twenty-six (talk about ancient) had not wanted to dump Sammy. She had wanted to marry him very much. Not because she loved him, alas. But because her little clique of friends – not Helen, but Helen was different – were all engaged, or just married. Worse, her younger sister, aged twenty-three, lived in a big white house in Pinner, and she and her husband (a doctor) were expecting their first freakin' baby.

Being single made Michelle look like a loser. She knew they all talked about her, pitied her. She was desperate to be part of the pack again, to discuss conservatory furniture, What My Husband Bought Me, child-friendly areas with good schools. Despite that, Michelle couldn't think of much worse than being tied to a small person. When they went to Pizza Express for their girls' nights out, Michelle ordered a salad. All the rest tore into Four Cheese This and Pepperoni

That, getting grease on their wedding rings, because, it seemed to Michelle, they were loved unconditionally and no longer had to worry about growing grossly obese and having to be rolled down stairs.

(It didn't occur to Michelle that even if her married friends weren't loved unconditionally, their husbands would think twice about divorce, as they were sensible men who did not wish to live in wretched penury for the rest of their days.)

So. For Michelle it was a brave decision. It would have been nice, therefore, if her parents had appreciated this and supported her. One would like to assume they wanted their eldest daughter to be happy. And yet they made their disapproval unpleasantly plain. Now. To a reasonable soul, the explanation Michelle provided was unassailable: 'Sammy bores me rigid – I can't stand to be in the same room as him, and if he kisses me in that gross, slobbery way of his, I get this, like, lurch of revulsion'. Really. Who could argue with that? You'd have to be some kind of debating champion.

Lewis and Maureen excelled at bridge, which I hardly feel qualifies. And yet, they saw fit to object. They even dragged Jemma (she of the white house and banker husband) into the fray. The poor girl – not for her, the pregnant bloom – she had haemorrhoids and looked like a beach ball. It was hardly fair to force her to 'talk sense' into Michelle. The sisters had never been close. The final insult was that Jemma's normally miniscule bosom had temporarily outswelled Michelle's. There was a feeble attempt to persuade Michelle that the lurch of revulsion might actually be a lurch of excitement. Then Jemma drove home in her Freelander in tears.

So Lewis and Maureen went on the offensive. Very offensive. A lot of piffle about being sensible. Good prospects. A nice boy. At your age. Settling down. Look at your sister.

Too choosy. On the property ladder. Get a reputation. Other things to consider besides *romance*. Too late. Grandchildren. Even Roberta and Leon's daughter. Did well for herself. People keep asking. *People keep asking!!* Pardon, but I insist on drawing your attention to that one. Of all the cheek! Call themselves parents?! So what if people keep asking? Let them ask! Not that it's any of their goddamn business!

Forgive me. I just find it insufferable that Lewis and Maureen were less bothered about Michelle's life than the prying opinions of their neighbours. Why, if this wasn't a free country, they'd have bullied her up the aisle to spend the rest of her days with a man who repulsed her, just so that when Mrs Lily Frosh up the road enquired after their daughter, they'd be able to provide an answer that they felt didn't imply failure on their part, that wouldn't have her tutting and shaking her head and whispering to Irene Frankel in synogogue, who would then pass it on up the row to Nina Koffler (the poor rabbi, he might as well have read the sermon to himself) until the whole congregation was aflame with the shocking news that the Goldblatt's eldest girl *still* couldn't find a nice Jewish boy, and what *would* become of her . . . ?

She met Marcus. Ha.

(So as you know, I sighed just then but it didn't translate to the page). The reason is . . . well. I have to confess. Michelle and Marcus figured in a previous tale I wrote about Helen, and I'm afraid I wasn't too kind to Michelle. She appeared to be that spiteful, infuriating friend – most women have at least one – who a girl hangs on to for no decipher-able reason other than masochism. Helen's father died and Michelle didn't call or come to the funeral. When she finally deigned to ring, it was to invite Helen to her birthday 'boogie'.

When Helen confronted her about her silence/absence, Michelle told her, frostily, that 'women in my family don't attend funerals'. As Helen rightly observed, this would cause a problem when one of them snuffed it.

Nor did Michelle distinguish herself throughout the rest of the book. Indeed, from Helen's viewpoint, it seemed that the prime reason Michelle got together with Marcus was to spite her. Oh boy, is that a bad reason to get together with any man. (Helen's nine year crush on Marcus, her landlord and flatmate, had recently ended in an excruciatingly awful one-night stand, the consequence of which was mutual loathing). Helen – who in her defence *was* in the clutch of grief, even if she didn't realise it – was pretty scathing about Michelle from start to finish. At the time, I endorsed every word.

But, gosh. I guess that back then I didn't know the details of Michelle's background and upbringing. (A shocking admission from an author, please keep that information from my publisher). Now that I do, I feel I understand her better, I even like her. Feel a little sorry for her. Oh, but she'd hate that. A fine attribute in a person, don't you think? Self-pity in others is so life sapping. You have to invent a million lies to tell them and it draws the energy out of you like an all-day wedding. Michelle had pride. I think the whinging about Sammy owed a lot to the fact that Michelle liked to talk about herself.

Ah, well. Back to Marcus. What can I tell you? He was different from Sammy. Certainly, he was more suited to Michelle, which was good. Marcus was a fitness instructor, ambitious, fit, good body. (His penis was kinda small, so he was lucky that Michelle was no *Sex and the City* Samantha. Michelle was more concerned with the size of his wallet.) Not, I hasten to add, that Michelle was a moneygrabber. The last thing I want to do is to reinforce a racist stereotype. For one thing, my mother would kill me. My old colleagues on the *Jewish Chronicle* wouldn't be too impressed either.

No. Michelle was unpretentious and she didn't see the moral good in pointless struggle. Let's not forget, she'd been schlepping Sammy around for the greater part of a decade, and his idea of a good time was a takeaway eaten on a sofa in front of *Jay and Silent Bob*. She wanted to be treated nicely. She liked luxury, and who doesn't? And it wasn't as if she didn't plan to work herself. She had taken a course and hoped to set up as a freelance beautician. It was a pleasure to find Marcus, who took care of his appearance, liked to be seen at the finest restaurants (he was yet to be caught *eating* in one) and whose disposable income was at her disposal.

Thus far, they were perfect for each other. I have to admit that Michelle did enjoy needling Helen. Let's put it down to Michelle's own insecurity. Remember, her parents were not the sort we all hanker after – proud and loving, no matter what kind of a beast you are. You can imagine that when she was little, they whipped away their approval whenever she was wilful, ie, disagreed with them. It must have shaken her confidence.

And if your self-opinion is a little wobbly, you're more inclined to care what other people think. Michelle needed Helen to be jealous of her 'catch', and thus reinforce her hope that Marcus was a man worth pinching. (Not that Helen had any real claim, bar having trodden in that muddy puddle before Michelle put her foot in it, so to speak).

Michelle was happy. She enjoyed showing Marcus off to all her married Pinner friends, whose own men were already developing paunches – watching football instead of playing it, eating two pepperoni pizzas where their wives confined themselves to merely one – and they admired his triangular torso, despite themselves. (Then they sped home and blew up in a rage at their husbands for eating chocolate. A sweet tooth, it was so . . . unmanly, and when was the last time you ran on a treadmill?) By a quirk of fate, Marcus was Jewish, so at last her parents gave Michelle some peace, and Rabbi Markovitch was finally able to make himself heard in synogogue.

And how did Marcus feel about our lovely Michelle? Good news. He was smitten. This was unusual because Marcus tended to wander from woman to woman rather like a dog wanders from tree to tree. An exciting new scent would catch his attention and he'd amble off. *Sorry!*

Marcus got away with this impudent habit because as well as being pleasing to the eye, he wasn't a man who had problems talking. He was witty, acid, and he loved to gossip, particularly about the celebrity clients at his health club. Marcus gave a fine impression of a man who was, as they say, in the loop. And in this cynical, media-savvy age, where we no longer believe what we avidly read in the papers, a lot of women found it thrilling to have a boyfriend who literally touched the stars. At first. Eventually, they tired of going out with a big girly gossip who had the conversational habits of a fishwife. So, Marcus's fickle nature suited both parties.

As for Marcus, he surprised himself at how much he let Michelle get away with. But he was in love. Michelle made him feel *fabulous*. She never made disparaging remarks about his private parts – unlike some women. She never tired of discussing famous people. Secretly, Michelle found his loquaciousness an acquired taste (she was accustomed to autocracy in dialogue), but she adjusted. Then she discovered its advantages. As a woman whose dreams were frequently populated by variations on Ben Stiller, Liza Minelli, Kate Moss, and Rob Lowe (nothing kinky, all they ever did was have intimate chats with the dreamer) Michelle was in her element with Marcus.

She was devastated, *devastated* I tell you, when J-Lo and Ben 'postponed' their wedding. 'But,' she wailed to Marcus, 'they were really in love!' Helen's spoilsport friend Tina tried to tell her it was a publicity ploy with tax breaks but Michelle wouldn't hear of it.

Every Hollywood split, Michelle felt in her heart. She was surprised and a little disappointed in Harrison Ford when he left his wife after all those years to shack up with Ally McBeal. She still bore a grudge against Jennifer Aniston (Brad and Gwyneth were so good together, why couldn't he see that?). Demi and Bruce, the break-up? Shattering. But she was holding out for a reconciliation, their relationship was so cordial now. And she couldn't *quite* warm to Cruise & Cruz. The Tom and Nicole arrangement had been so cosy. She couldn't imagine either one asking for a divorce. Did Tom stamp into the bedroom and shout it, '*I wanna DIVOOOORRRCE!*' or was it a subdued announcement, sitting down, over coffee, '*Look. I think we should . . .*' ?

Marcus understood that these people were the landscape of Michelle's emotional life, that she was easily as close to them as to her blood relatives. Closer, probably. And that was fine by him, because he was pretty pally with them too. It gave them a warm feeling to see in their precious *Hello!* magazine that Steven had invited Gwyneth to his son's barmitzvah. Bet Jennifer wasn't on the guest list. Their conversations regarding the stars, their choices, their highs and lows, were interminable. Marcus swore that Meg would *never* get over Russell's marriage to that Danielle girl; Michelle, '*Oh!* like, totally, I mean, who *is* she, a freakin' *nobody* . . .' When Michelle prompted Marcus to ask her to marry him, he accepted. Michelle was beautiful; she ate small portions (some women ate like pigs); she was proud of him, his career; she admired his dress sense; she wasn't sexually voracious (so uncouth in a girl). She *was* messy – Marcus was insanely neat – but that was rectified by a cleaner, and she was awed at his instinct for what made a house *home*. His Poggenpohl was dear to him. I'm not being rude here, it's a *super* exclusive kitchen range, pricey, but so worth it (I'm quoting Marcus, as alas, my own kitchen is cheapy-cheap from Ikea).

Once the monster diamond ring was secured from Tiffany, and Marcus had recovered from the shock, they held an engagement party – with a modest gift list, at Harrods. Certain people, I'm sad to say, speculated on how long the alliance would last. Laid bets, even. (All the while heartily tucking in to the smoked salmon bagels, and fishballs, paid for, of course, by Michelle's suddenly fond parents). It's human nature to bitch about marriage – fair enough, as it is human nature to bitch about most things – but one or two acquaintances seemed to have a vested interest in its failure.

They murmured amongst themselves, bagel crumbs at the sides of their mouths, that Michelle was, *mmm*, quite self-obsessed. And so was Marcus. Michelle was, you know, a tad selfish. And so was Marcus. Michelle wasn't what you call, *ahem*, a great intellectual. Nor was Marcus. Michelle could be so catty. And so could Marcus. Think he'd cheated on her yet? It made you wonder what was missing in these so-called friends' own petty lives to make them so keen for misery to afflict the lives of Michelle and Marcus.

I get confused with the use of irony, but I'm almost certain it was ironic that the only people present at the wedding (besides the bride and groom) who *didn't* entertain thoughts of imminent disaster, infidelity, divorce, and divorce settlements were Lewis and Maureen Goldblatt. Now that their eldest girl was striding up the aisle in an elegant cream princess dress, wearing a tiara encrusted with seed pearls, towards a handsome man who looked only a little scared to see her, they felt that all was right in the world, and always would be.

This, as anyone with half a brain knows, is a highly dangerous assumption. Life can be, as the poets tell us, a right bastard. There is no guarantee of happiness, however special you feel you are. Fate has fickle fingers (whatever the hell that means). Even if you've had more bad luck than other people, and feel you've done your share of suffering, who knows. Maybe destiny has it in for you, and is about to heap yet more agony upon your shoulders. God does *not* give you as much as you can carry. Often He gives you a great deal more, which is why at least half of us are clinically depressed and on Prozac.

If you're in any way superstitious, the Goldblatts' open satisfaction at the marriage of their eldest daughter was a harbinger of doom. Not to mention that neither Marcus nor Michelle are prototypes of loveliness, and so one rather feels that they *deserve* to fall flat on their faces.

In addition, what could be more unfashionable than to claim a happy union for this most bourgeois of couples? What could be more unlikely? Marriage, as we're all told till we're sick of hearing it, is a difficult, complex state, often impossible to negotiate, strewn as it is with trip-wires and pot-holes and suspicious dinner receipts in back pockets.

What hope for two middling-intelligent, medium-unpleasant people such as Michelle and Marcus?

Well, here's the thing. Fate is not in charge here. *I* am. And I approve of marriage. It's often romantic, optimistic, a beautiful gesture. Also, call me soppy, I believe that there's someone for everyone. Marcus is not *my* cup of tea. But he was Michelle's. As for Michelle, plainly, she's a pain in the behind. I wouldn't choose her as *my* wife. But Marcus did, and discovered, to his surprise, that he'd made the right decision. Perhaps it was a fluke. Because really, to assign those two a happy ending is wrong and unfair – there are so many far sweeter, more deserving candidates out there, currently enduring woe after woe. I confess. At first, I was fully convinced that Marcus would betray Michelle with a client, or that Michelle would embark on a steamy email affair. I was all set to conclude on a note of despair and a stern moral warning. What can I say? I found, like they found, people grow on you.

Sarah Mlynowski is the bestselling author of *Milkrun*, *Fishbowl*, *As Seen On TV*, *Monkey Business* and the teen novel *All About Rachel: Bras & Broomsticks*. She also co-edited the American and Canadian editions of *Girls' Night In*. Originally from Montreal, she now lives and writes in New York City.

Say hello at www.sarahmlynowski.com. She'd love to hear from you.

KNOW IT ALL

Sarah Mlynowski

My new roommate, Dee, claims she can see the future.

It's Thursday morning, and she's in the kitchen pouring herself a glass of my OJ. 'You should take an earlier flight to California,' she says, gulping it down.

'Why?' I'm crouched in front of the closet next to the kitchen, already late for work, debating whether taking six pairs of shoes on a three-day trip is absurd.

'There's going to be a blackout tonight,' she says. She's wearing pigtails, and the bright pink pajamas and matching flip-flops she never takes off.

'Yeah? Did they say that on the news?' If I have to, I can probably catch an earlier flight. My mother is swimming in airline points. To cheer me up about the Brahm breakup, she offered me a business-class ticket to visit the world's most perfect – and sadly former –roommate, Janna, in California for the weekend.

Dee shakes her head no and pours another glass. Does she think orange juice grows on trees? A friend of a friend of a friend, she moved in three weeks ago. She's no Janna, but so far she seems normal.

'It wasn't on the news,' she says. 'I dreamed it.'

'Very funny,' I say, and reluctantly eliminate one of my three pairs of gorgeous but impractical stilettos.

'No, really. I'm a little bit psychic.'

'If you say so.' I turn to her and smile. 'Can you be a little bit psychic? Is that like being a little bit pregnant?'

'I have premonitions,' she says, her lips pursed and serious.

My smile falters. I might have chosen a wacko for a room-mate. 'What kind of premonitions?'

She shrugs. 'Random stuff. Usually about things people talk to me about. Like your flight. I dreamed about us watching DVDs on my laptop by candlelight. You were complaining you'd missed your plane. So I'm assuming there'll be a power outage.'

'You dreamed about us watching a movie? Dee, you need to get out more.'

Weirdo.

At a little after four o'clock, I'm lugging my still-stuffed-with-shoes suitcase towards the front door, when the hall lights go out. Did a bulb just pop? A quick check reveals that the microwave clock is blank. No power. Damn. My flight departs in two hours, I'm late and I still need to flag a cab. I lock up, tow my ridiculously massive suitcase to the elevator and press the down button. Two minutes. Five minutes. After ten minutes, I force myself to accept the atrocious truth: the elevator works on electricity. And I have to take the stairs. All twenty-eight flights of them.

Crap.

Since my bag weighs at least four hundred pounds, I can't actually lift it and must instead drag it down each individual stair, controlling the momentum by bumping it against my hip. One, bump; two, bump; three, bump . . . twenty steps per floor. Twenty-eight floors.

Bump.

By the time I get to the lobby, it's 4:52, my arms feel like rubber, and I'm an excellent candidate for a hip replacement. But I have an hour, I can still make it.

Outside I frantically search for a cab. And search. Until I realize the traffic lights aren't working. The entire block has no power. Then, like a patio umbrella in the middle of the desert, a taxi catches my eye. I wave the driver over.

He rolls down his window. 'Where you going?'

'Airport.'

He laughs and drives away.

At six, I lug my bag back to my building. I've missed my one and only chance at business class.

I find Dee home from work, back in her matching pink outfit, in the fetal position on the couch, reading by candlelight. Sweating profusely from my real-life Stairmaster, I spread myself across the carpet like melted peanut butter on toast and remember her premonition about the blackout.

'I told you, I'm psychic,' she says, as though reading my mind. 'And I have a feeling the airports are closed, so your ticket will be reimbursed.'

Yeah, right. I roll my eyes.

'Tell me about the picture in your room,' she says brightly. 'The guy with the messy hair.'

'Brahm?' I'm surprised at how open she is about her snooping. 'He's my ex. We broke up last month.'

'Why?'

Apparently, she's snoopy *and* pushy. 'He wanted to move

in when Janna left. I wasn't ready.' I shrug as though it's no big deal.

I recalled the night Brahm and I broke up. We were in my bed and he was kissing my throat, telling me we could use Janna's room as an office or maybe a spare bedroom, why not, we'd been together for two years, he wanted to take the next step, he wanted to live with me, cook with me, clean with me.

I couldn't breathe, as if my room was bursting with hot post-shower steam. I loved him, but was I in love with him? I felt a nagging at the back of my throat, like a vitamin you still feel two hours after you've swallowed it.

I loved his short, curly hair that stood up in opposing directions. I loved the way his eyes closed when he laughed. How he ate pickles with everything. Sandwiches, pizza, macaroni cheese. I loved the way he wrapped my curls around his fingers when we watched TV.

I loved the way he talked about us. For my twenty-fifth birthday, we tried oysters for the first time. I couldn't believe we were supposed to slurp them down without chewing. 'That's how I feel when I'm with you,' he said, grazing my hand across the table. 'Swallowed whole.'

I wanted to feel swallowed whole, too, but I didn't. Yet I knew what he meant. I'd once lost myself entirely to someone, but the object of my devotion informed me he didn't feel the same. I couldn't get out of bed for weeks, until Janna forced me into the shower, turning on the water, telling me that His breaking up with me was the right thing to do if He didn't feel the way I did.

'It must have been hard to let go,' Dee says. Not sure if she's referring to me, Brahm or Him, I don't answer. 'Come,' she adds. 'I rented *Ocean's Eleven* and *Intolerable Cruelty* and charged my laptop. Let's watch DVDs like we're supposed to.'

I nod, too tired to be freaked out. And anyway, I love George Clooney. He kind of swallows me whole.

The next morning Dee pushes open the bathroom door while I'm brushing my teeth. 'I had a dream last night, but you're not going to like it,' she says. 'It's about the guy we were talking about.'

I spit a gob of toothpaste into the sink. 'George?'

'No, your ex. Brahm. I dreamed that he was at a place called Jeremiah's.'

'The store in the Village near his apartment? How'd you know where he shops?'

'I told you, I dreamed it.'

My back tingles, like hundreds of mosquitoes are feasting on my skin. 'And?'

She sits on the toilet. 'It was open even though there's no power. He walked in and bought a flashlight and a jar of pickles.'

The man loves his pickles.

'And then the woman said that in case the pickles made him thirsty he should buy some water. That's why she was there. For some H_2O.'

'The woman? What woman?'

'The woman in line. She was wearing a camel V-neck. She had straight red hair and a million freckles. And bright green eyes.'

What kind of a sicko is Dee? Did she make this up just to upset me? 'And?'

She lifts her gaze to the ceiling as if she's watching a movie up there. 'They're talking about where they were when the power went off. The guy behind the counter hands him his bag, and Brahm asks the redhead if she wants to join him for a pickle-and-water picnic.'

Maybe she really did dream this. I could have mentioned his pickle obsession in my stair-induced stupor, and she conjured it up in her sleep. 'So what happens next? Am I invited to the wedding?'

She laughs. 'They just met, Shaun. Don't be crazy. She says why not, and they walk to Washington Square Park and sit on a bench and eat their pickles. But they can't keep their eyes off each other. They have this instant connection, you know? Has that ever happened to you?'

'And then?' I ask.

'He asks her out for tonight. Then I woke up.'

My new roommate is a freak, and I am dismissing her entire freakish dissertation from my mind. I will not give her, or her dream, or the supposed new love of Brahm's life any more thought.

I freak out at noon. What if Dee really is psychic?

I throw my novel on my bedroom floor. She's not psychic. There's no such thing as a third eye. My roommate is a Wall Street receptionist. She's not Nostradamus.

I'm putting the entire Brahm conversation out of my head.

At one I decide that I, too, need a flashlight. From Jeremiah's. Who knows when the power will come back? I speed walk since the subways still aren't working. When I push the door to the store open, I see no redheads. Ha.

I wonder what Brahm is doing today. When I spoke to him last night he said that since his office is closed because of the power outage, he'd probably just bum around. He wanted us to hang out, but I told him it wasn't a good idea. I don't want him to get his hopes up.

I know I shouldn't be talking to him past the more-than-friends hour of eleven. But I don't speak to him every night. Just last night, and the night before, and the night . . . oh, crap. Maybe it *is* every night. It's not my fault. He calls me. And we were friends for three years before we started dating, so we can't just *not* talk. His voice makes me feel warm, and safe. And I need an end-of-day phone call to signify bedtime, otherwise I lie in bed all night listening to the cacophony of honking and car alarms that sound like a five-year-old kicking a piano.

I buy my flashlight, but continue wandering around the store, my eyes peeled for Brahm. I don't want him to get his hopes up, but I don't want him to meet someone else. By the time I've combed every aisle at least twice, I'm relaxed. And feeling stupid for showing up. I'm cramming my bagged flashlight into my oversized purse when I hear a woman's voice say, 'Six jugs of water, please.'

Standing at the counter is a redhead in a camel V-neck.

My body starts shivering, like the temperature just dropped thirty degrees. How did Dee know? Did she set this up?

I peer closely at Ms. Redhead, about to ask if she's a friend of Dee's, when through the window I see the familiar messy hair. I leap into action, sprinting out the door before Brahm has the chance to open it. He's wearing his black T-shirt with the white lightning bolt, the one I once told him is my favourite, the one he wears to death. A smile lights up his face when he sees me.

'Hi,' I say, trying to suppress the shock I feel by keeping myself bleached of expression.

'Shaun,' he says, happily. 'What are you doing here?'

'Buying a flashlight.'

The redhead pays for her water.

'How's your day?' I ask, glancing at her out of the corner of my eye. I hold my breath.

'Not bad. Do you want to hang out in the park for a bit?'

The redhead leaves and I exhale.

Shouldn't lead him on, shouldn't lead him on. 'I can't, I have to get home.'

His face falls. I wave goodbye. As I walk back to my apartment, a weird feeling comes over me, like I've been transported into *The Twilight Zone*. I'm not sure if Dee is psychic, if she set this up, if I just ruined Brahm's life.

Maybe this never even happened. Can I pretend this never happened?

A week later, when the power has been restored and the chance of my finding a free weekend to reschedule my trip to California is pretty much nil, Dee once again barges into the bathroom, clad in her usual pink PJs and matching flip-flops. Instead of pigtails, this time she's wearing her glasses on her head like a hair band. Her third eye, perhaps?

I'm on the toilet, and I'm too tired to yell at her to leave. I was on the phone with Brahm until 3:00 a.m. talking about the weather, TV, how much he misses me. 'Can I help you?' I ask her.

'I had another dream about your ex and the redhead.'

I feel queasy, like I'm on a sailboat in choppy waters. 'What happens?'

'He's on the subway after work, and she's rushing down the stairs on Thirty-third to get on. Brahm spots her running toward the car and, throwing his suitcase between the subway doors before they close, he helps her inside. They share the same pole and feel that connection again. He asks her out.'

'No way.' He wouldn't ask out a random woman on the train.

She shrugs. 'That was my dream. But why didn't they already meet at Jeremiah's?'

I pay special attention to the toilet paper. 'Guess you were wrong.' I don't mention my Jeremiah's intervention in case I screwed up the fate of the universe.

'Guess so.' Perplexed, she exits the bathroom.

Is she for real? Will I miss him if he dates someone else? Will I be able to sleep at night when he no longer calls?

I must stop them from meeting.

At a quarter to five I leave the ad agency where I work to lurk outside the cosmic subway station. At 6:34 I spot the redhead from Jeremiah's. I admire her red sling backs before stepping directly in her path. 'Excuse me.'

She has a round face, with eyes the colour of the inside of a cucumber. 'Yes?'

Um . . . 'Can you tell me how to get to Central Park?'

'Sure.' She leans in close and gives me directions.

Many follow-up questions later, I thank her and let her disappear down into the station. I wait a few seconds and follow. I peek over the turnstile, and spot her waiting by a bench.

Hurray! She missed Brahm's train. That's it. It's the end of this redhead and Brahm. Mission accomplished. I've altered the fate of the universe. I glance over my shoulder nervously, refusing to feel guilty as I make my way home.

Mmm. Bacon.

On Saturday the aroma of crisping meat awakens me.

Funny, I would have pegged Dee as a vegetarian. Being in touch with the earth and all that stuff. What do I know? Maybe she's more of an evil witch. I stretch and stagger into the kitchen.

'Want some breakfast?' she offers.

'Sounds divine,' I reply, putting my anti-Dee thoughts aside in honor of this splendid meal.

She scoops two eggs out of the pan and slides them onto a plate. Then she makes a smiley face by adding a curved slice of bacon as she asks, 'Can you explain something?'

She's already halfway through a glass of my OJ, but I don't mind, since my meal smells so delicious. 'Sure.'

'Why is it that I had another dream last night about Brahm and the redhead?'

Again? Enough already. 'What happened?' I try to keep my voice steady, as though none of it matters.

'I dreamed that they're at the Astor Place Barnes & Noble and both reach for the last copy of the new Grisham novel.'

'And?'

'They compare Grisham's literary work with his legal thrillers, and she asks him to join her for a coffee.'

'She asks him out?' Getting aggressive, is she?

'What I'm wondering is why I keep dreaming they're meeting for the first time. They should have already met twice by now.'

I shrug. 'Maybe you're not as psychic as you think you are.'

She cracks two more eggs into the frying pan. 'No, that can't be. Have you spoken to Brahm recently? Do you know if they've met?'

I stuff my mouth with bacon so I can't be expected to answer.

'Wait a sec,' she says, mouth widening as if she's about to yawn. 'Did you somehow prevent them from meeting?'

I chew extra slowly. Swallow. Fake chew. Fake swallow. 'Would there be consequences if I did? Is it wrong to mess with the future? I mean, you told me to take an earlier flight to California, right?'

'I'm not entirely sure how it works,' she admits. 'Last week, I dreamed that my sister missed my father's birthday, so I reminded her and she called him.' She shrugs. 'No harm done. No cosmic implications.'

I breathe with relief. I haven't botched the fate of the world. Unless the redhead and Brahm's future offspring would have found a cure for cancer, or invented a flying chair or something. I take another deep breath and confess in a rush, 'I've been stopping their meetings before they could happen.'

She calmly turns over the eggs. 'Why? Didn't you break up with him?'

'Yeah, but the idea of him kissing someone else makes my skin crawl. I can't sit by and let them meet. I just can't.'

She nods. 'Fair enough.'

I arrive at Barnes & Noble a half hour later. After two chai teas and a scone, I spot Ms. Redhead browsing in the romance section on the second floor, and I make a mad but hopefully subtle dash over there.

'Hey,' she says. 'Didn't you ask me for directions yesterday?'

Damn, she recognizes me. She's going to think I'm a psycho stalker. I *am* a psycho stalker. 'Thanks again.'

'No problem. It's so weird that you're here. The universe must be trying to tell us something.'

I lower my gaze and pick up a book.

'Are you visiting New York?' she asks.

'Me? No.'

'Really? And you needed directions to Central Park?'

Damn. 'Um . . . I have no sense of direction.' Change subject, change subject! 'Do you read a lot?'

'Yeah. Mostly mysteries and romances, I like happy endings.'

'Don't we all.'

'I'm heading to the café. Want to join me? I'm Simone.'

Apparently Simone would have asked *anyone* to join her for coffee today. 'Sure. I'm Shaun.'

In the café once again, I order another chai and she orders a cappuccino. Even though I want to hate her, I like her. She laughs at my jokes. Asks me about my job. She just moved to the city and wants to meet people. She gives me her business card and tells me to call her.

Thirty minutes later I spot Brahm at the magazine rack. He doesn't see me. Tucked under his arm is the new Grisham novel.

'Operation Stop Brahm and Simone, take four,' Dee says two mornings later, pounding on my door.

'Not again,' I whine.

'They unknowingly sit next to each other at the Union Square movie theatre, and they start chatting.'

I feel sick. Possibly because I had sex with him last night. Okay, I know I shouldn't have, but we were on the phone until two, and he said he missed me and wanted to see me and I thought, Why not? I told him he could come over if he wanted to, and to wear the lightning bolt shirt, and twenty minutes later he was kissing me. And it felt so nice and safe.

I can't let him meet someone new, I just can't. 'I don't understand, why do they keep meeting?'

'I don't know.'

'What do you mean you don't know? What kind of psychic are you? Eventually it'll stop, right? They can't keep bumping into each other indefinitely, can they?'

'I don't know.'

I need to put an end to this. I search in my purse for Simone's business card and call her. 'Hey, it's Shaun. Your bookstore buddy? Want to catch a book signing tonight?'

'Sure,' she says. 'I was going to see a movie, but a book signing sounds great.'

It's Thursday morning and Dee throws open my door.

I pull the pillow over my head. 'Go away,' I moan.

'He gets out of a cab at eleven p.m. on Houston and Broadway. She gets into it.'

I call him at ten and tell him I'll meet him for a drink. By eleven I'm drunk and under his satin sheets. He plays with my curls and tells me he loves me. I pretend I'm asleep.

On Friday morning Dee wakes me up at six. 'Starbucks. Forty-second and Third. Forty minutes. He spills coffee on her shirt. Go.'

Saturday morning, ten a.m.

Flip-flop! Flip-flop! Dee stomps from her room to mine and whips open my door. 'I can't take it any more! I can't stand dreaming about Brahm and the redhead continuously. It's driving me crazy!'

What, it's my fault she's psychic? Like I can control what she dreams? I jump out of bed. 'Where are they?'

'Shaun,' she says, 'you have to let go.'

'Tell me where they are.'

She sighs. Loudly. 'They're sitting at a table on the patio of French Roast in the West Village.'

'How are they sitting together if they don't even know each other yet?'

I must look crazed, because Dee says, 'I don't think you should intervene this time.'

'If you didn't want me to intervene, you shouldn't have told me.'

She shakes her head. 'I'm not making your choices for you.'

The phone next to my bed rings and I turn my back to her and snatch it up. 'Hello?'

'It's me,' Brahm says. 'Have you eaten? Want to go for brunch?'

'Sure,' I say slowly, trying to process this phone call. 'Where do you want to go?'

'How about French Roast?'

Huh? 'Sure. Thirty minutes?'

Thirty minutes later, panicked that I'm late, and exhausted from the run, from the week, from these damn interventions, I see Brahm's curly-haired head. He's sitting on the terrace, his face tilted toward the sun. Every few seconds he looks down and eagerly scans the street, searching for me.

He's wearing the lightning bolt shirt.

And suddenly I remember that I was once a girl who wore my hair up every day for a year because He, the boyfriend before Brahm, remarked in passing that he thought my neck was sexy.

I have to let him go. Have to let him move on. I want him to be with someone else. Someone who feels swallowed whole.

My heart breaks and I flip open my cell. I dial. Slowly.
I know someday I'll feel it again, too. But until then?

Maybe Dee and I'll take a vacation. I'll trade in my business-class ticket for two economy seats to California. Or maybe Vegas. Bet Dee kicks ass at the tables.

She answers on the first ring.

'Simone?' I ask. 'What are you doing for brunch? There's someone I'd like you to meet.'

Karen Moline is the author of two novels, *Belladonna* and *Lunch*, several *Girls' Night In* short stories, dozens of ghostwritten and nonfiction books, and hundreds of articles for a wide variety of magazines and newspapers in many different countries. She lives in New York City with her son.

HELL AMONG
THE HOLLYHOCKS

Karen Moline

Sometimes it takes only a small slip for life to unravel.

My boyfriend Jordan and I sat in Saturday evening traffic in the Hamptons, en route to a dinner party chez his chums Julian and Susannah. They owned a splendid house overlooking the bluffs, the sea an endless expanse below, near Beach Road in Montauk. You know, one of those picture-perfect pads with immense bay windows, draped with antique saris in gossamer silks; sculptured marble columns holding huge pseudo-Grecian urns filled with vast arrangements of fluttery black tulips (out of season, but Susannah had contacts in Holland who owed her a favor); and sofas upholstered in broadly-striped linen, Spanish piano shawls artfully thrown over the sides so the fringes hung just so.

'What's with all the *fringe*?' Jordan had whispered the first time we went there, two summers ago, when we'd been only dating for a month and were deliriously in love. 'It's so *drippy*.'

Drippy became our code word for over the top.

'God, this traffic sucks,' Jordan said as he lit a Marlboro.

'Small price, pal,' said his friend Morgan Rafferty, a landscape architect known to everyone as Raff, as he winked at me and his girlfriend, Gabrielle.

'Quit your belly-aching,' Gabrielle said fondly, pushing her flamboyantly copper-coloured hair out of her face. She wrote for the Sunday Style section of the *New York Times*, but was spending the summer trying to write a novel. 'I personally welcome any diversion away from my dreary days. I mean, I stare at my computer. I write about two words. I put on sunscreen. I count my freckles. I write another two words. Then I decide to be productive and tackle the mess Morgan calls "*le jardin*". It really is shocking how a landscape architect can have such a pathetic assortment of boring flowers clumped around.'

Morgan laughed. 'I only rented the house for two months, sweetie,' he said affectionately. 'I can't be bothered with some other idiot's idea of over-planting the clematis and nasturtiums.'

'Hell among the hollyhocks,' she said with a snort. 'Sounds like a good book title, doesn't it? The chumps we rented from have a thing for quick-growers. Everything *climbs*. And climbs *quickly*. It if doesn't go up, they yank it.'

'Must smell delicious,' I said.

'Yeah, it does. Enough to make me long for a cigarette. And I quit exactly four months, two weeks, and three days ago. I would just kill for a smoke right now. So, thanks, Jordan.'

Jordan laughed and blew her a smoke ring.

Morgan handed her a piece of Nicorette gum, which she gratefully popped into her mouth. 'Anyway,' she went on. 'I can't think of a damn thing to write, right? So I schlep out to the *jardin* to commence yanking the weeds. And guess what I found?'

'What?' Jordan asked.

Gabrielle fished around in her bag, then held up a joint. 'I found the pot plants hidden behind the hollyhocks!' she announced. 'See – sometimes procrastination has its rewards!'

'Guess *le jardin* isn't such a wasteland, after all,' Morgan said smugly.

'Sure ain't,' she replied. 'This makes it all more than worthwhile. And, sweetie,' she said, turning to him, 'we must remember to leave an especially big thank-you present, like a bong or something, for the now-beloved owners of *Maison du Pot*.' She smiled happily. 'So, should I light this now, or save it for later?'

'Later,' Morgan said emphatically. 'We're going to be having a feast, and if I get stoned now, I'll eat like a pig.'

'You sound like a girl,' I said.

'He *is* a girl,' Gabrielle said, teasing. 'You should see him after his daily tick inspection.'

'Ticks are no joke,' he said sternly. 'And that goes for the stupid deer that carry them, too. They're nothing but a buncha bug-infested Bambis.'

'Do you think '*Bug-Infested Bambis*' would be a good book title?' Gabrielle asked.

'There's tons of deer out by Julian's house,' Jordan said. 'He had to put fences all the way around the property to keep them out of the yard. See – these gates are new.'

We pulled up in front of the driveway, and I got out to open the gates.

'Very chi-chi for Montauk,' Gabrielle commented.

When we got to the house, we joined Julian and Susannah for a drink on the terrace, and they introduced us to some other friends: Milo Weatherby, who ran one of the largest PR firms in London, and his wife, Sasha, an interior decorator;

Michael Berger, a painter; and Claire Peyton, a hat designer. It was a cloudless, beautiful evening, and the surf was flat and placid. Wonderfully, the champagne was not.

'Have you ever seen the World War Two bunkers on the cliffs?' Jordan asked Milo as we stood around chatting. 'They're relics of our non-defence plans against the German invasion.'

'I'd love to see them,' Milo said.

'Anyone up for a walk?' Jordan asked.

'I am,' I said.

'Me too,' Gabrielle said.

We sauntered off down the driveway, making sure to close the gates firmly behind us, then followed the road until it narrowed to a cliffside path. Jordan, who designed golf courses, was busy discussing teeing off in the Scottish Highlands with Milo when Gabrielle sighed deeply.

'Are you okay?' I asked.

''Course not!' she said melodramatically. 'I would just kill for a goddamn cigarette! I mean, here we are out in nature, and it's all gorgeous and everything, and all I can think of is a goddamn motherfucking cigarette! Where's my motherfucking gum?' She searched in the pockets of her jeans. '*Shit*! I must've left it at the house. Well, so much for the bunkers. They can wait, and I can't! Give 'em my regards!'

With a brisk wave, she headed back to the house. I walked slowly on the path up the cliff, then turned to look back at the expanse of sea at my feet. Aside from one fisherman, busy with his rod way down at the other end of the beach, there was no one else in sight. Just the endless expanse of sea and sky, calm and azure, a slight mist starting to rise as dusk approached. And then I saw the most astonishing sight.

Six deer were frolicking on the beach below me. Four

bucks and two does, cavorting around as if they were over-grown puppies. They jumped up on each others' backs, playfully nudged each other into the surf, then ran down the sand, into the water and then back over the dunes, as if they didn't have a care in the world. Then they'd jump back up on each other, and start prancing and carousing again.

I'd never seen anything like that before in my life, deer playing in the sea, and I stood watching for a long time, frozen with delight. I felt as if I had been given a gift, that I had stepped into an enchanted fairy land. Just me, and the placid blue sea and the deepening blue sky, and these joyful, amazing animals, chasing each other up and down the beach.

When I heard Jordan and Milo's voices behind me, I turned to them and smiled. 'Look down there,' I said, pointing to the deer, gambolling in the surf.

'Wicked,' Milo said.

'No wonder Julian put up the fence,' Jordan said, frowning slightly. 'They're everywhere. Full of ticks, the dumb drippy things.'

'A bolt-action rifle would take care of that,' Milo said, pretending to pull a trigger.

They laughed, and all the magic I'd felt at such an enchanted moment disappeared in a flash.

'Coming, babe?' Jordan asked, oblivious to my disappointment.

'In a minute.' I turned to watch them go, but when I looked back at the beach, the deer had vanished.

When I got back to the house a short time later, Gabrielle was regaling all with stories of her escapades in Style Land.

'Would you like to come riding with us tomorrow?' Sasha asked her.

'I think I'll pass. I love horses,' Gabrielle confessed, 'except for the slight problem I have sitting on them.'

Sasha laughed. 'Well then, go to the beach. You do look rather pale.'

'Excuse *moi*,' Gabrielle retorted. 'I work very hard on my non-tan, and trust me, it's not easy being a paleface in the land of golden honey. Especially out here, surrounded by so much sun-fried *glamour*.' She shuddered. 'I still haven't recovered from those hideous, formative teenage years, when we moved to Gilroy, California. Garlic capital of the world.'

'Must've smelled great,' Jordan said. 'But then you weren't very far from the golf course at Carmel.'

Gabrielle looked at him, aghast. 'Me, play golf? In Carmel with the rich people? What, are you mad? No, pal, I was busy inhaling the garlic fumes and dodging the fruit thrown at me by the locals. The proud future prune farmers of America.'

'What do you mean, prune farmer?' Milo asked. 'Prunes don't grow on trees.'

'Prune plums do.'

'Prunes make you go all woody,' Sasha said with a shudder.

'Only guys get woody. Or at least some guys,' Julian said smugly.

'I mean pulpy,' Sasha said.

'Prune pulp. Yuck!' Jordan said.

'Better than prune whip.'

'What on earth is prune whip?' Sasha asked.

'You don't want to know,' I said. 'But I did meet someone once who named her kitty Prune Whip.'

'At least prunes work better than Preparation H,' Gabrielle said, looking at me with a wink. 'But Preparation H does work on tightening those unsightly wrinkles around the eyes.'

'Gross,' Morgan said. 'You put haemorrhoid cream near your eyes?'

'Not *me*, darling. The models I'm forced to write about. You'd be amazed at the little tricks they have up their Marc Jacobs sleeves.'

'No wonder they never eat,' Susannah said, taking a mouthful of lobster *fra diavolo*. 'They're too grossed out.'

'No, they're too *tight*,' Morgan retorted. 'Can't get their mouths open after the Preparation H takes effect.'

'Speaking of tight, have you seen the leash that Renata keeps Chris on?' Julian asked.

'Who are they?' Milo asked.

'Chris is an architect friend of mine and Jordan's,' Julian replied. 'And Renata is his girlfriend. Previously his ex-girlfriend. She's just after him for his money.'

'Christ keeps all his exes on a string,' Jordan said. 'They always get back together, and it's fabulous for two weeks, and then all of a sudden they remember why they split up in the first place, and the drama begins again.'

'I thought grown-ups didn't see exes any more,' I said carefully. 'That's how they turn into exes.'

'I swear, there needs to be a test to give these guys,' Claire said. 'Some standardized list of fifty questions to see what sociopathic tendencies they have so we can be forewarned.' She smiled grimly. 'They skim through life on their charm, their alleged sexual prowess, and their very glib tongues. They flit from one situation to another because if they light in one place for too long, someone's bound to see their glaring flaws. The problem is that they're so charming that it's hard to imagine the destruction they'll let loose on your psyche. If you're dumb enough to fall for one of them. Like I did. But I wised up. And I got out.' Her smile faded.

'But when is the right time to become an ex?' Michael asked. 'Since I seem to be the only divorced person here.'

'Whatever gave you that idea?' Milo asked. 'I've been divorced three times already.'

'Sounds like you need a good PR,' Gabrielle teased.

'I have one,' he said, leaning over to give Sasha a kiss. 'The very best.'

'Oh, I don't know when the best time to leave is,' Susannah said. 'Probably around the time that he's indicted.'

We laughed again.

'Marriage isn't always what it's cracked up to be, especially for the desperate singles who think it's going to solve all their problems,' Sasha said.

'Trust her on this one,' Milo said, wagging his fork at Michael, 'before you do anything so rash as to take the plunge again.'

'Thank you, darling,' Sasha said, rolling her eyes. 'Well, I must say, we do have a friend, Anastasia, back in London, who just got married for the fifth time. To her personal trainer.'

'He's got muscles where men don't have places,' Milo confided.

'They had this glorious country wedding, in this beautiful manor house, with a private chapel and a tiny little cemetery nearby,' Sasha went on, ignoring him. 'Well, when she threw the bouquet, all the bridesmaids were huddled around, shoving each other. The one who caught the bouquet fell backwards onto one of the graves. She was simply dying to get married!'

We all laughed again, then Julian turned to me. 'Speaking of wankers, Kat, there's something I've been meaning to ask you.'

My heart sank. The last thing I wanted to talk about was work.

'Do you have a checklist for donors?' he asked.

'What do you mean, donors?' Michael said.

'Katalina works in a sperm bank,' Julian told him, 'interviewing the donors.'

Michael's eyes lit up with natural curiosity. So did Claire's. Then the two of them looked at each other, and blushed. That made me happy, sensing that invisible shiver between the two, thinking that they might really start to like each other, so I instantly stopped fussing that Julian was baiting me. I smiled widely. This was going to be fun.

'Of course I do,' I said, trying to make myself look all innocent. 'The first question is always: "Are you extremely horny?"'

'No way,' Julian said.

'Are you doubting me, darling?' I retorted, and Julian shook his head. 'Good. The second question is: "Do you understand that you will be compelled to continuously spill your life force, with no possibility of ever having it come back again?"'

Milo laughed out loud.

'The third question is: "Does your wife or girlfriend or favourite hooker know what you're planning on doing?"'

Even Susannah had to laugh at that one.

'Shall I go on?' I asked everyone, and they nodded. 'Fine. Here's the rest of my checklist: "Why are you sweating? Are you aware that once you commit to us, your life will no longer be your own? Do you understand that you will become addicted to those precious moments spent here, that there is no twelve-step programme to help the jerk-off-for-money addict?"' I paused. 'And here's the kicker: "Should you make dozens of women pregnant, will you accept the fact that you'll never know who any of your children are, and can take no credit for them whatsoever?"'

That instantly silenced the room, as I knew it would.

'You see,' I said, 'that's why it's so important to have the proper checklist. For sperm, and for everything else.'

'Too true,' Sasha said, to break the silence. 'Milo had a checklist for what he wasn't going to marry again. Luckily for me, I found it hidden in his pocket, and threw it in the trash!'

We all started laughing and talking and drinking again, and, hours later, Jordan somehow managed to drive us home and we drunkenly rolled into bed, and instantly fell asleep.

But then I awoke to hear something odd. It was the sound of the ocean, rolling in, closer and closer, as if it were a lake. It made no sound; there was no soothing murmur of waves, no seagull's cry. It was just water, creeping up to the house where we slept, silvery in the moonlight. I got up and stood near the window, watching, as the water drew closer, but I could do nothing to stop it. It was hot, and still, and the thin curtains, as silver as if they had been spun out of gossamer moonlight, started to sway gently, back and forth. I looked at them and wondered idly how they could be moving when there was not a puff of a breeze, or how, in fact, the ocean could be anywhere close to this house that sat on a street far inland from the sea, but I was rooted to the spot, frozen. Then I realized we were entirely surrounded by water. It was lapping closer, closer, but I couldn't move and –

I woke up with a start and sat bolt upright in bed, my breathing deep and ragged. Jordan lay beside me, deep in slumber, one hand flung back over the pillow.

I got up, then went to the kitchen to make a cup of camomile tea, knowing that such an anxiety-laden dream hadn't been caused by all the red wine at dinner. Something had shifted. This weekend, we'd barely talked, about everything and nothing, as we usually did. What was it he'd said?

Drippy.

He'd said the deer had been drippy. The lovely, enchanted frolicking deer.

I crept back into our room, and packed up my bags. I imagined the talk we should have had, walking on the cliffside path to where the concrete shells of aging bunkers stood, covered in graffiti and ivy. Except this time the walk along the cliff would be irreversible. There would be no frolicking deer. Only heartbreak and goodbyes.

Then I tiptoed down the stairs, and went out into the night.

Santa Montefiore was born in England. She is the author of *Meet Me Under the Ombu Tree*, *The Butterfly Box*, *The Forget-me-not Sonata*, *The Swallow and the Hummingbird* and *Last Voyage of the Valentina*. Her new novel, *The Gypsy Madonna*, will be published in March 2006. She lives with her husband, historian Simon Sebag-Montefiore, and their two children in London.

A WOMAN OF MYSTERY

Santa Montefiore

When Celestia Somersby moved into Old Lodge, the sleepy, insular village of Westcotton was roused to wakefulness by a blazing curiosity. It wasn't that they hadn't witnessed the arrival of strangers, though being a small, remote town on the Devonshire coast there was little to entice people, except the odd few who came for the peace; it was because Celestia Somersby was a woman of mystery. 'She's very beautiful,' said Betty Knight, standing back to admire the expanding flower display she was arranging in the nave. Vivien Pratt screwed up her nose and leant on her broom, surrounded by leaves and twigs from Betty's overenthusiastic creation.

'In a severe way,' she replied with a snort. 'I don't think that black she wears is very becoming. Makes her look pale and drawn. Older, too,' she added, and there was an ill-disguised timbre of pleasure in her voice, for she was sixty-five and looked it.

'You can't deny she's elegant, though. I used to wear long skirts with boots like that when I was young.' said Betty with a sigh.

'It's not your age, dear,' said Vivien, passing her reptilian eyes up and down Betty's squat build. 'It's your girth. You shouldn't indulge so. I'm not this thin by nature but by abstinence, Betty. Jesus taught us that, and he was thin, wasn't he? No cream buns and pies from Ethel's Pantry for him, just the odd fish and crust of bread after the five thousand had troughed.'

'Do you think she's a divorcee?' Betty pulled her stomach in then let it out with a heave as a wilting lily diverted her attention.

'She wears a ring, you know. I saw it. Though there's been no sign of a man. Must be divorced. Otherwise why would she look so sad?'

'If Cyril gave me a divorce, I wouldn't look sad. I'd be positively gleeful. Thirty years of sitting about like a fat walrus. I'd be more than happy to roll him back into the sea.'

'You'd be lost, dear, have no illusions. That woman's a walking tragedy; you can see it on her face. A smile would do much for that sallow complexion.' Vivien didn't bother to reflect on her own smile, lost long ago with her sense of fun. Slowly she began to sweep.

'She hasn't said so much as a hello to anyone. Just lots of sightings, though no one seems to know what she does or why she's come. There. I think Reverend Jollie will appreciate my effort this week. I do love spring, don't you? Still, she'll come to church on Sunday, I'm sure. We can all get a good look at her then.'

'My dear, if she hasn't had the decency to introduce herself by Sunday, I shall think her very rude indeed. She shan't be welcome here.'

'That's not for you to say, Vivien. This is God's house.'

'Then I shan't invite her back for tea. She'll know she's caused offence then, won't she.' *And she'll know who calls the shots around here, too.*

By Sunday the whole village was whispering about the enigmatic Celestia Somersby. She had wandered into Agatha Tingle's shop and bought a basket of provisions, infuriating the docile shopkeeper by hiding her features beneath a black sunhat and dark glasses. She had said nothing, just paid, handing the older woman crisp pound notes with long white fingers. Agatha gossiped with Betty and Vivien over tea in Edith's Pantry, dissecting every detail, from the goods she had bought to the strange old-fashioned buckle shoes she wore on her feet, while Vivien sipped weak tea and Betty bit into a large slice of chocolate cake. What they didn't know, however, was that Fitzroy Merridale had seen her down on the beach, walking wistfully with her feet in the surf, her long black dress billowing about her ankles, the chiffon scarf tied about her hat flapping like the wings of a bat and that there, in the roaring wind and the crashing waves, he had lost his heart. It had been a wonderful moment. An awakening from somewhere dull into somewhere bright and full of possibilities.

Since that exquisite sighting, Fitzroy had been able to think of little else but Celestia Somersby. He had sat in the Four Codgers pub and listened to the mutters of speculation. Some said that she was divorced, others that she had murdered her husband. He believed none of it and took pleasure from the fact that she hadn't deigned to speak to any of them, because he knew instinctively that she would talk to him. After all, he was one of the few in town her age. Westcotton was an old people's town. He had only moved there to write, having found no inspiration in London. He was also bold. *Why*, he mused, *was it up to her to approach them? Surely as the newcomer they should make the gesture and welcome her into their midst?* He sat in the pew, on the cold hard seat of ancient wood, and looked about him. Agatha, Betty, Vivien, Edith and a gaggle of other grandmothers in feathered hats and pastel dresses. Their husbands were fat and weathered or thin and dominated. A few young couples with fidgeting children, following in the deep, stodgy footsteps of their parents. There was nothing for Celestia Somersby here. Why had she come?

When Reverend Jollie stepped into the nave, his long gowns disguising a belly full of Edith's scones, the disappointment that was felt by every member of his congregation caused the very air in the church to drop. Betty glanced warily at her flowers, afraid that the lilies would wilt too, for everyone had expected their first proper sighting of Celestia Somersby. She had not come.

Reverend Jollie was aware of their frustration because it reflected his own. He had indulged in fantasies of a more godly nature than Fitzroy Merridale, envisaging her confessing her sins, of which there were bound to be many, onto his chest. He was appalled at his own weakness, for since Celestia Somersby had arrived in Westcotton, he had wished he were Catholic.

With a heavy sigh he raised his palms to the sky and addressed the sheep in his flock like the good shepherd that he was. 'Welcome, friends . . .' Just when his enthusiasm was on the point of stalling, the large doors of the church opened with a deep groan. At once the air was charged with expectation. Reverend Jollie watched his congregation turn their heads to face the entrance now gaping open like the toothless yawn of an old man. Fitzroy Merridale's heart stopped for a second, as did his breath, suspended between anticipation and disappointment, willing it to be her. He craned his neck past Cyril Knight's thick shoulders and saw, to his delight, the slim, hesitant figure he had dreamed about since he saw her walking barefoot up the beach. She remained there for what seemed like a very long while, her arms outstretched on either side, her gloved hands holding the doors open. She wore black, and her white face and neck glowed luminous beneath the veil that was pinned to her hat. Only her crimson lips and the pink apples of her cheeks retained their colour. With a purposeful stride she walked up the aisle, passing the many pairs of eyes that strained for a better view of her face. To Reverend Jollie's astonishment she knelt before him, for he still stood in front of the altar, and crossed herself, inclining her head as the Catholics do. He experienced a frisson of excitement then let out a controlled, though staggered, breath. She smiled, a small but unmistakeable smile, before turning and walking back down the aisle to a seat at the back. Fitzroy grinned with admiration. What a cool, confident display that was and how dignified. He had noticed her slim ankles and the high heels on those old fashioned buckled shoes. He wondered what she looked like with her hair down, cascading over naked shoulders.

Fitzroy wasn't the only man in the church unable to concentrate on the service. Even Reverend Jollie flustered over the sermon like an overexcited girl, anticipating communion when Celestia would at last raise her veil and cast her dark eyes to him in submission. He was to be disappointed, however, for although she knelt before him she did not raise her veil or her eyes, which remained lowered and demure.

'Well,' huffed Vivien once the service was over and they were all standing about in the sunshine. 'She might have introduced herself. What does she have to hide, I wonder. I shall not invite her to tea.'

'I don't think she'll mind,' said Betty with a laugh. 'She doesn't look the type for tea. Much too common for her, I suspect, as are we.'

'Oh, for goodness' sake, Betty. You talk such nonsense. Your father might have been a plumber but mine, my dear, was the son of a gentleman.' Betty raised her eyebrows cynically. She knew better than to argue with Vivien Pratt.

Fitzroy had noticed Celestia leave during the blessing and had slipped out behind her. As she walked briskly down the path towards the green he hurried after her. 'Miss Somersby,' he said, catching her up. 'May I introduce myself?' She continued to walk until they were out of sight of the church. Only then did she turn. He was surprised at her small stature, for her charisma gave the impression that she was taller. She did not lift her veil, but he saw her eyes shining behind it. 'My name is Fitzroy Merridale. I want to welcome you to Westcotton.'

'Thank you.' Her voice was soft and deep, like brown suede. He noticed she looked around furtively.

'May I accompany you home?' he asked. She nodded and proceeded to walk across the green. 'I don't imagine you know anyone here.'

'That is why I have moved,' she said and her words weighed heavily with significance.

'I see,' he replied, intrigued. 'I hope you don't mind my approaching you. You just seem so . . . alone.'

'I am alone,' she said, then sighed. 'It is nice to talk to someone.' Fitzroy felt his insides flutter as if they were filled with bubbles.

'I'm a bit of a loner myself. I'm trying to write a novel, but it's not really working. I live in a cottage by the sea. I saw you the other day, walking along the beach.' He was sure she smiled beneath her veil. Encouraged, he continued. 'You had taken your shoes off and your feet were in the water. It must have been cold.'

'I didn't notice,' she replied.

'Well, I live near there. It's meant to fill me with inspiration, but I just stare out at a void. You inspired me, though.' She stopped and looked up at him.

'Did I?'

'Yes, you gave me an idea for a story.' He felt himself blush and put his hands in his pockets. 'I've already begun.' She stared at him for a long moment then walked on.

'Why don't you come back for tea? It's not much, but it's home.'

The house was pretty, with tall ceilings and sash windows overlooking a large garden surrounded by lime trees. Once inside the wall that encircled the property, they were entirely alone. Fitzroy followed her into the house. He watched as she took off her hat in front of a gilt mirror in the hall. She unpinned her hair so that it fell in dark waves over her shoulders and down her back. Then she slipped off her gloves and unbuttoned her coat with delicate white fingers. When she turned to him he was struck by the surprisingly pale colour of her eyes. Like water in a tropical sea. Her mouth twisted once again into a small smile and he felt the colour rise in his cheeks. She was more beautiful than he had imagined.

He followed her into the sitting room where a fire smouldered in the grate. There was a piano upon which large church candles were placed in clusters. The melted wax revealed that they were often lit. 'Do you play?' he asked.

'Of course,' she said and sat down on the stool. As she launched into an emotive solo, her face was suddenly darkened by some unspoken sadness.

'Play something happy?' he asked. She raised those strange pale eyes to him and shook her head.

'I'm afraid I can't play what is not in my heart.'

'Then don't play,' he said impulsively. 'Please don't play if it makes you sad.' Once again she smiled, but this time it was the smile one gives in the face of a beautiful sunset. A smile tinged with sorrow. She got up from the stool and walked up to him. The look in her eyes was intense. He turned away.

She raised her hand and ran it down his cheek. 'You're a sensitive man,' she said and then she kissed him. He didn't pull away or question his good fortune, but wrapped her in his arms and pressed his lips to hers. He breathed in the scent of her skin, warm and sweet like the smell of bluebells, and closed his eyes.

Suddenly she pushed him away. 'You must go!' she said hastily, shaking her head as if ashamed of what had come over her.

'But Celestia!' he pleaded.

'Not here. Not here, Fitzroy. I can't. It's wrong.' She staggered back and leant against the piano, her hand pressed against her forehead.

'What's wrong? Are you married?'

'No.'

'Are you divorced?'

'No.'

'Are you a widow?' She stared at him with frightened eyes and hurried into the hall.

'You must go!'

'Will we meet again?'

'There's a cave on the beach, you know the one. I'll meet you there tomorrow at noon. Don't breathe a word to anyone!' Fitzroy promised then departed. The door closed behind him and he was left bewildered. If she had been mysterious before, she was even more mysterious now.

The following day Fitzroy went down to the beach and waited for her in the cave. He waited and waited, but she did not come. When finally he was on the point of leaving she hurried in through the narrow entrance and fell into his arms. 'I'm sorry,' she breathed, kissing him fervently. 'Forgive me!' He did not bother to ask why she was late. He did not care. He had her in his arms and he was happy.

The following weeks passed in the same manner. They met in the cave and she was always late. But he had learned to wait for her. They didn't talk much and every time they parted he felt he knew her less than before. In the evenings he went to the Four Codgers and listened to the talk. The rumours had grown. They called her the Black Widow and were certain she had killed her husband. Maybe one, perhaps more. Fitzroy sat smiling to himself. He knew her better than any of them. At the end of May, when the air was filled with the sugary scent of summer, Fitzroy invited her back to his cottage. 'I want to make love to you,' he said. At first she was hesitant, as if betraying another or breaking a vow, but then overcome with desire she agreed. In the amber light of evening he unburdened her of the black clothes she wore, unwrapping her slowly as if she were a precious gift. Her skin was soft and creamy and blushing with youth. *You are too vibrant a woman to be subdued by black*, he thought as he kissed her flesh. Then he noticed a scar on her chest. It was pale, barely visible. It was the texture that made it stand out. Afraid of wounding her, he said nothing. After they had made love they lay entwined, engulfed by an unsettling mixture of joy and sorrow, as if instinctively aware of the transience of their affair.

Then one night in the Four Codgers Fitzroy heard them talk of another man. One who came and left her house in a car. He was dark, in his late forties. He never stayed for long. Fitzroy was consumed with jealousy. He marched over to Old Lodge and knocked on the door. When she did not open it he pounded with his fists. 'Who is he?' he bellowed into the night air. Before walking away he noticed a brief flash of light from upstairs and the hasty drawing of a curtain.

The following morning there was a furore on the beach. Policemen and onlookers and dozens of people he did not recognise. When he approached, Vivien Pratt drew him aside. 'Don't,' she said, shaking her head. 'It's that woman. Celestia Somersby. She's dead.'

'Dead?' he gasped, feeling his world unravelling about him.

'Drowned.' Then she hissed. 'They say it's suicide. I don't know. Might have been murder.' Celestia Somersby, or Jane Hardwick as she was really called, was not buried in Westcotton. Fitzroy found her brother sorting through her things at Old Lodge. 'She was a Londoner at heart,' he said sadly. 'She was once an actress. A good actress too, before the accident. After that she was too frightened of the stage to continue. She turned her life into a drama. Moving from place to place where no one knew her. Where she could be anyone she wanted to be so long as she was playing a role.'

'Why did she kill herself?' Fitzroy asked and the pain must have echoed up from the hollowness in his heart. Her brother looked at him for a long moment then smiled compassionately.

'She fooled you too, didn't she?' He sighed and picked up her photograph. 'She died, my friend, because she couldn't sustain that bizarre life forever. She wanted to be Celestia but Jane was always one step behind her. I think she preferred to die dramatically than live modestly.'

'But I loved her.'

'No, you didn't. You loved someone who didn't exist. Even she had lost sight of who she really was. But in a way she got what she wanted. A dramatic life and a dramatic death, and she will live on as Celestia in your memory and in the memory of the others who gave her their hearts. Only I will remember her as Jane, but she never cared much for me. I was a constant reminder of the truth and she cared little for that.'

Elizabeth Noble is the author of two novels, *The Reading Group*, and *The Tenko Club* (Hodder & Stoughton). Her third, *Alphabet Weekends*, is out in January 2006. She lives in a haunted vicarage in Surrey with her incredibly tolerant husband David and her two young daughters, Tallulah and Ottilie, who are actually more frightening than the ghosts. As she careers towards 40, her girl's nights out have definitely become more womanly (and the more precious for it) – and, yes, said fabulous women were involved in a 'research' trip to Las Vegas for this story, and, no, she's not telling . . .

WHAT GOES ON TOUR . . .

Elizabeth Noble

They had been doing this to her all her adult life.

Ever since those first years of training, when they were all sharing a grotty flat in the nurses' quarters in Lambeth. Young, free and single – ish. Spoiling her fun. Cramping her style.

There'd been that policeman, the one who'd unzipped her dress at the dance, and who'd stumbled back with her to her room. Her three best friends had stood outside and hammered on the door, calling her name, until he'd given up, pulled his trousers back on, and gone home.

And there was that anaesthetist, the tall one with the Tintin hair and the aquamarine eyes. He'd been taking great care of her vital signs until they'd had him bleeped, the bastards, just before the crucial moment.

But not this time. This time was her fortieth birthday, and this time the three of them were not going to stop her.

He was gorgeous. Well, good looking. In a dumb sort of way. Swarthy. With the glossy kind of hair that is only a few degrees away from greasy. And a wide nose. Even wider

403

shoulders, and an ass that was undeniably smaller and tighter than hers, which would absolutely rule him out as a lifelong partner, but which made him pretty much perfect for the one night stand she was utterly determined to have. Because what goes on tour, stays on tour. The t-shirts said so.

They were probably for children, really, the t-shirts. Or emaciated women. Hers particularly was too tight, so that the spangly words were stretched luridly across her bosom and quite hard to read. They had found them in a tacky gift shop on the strip, alongside the birthstone dice and the rip-off designer sunglasses.

This whole trip had been her idea. A fortieth birthday long weekend in Vegas. With who else but the three women she had known all of her adult life?

She was sick of her adult life. Sick of her immaculate semi, with the beech-effect laminate flooring throughout. It was so bloody safe. Keith was so bloody safe. Reliable, sensible, practical. Yes, she knew how lucky she was to have him. Everyone was always telling her, weren't they? Even her own mother used to say, 'He's been the making of you, has Keith. Lord knows where you'd have ended up without Keith. Who could have asked for a better provider and a better father?'

Well, she wouldn't have. He'd provided laminate flooring throughout, hadn't he, and who would dare shoot for more than that? And of course he was a fabulous father. The kids would rather have him than her, truth be told, unless they were ill, or hurt themselves. She might have asked for a better lover, mind you. Not that she discussed that with her mother. Even if she knew it wasn't all Keith's fault that their sex life had been whittled away to a quick fumble every second or third Saturday in the dark between the football and a curry. Usually one of them kept at least one item of clothing on.

A pyjama top, or socks. It was hardly the sort of thing to set your pulse racing.

Not that any of her friends' lives were so different. If anything she was a little better off than the others. Angela had those lumpy stepchildren who arrived every Friday night and wedged themselves into her three-piece suite for the entire weekend. Frances spent her whole life at the gym, claiming that she was trying to hold back the years, but really just trying to hold back Malcolm, who was usually breathing lager and cheap cigars all over her. And Trish? Trish had a nice enough husband, who'd laminated the kitchen floor, at least, but she was still working nights at the hospital to pay for it, and for the golfing holidays Bernard always insisted they took, although she didn't know a driver from a wedge.

What the hell was it all about? It wasn't that she wanted to do a Shirley Valentine. Not really. Not never go home. But they were here, right now, weren't they? Now that she was turning forty, she had this tremendous sense of something if not exactly lost, then never actually found. She'd missed something. Not just all those one night stands she'd been interrupted from, although that was part of it. She'd had a happy life. She'd liked her job, really liked it. She'd had the white wedding and the home, and the husband who didn't cheat on her and brought wages into the house each month and took her out on birthdays and anniversaries. And the children, the beautiful, rotten children she loved as much as any mother could. And these friends, who knew her well and loved her anyway. She just hadn't had an adventure.

This was supposed to be an adventure. And it had been, a bit. Not having your husband and children made it different, for starters. Doing what you wanted to do, all day. They'd drunk cocktails with umbrellas, they'd played roulette, they'd wandered around the outlet mall for hours and lingered in coffee shops, nattering. They'd spent as long as they wanted getting ready to go out, like they used to, giggling and drinking wine in their underwear, swapping lipsticks and necklaces. It had been nice.

But an adventure?

It was in the nightclub that her mood had changed. They had no business being there, of course, not really. They were too old. They didn't know the songs, and they didn't know how to dance in that way the kids did, with one arm waving rhythmically above your head, like you were doing an impression of an elephant. And all that bumping and grinding stuff. So they stood awkwardly, leaning against the mesh of the balcony above the dancefloor, and watched. You couldn't have talked.

There was a young couple in one corner engaged in vertical foreplay, oblivious to the gyrating crowd around them. Their attempts to dance were half-hearted. Her arms were above her head, fingers clinging on bars, and he was rubbing himself against her, vaguely in time to the music. When he came in to kiss her the kisses were deep and desperate, and they trailed down her neck into the top of her shirt. Then he would draw back and stare at her. Open, staring eyes. She couldn't stop staring at them, until Frances pulled at her arm. Trish was miming sleeping actions, and Angela had her arms folded.

They took off their stilettos outside Caesar's Palace and the cold pavement felt wonderful beneath their feet. Her ears were ringing, a little.

'Did you see that couple in the corner?' Trish asked.

The others giggled. 'Filthy little sods!'

She sighed. 'Lucky little sods.'

'What do you mean?' Angela nudged her.

'I mean, it's been seventeen years since I had a first kiss. Seventeen years. Don't you remember how amazing a first kiss is?'

The others were quiet for a moment.

'I do.'

'Me too. Your knees go, don't they? You tingle all over.'

'There's nothing like it.' Even Trish conceded.

They'd stopped now. It was a gorgeous balmy night. Behind them, fountains sprang into action in front of one of the big hotels, and overhead, the omnipresent helicopters zoomed up and down the strip. It was like nowhere else, this place. Adventures could happen in a place like Las Vegas.

'Supposing you could have a first kiss here. Nothing else. Just a kiss. And no one else would ever know. No one would get hurt. What goes on tour stays on tour. You'd just have that knee-trembling, body tingling, unbelievable first kiss and then you'd go home. That's it. Would you do it?'

She wasn't looking at the others. They didn't answer straight away.

'Course not,' Trish was the first. 'I mean, be fair. I'd bloody kill Bernard if he kissed someone else. So, no. It wouldn't be right.'

'I couldn't,' Angela grinned ruefully. 'I know what you mean, but I don't think I could go through with it, not when it came down to it.'

'I wouldn't want to. Can't think of anything worse than being out there on your own again. You're only remembering the first kiss, and how long does that last? A few minutes. Nah,' Angela shook her head dismissively. 'Not worth it.'

That was that then.

'What about you?'

She shrugged. 'Not much chance of that, hanging around the moral high ground with you lot, is there? It'd be like the bad old days all over again. You know those cartoons where people have good angels on one shoulder, telling them the right thing to do, and devils on the other, pushing them the other way? I've never had a devil. The devil in me has always been outnumbered by you three blinking angels. Spoiling my fun.'

'Don't you pin that on me,' Frances smiled. 'You're forty now, love. You wanna do it, you do it.' They all grinned. 'After all,' and the rest joined in, 'WHAT GOES ON TOUR, STAYS ON TOUR . . .'

And the moment passed. They linked arms and started off again towards their hotel. And she almost forgot about the couple in the nightclub.

Until she saw him the next night. He'd been dancing in one of the free shows that played on the casino floor on the hour. He'd come up through the floor, on a platform with five or six others. Topless, in leather trousers, with just a bow tie around his neck. She hadn't been particularly struck by him then. She had never been into that sort of thing. It was silly.

But now he looked different. The leather trousers had been replaced by faded jeans, and the muscles were less defined beneath an old-looking t-shirt. He was drinking deeply from a bottle of beer and watching the next show, smiling. He looked normal. He was more animated, somehow, watching his friends perform, than he had been on stage himself.

She was staggered when he started smiling at her. She told herself that, of course, this was how they all got laid. Turn the sad housewives on with the leather and the dancing, then pick them off one by one when you come off your shift. But she didn't want to believe it. And he was good at making it seem unlikely. Making it seem like she had really hit him like a bolt of lightning in the middle of this cacophony, made his world stand still for a minute. Trish elbowed her. Angela was mouthing 'Sad old woman' at her, and smiling. They turned away, heading towards the bar. They didn't recognise the moment.

The first kiss was just as fabulous as the four of them had acknowledged it was bound to be. The gentle, warm, tentative lips of a thousand novels, the feel of a new hand on the back of your head, a new mouth opening into yours. The show, the crowd, the *Wheel of Fortune* slot machine they were leaning against, all fading away. She almost cried when she felt her knees go. Seventeen years.

'Come with me. We have rooms, round the back.' It was the memory of all the times when she hadn't gone that propelled her round the corner, off the casino floor, away from the gaudy lights and the loud music and into a world of grey corridors. And then they were in his room. The leather trousers were over a chair, and there were photographs on the wall, but he turned the lights down as soon as the door was closed, and was kissing her again, unwrapping her from her clothes with flattering alacrity.

They'd be here in a minute, the three of them. God job it wouldn't take much longer than that. She felt drunk. She probably was. But it was this, this that was making her feel light-headed. He wanted her. His hands were everywhere, urgent and warm. His kisses landed wherever he could hold her still. She wanted him. It was years since desire had been this sudden, this unexpected. It wasn't Saturday. She almost laughed. It was Wednesday. She hadn't had sex on a Wednesday in a long, long time.

No knocking. They weren't coming to stop her. And he clearly wasn't wearing a pager. Just a suntan, which now that she was close up to it, looked just a little streaky around the armpits; a lascivious smile; and a quite terrifying, wobbling erection. It was unnaturally hot against her thigh.

Still no knocking. They couldn't knock, of course. They didn't know where she was. And she wasn't carrying her phone. She'd put it, defiantly, in the hotel safe with her passport as soon as they'd arrived, so that Keith couldn't bring her down with queries as to the whereabouts of the washing powder or the cooking instructions for shepherd's pie. There was absolutely nothing to stop her going through with it.

She didn't, of course.

If they hadn't shown up outside her door, or paged, or dragged her out of nightclubs, all those years ago, would she have done anything differently? Had she ever had the spirit? Had she spent all those years believing things about herself that weren't true? Was this what she was now, or what she'd always been?

She couldn't do it. Instantly her stomach burned with it, and the other sensations faded away. She couldn't do it. She wasn't fearless, she wasn't lost in a moment, she wasn't a free spirit. Not any more. Not now. And she didn't know whether that was a triumph or a tragedy.

It was hideously embarrassing, extricating herself. He looked momentarily crushed, and she wondered briefly whether he would go hunting again that evening, or just stay there, wondering what was wrong with the English woman who had been led so willingly and stayed so briefly, and who had backed out of his door, half-dressed and muttering apologies. Crying and laughing.

'Where've you been?' Frances asked her. 'Got you a drink in.' Trish was pushing a glass towards her.

Angela looked at her, eyes narrowing. 'You alright? You look like you've been crying.'

She pulled her t-shirt down roughly, and took a long drink. 'Crying? No way.' She winked lasciviously. 'You know me, girls. I've been having a bit of an adventure . . .'

Freya North gave up a PhD to write her first novel, *Sally*, in 1991. For four years she turned deaf ears to parents and friends who pleaded with her to 'get a proper job'. She went on the dole and did a succession of freelance and temping jobs to support her writing days. In 1995, throwing caution to the wind, Freya sent three chapters and a page of completely fabricated reviews to a top literary agent, and met with success: five publishers entered a bidding war for her books. In 1996 *Sally* was published to great acclaim and Freya was heralded as a fresh voice in fiction. Her next books, *Chloë, Polly, Cat, Fen, Pip* and *Love Rules* have all been bestsellers.

LADIES' NIGHT

Freya North

oi u slag! have u nicked my shoes??? my gold, strappy, fuck-me shoes??? ☹ Bev x

oops!! guilty!! sorry!! will bring 2nite + repay you in chocolate!!! ☺ Suze xxxx

Nine exclamation marks, Bev counted, and four kisses. She marvelled at the emotion flowing through Suze's text message, the legibility of her chirpy personality that gamely contradicted the usual concision of this form of communication. In the space of one text message, Bev no longer bemoaned Suze's purloining of her favourite fuck-me shoes. Bizarrely, the crime itself and the subsequent good humour of both the prosecution and the defence presented via the medium of text messaging, elevated the status of these two women beyond merely work colleagues into the realm of friendship. Bev and Suze had worked in the same place for six weeks, first exchanged text messages a fortnight ago, but had only inserted expressive punctuation, wingdings and affectionate insults over the last few days. Steal my shoes and become my pal you silly slag!!! ☺

Bev opened her wardrobe, pondered her mood and considered what she'd wear that evening. She regarded her pvc thigh-high boots, thought about her fuck-me shoes and laid out a selection of short skirts and glitzy tops that would go well with either. Currently, she wore jeans and trainers, and very comfortable she felt too. She'd change later. She'd get ready with Suze: music playing, make-up bags at each others' disposal, a glass of wine. She piled clothes and footwear into a holdall, fed the cat, set the video to record *Sex and the City*, and headed out. She was quite looking forward to the evening. It should be a good crowd.

```
Fancy a nite of good wine + fine women? Or else
a few pints + coupla tarts . . .?! P.
```

Bugger all else to do tonight, Ian thought, staring vacuously at his computer with a deceptive expression he'd perfected over the years, which implied the spreadsheets he was looking right through were actually the most scintillating sight, the highlight of his working day. He considered Pierce's text message. He suspected that a night on the tiles might do him the power of good, that a little bit of inebriation would be medicinal, that to fling himself on the rebound could be just what the doctor would order. Or so Pierce would have it. Trust Pierce. Ian rapidly justified that because Pierce was midway through a PhD, he could trust him because he was practically a doctor. Of sorts. He decided not to consider the relevance of Pierce's PhD in the Glacial Vagaries of California; Pierce was a great friend and his cure for a broken heart was likely to be a good one. So if Pierce prescribed fine wine and good women, or a couple of pints and a few tarts, then who was Ian to argue. Pierce was the expert. He was the confirmed bachelor. A night owl. He was almost a doctor. Pierce was a great mate. Ian texted his reply.

```
Cool. Coach + Horses 7pm. I.
```

He continued to stare at the monitor, eyebrows raised, sucking in his lower lip, nodding or frowning every now and then as if enthralled by the columns of numbers. All the while, it was an image of Cathy which filled his mind's eye. Cathy dressed to the nines and looking gorgeous. Cathy heading off for a girls' night out in her bid to move on and forget all about him. Cathy with her tongue down some other bloke's throat, some other bloke's hand travelling over her – no no no, banish that thought, cancel that image, look at the monitor, look at the monitor. Spreadsheets. Go away Cathy, get out of my life. Why can't you just be gone?

But just say *she* was going out tonight. Where might she be going? Would she perhaps wonder if *he* was going out tonight, too? She'd know he'd head for the Coach & Horses. She'd know where to find him. If she wanted to find him. Ian was easy to track down and he intended to remain so. He sighed. It appeared she wasn't even looking for him. Texts, email, snail mail, home visits, phone calls, drunken serenading, flowers, stalking – initially tolerated, soon enough rebuffed, now studiously ignored. He hadn't seen Cathy for over a month. Apart from the tantalising image of her which he could superimpose at will over these sodding spreadsheets.

Suze was already there when Bev arrived. Bianca was there too. Lisa was just leaving but said she'd be back in a couple of hours and did anyone want anything from the shops. Karin was sitting at the table nursing a headache, dosing herself

415

with paracetamol, a cold, damp flannel across her brow. Mel
was brewing tea and buttering toast for everyone.

'Sod Dr Atkins,' Bianca said. 'The night is young, we need
our energy, so load up on carbs, ladies.'

'Where's Kay?' Bev asked.

'Dropping her kid off at her mum's,' Suze replied, heaping
sugar into her tea. 'Said she'll be here at 9ish.'

'And Alisha?' Bev asked.

'God – didn't you hear? Remember how Ron swore to her
that he was leaving his wife at the weekend – even texted
her on Friday morning saying all systems go?'

'Oh Christ – no show?'

'Nope. Nothing. Not a word. His mobile is now out of
service. She's heartbroken – gone back up north for a bit.'

'The bastard. Poor Alisha. Nothing seems to go right for
that girl.'

'Anyone have an address for her, in the north? We could
send some flowers.'

'I do,' Karin said, raising her hand like a schoolgirl, 'Christ
my *head*.'

'Eat toast,' Mel said sweetly, 'drink tea.'

'So it'll just be seven of us tonight?' Bev asked.

'The magnificent seven,' said Bianca.

'What's the time?' Suze asked.

'Just gone seven,' said Bev. 'I'm going to change. I'm
thinking top-to-toe pvc tonight. Coming, Suze – or is
Suburban Housewife your look for the evening?'

Suze took toast for the two of them and tottered out of
the kitchen in a pair of baggy velour tracksuit bottoms, a
Phil Collins tour t-shirt and Bev's favourite fuck-me shoes.
The sight of her appeared to lift Karin's headache.

'Looking good, lady,' Karin wolf-whistled after Suze.

'Looking *hot*!' The remaining girls in the kitchen laughed and heckled.

'Armani and Marni, Gucci and Pucci – they all take my lead,' said Suze deadpan, with a wiggle that was engagingly saucy despite the limitations of beige velour and Phil Collins.

Ian was already at the Coach & Horses when Pierce arrived promptly at seven. Unseen, Pierce assessed the look of the man, ordered himself a pint and ordered Ian a double scotch. He took the drinks over.

'You are *nursing* your pint,' Pierce greeted him with mock consternation. 'You are *brooding* over your beer. There'll be no nursing of pints tonight, my boy. No drowning of sorrows. No drowning, just downing, my son. And here – you can start with this.'

Ian regarded the double scotch with his bugger-all-else-to-do expression and tipped the contents of the glass straight down his gullet. He gave his head a brisk shake, smacked his lips and blinked the smart from his eyes.

'That's my boy,' Pierce praised him. 'Now you can return to your pint and enjoy it.'

'Cheers, mate,' said Ian. 'Cheers.'

'How's work?' Pierce asked.

'Dull,' said Ian. 'How are the glaciers?'

'Cold,' Pierce said and laughed, though he was concerned that if that put paid to further conversing about work, they'd be moving swiftly on to the subject of women next. And though he would rather not waffle on about glacial progression in Yosemite National Park, he'd probably prefer to hear about Ian's spreadsheets than Cathy bloody Cathy. Lighting a Marlboro sparked inspiration of the highest order. Football! The beautiful game! There was always football.

Between work and women there always, *always*, would be football.

'Let's finish these here,' Pierce said, 'then go and catch the game at the George & Dragon.'

'Cool,' said Ian, welcoming the notion of ninety minutes utter focus on something other than his ex-girlfriend. It might even go into extra time, hopefully. Penalties too, if he was lucky. Perhaps an evening out with Pierce was a very wise thing to do. Football and alcohol had long been lauded for their healing properties when it came to the spirit of man; a combination of the two promised to be most potent.

'2–1 after extra time, I reckon,' said Ian, his voice brighter.

'Bollocks, man,' Pierce ridiculed. 'Have you seen their defence? 3–0. I'll put a tenner on it.'

Pierce and Ian slapped hands, downed their pints and left for the George & Dragon.

'Poor Alisha,' Suze said, rummaging around Bev's make-up bag for the eyelash-curler. 'She really had her hopes pinned on Ron.'

'I did warn her about men who fuck the payroll,' Bev said. 'It's nigh on impossible to meet the right kind of bloke at work.'

'It's difficult to meet nice blokes, full stop,' Suze said. 'Men can be such sods.'

'Don't I know it,' Bev murmured, deftly swiping liquid liner over her eyelids.

'I don't know,' Suze said thoughtfully. 'My ex was a complete and utter – well, you know the rest. But though he may have broken my window and my cups and saucers and my nose – he didn't dent my heart. That's intact, and it beats in hope.'

Bev regarded Suze; pointed the mascara wand at her. 'Secretly, you're just a slushy die-hard romantic, aren't you?'

'Totally,' Suze admitted, briskly pinching her cheeks along the bone for a becoming blush. 'No one treads on my dreams. I read somewhere – on a tea-towel actually – that we're not given dreams without the power to fulfil them.'

'So one day a dashing knight will come and sweep you off your feet and carry you off to a land of love and plenty?' Bev challenged, trying not to sound too sceptical, simply trying to sound audible whilst applying slicks of lipstick the shade of crushed raspberries.

Suze shrugged and smiled. 'You never know. Don't you believe in fairytales?'

'No I do not!' Bev chided. 'You've been watching *Pretty Woman* again, haven't you?'

'Richard Gere's in town, according to *Heat* magazine,' Suze deadpanned.

'So you'll be wanting my fuck-me shoes again tonight, then?' Bev said.

'Please,' said Suze, with her winsome smile. 'You don't mind?' She stretched out her leg, still clad in vile velour, and rotated her ankle to best display Bev's shoes in all their glory.

'Go ahead,' said Bev, oozing herself into a skirt. 'They suit you.'

'Thanks,' said Suze. 'You can borrow my tracky bottoms whenever you like.'

'Don't go getting any ideas about my boots,' Bev said, zipping them on, then lying back on the bed with her legs in the air while Suze giggled. 'Are you working this weekend?' Bev asked, contemplatively sniffing at three scent bottles before choosing one for an ample spritz.

'Nope,' said Suze. 'You?'

'No,' said Bev. 'Shall we do something? See a film? Have a curry?'

'That would be great!' Suze enthused.

'No chick-flicks, though,' Bev warned her. Suze shot her a sweetly sulky pout. 'Come on, my tea's cold. Let's go down for a glass of wine.'

The match had run on into extra time and by the final whistle, Ian and Pierce had drunk enough to make remembering who owed who the tenner a tense philosophical conundrum. They debated it at length over another pint and called each other bastard and wanker and generally insulted each other affectionately.

'Here, take twenty, you student twat,' Ian said, mistakenly brandishing a five pound note. 'Plenty more where that came from.'

'Save your pennies! Put them away!' Pierce boomed. 'I don't need you to *pay* me. I *own* you.'

'They're looking at us,' Ian said, in not much of a whisper.

Pierce glanced at three women perched on barstools with their handbags in their laps. Though he'd had enough to drink to misconstrue the girls' expressions of distaste for lust; he hadn't drunk too much to preclude an idea springing to mind. 'Of course they're looking at us,' Pierce said to Ian. 'They're on the pull and we're a hot prospect.'

'But there's three of them,' said Ian, 'and only two of us.'

'So?' said Pierce with a wink. Ian looked a little perplexed. He looked a little uncomfortable. He didn't look particularly enthusiastic. Oh fuck, it looked like he was about to nurse his pint and sob for Cathy to come home.

'It'll do you good,' Pierce told him sternly. 'The rebound is an essential part of the healing process. It's a rite of passage. It's the right thing to do.'

Before Ian could even assess whether any of the three girls

420

tickled his fancy, Pierce had swaggered over to them. Ian busied himself with finishing his pint and lighting one of Pierce's cigarettes, and through the haze of smoke, he decided he didn't much fancy any of them. Nor, it seemed, did they fancy him or Pierce because Pierce was now returning alone with a fixed and awkward grin. 'They were a bit rough close up,' he told Ian with contrived nonchalance, 'so I made my excuses.'

'Another pint?' Ian suggested.

'Yeah, why not,' said Pierce. 'The night is young and delights await in the darkness.'

'You do talk a lot of shit,' Ian laughed. And then he kept grinning, because the laughing felt good.

Kay arrived at much the same time as Lisa, who'd returned from the shops with white wine and chocolate.

'Did you hear about Alisha?' Lisa asked.

'I did,' Kay said gravely. 'The bastard. Wish she was here so we could give her a hug.'

They walked into the kitchen, which was actually more like a lounge, as if the stove and fridge were clever and discreet afterthoughts of convenience.

'Hiya,' said Kay, giving the girls an encompassing wave.

'Wine! Chocs!' Lisa declared to a round of applause. 'Bloody hell, Bev, how do you do that? Spray it on and peel it off? Can you breathe? There's more rubber on you than at KwikFit.'

'I guess that makes me a Pirelli Girl,' Bev said, while all eyes admired her, sitting surprisingly demurely in her rubberized splendour.

'It suits you,' said Bianca.

'Wish I could get away with that,' said Kay, with a forlorn

pinch at her stomach. 'I'd be more Michelin Woman than Pirelli Girl.'

Wine was poured and chocolates were shared.

'To Alisha,' Bianca raised her glass and the girls toasted her.

'It's a nice night,' Suze said, peering through the slats of the Venetian blind. 'Quiet.'

'Who's for poker?' Bev suggested to a chorus of approval.

'I'm a bit very pissed,' Ian said mournfully.

Pierce burped his reply.

'And you wonder why you're single?' Ian responded, with much theatrical waving of the air between them.

'I'm single because I can't be doing with the headache you went through when you were *with* Cathy and the heartache you're suffering now you're *without* her,' Pierce said.

Ian shrugged. 'Gives life its meaning, its depth, I guess.'

'It *is* over,' Pierce announced gravely, 'but that doesn't mean that your life is. OK?'

Ian shrugged and nodded. He pinched the bridge of his nose and closed his eyes as he sighed. He looked tired. Not so drunk now, more sad, rather attractive. Ian, four years his junior, appeared older, wiser, more weathered, more worldly – the very image, oddly, to which Pierce aspired. Girls loved that look, didn't they. Just then, Pierce slightly envied Ian the experience of love, the depth of emotion that had led him to this terrible but rather romantic wretched state.

'Are you still holding a torch?' Pierce asked. 'For her?'

Ian sighed and shook his head. 'I guess not. Not anymore. But I'm still hurting. And fuck am I empty.'

Pierce considered Ian's words very carefully. 'The rebound

is a bit overrated,' he said at length, 'and it can be actually
a bit messy. Which defeats the purpose. But if I told you I
had the perfect solution – something that's no strings, no
holds barred, something naughty but nice, downright dirty
but good clean fun – what would you say?'

'Not Spearmint Rhino?' Ian groaned.

Pierce pulled a face. He rose, looked for his wallet, checked
a text message on his mobile phone, slipped his cigarettes
into his back pocket. 'You need to be bad to feel good again.
Come on,' he said to Ian. 'You trust me, don't you?'

'Of course I do,' said Ian, patting him on the shoulder.
'You're practically some kind of doctor, mate.'

Evie came into the kitchen-cum-poker-den.

'Slow tonight,' she said.

'Not for some of us,' Bev said, raising her eyebrow
triumphantly at her little towers of pennies.

'It's because it's such a nice evening,' said Suze.

'I still have a headache,' moaned Karin.

'Why don't you go home?' Evie suggested, but the doorbell rang over Karin's reply that she'd give it another half an
hour. 'Excuse me, ladies,' said Evie, going to answer the door.
Two young men presented themselves.

She'd seen the scruffy blonde one a few times before. He
mostly came by himself, usually much earlier in the evening;
late afternoon, she seemed to recall. He and his friend looked
a little dishevelled but they were making a commendable
effort to seem quite the urbane gentlemen.

'Good evening, Madam!' the blonde man greeted her.

'Good evening to you,' his friend said.

'Won't you step inside,' Evie invited them, with excessive

cordiality. 'Come into the Drawing Room. Would you like a drink?'

The blonde bloke settled himself into the black leather armchair and ordered scotch for himself and his friend.

'Relax,' Evie smiled. As she left the room to fetch the drinks, she flicked a remote control.

The plasma screen was on the wall but Ian stood with his back to it. He had not taken a seat yet, let alone sprawled himself in the same relaxed fashion as Pierce.

'You heard the woman,' Pierce said. 'Sit down, relax!'

Ian sat and observed the melee of hard-core superstars, silently writhing around on the plasma screen. He suddenly thought that porn with no sound was as ludicrous as *Top of the Pops* with the volume turned down, but he didn't share the thought with Pierce, who kept eagerly glancing at the screen with the expectation of one of Pavlov's dogs. Ian half thought of asking himself what the fuck he was doing here but the simple answer was that he was here to fuck. He'd had too much to drink to philosophise, too much to drink to object and enough to drink to feel quite horny; to feel titillated rather than disturbed by the ease of it all.

'She looks like my old Maths teacher,' said Ian, nodding towards the screen.

'She looks nothing like mine,' Pierce laughed. 'My old Maths teacher was called Mr Kieffer and he was 112 years old.'

Evie went into the kitchen-lounge. 'Two young ones,' she told the girls.

'What do they want?' Karin groaned. Recently the young ones had seemed to plump for the more mature plumper option – only tonight she was the only mature plump lady and she had a cracking headache.

'Scotch,' Evie smiled.

'I meant –'

'I know – I haven't asked them yet.' She fixed the drinks and took them through.

'And what else can we serve you gentlemen tonight?'

Ian glanced at Pierce who was licking his lips as if about to peruse a menu.

'We have Jade and Amber, they are our youngest girls – nubile and fun, of athletic build, both blonde,' Evie announced, like the compere of a beauty pageant. 'Velvet and Ebony are our dusky and voluptuous brunettes – they offer exotic services and can be hired together. Coco has recently arrived from Thailand and brings many traditions from the Far East. We also have Miss Whiplash if you would like some S&M tonight.'

'Well, I don't know if I speak for us both, but I rather like the sound of the dark and dusky maidens,' Pierce announced, looking at Ian, who shrugged in his bugger-all-else-to-do way. 'Though gentlemen do prefer blondes,' Pierce continued, arching an eyebrow to signify his honed wit. 'And being a philanthropist, it would be most interesting to *uncover* the delights of Thailand.' This time, both eyebrows shot up his forehead and he chuckled at himself.

'Ebony and Velvet, Amber and Jade, and Coco, will come in and introduce themselves.' Evie announced and she left the room for the kitchen-lounge.

'I didn't mention our mature lady,' Evie tells Karin, who blows her a kiss in gratitude. 'But they would like to see blonde, brunette and Thai.'

'Evie!' Bianca and Lisa protest, gesturing to the crucially

425

strategic state of the backgammon board between them.

'Well, if they ask if your carpets match your curtains, just say no,' Evie laughs. 'Tell them you're fake. You're bottle blondes.'

'But I'm natural,' Lisa complains.

'And I shave,' Bianca sulks.

'They don't need to know that,' Evie tells them. 'Go on. I'll stand guard over your dice and I won't move a thing.'

Bianca and Lisa, Suze and Bev and Mel walk along the corridor together.

'You can always fart,' Bev tells the blonde girls. 'I didn't fancy a punter once but I had this vibe he was going to pick me so I let out a great big rort. I was back watching television before you could say excuse me.'

The girls giggle.

'You fart, I'll burp,' Lisa whispers to Bianca.

They all giggle again. Then the five of them flick their hair, give a little jut to their busts, a wiggle to their hips and they file into the Drawing Room.

They stand in a line and say hello with either a coquettish wink, a sultry pout or a come-hither look. They turn around, one by one, and offer a seductive goodbye before sashaying out again.

'I'm not sure about this,' Ian says to Pierce.

'It'll do you good,' Pierce assures him. 'I'll pay. Happy Birthday, Merry Christmas.'

'It's not the money,' Ian says.

'Mate – this is not the time for a morality melt-down,' Pierce says, a little irritated. He grins. 'I'm hungry. Nothing like a tasty Thai to meet my raging appetite.'

'Pierce, I –'

Evie returns with her anodyne smile.

'Coco for me, please,' Pierce says.

He and Evie turn their attention to Ian.

'He'll have the one in the fuck-me shoes,' Pierce declares.

Evie returns to the kitchen-lounge. The doorbell has rung again and she has asked the gentleman to take a seat in the vestibule for a moment. 'Suze and Mel,' she tells them. 'Mel, you're with the blonde. Suze, yours is a first timer, I reckon. Bev, one of your regulars is sitting in the vestibule – give Suze and Mel a moment. Mel take the Red Room, Suze go in Arabian Nights. Bev take Safari.'

The three girls file out. Karin looks at her watch and decides it's time to take another paracetamol. Bianca and Lisa return to their backgammon tournament. Kay flicks on the kettle and replies to a text message.

'See you in a bit,' someone leaving the room says.

'Have fun,' says someone who stays behind.

In the corridor, just before Suze and Mel enter the Drawing Room and Bev continues along to the vestibule, they wink at each other and pass gentle smiles between themselves.

Suze takes her punter up to the room rather optimistically decked out as Arabian Nights. She reckons he's about her age. He's had a drink but she wouldn't call him pissed. He doesn't look like he's up for the non-stop fun of his whooping, whistling blonde friend. But didn't Evie reckon he's a first-timer? Suze would agree.

'Is Ebony your real name?' he asks her as she shuts the door, runs a basin of warm water and beckons him over. Suze thought she was meant to be Velvet.

427

'You can call me whatever you like,' she purrs, unbuttoning his trousers and preparing to wash his cock.

'Could you call yourself Cathy? Please?'

Suze walks over to the bed and undresses until she's naked apart from Bev's fuck-me shoes.

'You're paying me, sunshine,' she tells him as she slides along the bed, gets up onto all fours, provocatively bucks her shapely rump in his direction and casts him a desirous look over her shoulder. 'Mummy. Whore. Your Majesty. Lara fucking Croft. Being called names is all part of the service, all part of the job. In with the price. You choose, Big Boy.'

'Cathy, please,' he says, clambering onto the bed, breathing fast, his hands warm and soft and everywhere. 'Cathy's fine.'

Adele Parks lives in London with her husband and son. She has published six best-selling novels to date: *Playing Away*, *Game Over*, *Larger Than Life*, *The Other Woman's Shoes*, *Still Thinking of You* and *Husbands*. Her books have been translated into seventeen different languages and are published throughout the world. Adele writes articles and short stories for a number of publications in the UK, USA and Australia.

For more information about Adele and her books, visit her website at www.adeleparks.com

WAKE-UP CALL

Adele Parks

I can't imagine why I'm here. What possessed me to accept an invitation to a college reunion? When the envelope dropped onto my doormat, my first reaction was to put it in the bin. Why would I want to meet up with people that I haven't seen for years? Surely, the point is, if we'd wanted to stay in touch, we would have.

I graduated ten years ago, and despite popular myth, student years were not the best years of my life. I remember them as a blur of damp accommodation, cheap curries, and a series of broken hearts and essay crises. While I send Christmas cards to about half a dozen old acquaintances, I only really have three true friends from college – one of whom lives in Australia and does something impressive as a management consultant. Another lives in India and does something worthy in a hospital in the Calcutta slums. And then there's Laura. Laura works as a junior copywriter in a small advertising agency, but dreams of writing novels. I'm a temp – a receptionist on my third career break and I dream about a knight in shining amour.

We share a flat and it was Laura who insisted that I attend this reunion.

'You can't not,' she'd argued. 'What else will you be doing that night?'

Which seemed to settle it.

We push open the bar door and I'm hit by beer and cigarette fumes. Laura starts waving to people. I don't actively recognise anyone, although one or two faces are vaguely familiar. We force our way to the bar and buy a bottle of wine. That's my idea, because if we find a table we can offer people a drink when they join us. Laura is insisting on smiling at everyone and she even thinks the nametags are a good idea. Mine's spelt wrong.

'It is you, isn't it?' I recognise Anna Crompton's voice without having to check the tag.

'Wow, Anna you look wonderful!' says Laura, flinging her arms around Anna. Anna smiles and although she shoots an up-and-down glance at both Laura and me, she doesn't return the compliment. I pass her the bottle of chardonnay and an empty glass and pray for the evening to be over.

'Are you married?' she asks, with all the subtlety of red, lacy underwear. Our silence is our confession. Neither Laura nor I are even regularly dating, which suits Laura and horrifies me.

'I got married last summer,' smiles Anna. Which I suppose explains why she's here. She never was one for team events, but she obviously saw this as a good opportunity to gloat. Her recently-married state also explains why she is glowing. I try not to resent it.

'Have you seen Sue?' she asks as she looks around the bar. Anna, Laura, Sue and I were not only in the same hall of residence, but we also all did the same course. This should mean we have plenty in common.

432

'There she is,' says Laura, pointing excitedly towards the door. Sue waves, blows kisses, and then flies towards us. She oozes activity. She always did. Sue is one of those people who always have thousands of friends to see and places to go. I lost touch with Anna because she's a horror to be with: I lost touch with Sue because I didn't have the energy to keep up.

Sue's still striking. If I'm pedantic and draw a distinction between beautiful and attractive, then she's attractive – but quite *especially* so. She's wearing her hair in a silky bob. She has an exquisite face, which she can rely on: enormous brown eyes framed with Bambi lashes, a wide nose and a rose red, lopsided mouth.

Everyone air kisses and then settles down.

'I hear you're married now, hey?' says Sue nudging Anna. This is all the prompting Anna needs. From nowhere she produces wedding photos and starts to give us a blow-by-blow account, from first kiss onwards. I remember when Anna wasn't above going out and getting wrecked, losing her shoes and if not quite flashing her boobs at passers-by, then at least insisting that she can pee standing up. Now, it appears, all she can talk about is matching towels from M&S and the importance of damp-proofing.

It's so depressing. And what's more depressing is that I'd pay a king's ransom to be so blissfully content with domestic dreariness, which makes me ashamed that women chained themselves to railings for me and burnt good underwear.

Laura entertains us with stories about the advertising agency and details her plans for getting her novel published. Her plans have been thwarted on a number of occasions. She regularly receives don't-call-us-we'll-call-you letters from publishing houses and agents. She puts this down to their inability to take risks. One thing can be said for Laura – she certainly isn't a quitter. I drift off as I look out of the window. The sun is doing its best – not exactly shining, more shimmering from time to time, whenever there's a gap in the clouds. I must have drunk too much. I'm feeling maudlin.

'What's up?' asks Laura.

I'm that transparent. I shrug.

'How's the teaching going?' asks Sue, politely.

'Teaching?' I'm confused.

'Didn't you always want to be a teacher?'

God, I'd almost forgotten wanting that. 'Er, never panned out. Couldn't face more exams after I got my degree.'

'Oh.' Sue nods, but she doesn't ask what I do instead.

'Are you seeing anyone at the moment?' asks Anna, but only because she knows the answer.

'I was seeing a lawyer until quite recently,' I comment. 'Didn't work out.'

'Why not?'

I shrug again. The problem is, it's difficult for me to explain *exactly* what went wrong. The difficulties, which must have been obvious to him, are indefinable to me. He'd said he wanted us to finish. That's all he said. Odd, because I'd spent my morning planning mini-breaks in Edinburgh or Prague – somewhere cold, so we'd have to cuddle. Somewhere old, so I could pretend to be cultured.

I'd asked him if he thought things were moving too quickly, if he thought I was commitment-shy. I offered him a range of options, from large-white-wedding to let's-just-be-friends. He didn't comment. We had the most silent break-up *ever*. I can't see him making much of a living as a barrister. His silence was particularly frustrating, because when I met him I was almost overwhelmed by how very interesting, articulate and clever he was. He had an opinion on just about every subject you can imagine, and it *always* impresses and thrills me when people can talk knowledgeably about politics, religion, history, sport – any, or a combination. All I can talk about with any certainty are feelings.

Laura always maintained that the lawyer was a bit overly fond of his own voice. But then she thought the management consultant was too materialistic; the web-designer, too flighty; the estate agent, too manic. Tinker, tailor, solider, sailor, none of them ever meets her criteria. I think she's too picky. She thinks I'm not picky enough. She's always going on about the fact that I deserve better, '*if only I could see that*'. I tell her the issue is getting other people – male people – to see me *at all*. That's challenge enough. She usually sighs at this point in the discussion and offers to make a cup of tea.

I wonder if the girls can throw any light on the break-up. I reach for the wine and pour myself a generous glass. 'I know that it's mostly my pride that's bruised. He was nice enough but . . .' I leave the sentence unfinished. *Nice enough* is condemnation enough.

'Just physical, then? Good sex?' asks Sue.

'Not even that.' We grin.

I decide against telling her that I can't remember when I last had good sex. The most I hope for nowadays is an absence of any out and out peculiarities: an over-reliance on sex toys, premature ejaculation, ingrowing toenails, hairy backs . . .

'How's Dave?'

Dave is Sue's husband. They met during Fresher's Week and have been together ever since. Thirteen years! The longest relationship I've ever had is four and a half months. Unless you count Karl. But you can't really count Karl, as that only lasted two years because he lives in Germany.

'Fine,' She hesitates and then adds, 'I imagine.'

As she tries to light her fag the match breaks and she throws the box onto the table in a temper. None of us say a word. Laura holds up a lighter. There is so obviously something wrong that you can almost touch it in the air.

Finally she adds, 'We're getting divorced.'

'Divorced?' repeats Laura in astonishment.

'Did he have an affair?' asks Anna, angrily.

I'm too stunned to say anything. Sue shakes her head. She's debating whether old friendships, which have been neglected, are still relevant. It could be the distance between us that prompts her to go on.

'Nobody warned me. Nobody told me the important stuff, like why *doesn't* respect, peace and trust always add up to being in love? How can we possibly mistake excitement, passion and lust for love?'

'*You* had an affair,' says Laura, deadpan.

Sue nods and puts her head on the table. Her silky hair falls forward into a puddle of wine. She doesn't seem to notice or, if she's noticed, she doesn't care. I'm fascinated and repelled.

Our intimate party breaks up fairly swiftly after that. Some blokes who studied Geography ask if they can join our table and instead of shunning them as we always did, we eagerly welcome them. None of us want to face the intensity of Sue's confession. We drink a lot and then drunkenly swap telephone numbers, promising to not leave it so long next time

Laura and I treat ourselves to a cab home.

'You're quiet. Did you hate it?' asks Laura.

'I'm glad I went.'

'What even though your dream of Happily Ever After was blown apart when you heard Sue's news?'

'Especially because of that.'

Laura starts to chat about how grey someone or other is and how lined thingy-me-bobby is but how radiant blah blah is. I barely follow. My mind is full of plans. I don't say so, but I plan to get up really early tomorrow morning and get on the internet to research teacher training places. Because, while it might just be the alcohol giving me a false sense of optimism and a new perspective, I don't think it is. Sue's story, and Anna's too for that matter, didn't depress me, as I'd have expected. They poked and prodded me. Never again will I sit in a room and admit that my only news is that a mute barrister has ditched me. Even a divorce seems more of an achievement than doing nothing at all.

'You didn't mean it when you said we should meet up again, did you?' asks Laura.

'I might have. I think I did.' Laura looks surprised but pleased. 'The thing is, Laura, life is what passes you by when you're waiting for something to happen.'

Laura looks confused. 'Did you read that on a Hallmark card?'

'Probably, but it doesn't mean it's not profound.' Laura looks skeptical so I admit, 'Well, it probably does, but either way I've decided not to wait any longer.'

She doesn't understand but she puts her arm around me anyway. She'll get it. I'll show her. I'll show myself.

Victoria Routledge was born in the Lake District and she prefers it when it's raining. She also likes cars, strong coffee and spooky old houses. Victoria's fifth novel, *Constance and Faith*, is published by Pocket Books.

THE LEADING LADY

Victoria Routledge

Etterbeck Women's Institute Hall, one wet night in February.

'. . . yes, it's absolutely coming down stair-rods, now, isn't it? Where does all this water come from? Still, it means we get a jolly good turn out if it's too wet for the crown green bowls. That's the only explanation I can think of for an attendance like this on a *Crimewatch* night. Goodness me, there must be over twenty ladies here!

Well, perhaps they have come to see you, dear, yes. Who knows? We do have one or two bookworms in our membership. Don't get out much, you know. No fines on large-print books either . . .

Hello? Ladies?

They're not normally this rowdy, Mrs Bannister, I can assure you! I think we may have some interlopers tonight from the sugarcraft society. I don't want to use this bell, but if I have to . . .

Hello? Can I have your attention to the front? Please? Thank you! Thank you, Mrs Eelbeck! If you've quite . . . Yes, if you could see my lips moving, it means I *was* talking. Mrs Granger, could you adjust her hearing aid for her? I don't think she's quite tuned in to WI FM, if you get my drift.

That's better. I said, that's better, Mrs Eelbeck!

No, I have not had my hair set. Really . . .

May I welcome one and all to our February meeting, which tonight includes a convening of the Etterbeck Ladies book group, and let's extend an especially warm welcome to our newest member, Mrs Parkinson, who has recently moved into Audrey Richard's old bungalow. Just another twenty years to go and you'll be one of the village, dear! I'm joking, of course.

Yes, I *am*, Mrs Riley!

We're a *very* inclusive group, Mrs Parkinson. We have all sorts here! As you can see.

Just a few notices before we launch into our literary appreciation this evening. First of all, let's remember in our thoughts, Audrey Richard. We have decided to donate the money raised by the Guess The Weight of the Cake raffle to the RSPCA. It's what she would have wanted. (How heavy was it? Eight pounds ten, Mrs Gore. Yes, I *know*. The *currants*, apparently.) And let's all bear in mind just how dangerous aquariums can be when you've got Basset hounds. A lesson there for us all, especially you, Mrs Ricketts. Your Tilly . . . still barred from the obedience class, is she? Well, think on, dear.

(I hope it's all dried out now, Mrs Parkinson? Oh. The estate agent didn't mention . . . Oh, I see . . . Well, it's nothing Febreze and a good airing can't nip in the bud, I daresay.)

Thank you. Now, may I remind everyone that this week's competition is for Oldest Teapot, and will be judged by our guest, Mrs Bannister. After last month's furore over Prettiest Spectacle Case, you're limited to two entries each.

Yes, I'm sorry, only two, Mrs Tyler.

Well, yes, I can see you've brought more than two, but if you put them all out there won't be room for anyone else to . . . Yes, I can know your father was the area's top tea importer but that makes you semi-professional, dear, so maybe you shouldn't be entering at all!

Up to you, dear. If you could limit yourself to two . . . Well, I imagine Mrs Bannister is as able to adjudge the age of a teapot as anyone else, unless you'd rather step aside from the competition and judge it yourself . . . ? No? Well, suit yourself.

So, everyone else, if you could place your entries on the competition table, Mrs Bannister's final decision will be made over refreshments. Our hostesses this week are Mrs Granger and Mrs Parkinson. I hope you're prepared to have your sponge examined by experts, Mrs Parkinson! We have been the Rannerthwaite regional WI baking champions four years' running! Not that I want you to feel under any pressure!

So, if we could . . . Is someone whistling? Am I hearing things?

Oh, it's Mrs Eelbeck's hearing aid. Mrs Granger, would you . . . ? Just down a little . . . that's much better, thank you. I said, thank you, Mrs Eelbeck.

Any volunteers to visit Mayton Institute's spring fair next month as Ambassadors of Friendship? No? We have to send *someone*. No? Anyone? Now, I don't think that's a Christian thing to say, Mrs Tyler. It's a good while since the curd incident. Four years at least. We can't hold it against them for ever! No, I'm serious – we can't. Well, if no one will volunteer, I'll put names in a hat after tea, and I'm afraid it'll be compulsory.

I said nothing about pustules, Mrs Eelbeck. No. No, I

didn't. Really, I didn't. Well, why on earth would I? Up a notch, please, if you would, Mrs Granger . . . thank you so much.

Anyway, on to the main business! Now, Mrs Bannister is, as you know, our very own local "celebrity author", having had three of her "saga pot-boilers" published. Some of you may know her as . . . Well, that's what they're referred to in the trade, aren't they, Mrs Bannister? "Pit-fic"? You prefer regional family epics? I see. Well, they *are* your books, I suppose! Anyhoo, at the request of various members, Mrs Bannister has graciously agreed to lend her professional opinions to our discussion this evening and if, only *if* though, any time remains to us at the end of the meeting, she may answer some questions about writing.

At the *end* of the meeting, if you wouldn't mind, please, ladies.

Now, just to bring Mrs Bannister up to speed – who's minuting? Mrs Andrews? Well, can someone give her a biro, please. We had a very spirited debate about what we should select as our Novel of the Month, and there were one or two members who suggested one of Mrs Bannister's own little pot-boilers! Yes, really! Well, not so little, I suppose. Quite the doorstops, those books! Do they pay you by the ounce? Only joking! But, anyway, I said how embarrassing it would be for you to hear us picking it to pieces, so –

Or having to listen to compliments, yes, Mrs Tyler, that's true as well, I suppose, though there's no need to suck up to Mrs Bannister! She's going to judge those teapots fair and square!

Don't minute that, Mrs Andrews.

As I say, we had a very lively debate, with several intriguing titles being proposed, including my own magnum opus, *The*

Love That Knew No Bounds! But as it's still being considered by several top London agents, I decided to plead modesty and hide my light under a bushel. I know, I know – next year perhaps.

(Minute that, Agnes. Thank you.)

So, getting back to the matter in hand, Mrs Bannister, we plumped for Mrs Rance's suggestion, and this month we've all been agog at the adventures of Harry Potter. Some more than others, I would hazard a guess. And the topic that little know-it-all man at the library has suggested for us to discuss is, let me just get my spectacles on, is . . . 'The reality of magic: how much magic is there in everyday life?' (How *ridiculous*. He's not running the Open University. Someone should have a word . . .) So! Who'd like to start us off?

Anyone? Don't be shy!

It was quite a long book, yes, Mrs Duckworth. Although length is not necessarily a mark of great penmanship! Well, yes, I suppose it did make it good value, but still . . . Any thoughts on the, er, reality of magic? In everyday life?

Excuse me, but if anyone has questions for Mrs Bannister, would you mind directing them through the chair. Through me, Mrs Eelbeck. Me. Through. Me. Dear. Thank you.

How did she feel when she saw her book in the shops? Well, I imagine she felt very pleased, didn't you, Mrs Bannister? Very pleased and ever-so-slightly humble at the thought of all those people out there reading it and forming judgements about your . . . very distinctive style.

Yes, I enjoyed it too. We all enjoyed it. Didn't we? Of course I've read it, Mrs Eelbeck! *Friend or Family*?

Friend of the Family. My mistake, I beg your pardon. Easy mistake for anyone to make though, the amount of nasty little squabbles there are in it! All that bickering – you'd think they loathed each other!

Yes, well, it *was* an excellent story. A little melodramatic in parts, perhaps, but maybe that's what made it such a hit with the soap opera crowd. I myself felt there was no need for some of the language, but I daresay that's what sells. Yes, Mrs Tyler, I *have* read it, more or less. The first few chapters, at any rate. No offence, Mrs Bannister, but it's not really my cup of tea. I myself lean towards literary fiction. Anyhoo, shall we get back to the . . .

Another question? Well, make it a quick one, Mrs Pattinson. Now, that's a very good question. How *did* you get published, Mrs Bannister? Sorry, dear, that came out badly.

I see.

Mmm.

Well, that's fascinating, but time is against us as always, and I'm sure everyone would like to get back to the matter in hand, which is . . .

Now it's funny that you should bring that up, Mrs Granger, because that, for myself, was the weakest part of the book. I myself felt that the character of Linda was far from credible. I mean, women like that simply don't exist! What a fishwife! All that bossing and shouting . . . And some of the expressions!

Goodness me, you do seem to have brought a fan club with you, Mrs Bannister. One more question, ladies, because I'm sure there are plenty of people here who spent a great deal of time ploughing through Harry Potter and all those goblins and what-have-you when they could have been getting on with more pressing tasks like editing their son's wedding video. Yes, I am talking about myself here! I know it was last year, but my own writing commitments have taken priority, and believe me, there was a lot of editing to be done on that video. I was far from happy about some of the singing. Not that I'm criticising your organ-playing, Mrs Barber. Well, not much. Ladies! One more question, and that is it.

Where does any writer get their inspiration from? From their imagination, I should think! It's certainly where I get my inspiration from. Mrs Bannister? From real life? Really? As I say, I've never met characters like yours in real life, dear.

I don't think it's necessary to elaborate with an anecdote, no, not even a very amusing one. Well, yes, I hope I can take a joke, but I don't really see . . . Well, no, I hadn't read quite as far as the scene in the church where . . .

. . . where the mother-of-the-groom stops the wedding to—

No.

No, I don't believe you would do something so . . .

Marjorie!

No, Mrs Tyler, I'm not choking. I'm just . . .

Yes, Mrs Granger, that's quite correct, Mrs Bannister is my sister-in-law. There's no need for Mrs Eelbeck to whisper, I can hear her from the front of the hall. I'd hate to hear her shouting.

Sister-in-law, yes. No *blood relation*. No, my middle name is not Linda. I don't know what you all find so amusing.

All right, so I may have *temporarily* stopped the wedding so the vicar could redo the vows with better enunciation, but that's no reason to assume that Linda is based on me! What? Even if she does . . . ? No, I hadn't read that far. And for the record, before anyone asks, I have never asked my mother to change her will, I have never thrown my children out onto the street, although I admit I have come perilously close to changing the locks a few times when our Colleen got her tongue done, and I have never, *ever*, taken my belt off to anyone, buckle end or not!

No, I don't know what happens at the end of the book, Mrs Mattock. I haven't got that far yet. I don't think I want to . . . Oh, should I? Really? Linda gets what? *Where?* Good God . . .

Pass me that orange squash, Mrs Tyler. I think I need it more than you.

Does anyone have anything else they want to ask? No? Good, well, in that case, shall we . . .

Have I ever worked as a dockside daisy? Well, what do *you* think, Mrs Eelbeck?

Mrs Eelbeck, I don't care if you *were* asking Marjorie, I think I have a right to reply. Well, if you don't mind my interrupting, Marjorie, evidently there are people here who *do* have trouble distinguishing fact from fiction, especially now you've planted that thought in their heads. You, for a start.

Yes, I *am* upset. I am absolutely speechless. I am struck *dumb* with shock. I simply don't have words to tell you how very unpleasant I find this. I honestly don't know what to say. Words fail me, Marjorie. After all we've been through with your Arthur! I mean, it's not as though you've not got plenty of material right there in your own front room. Have you been using that, eh? That funny business with the courgettes? And your Barry's leg? Hmm?

You may well blush, lady. And yes, *do* let's continue this conversation somewhere more private. What do you mean, there's something else I should know . . .

Film rights?

Patricia *Routledge*? As in Hyacinth *Bouquet*?

No, I am not "having an attack", Mrs Granger. I'll have you know this is yoga breathing.

Give me a moment.

(How could you, Marjorie? Now, *Penelope Keith* I could have understood.)

Is there any other business?

Any other *Institute* business? Fine, well – no, save it till the next meeting, Mrs Tyler, please! – in that case I call this meeting closed, and will see you all Tuesday next. Mrs Granger, pick a teapot – that one? Right, fine. Talk to the hand, Mrs Tyler! I said *talk* to the *hand*, Mrs Eelbeck! Yes, I am being rude! Now, Marjorie, the car, if you don't mind. No need to offer lifts, ladies, Mrs Bannister's coming home with me. No, there isn't time for you to tell them about your new book. Even if it is going to be in Tesco's next . . .

"No Blood Relation"?

Charming.

The car, Marjorie. Before I say something you might write down.'

Louise Voss is the author of four novels for Black Swan/Transworld: *To Be Someone*, *Are You My Mother?*, *Lifesaver* and *Games People Play*. She lives near Hampton Court Palace in south-west London, with her eight year old daughter and their flatulent cat.

Her website is www.louisevoss.com

BEST SERVED COLD

Louise Voss

Clive prised open his eyes at four-thirty pm, squinting from the slits between his matted lashes. His shift at the restaurant started in less than an hour, three different colour tube lines north of where he lay, queasy and fed up.

He climbed out of bed and gingerly reached for the uniform – black trousers, white shirt – he'd discarded at seven that morning, feeling the sickening memory of whisky pressing behind his eyeballs. He'd have to iron the shirt, or he'd be fired, but the trousers should be OK. That had been some session. Him and Burt, one of the sous-chefs. Surely they hadn't talked about Lisa for six hours solid? Or rather, Clive had ranted and Burt listened. How dare she dump him after two weeks? What was wrong with her? He'd only asked for that other woman's phone number, that was all . . .

'I've got a boyfriend,' the woman had said smugly, and it turned out that Lisa had been looming in the background the whole time, with the woman's bill on a little silver tray, and a face that would pickle walnuts.

Cursing Lisa, his job, and his hangover, Clive managed to

dress, iron the shirt, and simultaneously pee and comb his hair, in fifteen minutes flat. A voice in his head nagged him with the same boring persistence as his headache: why are you bothering? It's only a crappy job. Let her have the hassle of finding a replacement for you. Ditch the bitch (he forgot, temporarily, that it was in fact he himself who had been ditched).

It was a shame, because Lisa was very pretty. She had four different shades of blonde in her long stripy hair, which matched the colours of the restaurant's wooden floor exactly. After their first proper date, Clive had asked her if she'd had it done intentionally that way, but she just laughed, not answering. He'd concluded that she had.

In the end, Clive decided that trying to find a new job would be too much like hard work, so he hunched his arms into a thick woollen jacket, and took a last look in the mirror.

Clive's mirror was purposefully not full-length, so that he could admire the beauty of his sharp planed face, amber eyes, and black hair, without having to dwell on another part of his anatomy: his exceptionally bandy legs. Clive *hated* his legs. They were cartoon legs, worse than chicken legs, humiliatingly puny and grotesquely bowed. 'John Wayne' was his nickname at school, and not because he was a handsome burly cowboy. That was the main problem with being a waiter – too many opportunities for punters to look at his legs. If only desk jobs weren't so boring, he'd have gone for one like a shot.

Clive's restaurant (or rather, the restaurant of which his ex-girlfriend was assistant manager) was an upscale, modern eaterie, identical in ambience and menu to countless others in London. It was all halogen spotlights and roasted seabass, couscous, fennel fritters and coulis, and frequented by hordes of beautiful, rich women – which, for Clive, was the biggest perk of the job.

He made it his mission to see how many propositions he could attract in one night. When he and Lisa started going out, it became even more of a challenge to see if he could still pull. He'd managed it twice before she caught him out.

'Birds,' he said to his reflection in disgust. 'They're so damn clingy.'

After gulping down a carton of strawberry milk, Clive slouched off to the tube. He didn't feel at all well. In fact, his right leg seemed to be dragging very slightly, and he hoped he wasn't about to have a heart attack.

At five thirty-four, four minutes late, he was pushing open the heavy glass doors of Richmond's Place and heading for the kitchen.

'Where's Burt?' Clive called over the top of the servery to another of the sous-chefs, Mick. Mick was all right, apart from the fact that he was always moaning about his constipation. Clive had absolutely no patience with people who harped on about their ailments.

'Phoned in sick,' said Lisa, who materialised beside him. She was smirking – tactlessly, for someone who'd just dumped him, he thought. He couldn't help wondering if it was because of his bandy legs.

'Didn't you two go out last night?'

Clive hung up his coat and wrapped a large white apron around his waist. He wore his longer than the other waiters, in the hope that it would cover up the worst of his problem. Mick made a face at him behind Lisa's back, waving a thin but sharp vegetable knife in his direction, warning him not to get Burt into trouble. Everybody loved Burt. Clive couldn't imagine any of them sticking up for *him*, though.

'Yeah, we had a drink,' he replied, his fingers fumbling with the ties of his apron. 'Burt said he wasn't feeling great then – he went home soon after. Said he felt sick.'

Soon after had actually been six hours later but hey, Clive thought, it was all relative. And it earned him a wink from Mick.

'You look rough yourself,' said Lisa, fixing her unnaturally green eyes on his face. Clive was convinced that she wore coloured contact lenses, but had been unable to verify this, even on the occasions he'd stayed over at her place.

He stuck out his chin and ran a hand through his hair. 'Never felt better.'

'Good, because we need everyone to be on top form. We're packed tonight.'

By seven thirty the restaurant was already three-quarters full. Dido had been turned up from three to eight on the volume dial of the hidden stereo, and Lisa had dimmed the lights twice. Clive watched the bones in her wrist and hand flex beneath the thin covering of her skin as she twiddled the dimmer switch, and felt nostalgic for what might have been. He didn't normally 'do' relationships, but there'd been something special about Lisa. Dammit, he even felt sad.

But by the time he had served sixteen portions of that evening's special – bream on a bed of pureed cauliflower with lemon-glaze carrots – any vestiges of sadness had been bludgeoned away by the pounding of his head. The chunks of bream, with their blackened scaly skin, were making him queasy. They looked like he felt: crispy with lifelessness.

Just then a group of four attractive women moved through the doors together, fluid as jellyfish, waving their arms, talking and laughing. Lisa showed them all to one of Clive's tables, where she distributed menus and wine lists.

Clive momentarily forgot his hangover and began making bets with himself as to which of these women he could score with. They were all a little bit older than him; early thirties, perhaps, and all sexy – although that black-haired one was a bit skinny. There were two short-haired blondes, one slim with glasses, and one more chunky, with a long nose. The last woman, a brunette, was particularly lovely; buxom, but not in an obvious way. Sparkly eyelids, but not overdone. Her, he thought. I want her.

'*Excuse* me,' said an irate middle-aged man with such a big stomach that his shirt buttons were almost popping. 'If you've *got a minute*, we'd like to order.' His girlfriend, an emaciated old bird in a mini-skirt, tutted in agreement. She must have been at least forty-five, thought Clive with disdain. He didn't mind an older woman, but there came a time when females should admit defeat and cover up.

'Certainly, sir,' Clive said, whipping his order pad out of his apron pocket whilst simultaneously giving the customer's unattractive belly a hard stare, as if to say, *not that you need anything more to eat, fat boy*. He took the order, all the while straining his ears to try and eavesdrop on the table of women.

'He did what?' screeched the one with the glasses, her hand flying to her mouth. 'Oh, I'm sorry, but that man is just way too possessive of you.' She was addressing the gorgeous brunette.

Damn, thought Clive, she's already spoken for. Still, she hasn't met me yet, has she? He smirked faintly, noticing that his banging headache had subsided to a manageable throb.

'I *said*, what does that come with?' Fatboy was getting annoyed.

Clive checked his pad to see what he had automatically written down – the man's words having bypassed his brain completely and come straight out on the pad. Oh, right, he'd ordered the pheasant.

'It comes with sugarsnaps and baby new potatoes, sir,' he intoned, aware that his supercilious expression meant that he'd be kissing goodbye to a tip. Sometimes it was worth it, just to wind them up. Customers – he hated them. Unless there was something in it for him, such as a shag.

By the time Clive had taken the women's orders and poured their wine, he had gleaned that the brunette lived with her (possessive) husband in Camden; the black-haired one had recently become pregnant – she put her hand over the top of her empty wineglass when he approached with the bottle, and simpered, 'I wish I could drink for two as well as eat for two, but I'd better not,' and they all laughed; the blonde with glasses was celebrating a large bonus at work and would therefore treat them all tonight; and the tubby blonde had been feeling poorly earlier.

He thought he'd been doing pretty well on the flirtation front. He met their eyes, smiled, nodded attentively, made sure he was standing underneath a spotlight so that it would give his hair a luxuriant sheen. And they were all responding beautifully; giggling and peering over their menus like geishas simpering behind fans. He was in there, definitely – but with which one? Any of them would do, frankly, even that pregnant one, at a push.

Just as he was walking away to get the women a new bottle of mineral water, it happened. His hypersensitive radar alerted him to the fact that they had all suddenly fallen silent; and then – then – there was a great, unanimous gale of uncontrollable but swiftly stifled *laughter*! He wheeled around to catch the pregnant one pointing towards him, quaking with hilarity.

Clive's bandy legs – the subject, he was sure, of the hilarity – almost buckled under the humiliation, and his hangover immediately returned at full blast.

How dare they? Those judgemental *bitches*! Had they no sensitivity? He felt his peaky skin warm into a flush. Risking a glance towards Lisa, he saw that she was biting the insides of her cheeks as if trying not to laugh too – oh God, this was terrible!

He stormed through the restaurant and out of the fire door at the back, crashing down the heavy metal bar with the heel of his hand to open it, and blundering outside. He leaned his head against the rough brick wall, breathing heavily. *Bitches, evil bitches*. He contemplated doing a runner, never coming back – but then he had a better idea . . .

Revenge was a dish best not served on a bed of pureed cauliflower, he thought, his mind racing through a rudimentary plan. The worm would turn. He was going to teach these women that you didn't laugh at Clive Sampson and get away with it.

Ten minutes later the plan was underway. He began with the pregnant one and the long-nosed blonde. Those two were easy to sort – pregnant women were always moaning about their ailments, and the blonde had already complained of feeling sick. So Clive crept back inside and sidled across to the pegs where the staff kept their coats. Glancing around to make sure no one was looking, he slipped his hand into the pocket of Mick's overcoat. Just as he'd anticipated, his fingers closed around a packet of laxatives – and, much to Clive's delight, Mick preferred his laxatives in powder form.

It was no bother at all to surreptitiously empty all ten sachets of the medicine into two portions of mashed potato and mix it up.

His glee at the revenge plot almost made him forget the affliction which the women had been so cruelly mocking, but as he walked out with the two seasoned main courses, he was reminded again. It was almost beyond belief, the way that they appeared to find his unfortunate disability – for this is how Clive viewed his bandy legs – so hilarious.

He took a deep breath and forced his most beaming smile upon the women.

'Which of you beautiful ladies is having the sea bass?' he asked, inclining his head coquettishly, willing them to stop laughing. The long-nosed blonde and the skinny black-haired one put up their hands, still fighting back titters.

He slid their meals in front of them. 'Enjoy,' he said, before turning to gaze at the other two with rapturous attentiveness. 'Yours are just coming,' he murmured, his eyes flicking down the brunette's cleavage. She was delicious, creamy-skinned and perfect. Her husband really isn't going to be happy when he finds out she's been messing around with other men, thought Clive.

After he'd served a seafood risotto to the other blonde, and a skate wing to the brunette, he walked up to Lisa. Unbelievably, she too was still smirking.

'What's so damn funny?' he hissed at her.

'Nothing, Clive.'

He wanted to punch her. 'Right. Well. I'm just going on my break for ten minutes, OK?'

'Make sure you're back by the time table ten finish their mains, won't you?'

He nodded curtly and waited until she set off across the

restaurant floor. Then he dived into the cloakroom. Coat, coat, what sort of coat had the brunette been wearing? Something big and red, he thought. There were only two red overcoats amongst all the tightly packed outerwear in there, and he found what he was looking for almost immediately.

Oh, this is too easy, he thought as he pulled her travel-card out of her coat pocket. Her name was Jayne Harmony. Very glamorous photo – she looked as if she was about to slide a tongue over her hot, glossy lips. He slipped the card out of the clear plastic folder and examined the back of it. *28a Mitchell Gardens*, Camden, it said in small neat black ink, and underneath, bingo! A telephone number, which he copied down on his pad, before replacing the card in her pocket.

'Fag break,' he said to the chef on his way past. The chef glowered at him. He was arranging herbs around a steaming skate wing, white and terrifyingly skeletal on the plate.

Ponce, thought Clive, retrieving his mobile phone from his own coat pocket. Outside again, he lit a cigarette for appearance's sake, and took a deep drag. With the other hand, he dialled Jayne Harmony's telephone number.

'Hello?'

'Mr Harmony?'

'Who wants to know?'

'Jayne's husband?'

'Yes. Who is this?'

'I'm not telling you my name,' Clive paused. 'Perhaps you've already heard it, though. Perhaps when you're in bed with Jayne, she might have let it slip? Because she was always calling it out when *we* were together . . .' He let this sink in. 'Mr Harmony?'

'This is a wind-up . . .'

'No, Mr Harmony. Your wife was a great lay, by the way. She's decided it's time to move on to the next one, but that's her decision. I just thought you should know.'

The line went dead. Clive exhaled a plume of smoke, and smiled.

Back inside, he was unsurprised when the blonde with the glasses beckoned him over, a worried look on her face. She and Jayne Harmony were sitting alone at the table. Blimey, that was quick, he thought.

'Can we have the bill please? One of our friends isn't feeling well.'

Only one of them? He had to bite his lip to stop himself saying it. Their plates both had pleasingly sizeable chunks of the mashed potato missing. 'Sorry to hear that, Madam. Nothing wrong with the food, was there?'

Jayne Harmony smiled. 'Oh no, it was lovely. Wish we could stay for dessert.'

He smiled back. 'You must come again.' Clearing the plates, he braced himself slightly as he turned away, waiting for more laughter, but none came. They must be too preoccupied with their sick friend, he thought. As he passed the Ladies, the long-nosed blonde emerged. She looked pale and shaken.

'Is everything all right, Madam?' he enquired.

'Can you call an ambulance, please? Our friend is very ill in there. She's in the early stages of pregnancy – it could be serious.'

'Right away, Madam. Sorry to hear it,' he lied, mentally tutting to himself. An ambulance! For a bit of diarrhoea! Women were such drama queens. Talk of the devil, he thought, as Lisa bustled over.

'This lady's friend is unwell.' He moved away, letting Lisa take over, and prepared their bill, which he handed to the woman with glasses. She flipped a gold Visa card onto the little tray without even looking at it. She was too busy gazing towards the door of the Ladies and saying to Jayne, 'Should we go in and check?'

'No. We wouldn't be helping. We'll just let them know when the ambulance arrives.'

Both women looked upset. Good, thought Clive. He swiped the credit card through the machine – £120 – and then again – £400 – and took the first of the two printed receipts back out for the blonde one to sign. Pity he couldn't keep the £400 – Lisa would notice if he removed any cash – and the woman would probably get it back eventually, but it would be a hell of a hassle for her.

He was already planning the internet shopping he'd do when he got home. He could get anything delivered to that empty house next door – an iPod, perhaps. Maybe even a plane ticket somewhere exotic. He'd had it with this dump.

Her name was Rebecca Murphy. She signed the slip in a flashy squiggle, adding only a measly ten pound tip. Clive was affronted as he peeled off the yellow copy and handed it back to her. The tight bitch! Still, it only took a minute to copy her card number and expiry date into his notepad.

A voice behind him made him jump. 'Could we have our coats please?' It was the other blonde, looking a bit green around the gills. Jayne Harmony came up beside her.

'You know, Jayne, I think I'm coming out in sympathy with Eileen. I don't feel at all well.'

'Is it the same thing you had yesterday?'

'Might be. I've just suddenly got a really bad stomach-ache. Is Liz OK going to hospital with Eileen?'

Jayne nodded. 'I think so. I'd go myself, only I promised Steve I wouldn't be late. You know what he's like.'

'Look after yourself, then. Let's meet for coffee on Saturday. Eleven o'clock at Sergios?'

'Oh God, I've got to go . . .' The blonde bolted into the disabled toilet, just as a blue swirl of ambulance lights lit the restaurant, and two ambulancemen rushed in, carrying a stretcher. The diners' eyes were out on stalks.

Clive quietly lifted his coat off the peg and, for the final time, slipped out of the fire exit and caught the tube home, dreaming of the extended holiday he'd have on Rebecca Murphy's credit card.

By Friday everything was organised. He rang Lisa and told her he'd broken his leg, and wouldn't be back at work for three weeks. As predicted, she told him not to bother coming back at all. He tutted to himself – talk about loyalty to your staff! It was a joke. Courtesy of Rebecca Murphy he had a one-way flight to Goa all booked and paid for, plus a mini iPod, a new rucksack, new trainers, and a small tent. They'd all arrived by Next Day Delivery at the empty house next door (which he entered via a back window, to wait for his purchases). He was due to leave on Saturday afternoon.

One thing, though, still nagged at him. He didn't feel guilty or anything – why should he? They'd been laughing at him. But he suddenly really wanted to know how it had all turned out. If Rebecca had stopped her card. How sick the others had been. What Jayne Harmony's husband had done . . .

Against his better judgement, he found himself pushing open the door of Sergio's coffee shop in Camden at 10.45 on Saturday morning, his rucksack on his back, shades hiding his eyes and a baseball cap rammed low on his head.

He ordered a cappuccino and pretended to read a newspaper. At ten fifty-five Jayne Harmony walked in. She too

460

was wearing shades, but they didn't hide the livid violet bruise covering her cheekbone and eye socket. She sat down at a nearby table with her back to him.

Five minutes later, Rebecca arrived. The two women greeted one another sombrely, their muted kisses so different from the exuberant entrance into the restaurant the week before. Rebecca cried when she saw her friend's face.

'He went mad,' Jayne said quietly. Clive had to strain to hear her. 'Called me a slag, accused me of having all kinds of affairs . . . I think he's schizophrenic. I've left him. I'm staying at my mother's. I'm glad, in a way, that I've found out what he's really like. I always did have my doubts – you know that.'

Good, thought Clive. He'd done her a favour after all, then. Perhaps when he came back from his trip, he might look Jayne up, see if she fancied a drink or two. Now that she was free.

'And how's Eileen?'

'She's going to be fine. They said she was very lucky not to have a miscarriage –'

Something unfamiliar prickled at the back of Clive's neck – guilt. He dismissed it. There had probably been something else wrong with her, not laxative-related at all.

'Guess what? They did a scan, and it turns out she's having twins! Can you believe it? She's over the moon.'

'That's incredible. Well, she always did want a big family. Did you know that Liz had a stomach upset too? She's better now, though. Actually she's quite chuffed – she lost six pounds in four days.'

Clive felt faintly annoyed. His big revenge plot was turning out to be a damp squib. Of course he wouldn't have wanted the skinny one to lose her babies, but still, they all seemed

461

a bit overly fine. And Rebecca obviously had no idea about her credit card's adventures, either. Oh well, he thought. No harm done. I taught them a lesson. Now I'm off on a well-deserved holiday. He put down the newspaper and swung the heavy rucksack onto his back. Without leaving a tip, he began to walk towards the door. Rebecca opened her mouth as if to say something else, but Jayne interrupted her, her voice bright again.

'Still – we did have *one* good laugh,' she said.

Rebecca snorted into her coffee. 'How could I ever forget?'

They suddenly giggled, and both began to talk at the same time:

'That waiter . . .'

'That *prat* . . .'

'Thought he was God's gift . . .'

'Really fancied himself . . .'

'And all the time walking about–'

'*With last night's underpants sticking out the bottom of his trouser leg*!' they chorused hysterically.

Clive swallowed hard and walked past them, turning sideways to manoeuvre himself and his rucksack through the door. He headed for the tube to catch the Piccadilly Line to Heathrow Airport, unaware of the burly Detective Sergeant who'd be waiting for him at the check-in desk. Visa's computers had picked up certain irregularities on Rebecca Murphy's credit card, informed her, and she had told the police. If Clive had stayed in the coffee shop long enough to delve in his pockets for a tip, he'd have heard her telling Jayne all about it.

Fiona Walker began her writing career at just twenty one, and had instant success with her first novel. Since then she has written eight best-sellers, most recently *Tongue in Cheek*. In her trademark 'bucolic frolics', larger than life characters enjoy sex and laughter, as well as tears and temptation, in action-packed roller-coaster plots with the best loved-up endings in the business. Fiona lives in cheerful chaos in the Cotswolds with four horses and two dogs.

THE KATO LOVER

Fiona Walker

'How do I make Kate say "*oh*"?' he asked as he thrust away enthusiastically. 'How do I do that, baby? Make Kate say "*oh, ohhhh, OHHHH!*" Kate – oh!'

'Kato?'

'Yes, baby. I want to make Kate say "*oh*".'

Kate watched his face and fought giggles.

They were making love, she reminded herself. Think passion. Do *not* think Peter Sellers with a moustache, under attack.

'*Oh!*' she managed to squeak.

'Yes, Kate – *oh*! How do I make Kate say "*oh*" again – how, Kate – *oh*!'

She chewed back the delight. 'You could try hiding in the wardrobe, catching me unawares and then leaping on me.'

'*Eh?*' The tempo slowed briefly and then he plunged on. 'I was . . . thinking . . . Christ that's good . . . more along the lines of . . . you going on top.'

Kate, who had formed a very comfortable nest amongst the pillows, had no intention of moving. Tonight, she was on a missionary mission.

'You carry on like that, darling – it feels just great.' She tried to hurry him along. She had an early start in the morning. Her recent fight with the giggles was a fair second to the orgasm that would take forever to arrive. 'That feels great – *mmm*.'

Afterwards, she stared up at the ceiling in the dark and wondered if their sex life was ever going to get any better. It had been so wonderful once. She missed the laughter. She knew that she was guilty of becoming lazy and complacent, but Sandy was equally guilty of sameness. Their lovemaking had changed from bawdy five act opera to predictable soap – three episodes a week with an omnibus repeat at weekends. And the storylines kept coming round again and again.

Rolling onto her side, she remembered how much they had giggled at first, white-hot passion and mirth seeming so natural together. As the years passed, sex had to be timetabled into the short gaps between his shift-work and her nine to five, and it had become a far more intermittent, serious business. The spark that had once ignited carnal firecrackers now lit faithful and sombre church candles – the flame yet to be snuffed out, but the dirge well underway.

'We could try something a bit different next time,' she suggested tentatively.

'Is that what all that hiding in the wardrobe stuff was about?' he asked sleepily, as he spooned his belly against her back in a post-coital moment of openness.

'Maybe,' she seized the togetherness second. 'You remember Kato, the character from the *Pink Panther* films who leaps on Inspector Clouseau when he least expects it?'

There was a long pause as post-coital openness closed its tired eyes.

'You want me to attack you when you least expect it?' he humoured her.

'Not attack – ravish.'

There was another pause and then he gave the nape of her neck a drowsy kiss. 'Leaping out from a confined space practising martial arts is hardly seductive, Kate.'

Put like that, he had a point. She tried to explain it better: 'I thought you pouncing on me without warning might spice things up a bit?'

A tired yawn almost unlocked his jaw but closed proceedings. 'I'm not into wife beating, baby. Let's go to sleep.'

You beat me in the race to an orgasm every time these days, Kate thought silently as he gave her a sluggish goodnight kiss on the ear then rolled his spine to hers with a final slump and sigh.

Listening as his breath deepened in sleep, she imagined an athletic figure dressed in black hiding in the en suite and enjoyed a brief shiver at the thought. It was ages since she'd enjoyed a really good fantasy.

'You've done *what*?' her sister gasped the following week.

'I've taken a lover.'

'Good God, Kate. Does Sandy suspect anything?'

'This is a Kato lover. He's very discreet.'

Her sister studied her wisely and then laughed. 'Is this one of your imaginary friends?'

'I'm far too old for imaginary friends.' Kate winked.

He hid in the wardrobe the first time. Kate knew that he was in there – the fact that he had been forced to remove half her clothes and drape them over a chair in order to fit himself in gave the game away – but she still experienced a rare frisson of excitement and fear. Humming the tune to the *Pink Panther*, she moved around the bedroom as she undressed, helpfully indicating her whereabouts. When her back was turned, he stole out from his lair and kissed her throat.

'Don't look round,' he ordered, slipping a scarf around her eyes.

Kate almost fainted with anticipation.

'What exactly does this Kato lover *do*?' Kate's sister asked, taking in her bright eyes and beaming smile the next day.

'He catches me by surprise.'

'Isn't that rather alarming?'

'Not if you're hoping it will happen all the time.'

'What if Sandy catches you by surprise with your Kato lover?'

'That's the whole point.'

The next time, he hid beneath the bed and waited until she was almost asleep before rolling out and pouncing. Over the coming week, he holed up in the boxroom, the airing cupboard, the larder, the coal bunker, the garage and then the cupboard under the stairs – leaping out amid a clatter of ironing board crashing on vacuum cleaner. Whether hot tank sweaty, coal-dust grubby or surrounded by domestic appliances, he was the most exciting thing in her life, and she thought about him night and day.

He hid beneath the dining room table, behind the sofa and in the garden shed. He leaped out from the most unexpected places, charging even mundane tasks with sexual anticipation. Foreplay had never been so much fun.

*   *   *

'Oh, Kate!' Sandy gasped as she bounced joyously around on top of him, facing his feet, his big hands on her waist.

She eyed the wardrobe dreamily, thinking about her Kato lover who had just been hiding there.

'I love you, baby!' he called out. 'Oh, Kate, oh, Kate, oh, OH!'

Moaning in delight as she rode him home, Kate couldn't agree more. 'Kato! Oh, Kato!'

'You're looking fantastic,' Kate's sister eyed her enviously. 'Are you on a new wonder drug?'

'I've told you. I have a Kato lover. He's the perfect tonic.'

'Well yours has taken years off you. Can I borrow him?'

'Absolutely not.'

'Are you sure Sandy doesn't suspect anything?'

'Of course not,' Kate smiled. 'He's having a wonderful time. Which reminds me, he's on a late shift tonight. I want cook a special meal. I know he'll want steak and I don't have a clue, so . . . ?'

'Hot pan, knob of butter, sizzle three minutes each side – keep it very pink inside. Then take the meat out, swirl the butter in the pan, add red wine and peppercorns. Serve.'

'So I take them out when the middle's still pink, pan the butter and add the extras?'

Kate's sister nodded thoughtfully, eyes narrowing. 'Are you trying to tell me something?'

'Got to go!' Kate leapt up and aimed random kisses at two pale cheeks.

'Kate, I should tell you I'm meeting . . .' Her sister threw her hands up in despair as she was left alone '. . . Sandy later,' she tutted under her breath. 'Oh, Kate.'

*   *   *

That evening there was a note on the kitchen table. '*Why not surprise me for once?*'

Kate's eyebrows shot up. The suggestion made her anxious and euphoric at the same time. She might have to wait in a confined space for hours, and he had already used the best hiding places in the house. Yet he would surely love the thrill that she had in store for him.

She went for a quick scout around, dismissing the wardrobes and under-stairs cupboard as too obvious. If she was going to lie in wait for him it had to be comfortable and it had to be somewhere he would never think to look.

Her eyes alighted on the loft-hatch in the ceiling above the bed. They had boarded the attic space last year. It was perfect, she realised as she hooked down the loft ladder and trotted up it to recce her lair beneath the eaves of the roof. Now all she had to do was dress for the occasion.

Kato always wore a black polo-neck and trousers – part jewel thief, part Milk Tray Man. Kate adopted the colour-scheme as she selected a lacy bodice, g-string and stockings – might as well go for the full impact. She sprayed herself liberally with scent, gathered a torch, high heels, a magazine, a big bar of chocolate and some breath fresheners before ascending the ladder and pulling it up behind her.

On closer inspection, it was very cold and cobwebby in the roof, and the duvet stored up there felt damp and clammy as she wrapped herself in it. She hoped he wouldn't be long.

'I'm worried about her,' Sandy told his sister-in-law as they settled in a corner table at the village pub. 'She's been acting very strangely.'

'In what way?'

He cleared his throat, editing the more graphic details.

'She gets agitated every time I open the wardrobe; she keeps taking everything out of the cupboards – and she asks me to check under the bed and in the garden shed all the time.'

'Well, there have been a lot of burglaries in your area.'

He sighed. 'Perhaps I'm over-reacting, but I love Kate – oh, believe me, I love her.'

Kate's sister's eyes twitched. 'Of course you do. Kate – oh, she's a diamond.'

'Absolutely. She thinks I'm on a late shift tonight and –'

'You think your diamond might get stolen while you're away?'

Sandy balked. 'Look, I hate to drag you into this, but you know her better than anyone. I need answers. You must have picked up on it. I think she might be –'

'Having an affair?' The eyes twitched again.

He looked up sharply from his pint. 'I was going to say "having a breakdown".'

'Oh . . . whoops. Freudian slip.'

'You mean she *is* having an affair?'

Kate's sister was fed up with the carry on. With clues so blatant, she was amazed Sandy still hadn't twigged. It was time to throw some light upon the jewel that every thief wanted to steal and that dear, unwitting Sandy had firmly in his grasp. Her eyes were twitching uncontrollably now.

'You should know Kate by now, you fool. She has a very vivid imagination. She latches onto an idea and becomes obsessed. She used to have all these imaginary friends as a child and now she has 'dream' lovers in the same –'

'Who *is* the bastard?' Sandy raged. 'I'll kill him!'

His sister-in-law sighed and clasped a hand to her twitching eyes, knowing that he didn't understand what she was saying. 'She calls him Kato.'

*   *   *

At last! Kate could hear somebody crashing around below. She carefully laid her magazine and chocolate to one side, knocked back a breath freshener and straightened her suspenders. It was time to act.

He was moving about immediately below her now, making a surprising amount of noise. He appeared to be pulling out drawers and upending things. Why did Sandy always have to be so messy?

Kate pressed her hands to her lips to calm herself. This was supposed to be a sexual fantasy, not a domestic scrap. *She* was the Kato lover now. And she couldn't wait to get out of the chilly attic.

In her plans, she hadn't considered how best to lower herself from the roof hatch. Putting down the ladder and clambering out was hardly sexy – the sight of her white bottom dangling from above the bed wasn't her fantasy at all. She'd just have to dive out head-first and aim for a slick SAS landing on the mattress. Very Lara Croft.

She stealthily lifted the hatch and peered out.

It was dark in the room – strange, given that he appeared to be searching for something just out of her line of vision. Why look for it in the dark?

Still, it at least gave her much-needed cover. She licked her lips, crouched carefully by the hole beneath her, eyed her landing spot and sprang out.

Sandy spotted the white van parked just around the corner from his front drive, half-hidden in the trees. Bastard! He was in the house right now with Kate. Much as he longed to leap out of his own car and slash the van's tyres, he was in too much of a hurry.

The front door was ajar. He slipped silently inside.

The noise coming from upstairs was unmistakeable – grunts and groans and those little wails Kate let out when she was excited. God, they were going at it like animals!

Furiously, Sandy stormed up to confront them.

The sight of his wife in black lacy underwear, straddling a man dressed in black almost finished him off.

'You bitch!'

'Sandy!' she had the grace to look terrified.

'You harlot!' he bellowed.

She seemed to be trying to wrap a stocking around her lover's neck – auto-asphyxiation, Sandy registered in contempt. He'd never seen this side of her. What's more, she seemed to want him to join in:

'Quick, grab him!'

'Whoa!' He backed away, appalled.

'He's broken into the house!'

In the face of such overwhelming evidence to the contrary, Sandy snarled and stepped back further, punching out at a wall and then fighting tears as the pain from his smashed knuckles joined that from his broken heart.

'Don't think you can fool me with that one! You might be quick-witted, Kate, but it's bloody obvious what's going on here.'

There was a muffled groan from the man that Kate was still straddling. It was hard to make out what he was saying under his balaclava, but it sounded almost like *please get her off me!*

'How could you do this to me, Kate?' Sandy yelled. 'You were my life!'

'Call the police!' she looked up at him wildly as the man beneath her fought to struggle free.

'You were my life!' Sandy repeated.

Moments later, sixteen stone of balaclava-ed terror had crashed his way down the stairs to flee the house.

'You idiot!' Kate slumped back on her heels, her stockings shredded. 'You let him get away.'

'I'm so sorry,' Sandy muttered. 'I didn't realise you wanted him to hang around for a nightcap – and a threesome.'

'I'm calling the police.' She crawled to the phone.

'Good. Tell them someone stole my diamond from under my nose.'

The police tried hard to hide their smiles as they told Sandy and Kate that this was – *ahem* – not the first time a husband had mistaken an intruder for his adulterous wife's lover.

'I am not adulterous!' Kate wailed.

Sandy remained unconvinced. 'You have a lover – your sister told me.'

'I've never been unfaithful to you.'

'What about Kato?' he accused.

'He's a character in a film! I just used him as a fantasy.'

'You fantasised about *Burt Kwouk*?' He seemed appalled.

'Who?'

'He's the actor who played Kato.'

'No! He wasn't my fantasy. You were Kato. *You* were.'

'Liar!' He laughed disbelievingly. 'You're just trying to cover up a seedy affair –'

'Our sex life had become so mundane, Sandy.'

He cleared his throat, looking at the police inspectors who were swigging tea nearby. 'Not now, Kate – oh!'

She kicked him on the shin. 'Don't you dare accuse me of having an affair again! You thought my Kato idea was stupid, so I daydreamed about it instead. It was innocent fun. And tonight I thought I'd try it on you.'

'Well I wish you'd warned me.'

'How was I to know someone would break into the house?'

'Yes, all too convenient an alibi!' Sandy might be as macho and compassionate as a fire-fighter hooking a kitten from a high branch, but he was hopeless at arguments. 'You're just making this up – you always were a pants-on-fire liar!'

Kate's temper ignited fully. 'My pants hadn't been on fire for months before the Kato idea came along – that's the point!'

'Liar!' Sandy roared, playing to the crowd. 'Arrest her for wasting police time!'

The police didn't stay for a second cup of tea. Politely asking Kate and Sandy to leave everything where it was until their SOC team arrived, they beat a hasty retreat. The argument raged through the night and soon the mess created by the balaclava burglar was joined by the mess created when Sandy and Kate threw things at one another. Before long, the scene of the crime was beyond disturbed – it was demolished as they slung bra after belt after necklace after compact disc. Kate even tried for a couple of karate chops, but missed.

'How can you be jealous of something that was just a figment of my imagination?' she screamed at him.

'And how can you accuse me of being a boring lover? I'd do anything for you. You're the one who can never be bothered to make an effort.'

'*Hello*? I just hid in the roof for you and waited for hours!'

'Thanks, but I'd rather you dressed up as a French maid in future.'

'You sexist pig!'

'Cow!'

'Warthog.'

'Bitch.'

'Big pink panther.'

He was momentarily wrong-footed. '*Panther*?'

Realising that the animal analogies were used up, Kate fled, leaving the door swinging.

She begged temporary shelter with her sister. Not that the fighting ended there.

'I can't believe you told him I was having an affair!' Kate fumed on, picking out a new target over sauvignon and sympathy.

'I did point out that it was probably a figment of your imagination.'

'You *what*?'

'Well it was, wasn't it?'

Kate hung her head. Her sister always cut to the chase, unlike Sandy who could cut heartstrings and arteries without ever getting to the point. She guiltily remembered all the delicious times Kato had leaped from his hiding place around the house, intent on carnal pleasure.

'I just liked to imagine – when Sandy and I made love – that he'd been, sort of hiding.'

'*Hiding*?'

'Like Kato.'

'You fool, Kate – oh, you are weird sometimes. I'll have another word with him,' her sister offered with a wry smile. 'Sometimes you hide your true feelings in the oddest of places. Sandy loves you very much, I have no doubt, but he needs help understanding you. Who can blame him? Lord knows, it's taken the rest of your family a lifetime to figure you out.'

Sandy polished off another scotch and looked at the scribbled reply he had left that morning to Kate's note asking what he wanted for supper.

Why not surprise me for once?

Well she had done that, all right.

And then it hit him. His daft, dreamy Kate really had been telling the truth all along. She had wanted him to hide around the house waiting to seduce her unexpectedly, and he hadn't even noticed. When she had tried to be the Kato lover herself, she'd jumped on an unsuspecting burglar.

'Kate, oh, you fool – you gorgeous fool.'

He started to laugh. Poor, sweet Kate. He had to make it up to her.

And when he saw car headlights coming along the drive, he didn't hesitate. He slipped the back door off the latch and crept into the sitting room to hide.

'What do you mean, arrested?' Kate clutched her mobile to her ear in shock.

'The police had a patrol car cruising past our house. They guessed we might be targeted again – our burglar has been quite busy in the area, it seems. When they spotted me behaving suspiciously through the front window, they thought I was him.'

'What were you doing?

'Trying to hide in the ottoman. I gave your sister a terrible shock. She fainted on the hearthrug when I jumped out. Then the police stormed in and arrested me.'

Kate started to giggle and then stopped herself. But the laughter that came down the opposite end of the line knew no such self-control. 'Oh, Kate! Kate, oh Kate. We will make love in every cupboard dressed as Ninjas from now on if it makes you happy. Just come and take me home. I love–' He couldn't speak for laughing.

* * *

Neither Kate nor Sandy tried to hide from one another for a long time after that. They didn't hide their bodies or their feelings. They made love far more often and with far more effort. Sandy tried hard to be more spontaneous and Kate tried to explain better what made her go '*oh*'.

Occasionally, Sandy dressed all in black and crept up behind her, but that was as far as it went. Kate bought a French maid's outfit that made them both laugh far too much for hot action.

It was almost six months later that they found themselves spending a lazy Sunday afternoon in bed watching *The Return of the Pink Panther*. When Kato leapt out of the fridge to attack Clouseau in his apartment, they exchanged a long, excited look.

'You're where?' Kate's sister asked as she received a crackly phone call the following evening. 'Casualty? Oh God, is it serious?'

She listened for a long time. 'Kate, it's the middle of summer. How on earth did you both get *frostbite*?'

Daisy Waugh has written three bestselling novels, *The New You Survival Kit*, *Ten Steps to Happiness* and *A Bed of Roses* (watch out for the pricks). She is married with two children and lives in London and France.

BREAKING AWAY

Daisy Waugh

She could have given up smoking, got married, started a family or come into some money. She could have decided that the grey old city she'd been living in all these years, as blissfully discontented as the rest of her acquaintances, was no longer the city for her, and that she was going to fuck off to live somewhere nicer. Where the sun shone. And the vegetables still tasted. And the houses were cheap and didn't all look the same. And the streets weren't clogged with cars, and the pavements weren't covered in gob and gum. And where keeping up with one's friends – their bank accounts, their careers and their impeccable bloody 'lifestyle choices' wasn't quite so relentlessly disheartening.

Susie Hall, mid-thirties, professional, trundling through an averagely unpleasant West London life, with a nice boyfriend, plenty of successful friends and a well-decorated but nonetheless depressing – and absurdly overpriced – basement flat, had spent many evenings fantasising about all of the above. She dreamed of escape.

So it ought not to have come as a surprise when, one

Tuesday night in early spring, she put in a call to her two oldest, closest, dearest friends, Poppy Starke and Travis Holby. Poppy and Travis lived and worked together, and had done since their adulthoods began. Susie rang them at the office.

'*Poppy*!' Susie said. There was a note of creamy triumph in her voice which might have been a little irritating. 'I've got – I mean *we*, Sylvester and I – *we've* got *so much* to tell you. Can you and Travis meet us in the Bush Bar later tonight? Early or late. It doesn't even matter. Any time. Only please say yes. We want you guys to be the first to know.' She laughed a little breathlessly, Susie did – Susie, who usually sounded so calm. 'We've got *so much* good news I swear I'm not even going to know where to *start*!'

Now. Who could resist an invitation like that?

Poppy smiled. Broadly. Susie and Sylvester were broke (compared with Poppy and Travis) and rarely suggested meeting anywhere but Pizza Express. Drinks at the Bush Bar cost serious money. Or they did when you got glugging, as old friends like Poppy, Susie, Sylvester and Travis invariably did. So Poppy said, with sincerity, 'My God how *exciting*. What are you going to tell us? Can't you tell me now?' Susie said she couldn't.

'Bloody hell. You're killing me, Snooze. I'm not sure I can wait!'

Susie (Snooze) Hall and her boyfriend Sylvester had been enjoying quite a run of good news recently, registered Poppy quietly, as she and her old friend chatted on. For example Ikea, having messed up with the delivery of a sofa and armchair, had sent them a gift token, virtually unsolicited, for £150. Most people only got £50. Then Sylvester had found some deal to New York on lastminute.com, and they'd taken themselves off for a weekend of sex and shopping. Just like that. Which was fun for them. And then last week – this one had been a little harder to swallow – Susie, who worked quite low down at Radio 4, had somehow managed to find a small publisher willing to take on her collection of love poems. Which, for the record, Poppy had read and secretly told Travis she thought were *utter crap*.

Poppy and Travis worked in television, the way a lot of people do who can afford to live in nice big houses with solid oak floors in Shepherd's Bush. They owned their own production company, with offices in Soho, and currently had not one, but *two* shows running on different UK cable channels. The first was a thing for young mothers; people stuck at home mid-morning with no sensible means of escape. It featured a group of leather-faced women 'pundits' curled onto comfy chairs, gusting coffee-breath at one another and laughing uproariously at each other's lady-jokes. The usual drivel.

The other show was not quite so good: a late night sort of dating show, in which contestants had to guess one another's personalities by the shape of their naked bottoms. That one was bad. That one was devastating drivel. Poppy and Travis could laugh about it, and they did, for example with Susie and Sylvester. But at the same time it did pay the mortgage. And as anybody living in Shepherd's Bush would tell you, that is no mean feat.

Poppy and Travis weren't doing anything that Tuesday night, unusually enough, and the thought at four o'clock of getting pissed on the Bush Bar's Caipirinhas almost made Poppy dribble, made her yearn for eight o'clock. Ditto Travis, when she put a hand over the mouthpiece and shouted across at him. Travis loved cocktails almost as much as Poppy did, and he was sufficiently metropolitan not even to be ashamed of it.

So they were in for the long haul. One long night of celebrating Susie and Sylvester's exciting surprises, whatever they may be. And it would be fine. It would be *fun*. Besides, Poppy and Travis had enjoyed their own fair share of good news over the years, and Susie and Sylvester had always been there for them. For example, when they won the *Bums Away!* contract, Susie and Sylvester had sent them a whole case of champagne, and a giant bunch of helium balloons in the shape of bottoms. Which, as Travis said to Sylvester, and Poppy said to Susie, must have cost them a fortune they could ill afford.

Poor-old-Sylvester, Travis had taken to calling him recently, as Sylvester's worldly fortunes waned (and Travis's restaurant-girth expanded). Sylvester had started life so full of ambition and promise. But then he'd dropped out of journalism for some quasi-ethical reason nobody had been much persuaded by, and last month he had completed a year-long course in landscape gardening. Very nice and everything, Poppy and Travis agreed. Nobody would ever argue that Sylvester wasn't nice. But how was that going to pay the mortgage, or the school fees, or whatever?

It was actually getting to the point now, Poppy and Travis also agreed, where it could be quite embarrassing going out with them. For example, when they were in restaurants together, Poppy sometimes felt quite self-conscious about ordering expensive items from the menu.

Anyway, none of that mattered. Not tonight. Poppy and Travis adored their old friends. Ever since university, they'd been getting high together, making plans together, drowning their sorrows together and doing a whole lot of other things, some of which they didn't even like to talk about. They knew each other inside and out. Literally. And Poppy loved Susie, and Susie loved Travis, and Sylvester loved Poppy, and Travis loved Susie, and everybody loved everybody, and that was that.

Susie and Sylvester were already into their second round of drinks by the time their friends arrived. They had their arms linked and their foreheads almost touching and they – glowed. It was unmissable. And astonishing, honestly. After twelve years together, they still looked like a couple newly in love.

They glimpsed Poppy and Travis making their way over – late, as usual. And they might have pulled apart, if they'd wanted to. But neither of them did. Just for a second or two they pretended not to notice.

Beside him, Travis felt Poppy tense a little; felt the tremor of failure travel through her, the tremor of resentment that she and Travis couldn't look at each other in the same way. And he simultaneously felt his own buttock muscles clenching, as they always did at moments of stress or emotional awkwardness. (It was how he had come up with the *Bums Away!* brainwave, needless to say.) Travis truly believed that the human arse held secrets to its owner's personality. His own was spotty but toned – and a lot less flabby than the rest of his body, because of all the clenching. But what does that really tell us? Anything much? Possibly not. The point is, some people look out and see only poetry in the world. Others may see only pretension, injustice, cowardice, conspiracy, and so on. Travis wasn't so limited. He saw the world – all of it, including his own bottom – entirely in terms of how it might work on low-budget television.

'OK guys, break it up!' yelled Poppy merrily, swooping

for the usual hugs. Susie and Sylvester did a mini jump, as if they hadn't been expecting her. 'Sorry we're late,' Poppy said. *Kiss kiss.* 'Some sod in LA called just as we were leaving. I'm beginning to think they do it on purpose. Either that or they haven't yet clocked that the world is round and we work in a different time zone over here. *Oooph*!' She collapsed onto the banquette beside them. 'Well done getting a table,' she said, over the general hubbub. 'Budge up, Sylv. Christ! I'm *gagging* for a drink. Travis, darling, be a love. Don't sit – please. It'll only waste precious drinking time. Go and fetch us some caipirinhas.'

Travis looked faintly pissed off. Hesitated.

'Ooooh. *Please-please-please-please*,' she cajoled him, sweetly. 'Get a round for all of us.'

'I think I'll have something soft, actually, Travis,' Susie said significantly. 'Maybe some elderflower juice.'

But Poppy wasn't listening. 'In fact, get six,' she ordered. 'Get eight. They always take so bloody long to make.'

Sylvester paled. Did the maths. Said nothing, since – though they maintained the Going Dutch charade right up until the end of every evening they ever spent together – Poppy and Travis always wound up footing the bill. Which was OK, Susie and Sylvester thought, because they were all such old friends, and because everybody knew Susie and Sylvester did lovely gardening and lovely poetry and cared about the environment and things and were therefore always broke. 'But be quick, mate,' Sylvester shouted after him. 'Or Poppy'll have got all our news out of us before you get back.'

Travis returned fifteen minutes later with a tray full of caipirinhas and nothing soft, having failed to register Susie's elderflower request.

486

'*Travis*!' Poppy exclaimed, her voice full of leaden excitement, her teeth grinding with difficult smiles, unspoken hurt,
and all her untold reservations. 'You'll never guess.
Remember that awful guy James Russell? Works at the
Guardian?'

'Don't think so.'

'Anyway, he had dinner with Snooze and Sylv last week.
He's put in a bid for two-hundred thou for the flat! Cash
bid. Wants to be in next month. Can you believe it?'

'Really?' Travis said comfortably, balancing the tray,
looking for somewhere to rest it. 'I didn't even know it was
for sale.'

'Well it wasn't,' Susie beamed. 'That's what's so amazing!'

'So – well that's good news. Is it? I presume it is. Where
are you going to live?'

Poppy grabbed a caipirinha from Travis's tray and sucked
it up in a single gulp. 'The south of France, darling,' she said
brightly. 'They're going to live in the south of France.'

'Oh –'

'*Mmm*. And Susie's given up smoking.'

'*Susie*?' Travis began to laugh. 'Not *smoking*? This is all
a joke, right?'

Poppy slugged back a second drink, also in one. 'She's
pregnant.'

'*Oh*!'

'Yes. Isn't it fab? Fabulous. Isn't it *fabulous*?' Poppy said.

'. . . I know it's a bit sudden,' Susie murmured, having
finally peered through the haze of her own smugness and
noticed the unhappy faces of her oldest friends. 'But you
know . . . you get to a point in life . . . oh,' she giggled, unable
to contain herself even that long. 'And we're going to get
married, too! In Carcassonne, we thought. On one of the

little turrets. Have you been to Carcassonne? I think it's the most romantic place in the –'

'*Married*?' interrupted Poppy in astonishment. '*Married*? I didn't think you believed in marriage. But you do!' she added quickly. 'Goodness. Well. All these surprises. Anyway I'm so happy for you,' she said, really trying to be. Smiling at them. 'And I think you're both very, very *clever*.'

'Thank you,' Susie said.

And then Poppy turned to Travis. The smile on her face became a little more fixed. 'Sylvester says one of the main reasons they want to escape to rural France is because they can't stand any more British telly!'

Sylvester groaned. 'She's taking what I said out of context. *As usual*.'

'Most particularly,' Poppy continued, a glint in her eyes, 'British telly shows like ours.'

'It's not what he meant, Poppy, and you know it,' Susie said. 'We just meant . . .' She reached across, more or less unconsciously, and took Sylvester's hand. 'After James put in his bid we got to thinking just how lovely it would be to get away from it all, lead a quieter, simpler life; one that isn't so career focused. In a place where the pervading culture isn't so damn aggressive and so damn *dumb* . . .'

'See?' Poppy said.

'Oh, come on, Poppy. You know it as well as I do. The kind of telly shows you make are – I'm not saying it's your fault. We're not *blaming* you. It's what gets commissioned these days. But they're typical, aren't they? Of the way our culture is going? And we just don't want to be a part of that culture anymore . . . You can understand that, can't you?'

'Absolutely,' Travis said lightly. '*Absolutely*. Well –'

'. . . and then I realised I was pregnant. And honestly – to bring a *child* up in this kind of sniping, sleazy, backbiting environment . . .' She shrugged. 'Plus it all seemed so incredibly auspicious. Such perfect timing, the baby and everything. It just seemed *perfect*.'

'Well, well, well!' Travis said – at last. He pulled himself up to his full height and slapped Sylvester hard on the back. Very hard. 'What can we say? Congratulations, mate. Really. And you, Suze. Snoozy Suze. We're bloody heartbroken you're leaving. But seriously – *congratulations*!' He glanced across at the array of expensive cocktails in front of him. 'I think we should forget about these, and get some champagne down us right away. Don't you?'

After that everyone – apart from Susie of course, who ordered herself some grilled lobster, to make up, and then fresh figs and pasteurised cheeses, and pears poached in a rare pudding wine – got uproariously drunk. Appallingly, filthily, stinkily drunk. Travis and Poppy, who could drink more and faster than just about anyone, kept ordering more and more bottles of champagne. And delicious champagne it was too, Sylvester commented, glugging it back.

'C'mon,' slurred Travis again and again, and then again. 'It's not every day your best friends announce they're pissing off to the south of France. *Let'z-gedanuther-one*!'

'Actually, Travis,' Susie screwed up her face apologetically. 'I don't want to be a spoilsport, but I've really *got* to go to bed.'

'Me too,' Sylvester nodded. 'I'm wasted.'

They called for the bill, and a slightly sour silence fell. Suddenly Travis laughed. Not a particularly nice laugh, either. 'You're going to go bust,' he said. 'You do know that, don't you? Sixty-five per cent of English people who do what you're doing crawl back home with their tails between their legs within eighteen months. You're going to lose everything.'

'Don't be mean,' Poppy said vaguely, lighting herself one last cigarette. 'They've obviously thought it through.'

'Of course they haven't,' Travis snapped. He drained his glass. '. . . make a great TV series, though.'

'Shut up Travis,' Susie and Sylvester said simultaneously, and smiled at one another.

'Seriously, though,' Travis persisted. 'We could call it *Breaking Away*. Or *Breaking Up*. Or *Going Broke*.' He chortled '*Making a Prat of Yourself*. There are endless possibilities.'

'Piss off,' Sylvester said, more irritably this time. 'We don't want anything to do with your tacky TV shows. So forget it.'

And then the bill arrived. Travis pounced on it, as he always did. Slowly, he opened it up.

Sylvester belched. 'Nasty feeling about this one,' he said casually. 'We haven't exactly held back.'

Travis looked at the bottom line and whistled. It was usually at this point – it was always at this point – that Travis or Poppy shrugged, pulled out their platinum credit cards and told Susie and Sylvester the night was on them.

But this time nobody shrugged. Nobody pulled out anything.

'Jesus!' Travis muttered. 'You're bloody right, Sylvester. It's a biggie all right.' Travis showed it to Poppy.

'*Travis*! Poppy scowled. 'You ordered the most expensive – and *four* bottles of it! What the hell were you *thinking* of?'

Travis smiled. 'It was bloody good though, wasn't it?'

'Not £165-a-bottle good. No it bloody wasn't. Idiot. *I'm* not paying for that. You can bloody well pay for it yourself.'

Sylvester swallowed, uncertain if he'd heard quite right. £165? Obviously not. 'Go on then,' he said, making a good-natured show of reaching for his wallet. 'What's the damage?'

'You're not going to like it I'm afraid,' Travis said, sliding the bill across the table. Susie and Sylvester craned forward to have a look.

Susie gasped.

Sylvester's eyes bulged.

Words failed.

'. . . but I only drank elderflower juice!' Susie said at last.

She and Sylvester glanced nervously up at Poppy and Travis, waiting for the nod, for the stay of execution. Still it didn't come.

'But we can't pay for this!' Susie panted. 'It's half my salary!'

'Should've thought of that before,' Travis grinned. He leant towards them. 'Imagine, Suse,' he said softly. 'All that free publicity for your poems. How could it possibly be tacky?' He turned to Sylvester. 'And your gardening – thing. You'll have clients flocking. You'd be celebrities!'

'Yuck!' said Susie, blushing.

Sylvester shuddered.

'Say you'll do it,' Travis fingered his credit card.

A pause. A long pause.

And while they waited Poppy Starke stretched across the happy couple and kissed Travis full on the lips.

Isabel Wolff read English at Cambridge, and worked as a broadcaster and journalist before becoming a full-time writer. She is the author of six bestselling romantic comedies, including *Rescuing Rose*, *Behaving Badly* and *A Question of Love*, and is published in over twenty languages. She lives with her family in West London and spends most of her spare time playing table-football – at which she excels.

For more information about Isabel and her books, please visit her website www.isabelwolff.com

IN AGONY

Isabel Wolff

'Problems, problems,' Jane muttered as she opened her mailbag on Monday. 'Problems, problems,' she repeated testily. 'As if I don't have enough of my own.' The thirty or so letters seemed almost to vibrate with indignation, resentment and rage. There were brown envelopes and white ones, airmail and Basildon Bond. There were typed ones and handwritten ones, some strewn with smileys and hearts. Jane's practised eye had already identified from the writing the likely dilemmas within. Here were the large, childish loops of repression, and the backwards slope of the chronically depressed. There, the stabbings and scorings of schizophrenia and the cramped hand of the introvert. Jane fancied she could hear them, like childish voices, whining and pleading for help.

'*Dear Jane,*' she read, '*I have a problem . . . Dear Jane, I just can't sleep . . . Dear Jane, I'm so terribly lonely . . . Dear Jane, I feel so bad . . .*' *Dear Jane*, she thought to herself bitterly. Dear Jane. Dear, dear, DEAR. 'Oh dear,' she repeated testily as she turned on her computer. 'Off we go again.'

For Jane was neither an enthusiastic, nor even sympathetic, agony aunt. She had always regarded the *Post*'s problem page – she still did – with something close to contempt. 'But here I am – in AGONY,' she muttered. She longed for some anaesthetic to ease the pain. But '*Ask Jane*' was undeniably popular; more importantly, it paid the bills. Because for two years Gavin hadn't earned a penny, having given up his job in the City to write. He'd been 'trouble shooter' at Debit Suisse. 'But I'm the real trouble-shooter now,' thought Jane. And it sometimes amused her to think that Gavin's literary career was subsidised by the co-dependant, the abandoned and the bald. Jane had been a journalist for ten years; but her spell as an agony aunt had never featured on the imagined trajectory of her career. She had visualised a seamless progression from the diary to the newsdesk, to signed interviews, to glamorous features (with photo byline) and thence to a highly visible – and frequently controversial – column in some respected broadsheet. Her readers would gasp at her erudition. No subject would elude her grasp. She would pontificate on Britain's entry to the Euro, on drugs and welfare and defence. Her trenchant opinions would be regurgitated at lively dinner parties in Islington and Notting Hill. She would be invited to appear on *Newsnight*, on *Today* and *Question Time*. Instead, she found herself dealing with premature ejaculation, nasty neighbours, infidelity, impotence and debt.

This unexpected professional detour had happened entirely by chance. Two and a half years previously, Jane had been doing a reporting shift on the newsdesk of the *Sunday Post*. As she put the finishing touches to what she thought was a rather good profile of Cherie Blair, she noticed a sudden commotion. People were running. Doors were slamming. An atmosphere of tension and panic prevailed. Enid Smugg, the *Post*'s ancient but hugely popular agony aunt, had gone face down in the trifle at lunch. Before Enid's stiffening body had even been stretched out of the building, Jane had been deputed to complete her page. Keen, above all, to appear willing, she had gritted her teeth and agreed; and despite her lack of experience, or even natural sympathy, she'd acquitted herself pretty well. Too well, she now realised bitterly, because she'd been stuck in the job ever since. Still, fifty grand was good money, she reminded herself, and God knows they needed the cash. Their flat in Regent's Park was gorgeous, but the mortgage on it was vast. But Jane adored her husband, Gavin – 'Gorgeous Gav' – and she believed that his boat would come in. Moreover, she was secretly quite happy to be the bread-winner – it placed Gavin firmly in her debt. And she especially liked the fact that he no longer went to work. Jane had been to Gavin's office a few times and had been disconcerted and demoralised by the sight of so many sweet-faced, lithe-limbed blondes. For Jane was a very plain Jane – tall, big-boned and rather flat-faced, and she knew she'd married out of her league. She quite liked having her handsome husband safely at home, out of harm's – and temptation's – way.

But above all, she luxuriated in the knowledge that it was her professional sacrifice which enabled him to write. He'd probably dedicate his book to her, she mused contentedly. When it was published. Which it would be, quite soon. The phone would ring one day and it would be an editor from HarperCollins or Faber, begging Gavin to let them publish his intergalactic thriller, *Star-Quake!* Jane had to admit that Gav's books weren't quite her thing. But then she'd never really been a Sci-Fi fan. Gavin was an avid amateur astronomer and was aiming to become the new Arthur C. Clarke. Jane had a sudden, happy vision of them attending the Royal Premiere of *Star-Quake!* in Leicester Square. There they were, standing next to Nicolas Cage and Michelle Pfeiffer in the line-up to meet Prince Charles.

Gavin had not yet allowed Jane to see his manuscript. But a few nights before, when he'd left for his astronomy evening class, she'd gone into his study and sneaked a look. She'd found the story a little hard to follow, with its huge floating aliens, exploding supernovas and fur-clad talking snakes. But still, it was genre fiction, Jane reasoned, and there was a huge market for that. In any case, she supported Gavin unquestioningly, because she adored him. She always had. That's why she was prepared to be 'in agony' as she jokingly put it – so that Gav could fulfil his dream. And at least – and thank God for this – none of her friends knew that '*Ask Jane*' was her. For she had resolutely refused to have her surname or her photo on the page. '*Got a Problem? Ask Jane!*' it announced above a photo of a disembodied – and clearly female – ear.

Jane had assumed, when she first started doing the agony column, that her stewardship of it would be short-lived. She'd imagined that before long, some celebrity would be hired to take over, or some famously humiliated political wife. For a while there'd been talk of Trisha from daytime telly, and even of Carol Vorderman. But weeks had gone by, then months and here Jane still was, over two years on. But not for much longer, she thought to herself happily, because soon Gavin's writing career would take off.

'You're my rock, Jane,' he'd say with a smile which made her heart swell and tears prick the back of her eyes. 'You're my asteroid – no, my shooting star.'

Well, she certainly shot from the hip. Or rather, from the lip. But that's why people wrote to her. They wanted firm, robust advice. She turned back to the day's bundle of letters with a weary, regretful sigh. Christ, it was tedious – and it wasn't as though any of the problems were *new*. She had long since covered every conceivable dilemma: low libido, domestic violence, bad breath, bereavement, debt. Pregnancy, both wanted and unwanted, nasty neighbours and thinning hair. She'd helped *Divorcing of Dagenham, Paranoid of Petersham*, and *Borderline Bulimic of Bath*.

'Who have we got today?' she muttered. '*Phobic of Finchley? Suicidal of Solihull? Jealous of Jupiter* would make a nice change,' she added sardonically, 'or maybe *Miserable of Mars*.' Jane never felt guilty about her lack of sympathy for her readers. If these people wanted lovely, sweet, kind Bel Mooney, then they could damn well write to her instead. But 'kind' simply wasn't Jane's style. Her advice was uncompromisingly tough. She prided herself on being as sharp and to the point as an assassin's blade. Oh yes, Jane liked to tell it straight. She didn't mess about. First off was Sandra from Suffolk. Not getting on well with her husband's mum.

'*Dear Sandra,*' Jane typed. '*It's a GREAT pity you spoke to your mother-in-law like that. Let's face it, calling her a 'twisted old battleaxe' is NOT going to make relations more cordial! May I respectfully suggest that you try and THINK a little before you open your big trap. In the meantime I enclose my leaflet on Tact.*'

Jane re-read her letter, sealed the envelope, tossed it into her out-tray, then turned to the next. Oh God – another fatso with low self-esteem.

'*Dear Terry,*' she wrote. '*I know you'd like me to tell you that looks don't matter, and that some nubile blonde is going to fall in love with your "great personality". But the fact is, poppet, that no self-respecting woman is going to be seen dead with a guy weighing eighteen stone. Here's the Weightwatchers number for your area. Ring it right now and lose the lard.*' On further consideration, she decided the letter might be a little harsh. So she scribbled, '*Do let me know how you get on*' at the bottom, to soften it a bit.

Not that anyone ever did 'let her know'. They never got back to her. Her replies went out into the void, like meteorites hurtling through space. In the two years she'd been 'in agony', she'd never heard from anyone again. Occasionally, she would wonder why, but she had long since concluded that the brilliance of her advice obviated the need for further help.

Now she earmarked the four letters she would feature on this week's page – money trouble, transvestism, booze and menopause – then turned to the final letter in the pile. 'Oh God, *Betrayed of Barnes*,' she said irritably. 'You poor thing – boo hoo hoo!'

'*Dear Jane, I don't know what to do,*' she read. '*I've been married for seven years and love my wife dearly but fear she has started to stray. She is far more attractive than I am and I often feel insecure.*' Jane felt a sudden pang of recognition which she did her best to suppress. '*I have no hard evidence,*' the writer went on, '*but I believe she's seeing a colleague at her TV company, because she talks about him a lot. It's 'Ronnie this' and 'Ronnie that' so I assume it must be him. What's more, she's been dressing particularly well lately, with a new hair-do, and once or twice I think I've detected alien aftershave on her clothes. I have never been possessive,*' the man continued. '*I've always encouraged my wife to see her friends, go to the gym, attend classes etc. but I'm now so* anxious that I feel ill. Please, please advise me Jane. Yours in desperation, Alan.'

'Well Alan,' Jane wrote back. 'It seems to me you've got three options. You can a) stick your head in the sand and hope the problem will go away. But the problem with having your head in the sand, sweetie, is that you leave your backside dangerously exposed. Or you can b) confront her. But if you do, you'd better prepare yourself to hear something you're not going to like. Or you can c) have her followed. Go to a private detective – just look one up in Yellow Pages – and get a Dick Tracy on the job. At least that way you'll know for sure. So bite the bullet, Alan, and best of luck.'

Jane finished the letter with a sense of satisfaction. She'd given him the best advice she could. She wondered what the upshot would be, but knew that she'd never get to know. So she was rather surprised, a fortnight later, to hear from Alan again.

'Dear Jane,' he wrote. 'Thank you for the excellent advice you gave me recently. I had my wife followed, as you suggested, with surprising results. It turned out that her colleague, 'Ronnie', was in fact a woman – Ronnie is short for Veronica apparently.' Well then you're a lucky bunny Alan, thought Jane as she raised her coffee cup to her lips.

'However,' she read on, 'my suspicions about my wife were sadly proved right – in an unexpected way. The detective's dossier revealed that she HAS been having an affair, with a man who attends the same evening class. It appears they share a passion for amateur astronomy. He's a married man, very attractive, a former banker, who's trying to write a novel. I'm devastated, as you can imagine. But what I need to know NOW is, should I get in touch with this man's wife?'

Deborah Wright's first novel, *Olivia's Bliss*, won the *Ireland on Sunday*/Poolbeg *Write a Bestseller* competition in 1999. Her second novel, *The Rebel Fairy*, was published by Time Warner Books. A modern version of *A Midsummer Night's Dream*, it was summed up by *Now* magazine as 'Deborah Wright does for the fairy world what JK Rowling did for wizards'. She has also published *Under My Spell*, a comedy about witchcraft, and *Love Eternally*, a romance about a depressed ghost who finds love and happiness after death.

For more information visit Deborah's website at www.deborahwright.co.uk

IN BED WITH LORD BYRON

Deborah Wright

The day I broke up with my boyfriend was the day I decided to invest in a time machine.

Buying the time machine was relatively easy, as you can imagine: I just clicked onto eBay and discovered an auction ending in an hour's time. The seller, a man called Brian Pincher, described his machine as:

> Six months old and only used once. I took a quick trip back to lose my virginity to Dolly Parton but realised, to my dismay, that I am a nervous flier and ended up puking all over her guitar during a rendition of *I Will Always Love You*. The pain of this memory, which has since crippled my confidence with women, has put me off ever using the machine again. But I hope it can give someone else a little happiness.

Perfect, I thought.

The bidding was ferocious, and I ended up paying £900 for it. Another one to slap on my bulging Visa card. When

501

the machine arrived, I was slightly alarmed to discover it came as a box of parts, all needing to be put together. I was just sweating over inserting tube A into circuit B, when suddenly my phone rang and the answerphone clicked on.

'Hi, Deborah, it's Anthony here. So, um, yeah, I can come along to the dinner party you're having on Wednesday . . .'

I sat up, a lock of sweaty hair falling into my face. I'd entirely forgotten that I'd suggested the dinner party, as a 'let's be friends' gesture.

'And I'd like to bring, um, my new girlfriend, um, Kerry.'

Kerry? We'd only been broken up a day and he had found someone new?

Then again, I had been the one to break off our relationship. It wasn't that there was anything wrong with Anthony. He was tall, dark and handsome. He had a good job, working in the city. But that was the *point*. We were so good together; and yet I felt bored. Call it the grass-is-greener syndrome if you will, but I always suffered this restless ache that Mr Perfect, someone who was just that little bit taller and darker and more handsome and funnier than Anthony, might be just round the corner. Now I was finally going to get it out of my system. I was about to woo one of the world's greatest lovers.

I couldn't help feeling that the machine, though a delightful shade of scarlet, was somewhat flimsy, though. Spotting the trademark MFI on one corner was perhaps a clue as to why.

My next question was: what date to put in? I wanted to meet Lord Byron when he was in his prime. Men are supposed to be the best lovers at the age of eighteen, but I had no wish to end up in Harrow, watching Byron caught up in a whirl of homosexual politics. My experiences at Oxford had also taught me that public school boys should always be avoided at all costs.

Finally, I decided to programme in April, 1813. Byron would have just been writing *Childe Harold*, and would be at the tender (but not too tender) age of twenty-five. I exchanged my jeans for a ballgown, slipped a copy of my own novel, *The Rebel Fairy*, into my pocket, along with Leslie Marchant's *Byron: A Biography* (all 3 volumes – bloody heavy), so that I could flatter Byron with a deep understanding of his childhood and ennui, and off I went . . .

DEBORAH'S DIARY: 2005 / 1813
Day One of the Seduction of Lord Byron: 3pm, 5 July, 1813

Thoughts before going into battle
  Interviewers are always interested in whether books are autobiographical. But what's far more interesting is what happens to the author after the book is written – the way the book shapes the author's identity. As Oscar Wilde summed up: Does art mirror life or does life mirror art?'

I realised that there was probably a wide gap between Byron and his poetry. Obviously, it is the mark of a good author that they write with so much charisma that at the end of the book, the reader longs to meet them. The book seems to shine and scintillate with their personality. Hence – reading Jilly Cooper makes you long to walk with her in the Gloucestershire countryside; reading Jostein Gaarder makes you want to discuss life, the universe and everything with him for hours on end; and reading Will Self makes you want to take him to a Häagen Dazs café and discuss whether his *Cock & Bull* is as impressive as his novels suggest. Whether or not there is a gap between the creators and the creations doesn't matter; we are seduced and sucked in. Byron, too, perfected the art of the literary image; in writing *Childe Harold*, he fashioned a caricature of himself. Women read the poem and fell in love with him, assuming that Byron was Childe Harold – the brooding, melancholic, world-weary libertine – aided by the fact that within the poem itself the narrator and hero blur together until finally they merge around Canto 13 and become one.

Who can tell which of Byron's facades, the various costumes he put on, are real or masquerade? Tonight, I was determined to try and find out.

3am: House of Tom Moore (a fellow poet and close friend of Byron)

I entered the ball *in media res* – entered to hear shrill banshee screams and breaking glass. A woman was led from the room leaving a trail of blood behind her. A thousand heads watched her go, mouths agape. I realised then that the lady was the famous Caroline Lamb – Byron's latest lover, whom he had clearly grown bored with. All very ominous. And then I saw him, across the crowded ballroom. The man himself. Mr Mad, Bad and Dangerous to Know.

I could hardly believe it when he came over and introduced himself. He was indeed beautiful. He was not as tall as I had imagined, nor was his limp as exaggerated. But he certainly had presence. I couldn't think of what to say to him. I was about to start debating the topic of whether he was really a Romantic poet or an Augustan at heart, when he started knocking back glass after glass of wine. He seemed shaken after the Caroline ordeal.

'Maybe you should lay off the booze,' I suggested nervously. I couldn't help remembering that when Byron died and his body was cut open, the sutures of his skull were found fused together – normally a sign of old age, though he was only thirty-six. 'You might end up in AA.,' I slipped up.

Byron had no idea what I meant, but he didn't seem to care. 'Cant!' he cried. 'I shall drink as I like!'

And with that he smashed his glass and pulled me out to his carriage, ordering the driver to take me home. I said I had no home, and he gentlemanly offered to take me to Tom Moore's house, declaring that I would not be refused accommodation. I told him that he was a gentleman and I could never repay him. He told me that I could repay him with a kiss.

I blushed and looked away. We sat in the carriage, him watching me, me staring out of the window watching his reflection, silvery against the blue landscape. Our knees were brushing. Even though the night air was freezing, tiny beads of sweat were breaking on my forehead. As the carriage wheels started to slow, he leaned forwards and took my wrist, stroking the veins delicately. We kissed the rest of the way home. At Tom Moore's, I staggered about in post-kiss bliss. Moore gave me a quizzical look and Byron steadied me with his hand on my back, making a joke about me being drunk. 'Drunk on love,' he whispered, as he kissed me goodnight.

The next morning, Byron paid me a visit and declared that he would do anything to make me happy. 'Alright,' I said. 'Come back to 2005 with me. I think you'll enjoy it.'

Back in Surrey, England

For three nights in a row, I made Byron suffer. Determined not to become another Carolyn Lamb, I inflicted The Rules on him. No matter how he tried to woo me – whether it was with flowers, verse, or chocolates, I refused to give him more than so much as a kiss. At first he was cajoling; then he began to get quite peevish and starting muttering remarks about going back to be with Augusta.

Then Wednesday came, and I woke up with a jolt. I had completely forgotten that tonight I was meant to be having a dinner party, with Anthony and his new girlfriend, Kerry. I went into the living room and found Byron on the net, ego-surfing. Having typed his name into Google, he was delighted to discover he had 1,070,000 hits.

'God, this broadbent is so much fun,' Byron murmured.

'Broadband,' I corrected him. 'Look, I'm having a dinner party tonight and I really need you to be on your best behaviour. For one thing, I can't introduce you as Lord Byron.'

'But why not?'

'Because they'll think I'm mad.'

'But you are mad. Surely if they're your friends, they've already worked this out?'

'I'm just going to say you're George, alright? Look, just keep remembering this rhyme in your head,' I improvised wildly. '*I'm not a famous poet, I don't like lovemaking / My name is George and I work in computing.*'

'I don't think I'd care to remember such a frightful piece of poetry. The scansion doesn't work at all,' Byron's eyebrows knitted together in an elegant, faintly disdainful frown. 'Perhaps you ought to be dating Andrew Motion, not me.' He laughed as I threw a discloth at him and stormed out. I wasn't quite sure why I felt so jittery about the dinner party. I spent two hours getting ready, and everything I tried on or took off was assessed in comparison to an imaginary Kerry. My picture of her began to escalate in my mind until I felt she could be no less beautiful than Aphrodite rising out of the ocean: hair aflame, face an oval of perfection, body a sea of curves. By the time I'd finally decided on my little black dress, I was nearly hysterical with nerves. Twice, I picked up my mobile and nearly called Anthony to pretend I was sick and wanted to call it all off. Then 7pm came and the doorbell rang.

'Hi, Deborah,' said Anthony, giving me a kiss on the cheek. To my surprise, I felt a flutter in my stomach – I had forgotten how dark his eyes were. 'This is Kerry.'

Relief soothed the anxious grinding of my stomach muscles. She was pretty, but not *that* pretty. She had short hair, for a start – an autumnal haze of highlights – and Anthony had once confided in me that he hated short hair on women. I looked at Anthony, but he was gazing at Lord Byron. I groaned silently. Though Byron had put on a pair of jeans, they didn't really go with his eighteenth-century coat and cravat.

'Hi.' Anthony shook his hand. There was a slightly twisted smile on his lips. I felt a flutter of alarm. Could that smile mean something beginning with j . . . ?

'Hi,' Byron said, rising. For one moment, as he puffed up his chest and his chin, I saw the vulnerability beneath his arrogance. Then, seeing Kerry, he gave her a wolfish smile.

'Hi,' she said, as if sensing the ruffles of awkwardness and doing her best to smooth them over. 'Great to meet you! I'm Kerry.'

'I'm Byron,' he purred softly, ignoring the frantic look I gave him.

'Oh, Brian – oh cool, I once knew a Brian and he was great,' she enthused.

We sat down to eat.

'So, what do you do for a living?' Anthony asked.

'He's a –' I began to interject again, when Anthony said, smiling gently: 'I think Brian can answer by himself, Deborah.'

'Uh huh,' Kerry echoed under her breath, and I had to force myself not to give her an utterly monstrous look.

'I'm a poet,' said Byron importantly. At which point, about a hundred women would have collapsed at his feet. But this is the twenty-first century and if you announce at a dinner party that you're a poet, people will react with polite distress.

'Well,' said Anthony, 'good for you. But it must be tough trying to get recognition, right? I mean, I had a friend at uni who decided to become a poet and he spent years scraping by, sending things out to magazines and radio stations and never getting anywhere. By the time he finally managed to get something accepted by Bloodaxe, the bailiffs had taken away half his flat.'

By now Byron was nearly purple.

'He has had stuff published,' I said quickly. 'And it's been well received.'

'Oh wow, what about?' said Anthony, pointedly addressing the question to Lord B.

'He likes writing about nature,' I said. 'About birds and trees and that sort of thing.'

'Sounds very Wordsworthian,' said Kerry, and I saw Byron's fingers tighten around his knife as though he wanted to plunge it into someone's chest.

'I can assure you that Wordsworth has never been an influence on my work,' said Byron acidly. 'Blake – a fellow genius – once blamed a lifelong bowel complaint on reading Wordsworth's poetry.' We all laughed.

The dinner party came to an end. We waved them goodbye and I stood on my doorstep, watching them walk down the street. Anthony took off his coat and put it round Kerry's shoulders and I felt as though someone had stabbed an icicle into my heart. Then I felt a warm breath on the back of my neck. Byron had come up behind me. He took my hair, twisted it into a tight coil and pinned it up with his fingers. I watched Anthony again as he disappeared into the darkness. I felt Byron place a tender kiss on the back of my neck. And that was when I made the mistake.

Reader, I slept with him.

11:30pm

A post-coital chat between me and Byron, on literature:

'So, what poetry are you reading?' he asked me.

'Uh?' I gasped, bumbling about. 'Er . . . Coleridge.'

'Coleridge! What an idiot! Coleridge, explaining metaphysics to the nation – I wish he would explain his explanation.'

I burst into fits of laughter and he smiled, kissing my shoulder.

'That's from *Don Juan*!' I cried eagerly, then realised: fuck, it's 1813, he hasn't written that one yet.

'Don Juan,' Byron frowned as if suffering from inverted déjà vu, sensing that title would one day be meaningful to him. 'Hmm. I like that. I must write it down.'

'I think it would make a good poem,' I added cheekily. 'The adventures of a rake, travelling all over Europe, a little quietly facetious about everything.'

'Not bad at all,' Byron kissed me again. 'I may well use that idea at some point.' 1818, to be exact, I thought.

'Deborah – you're more than just a pretty face.' And with this affectionate cliché, he promptly fell asleep.

I lay awake. I tried to analyse the feeling in my stomach. I felt empty, as though filled with smoke. I couldn't believe that, during our lovemaking, I had had to fake an orgasm. This was Byron, for goodness' sake. But all the way through, I had been unable to stop myself from thinking about Anthony, about the way he kissed me, the way he touched me, the way he used to enter me and stare deep into my eyes and whisper 'I love you'. Beside me, Byron snored loudly.

The Morning After

Byron woke me up the next morning with a gentle kiss. I blinked blearily, noticing that my own novel, *The Rebel Fairy*, was looking reassuringly dog-eared and well-read. He had obviously found it amongst my clothes and was now reading it.

'Did you like the book?' I asked, expecting bemusement rather than praise. Perhaps he might even think me a genius. Perhaps I ought to go back to 1813 and republish *The Rebel Fairy*. Perhaps Byron might pass it on to his publisher, Murray. It could be published as a sort of light-hearted *1984*, a look to the future. For a moment I pictured the reviews: '*The ability of this young novelist to predict affairs of the heart in future centuries is extraordinarily perceptive!*' Byron and I would become a famous literary couple; we would marry and produce children who won the Booker Prize.

'Well?' I repeated. 'Did you like *The Rebel Fairy*?'

'Load of tosh!' he said. 'The woman who wrote it was obviously a born-again virgin. And what's all this about *fairies*? I tell you, I knew *real* fairies when I was at Harrow, and they most certainly didn't have wings!'

And with that, he tore out the first few pages and pretended to eat them, flecks of paper spraying from his mouth, crying, 'Delicious!'

Over the following week, my relationship with Byron went from bad to worse. I hardly ever saw him at all, for history had repeated itself. Byronmania had swept the country. After Byron had gone out on the town to Chinawhite, the inevitable occurred: a brief love affair with Jordan had ensued. He was splashed over every tabloid in town, whilst the magnificent ode he published on her bosoms (not having heard of plastic surgery, he was convinced they were a divine miracle) was revered in every broadsheet.

Then, after penning a poem that was published in the *Guardian*, challenging Andrew Motion to a duel, Byron was invited onto *Celebrity Big Brother*. Eight million viewers fell in love with him all over again as they watched him bicker with Jeremy Edwards, flirt with Caprice and discuss the origins of his deep-set chauvinism with Germaine Greer. The night of the *BB* final, I sat on my sofa, the cat on my lap. To my horror, the camera zoomed in on Byron lying in bed beside Germaine Greer.

'Since arriving in 2005,' Byron whispered, 'I've slept with many a pretty face. But you, Germaine, are the first woman I have bedded who has *brains*.'

The telephone rang. Anthony's voice rippled out.

'Um, Deborah, I think you ought to switch on the TV,' he said.

'I'm watching,' I sobbed. 'I suppose you and Kerry think it's hilarious.'

'I haven't seen Kerry,' Anthony said quietly. 'The night I brought her over, she went on and on about bloody Byron all the way home. She just sits at home, masturbating over his poetry. So . . .'

'Oh,' I said, suddenly feeling deliriously happy.

'Shall I come and keep you company?' he asked gently.

'Yes, please.'

'And just ignore Byron. Everything he says is cant.'

The last thing I did before Anthony came over was to hack my machine to bits and put them in the bin. No more fantasies, I thought with a smile, as the doorbell rang. From now on, Mr Normal will do just fine . . .